To Turn Full Circle

To Turn Full Circle

Linda Mitchelmore

Published 2012 by Choc Lit Limited
Penrose House, Crawley Drive, Camberley, Surrey GU15 2AB, UK
www.choclitpublishing.com

A CIP catalogue record for this book is available
from the British Library

ISBN-978-1-906931-72-8

MIX
Paper from
responsible sources
FSC® C014728

Printed and bound by CPI Group (UK) Ltd, Croydon, CR0 4YY

For my son, James, and my daughter, Sarah
– ever my shining stars.
And in memory of my father, Olmen Arthur,
who always believed in me.

Acknowledgements

No road is long – so the saying has it – with good
company. And on my particular journey to publication
I've met so many lovely people it would be impossible to
list them all – another book would be needed!

Huge thanks must go to June Tate for inviting me along on
writing holidays in Italy and Corfu; so much fine wine and
food, so much laughter, so many good friends made.
But I did learn something, June – and here's the proof.

When Katie Fforde awarded me her bursary it was a
massive boost to my confidence that hey, maybe I could do
this. Thanks, Katie.

All writers need writing 'buddies', I think, and I have two
of the very best in Jan Wright and Jennie Bohnet
– thank you, and *merci*.

My cousin, David Haas, dragged me kicking and screaming
from my 'loom' to embrace technology and the internet –
I will be forever in your debt, boyo.

Brixham Writers might be a group of the smallest order but it is perfectly formed and I'm proud to be amongst you, girls and boys.

The Romantic Novelists' Association gets my thanks, too. Joining you has been money well spent, and you opened up my world with your friendship and encouragement – especially my most consistent mentor of all, bella Stella – she knows who she is.

And now to Choc Lit – my destination, but by no means the end of the journey: my life as a novelist is just beginning. Thank you one and all for taking me into your fold.

You know that favourite chocolate you save until last to eat? Well, my husband, in this list, is that chocolate. Thanks, Rog, for fielding the 'phone for me, for copious cups of coffee, and for never, ever, as I battled on to publication, for even thinking it might be a good idea if I gave up. I wouldn't have anyway!

Chapter One

'Well, well, well – look what the cat's brought in,' Mrs Phipps said when Emma eventually made it down to the kitchen. 'Taken you six weeks to walk this far it has.'

'As long as that?'

'Didn't I just say as much?'

'Yes, Mrs Phipps,' Emma said. 'What day is it? Sunday?'

'Monday.'

Emma struggled to remember which month it might be. And the date. She pressed her lips together as she concentrated. Her mama's and Johnnie's funerals had been on a Friday and …

Mrs Phipps cut into her thoughts. '12th April to save you addling your brain.'

'I've survived this long, thinking about the date's hardly going to kill me now.'

Despite her spirited response, Emma's voice sounded weak to her own ears. She thought about checking it was still 1909 but didn't think she'd be able to stomach the look of derision Mrs Phipps would undoubtedly give her.

But she was on the receiving end of that look anyway. 'King's been to Germany and back while you were idling away upstairs.'

'I wasn't idling. I was convalescing.'

And still am.

It had been struggle enough for Emma coming down the stairs, her knees stiff after weeks of lying in bed, her legs so thin she was afraid they wouldn't carry her to the bottom step. She'd almost dropped her carpet bag. Mrs Shaw – the doctor's wife – had fetched it for her from her home, Shingle Cottage, after Emma had asked her to because it contained her 'treasures' and she wanted them close by her. Thank goodness Mrs Shaw had thought to look for a change of underthings in Emma's room and had put those in, too. But that had been all. No one had expected that Emma would be ill for so long, least of all Emma herself.

The bag was hardly heavy but Emma had been grateful to leave it in the hallway at last while she went in search of a hot drink and something to fill the cavern in her belly, her nose following the smell of frying bacon. How long had it been since she'd eaten anything decent? she wondered. All Mrs Phipps had served up was thin soup with bits of gristle floating in it.

'Pleurisy you've had,' Mrs Phipps said. 'And a fever. It comes on with shock sometimes, the doctor said. And you made a right spectacle of yourself at the funeral. I expect you want to know what happened, and how ...'

'Not particularly,' Emma said.

Bits of things kept coming back to her – unwelcome, the way heart-burn is. She remembered St Mary's had been packed for the joint funeral. Emma shook her head to banish the unwelcome memory.

But Mrs Phipps was intent on dragging it all up again it seemed. 'Fainted clean away you did, maid. And hot afterwards. I've never touched anything so 'ot that didn't have a kettle or pot boiling away on the top of it. I put my hand to your forehead and I swear I yelped with the shock of it.' Mrs Phipps banged a saucepan of water down on the range. 'Thank goodness Dr Shaw was there. Of course, when he asked the congregation who could take you in I was the first to offer, because didn't your dear, dead mother and I always say we'd look out for one another's little 'uns if times got hard?'

Mrs Phipps placed her hands on her hips, turned towards Emma. But Emma was prepared to let the woman prattle on knowing all of what she said was more than likely lies and that to challenge those lies would be pointless.

'Well, maid, didn't we?'

'I don't know, Mrs Phipps. My mama never told me what she spoke to the neighbours about.'

'Well, there's gratitude.'

'I am grateful to you, Mrs Phipps. For looking after me. Keeping me warm. I don't suppose there's a bite of breakfast left I could have?' Emma's stomach grumbled and groaned with hunger. She grasped the back of a kitchen chair for support. But Mrs Phipps was glaring at her. 'Please,' Emma said, remembering her manners.

'I could spare you a scraping of dripping on some bread.'

Emma swallowed hard. She thought she might retch at the thought of cold dripping, possibly filthy with the remains of goodness knows what from Mrs Phipps' cooking pot. 'I was hoping for a piece of bacon,' Emma said.

'Oh, were you?' Mrs Phipps sneered. 'And where be I getting bacon from, may I ask?'

'From Dr Shaw. I heard him say he'd be providing provisions for me and ...'

Emma left her sentence unfinished, giving Mrs Phipps time to assimilate the fact Emma had heard what Dr Shaw had said. The doctor was kindness itself – going far and beyond the calling of his duty to his patients. Emma's mama had been on the receiving end of that kindness many a time. And in return, she'd done sewing jobs for his wife without charging.

'Well you heard wrong.'

'I didn't, Mrs Phipps,' Emma said, gripping tighter onto the chair back. 'And my laundry. Where is it? I can't find any of the clothes I was wearing in the church when I ...'

When I couldn't bear to see my mother's coffin with my six-year-old brother, Johnnie's, small one sitting on top and I knew for sure then I wouldn't see either of them again, and

3

something overwhelmed me, bigger than the raging sea that took them both. Something dark and sinister that took my breath from me and stilled my heart.

But Emma couldn't say the words for fear she would be overwhelmed once more and she'd have to stay with Mrs Phipps forever.

'Well, my lady, you'd best forget anything you *thought* you heard the doctor say, you hear me? Especially if you're wanting a bit of breakfast.'

'Yes, Mrs Phipps,' Emma mumbled. 'But I can smell bacon's been cooked in here and not so long ago, so I'd like a piece. Please.'

She had a good idea where her Sunday dress had gone – the dress she'd worn to the funeral. To Mrs Phipps' daughter, Margaret, no doubt. Although a year or so younger than Emma, the girl was about the same size.

Emma smoothed out the creased fabric of a navy blue serge skirt that had been mended in at least three places which Mrs Phipps had placed on the bed ready for her to put on. It bagged at the waist and Emma had had to turn the waist band over twice to stop it sliding down over the tops of her shoes; shoes that had been her mother's which she'd worn to the funeral. And the cream Viyella blouse was no better; one cuff was frayed beyond mending and there was a button missing.

'I've never heard such audacity in one so young. That's what comes of your father having been a furriner, no doubt.'

'My father was a Breton, Mrs Phipps. The Breton language is similar to Welsh and Cornish. My papa ...'

'Oi! Don't you come your clever ways with me, my girl. All that educating is wasted on you now. Why you didn't leave the learning at fourteen like everyone else, I don't ...'

'Education is never wasted, my mama said. I stayed at school to help the little ones. Mama wanted me to be a teacher.'

Emma folded her arms across her waist. She could kiss goodbye to some breakfast now for her cheek, couldn't she?

'Did she now? From what I've heard, they won't be wanting you back at the school to help the little 'uns no more.'

'I don't believe you.'

Emma had been overjoyed when the headmistress had asked if she'd like to stay on at school after she'd turned fourteen, to see if teaching would be the career for her.

'P'raps, then, you'll believe this.'

Mrs Phipps handed Emma a letter. She opened it slowly and began to read. The school could no longer continue with her training to become a teaching assistant. The Board had had a meeting and concluded that Emma wasn't the sort of person suitable for the education of young minds. Emma shrugged. The letter hadn't said in as many words, but her guess was that the Board's decision had something to do with her mama's death. She hadn't been entirely sure that teaching *was* the career for her anyway – and now the decision seemed to have been made for her. Things were getting worse and worse, but what could she do but struggle on? She would have to find work of some sort – enough to pay rent and for food. But what?

'Ain't pretty, is it?' Mrs Phipps said, a sly smile on her face, as though she was glad it was bad news for Emma.

'No.'

'Well, seeing as you'm up and dressed you'd best be on your way. Is that your bag I see out there in the hall?'

Mrs Phipps jabbed a stubby finger towards the hallway and Emma's carpet bag. Emma shuddered. Mrs Phipps' fingers had nails that were none too clean. Emma wasn't sure now she wanted to eat another thing that Mrs Phipps might serve up.

But she was hungry – so hungry. She didn't think she'd be

able to make it to the front door never mind back to Shingle Cottage.

'The bacon, Mrs Phipps,' Emma said boldly. 'The bacon Dr Shaw said he'd instruct Foale's the butcher to deliver here for me. I'd like some, please. Just one rasher.'

''S all gone,' Mrs Phipps said.

Which was as near to a confession that Mrs Phipps had appropriated food sent for Emma as she was ever going to get out of her – the two-faced, lying, harridan. She'd only offered to look after Emma for what she'd known she would get out of it, hadn't she?

'I thought it might have,' Emma said.

'So it's bread and dripping or nothing.'

'Then I'll take the nothing,' Emma said.

Dripping had always made Emma gag eating it, and the thought of what state Mrs Phipps' dripping might be in was making the bile rise in her throat.

She let go of the back of the chair and willed herself not to feel faint. Then she retrieved her carpet bag from the hall, not that there was much in it save a brooch fashioned like a bunch of anemones that had been her mother's and a toy wooden horse that had been still clutched in Johnnie's hand when he'd been found. Emma had asked for her mother's rings – her square engagement ring with four, small diamonds set within it, and her thin wedding band – but had been told that they were missing when the body was pulled from the water. Emma had asked Dr Shaw about the rings and he said he'd check with the coroner who had said the same thing.

To Emma's surprise Mrs Phipps rushed out after her. She laid a hand on Emma's shoulder. 'Maybe I've been a bit hasty. I could send my Philip down to Foale's to ask for a bit more bacon. Charge it to the good doctor. And mebbe a bit of nice beef skirt to make a pasty for your supper.'

Emma imagined Mrs Phipps' filthy fingers and nails rubbing lard into flour to make pastry and shuddered. 'No, thank you,' she said. 'I've troubled you too long. If you could just tell me where you've put my coat.'

'Coat? I don't remember no coat.'

'It's red,' Emma said. She remembered her mother making it, telling her the material had once been an officer's uniform from when England had fought Napoleon. 'Don't tell your papa though, will you?' she'd laughed, hugging Emma to her at the joke. Fighting back tears because she missed her mother so, Emma went on, 'It's got black curlicue stitching on the collar.'

'Oh yes, I remember now,' Mrs Phipps said. 'In the church. The last I saw it was draped over the pew end. Next to Beattie Drew.'

'Mrs Drew would never take my coat,' Emma said.

'Did I say she had?' Mrs Phipps snapped, her eyes narrow slits, hard and flinty. 'Best you don't go around accusing folks of anything. D'you get my meaning?'

'I do,' Emma said, with a sigh. She pulled her shawl – at least Mrs Phipps hadn't appropriated *that* for her daughter – around her shoulders and tied it more tightly. It would have to do until she got home – there was bound to be a jacket hanging on a peg somewhere. Something smarter to wear than a shawl at least.

She lifted the latch on Mrs Phipps' front door. A blast of good sea air almost blew Emma off her feet – but how good it felt after so long in the mustiness of Mrs Phipps' front bedroom. If she took things slowly, breathing in deeply until she got back to Shingle Cottage it couldn't help but give her strength, could it?

It was only a short distance from Mrs Phipps' home in Cliff Terrace back to Shingle Cottage but it felt like miles to Emma.

Her bereavement and her illness had taken a toll on her and she'd had to stop to catch her breath more than a few times. But now she was catching it for a different reason – Seth Jago. If the first person she had to see after leaving Mrs Phipps' was Seth then she was glad it was him. He had his back to her, standing on a ladder, and the bright sunshine was making his crow-black, thick hair – straight as candles – glisten like wet coal. Rumour had it that Seth's pa was of Spanish descent. Certainly, Emma thought, gazing at him, Seth's skin was a lot darker than hers was, swarthy even.

Many were the times before Emma had been orphaned, when they had come across one another in the town, and would fall in to step together if they were going in the same direction. They never ran out of things to talk about. And once Seth had carried her basket of groceries from May's the grocer all the way back up the hill to Shingle Cottage for her. Emma had often had the feeling that he'd been hoping he would see her and that perhaps he might ask her to walk out with him. But circumstances had put a stop to that speculation.

The last time she'd seen Seth her brother's body had been cradled in his arms – half of her adored Johnnie's fair hair had been ripped off and his face was lacerated where he'd been thrown against rocks. Seth's face had been wet but Emma couldn't be sure if it was tears or the rain that had been pouring relentlessly down.

Two days later her mother's body had been washed up further down the coast.

'What are you doing, Seth?' Emma asked.

At her words, Seth turned on the narrow rung of the ladder and almost fell off. Thick, brown paint slid from his brush onto the window. He grabbed for a rung up above his head to steady himself, then jumped to the ground. He walked towards Emma, a shy smile on his face, but a smile that reached his conker-brown eyes all the same. He looked, Emma thought, as thrilled to see her as she was to see him.

'As you see, Emma. Painting window frames. But I've been interrupted now and glad to be. My, but it's good to see you.'

Emma felt a blush coming. Not just at Seth's obvious pleasure in seeing her but because he wasn't wearing a shirt. Emma could understand him wanting to be cooler because it was an unseasonably warm day for April. Hot even. But how broad Seth's chest was. How dark the hairs that ran from his chest down over his stomach until they disappeared into the waistband of his trousers.

'And me, you,' Emma said as the flush spread up the sides of her neck, pinked her cheeks. 'Thank you for the flowers.'

Mrs Phipps had put the stocks Seth had brought round in an old – and not very well washed-out – jam jar. But their ugly container had done nothing to take away the gloriously heady scent of the flowers.

'It was the least I could do. Mrs Phipps wouldn't let me in over the doorstep to see you, though.'

'And just as well,' Emma said. 'I wasn't a pretty sight.'

She stared down at her shoes – she wasn't a pretty sight now, either.

'Beauty's in the eye of the beholder,' Seth said, and Emma looked up at his words. He was still smiling at her – with his eyes, not just his lips. 'You're bound to have been affected by the loss of your ma and Johnnie.'

'Not forgetting my papa,' Emma said, her words coming out sharper than she'd intended them too.

But Seth hadn't lost his father to the sea, had he? Even though their fathers had been on the same boat – *The Gleaner* – that fateful day. And his father hadn't lost *The Gleaner* either because by some miracle it hadn't sunk, even though some of his crew had been tossed into the sea.

9

The boat had been overloaded with fish, so rumour had it, but nothing had been proved. No, it was only Emma's father, Guillaume, who had drowned.

Emma couldn't bear to look towards the harbour because she knew *The Gleaner* was likely to be there and her father was never going to jump from it, with a basket of fish for their own supper, ever again.

'Not forgetting your pa. Never. But you're a sight for sore eyes, Emma Le Goff, that's for sure,' Seth said, his smile widening now. 'I'm pleased to see you better. You're a lot thinner, but …'

'I'm pleased to see the cottage is being smartened up a bit,' Emma interrupted him. She didn't need reminding how thin she was – lying in bed at Mrs Phipps' her pelvis had held the sheet off her body it stuck out so much. 'You're making a lovely job of my windows.'

Seth looked away from her then. He stared into the distance, unable to meet her eye. 'They're not *your* windows, Emma. They're my pa's,' he said. 'You know Shingle Cottage is his …'

'I'm not stupid, Seth Jago. Of course I know that.'

'Then you'll know it has to go to one of Pa's crew. Someone's already been taken on. My pa owns most of the cottages in this row,' Seth made a broad arc with his left arm, then with his right, to show Emma just how much of Cove Road his father owned, 'all lived in by his crew.' He was speaking slowly, his voice gentle, and smiling at her again now.

He ran a hand through his hair and Emma wished he wouldn't because the sight of him doing it and smiling at her so kindly was doing funny things to her insides.

'But I live here. It's the only home I've ever known,' Emma said, swallowing back the beginnings of a sob. 'My pa always kept it so tidy. He would have painted the window frames if he hadn't drowned.'

And hadn't he always been so proud of the vegetables he grew in the little back garden? Every inch of ground filled with flatpole cabbages, potatoes, onions, leeks, radishes. Herbs, too – parsley, and thyme, and sage. And hadn't her mother always been so happy turning the insides upside down for the spring cleaning, singing as she washed walls and beat rugs and rinsed curtains in the tub? Making a home for them all. The only time she'd ever seen her mama sad was when she'd lost the babies she was carrying. Time after time she'd lost babies. Until Johnnie. He'd been the apple of her eye. Not her favourite, but special because she'd waited so long to have him – nine years after she'd had Emma.

But now they were all gone.

Tears burned the back of Emma's throat and she gulped to swallow them. Fear replaced them. What was she going to do? She had no home …

'I'm sorry, Emma,' Seth said. 'About your pa. He …'

'I suppose you've got to say that,' Emma said.

'Stop putting words in my mouth, Emma. It wasn't like that. The boat had been out three days and the catch had been good. But that made the going slow, especially when the wind dropped. So they had a drink or two to pass the time. Then, when …'

'Not my papa!' Emma stopped him. Her papa had never gone down the alehouses with the rest of the crew. He always came straight home to his family. And if he drank at all it would only be a glass of cider of a summer evening while he tended his vegetables.

Emma dropped her carpet bag on the path and folded her arms across her waist in an attempt to hold herself up, stop herself from collapsing with weakness and hunger.

'Emma,' Seth said, 'I can understand your anger. But if you'll just listen for a moment …'

'I don't think I want to hear it.'

'No? Well, I'll tell you anyway. Your pa died a hero. He jumped in to try and save Herbie Adams who couldn't swim. My pa threw a line and your pa grabbed it and tied it to Herbie Adams. Pa soon got Herbie on deck but when he went to throw the line again he couldn't see your pa anywhere – he'd gone under. And that's the truth.'

'Is it?' Emma said. There was something about Seth and the way he was standing so tall, so dignified despite being splattered with paint, his gaze holding hers, that made her want to believe him. But could she?

She remembered asking her mama more than a few times what had happened, exactly, that day her papa had drowned, and always her mama had said, it didn't matter, he was dead and he wasn't coming back, and she was to stop asking questions.

'That's the truth, Emma.'

'I wish I'd known when Mama was alive,' Emma said. 'I could have comforted her, perhaps. But *someone* could have told me.'

'They could. And for my part I think they ought to have done. But straight after – what with your ma taking it so badly – my pa didn't want to intrude on her grief. It's why he let you all stay on in the cottage instead of evicting you ...'

'Evict us? That would have been a cruel thing to do. He ...'

'Life often is cruel, Emma,' Seth said.

'So I'm finding out all by myself,' Emma said as the reality of her situation came crashing down on her head, along with the fear. 'I don't know that I need *you* to tell me.'

'Don't fight me, Emma, please. I feel bad enough about this as it is. I know all this is a shock.' Seth waved an arm towards the windows he'd been painting. 'But my pa's not all bad. He sent Dr Shaw around to your ma – paying the bill and that.' Seth halted, as though waiting for Emma to take in the information.

Yes, she remembered Dr Shaw sitting in the kitchen while her mother cried, telling her it was all raw for the moment but she had the children to think of now. She had to be strong.

Emma nodded.

'I remember the doctor calling a few times, but I'm sure my mama would have had money to pay him.'

'Maybe she did, Emma,' Seth said. 'I'm only repeating what my pa told me. Anyway, all the potions Dr Shaw could give your ma were no good because she jumped ...'

'She didn't jump. My mama would never have jumped. She must have slipped. The Coroner said so, too. Accidental death, he said. Ma and Johnnie wouldn't have been buried in the churchyard if she'd been a suicide, and you know it as well as anyone.'

'I'm sorry. I shouldn't have said that.'

'No, you shouldn't.'

Emma put her face in her hands. She wouldn't allow her emotions to show – and especially not to Seth Jago if she could help it. And she didn't want to permit herself to think what was forcing itself into her mind unbidden – the way filthy flood water creeps under doors and through windows – that her mother had been pushed. Although who would have done such a thing? Emma couldn't imagine.

She looked up, held Seth's gaze for a moment. He mouthed the word 'sorry' at her.

'Accepted,' she said. 'And if you don't put your shirt on soon, Seth Jago, you might burn, even though you look tanned already.'

'Do I now?' Seth said. He sounded pleased that Emma had noticed.

'I don't lie,' Emma said. She tried to walk past Seth but he dodged in front of her, blocking her way, his bare chest at eye level. Emma forced herself not to gaze at it.

'Let me pass. There's things inside I need.'

Once she'd got inside and made herself a cup of tea – although she'd have to drink it without milk because the milk in the larder would surely have curdled after all this time – she'd feel better.

'Emma, you can't,' Seth said. He grabbed Emma's arm.

'Let me go! Why can't I go in? Let me by, Seth. There are things of mine in there.'

'Not any more, there aren't. Pa has had all your stuff cleared out. He sold most of it to cover the weeks when he was getting no rent from the place. There's only the beds and a table and chairs left. A rug or two and some plates and cutlery.'

'Did you help him clear it out?'

Seth hung his head.

'How could you?' Emma shouted, making herself sound much stronger and in control of the situation than she felt. Not caring who heard her. But her heart was hammering in her chest – it made her feel faint and she had to take deep breaths to steady herself. 'You did, didn't you?'

'My brothers did most of it. But I won't lie to you. I did do one cart load, Emma, that's all. I had no choice. He's my pa. I had to do what I was told.'

'Even though you knew it was … was immoral.'

'I'm sorry …'

'I accepted your apology just now, but I won't accept this one. I don't think you know the meaning of the word sorry, Seth Jago,' Emma said. 'Now let me go.'

Seth loosened his grip, took his hand away. He reached for his shirt where it was draped over a lavender bush and pulled it on over his head.

'I'll show you,' he said. He walked down the path, took a key from his pocket and opened the front door wide.

Emma sucked in her breath and was afraid she'd never be

able to let it out again. Seth was right – there was nothing in the sitting-room but the table and two chairs, which had always been in the kitchen when Emma had lived there with the family. And there had been four chairs then, not just two. A few plates were piled in the middle and some knives and forks strewn across the table. Not even a tablecloth. Her mother would have been mortified to see her table without a freshly laundered cloth.

Emma raced through the room to the kitchen. There was a kettle on the range but nothing else. Not even a saucepan – and her mama had kept her copper pans so shiny and bright.

'I suppose your pa's dug up all the vegetables as well,' she said, yanking on the back door handle. It was unlocked and the force of her action made it bang noisily against the kitchen wall.

And then she saw it. The remains of a bonfire. There were a few remnants of cloth left unburned. And a book with its spine ripped off had escaped the blaze.

Emma began to cry then. It was like losing her parents and Johnnie all over again.

'So, you see, Emma,' Seth said, coming to stand beside her, 'why you can't stop here. This is no longer your home.'

He put an arm around Emma's shoulders and she wanted more than anything to shrug it off. But she couldn't. She needed the support. She leaned into Seth, felt the warmth of him. How she'd often dreamed of such a moment – but not in these circumstances.

And then she remembered that Seth was a Jago and always would be. She ducked out from under his arm.

'I'm not going to hurt you, Emma. I like you. You must know that. I thought you liked me.'

'I do. It's your pa I'm not keen on.'

'I'm not my pa.'

'But you've done his bidding?'

They stood looking at one another for a long moment. Then Seth put a hand either side of Emma's head, pulled her towards him and kissed her forehead. 'I'm so sorry, Emma, truly sorry. Sorrier than you'll ever know I've had a part – albeit a small one – in all this. But Pa needs this place for the new crewman. He's on his way from Slapton. He'll be here by nightfall. Come on. Let's fetch your bag. I'll carry it for you to wherever it is you want to go.'

'No, you won't. I ... I wouldn't want you to carry my bag if you were the last person on earth, Seth Jago. But there's no need for you or anybody to be carrying it for me because I'm not going anywhere! I'll be back for my bag – just watch me.'

Seth put a hand over his mouth to stop himself calling after Emma. He knew it would be useless anyway. Even if she did hear him, she'd probably ignore him. He'd never seen such fire in a person's eyes before.

And what beautiful eyes they were too – the colour of burnt barley-sugar but with greenish flecks in them. Eyes that looked huge in her gaunt face. She looked older – more womanly, more adult, more knowing – since the last time he'd seen her walking behind her mother's and her young brother's coffins as the cortège came slowly up the steep path from the lane to the church.

His pa had forbidden him and his brothers, Carter and Miles, to attend the funeral. When Seth had asked why, he'd received a hard clout across his face and been told not to question his father's orders. Ever.

But his father hadn't said that Seth couldn't stand between the graves, head bowed. So he had. And his heart had almost broken for Emma.

He'd made to follow the last mourner in, but had then turned and walked back home, ashamed of himself.

More shame seemed to pile on his shoulders, seep into his soul, now. He was doing his father's bidding again, wasn't he? Aiding his parent to throw the orphaned Emma out of the only home she'd ever known by painting it up for the next tenant.

Seth couldn't think how he could ever look Emma in the face again. And he wanted to. She had always had the ability to make him laugh, even when events at home made him feel as unlike laughing as it was possible to get. Just glimpsing her in the distance had made him smile When he'd turned on the ladder and seen her there he'd had to wrestle with his instincts not to rush to her, fold her in his arms, even though he'd never so much as touched her hand before. She was so beautiful, even given what she'd been through – perhaps more so now that a loss of weight through illness had heightened the shape of her high cheekbones. And she was so young. Who did she have to look out for her now? Him? But would Emma ever want anything to do with him, a Jago?

He watched her go until his eyes misted over trying to focus on her retreating figure. Her illness and her grief had weakened her. Her steps were short and slow – no longer striding and quick like the Emma he'd had to run to catch up with when he saw her scuttling along the pavement on her way to May's, or the bank, or the haberdashery. Now she had to grab hold of garden fences to keep herself upright as she went, head held high and with the sun highlighting the copper tints in her dark hair – hair the colour of polished mahogany.

Seth picked up Emma's carpet bag from the path and followed her.

Chapter Two

Gasping for breath now, Emma hauled herself up the flight of steps, flanked on one side by cottages and on the other by a high stone wall, that were a short cut to Boundary Road, where the Jagos lived. Although the steps were steep it was a quicker route than walking half way into the town and then back again. And time was of the essence for Emma. She bent her head, watching carefully where she put her feet on the slippery, moss-covered steps, and trudged on.

Everyone knew Reuben Jago's home – Hilltop House, the Victorian villa, large and imposing at the top of the hill. It would have – Emma was sure – a view that would take in the entire bay, if only she could get that far without collapsing with weakness to see it.

How dare Seth's father throw her out of the cottage. And why had he sold all her family's things? The photograph the journeyman had taken of them all standing by the front door, smiling and holding the pose for so long they'd all laughed afterwards saying they'd thought they were going to be stuck that way forever. Her mama had saved up and bought a silver-plated frame for it from Austin's. And the china jugs with primroses painted on them that her mother had loved so – where were they?

He wouldn't have sold them to cover the funeral costs, Emma knew, because her mama had always paid into a special insurance to cover the cost of family funerals. Emma had given the undertaker from Langdon's the book when he'd called to arrange the funeral. Emma had always thought the idea of saving for one's own funeral macabre every time the insurance man called on Fridays for the money.

And Emma's own clothes? Had Reuben Jago ordered her

clothes to be burned, too? *She* wasn't dead, even though it might have been best if she was. Back in Mrs Phipps', for the first few days, she'd refused to eat, hoping her refusal would hasten her own end. But then Dr Shaw's wife had crept into the bedroom and hand-fed her a sliver of Victoria sponge. Oh, how wonderful it had tasted, slicked with a smear of clotted cream and strawberry jam that oozed down her chin. She'd kept one, tiny, whole strawberry behind her teeth for ages, not wanting to swallow it, not wanting to let the taste of it, or the kindness of the doctor's wife in bringing it, go. She wished now she'd thought to ask Mrs Shaw to go back to Shingle Cottage and look out a change of clothes at least.

"'Ere! What are you doing up 'ere?'

Emma looked up from her trudge up the steps. Margaret Phipps. And wasn't that Emma's Sunday dress showing a good foot below Margaret's too-small coat? Not Emma's red coat that had always been kept for Sundays she was pleased to see, but no doubt Margaret had been given it and would be keeping that for best.

'Well? Cat got your tongue or summat?'

Emma ignored her. She took a deep breath and tried desperately to summon up a bit of strength to walk on. But then two more girls jumped out from a doorway and joined Margaret, blocking Emma's path.

'Answer her,' one of them said. 'Or have you gone deaf?'

'No. And my tongue's where it's always been,' Emma said. 'Let me by.'

'Will not,' Margaret said, lunging forward.

Emma caught the stench of days' old cooking on Margaret's hair – fair, stringy hair that didn't look as though it had been washed in weeks. She put a hand to her mouth to stop herself from gagging.

'My ma says your ma and your brother should never be in the churchyard 'cos they're suicides. And suicides go to hell.'

'They're not suicides,' Emma said. 'The Coroner said so. It was in the newspapers. But then, I'm forgetting – you can't read, can you? My mama ...'

'*Mama*? *Mama*?' one of the other girls said. 'What's a *mama* when it's at 'ome? Oh yes, I forgot – silly me. You'm a furriner, Emma Le Goff. Best get back where you came from.'

Emma sighed. She'd been born in the town, same as these girls had, but she wasn't going to waste her breath telling them something they already knew. Besides she didn't have the energy.

'So, when are they going to dig your *mama* and your brother up?' Margaret said. 'Seeing as suicides shouldn't be buried in holy ground. That's what my ma says.'

Emma knew she was outnumbered but she had to make a stand. 'Are you lot deaf or something? I've just told you, but I'll tell you again – the Coroner returned a verdict of accidental death.'

'Lies! Lies! Lies!' Margaret chanted, and the other girls joined in, their voices getting louder and louder.

Emma felt herself sway with the emotion of it, and no doubt the fact she hadn't had any breakfast and was hungry.

'If you've quite finished I'll be on my way,' Emma said, suddenly suffused with a strength she never thought she'd feel again. Her papa had often told her that he'd been frightened at sea in a storm, felt real fear, many times; felt he'd never be able to carry on – but then strength would come from somewhere. Well, Emma was feeling fear like she'd never felt before. Just one push from these girls and she'd be at the bottom of the steps – and there were at least a hundred of them to bump down, and have her bones broken on each and every one.

'Oh, will yer?' Margaret said.

'Yes,' Emma said.

She tried to shoulder her way through the wall of scruffily

dressed girls, but her knees buckled and she crumpled down onto the step, grabbing at a piece of over-hanging tree top to stop herself from falling further.

And then she heard footsteps, running up the steps towards her and her tormentors.

'Leave her alone! You hear me. Bugger off, the lot of you.'

Seth. Emma was glad to see him now even though she'd told him angrily not so many minutes ago that no, she didn't want him to carry her bag anywhere, even if he was the last person on earth. He was carrying her bag now, though.

'Ooooh, it's yer knight in shining armour,' Margaret Phipps said. 'Although I'd have preferred one of his *bigger* brothers. If you get what I mean, girls?'

'Shut your mouth,' Seth said.

'Make her,' one of the other girls goaded.

'I've never struck a woman, but don't tempt me.'

'Ooooh, I'm scared.' Margaret Phipps gave a mock-shiver.

But within seconds they'd disappeared down a narrow alleyway between two of the cottages that was a short cut back to the street below, screeching with mock-fright, because they knew Seth wouldn't chase after them.

'You all right?' Seth asked. He put Emma's bag down on the step and knelt down beside her. He didn't try to touch her, but he held out a hand to help raise her to her feet.

'I can manage, thanks,' she said, struggling to stand, refusing to take Seth's offer of help.

Seth shrugged. 'You're going to see my pa, aren't you?'

'You know I am.'

'It won't do any good.'

'I don't have a choice. And I want my things.'

'Ah, Miss Le Goff,' Reuben Jago said when Seth showed Emma into a very grand and imposing drawing-room. It had a high ceiling and a chandelier full of candles hanging from the centre of it. None of the candles had been lit, Emma noticed. 'I've been expecting you.'

'I want my things,' Emma demanded. 'My mama's china jugs, and our family photograph in the silver frame. And her copper pans. And her …'

'All sold,' Reuben Jago said.

'Sold?'

Emma looked at Seth, who held her gaze briefly before looking away. He hadn't been lying when he'd said his pa had sold her things, then? In a strange way, Emma took comfort from that.

'Sold?' she said again, pointing at the things in the room – the bookcase full of books, a small table covered with photographs in silver frames, chairs that were thick with wadding and piled with cushions in velvets and silks. 'Why would you want more money? Haven't you got enough things?'

'The rent, Emma,' Reuben told her. 'When your ma went and had her, er, little *accident*, there was no rent coming in. So I had to cover the loss somehow. I sold everything from Shingle Cottage I could to make up for rents due, and the rest …'

'There was money in a box under their bed. I know there was. There was more than …'

'I found it.'

'And you expect me to believe that the money in the box didn't cover all the unpaid rent?'

The man was lying and she knew it – he couldn't meet her eye when he spoke.

'My, but you're a mouthy one.'

'At the moment, yes,' Emma said. 'There's no one else to speak for me. But where are the rest of my things? My clothes? They were good clothes, most of them.'

'Good? Even the rag-and-bone man turned his nose up at them.'

Emma gasped in horror at his words. They *had* been good clothes. Her mama had only ever bought the best wool or cotton clothes from jumble sales and unpicked them, made them into something new for the family.

'Most of it was only fit for the bonfire,' Reuben Jago said.

'You *burned* my things? My books? Family papers?'

'All gone.'

'That's tantamount to stealing, Mr Jago. Did *you* burn them or did you get someone to do your dirty work for you?'

Emma turned to glare at Seth.

'A man doesn't keep a dog and bark himself, Emma,' Reuben said.

Emma looked from father to son, willing Seth to stand up for her in some way, but Seth was standing in the doorway, his mouth open and his eyes wide with surprise. She had a feeling Seth had been as shocked as she had that his father had – with one sentence – lowered him to the status of dog. But if Seth wasn't going to stand up for her, then she certainly wasn't going to stand up for him.

'And am I being stupid to assume that the money under the bed and the sale of my things covered the rent exactly and that there was nothing left over? Which, by rights, should be mine?'

Of course there had been money left over and they both knew it.

Reuben Jago yawned. 'I wouldn't go so far as to call you stupid, Emma, but you are rather ill-informed. And tiresome. Very tiresome.'

'No, Pa,' Seth said, striding into the room. 'Emma's right. The sale of her things must have raised more than enough to cover the owed rent. The copper pans alone ...'

'Enough, Seth. When I want your opinion I'll ask for it. Now, perhaps you'll remember which side your bread is buttered, son, and escort Miss Le Goff off our premises.'

'But I've got nowhere to go,' Emma yelled at him. 'I'll get a job and pay you rent. I'll …'

'Who's going to employ you? Look at you – a puff of wind would blow you over.'

'I've been ill, Mr Jago, which I'm sure you know. And *you* didn't send anything to aid my recovery, I couldn't help noticing.'

'I paid Dr Shaw's fee when he called to attend to you.'

'So you say. I don't believe anything you say any more, Mr Jago. You don't know what the word "truth" means.'

'Out!' Reuben Jago said.

Emma guessed she had gone a step too far with that comment, but she was so fired up, she just couldn't keep her mouth shut. 'My papa worked hard for you, Mr Jago. The least you can do to honour his good memory is let me stay there a little longer, just until I find somewhere else to live at least. I'll keep it clean like my mama did – all spick and span …'

'Your *mama*, as you call her, was a silly goose and didn't know when she was well off.'

'What's that supposed to mean?' Emma said, the fire going out of her that someone, anyone – and especially Reuben Jago – was saying anything bad about her mama.

'It means I want you out of my house. Now. Seth, did you hear me?'

'I heard you, Pa, but I think you're being heartless. Emma has nowhere to go. And she's right – her pa did work hard …'

'If you don't want the feel of my hand across your ear you'll do as you're told. Or you're no son of mine.' Reuben made to walk towards Seth but Emma jumped in between them.

'I don't want anyone to be hit on my behalf, thank you very much,' Emma said. And then risking a clout around her own ear she went on, 'For what it's worth, you're behaving as bad as the lads down Burton Street School.'

Reuben Jago looked shocked at her audacity, but he recovered quickly and laughed. A loud, theatrical, and meant to intimidate laugh. But Emma wasn't intimidated. She'd seen him for what he was – a bully. To her – and possibly her mother if he'd harangued her over the rent when she'd just lost her husband. And to Seth.

'Just give me my bag, Seth,' she said quietly. 'And I'll go.'

She held out her hand to take the bag but Seth gripped it tightly. 'No,' he said. 'Don't take this the wrong way, Emma, but I can see by the size of you that you haven't eaten properly in a long time. Have you?'

Emma's hands flew to her hips – how sharp the bones felt through the fabric of her skirt. She shook her head.

'Well then, I'll at least make sure you've got food inside you to go on your way.'

'Oh, Emma, lovie,' Beattie Drew said, taking Emma's hands and drawing her into the kitchen. 'Look at you. You've been crying that much the acid in your tears has taken a layer of skin off, you poor lamb.'

Emma still couldn't speak because her throat was raw from the crying, so Seth spoke for her.

'All the way,' Seth said. 'I didn't know where else to take her, Mrs Drew, so I brought her here.'

''S all right, lad. You did right in bringing her to me.'

'She hasn't eaten in a while, Mrs Drew,' Seth said. 'Have you got a bite of something you could give her? I'll pay you, of course ...'

'No, you won't,' Emma said, finding her voice. 'I don't want to be beholden to a Jago. I'll pay my own way. I've got a few shillings saved. I used to run errands for neighbours and saved my pennies. It's deposited at the Devon & Exeter Savings Bank. If your pa hasn't burned my bank book, that is ...'

'I'm sure the bank manager will help you if ...' Seth began. But Emma interrupted him. 'Oh, are you?'

'Will you two stop bickering,' Beattie Drew said. 'I don't want anyone to pay me anything. If a body can't help another down on their luck then it's a bad job.'

'I hope this won't get you into trouble, Mrs Drew,' Seth said. 'With Pa, I mean. What with you doing the cleaning up at Hilltop House.'

'No one need know, need they, Seth? But if you're afraid for your own skin you can go now.'

No one spoke for a moment and it was silent in the room, save for the tick of a grandmother clock in the hallway.

'Perhaps I *had* better go,' Seth said. 'Nothing to do with saving my own skin, Mrs Drew, but Pa's got three crabbers going out in the morning and it's my job to make sure the creels are stacked, and what with the brouhaha we had earlier I'm behind with my tasks. And then there are the windows I haven't finished painting yet ...'

''S all right, lad. We understand, don't we, Emma?'

Emma nodded.

'But before I go,' Seth said, 'I need you to know it wasn't me who lit that bonfire.'

'You could just be saying that,' Emma said. 'To save ...'

'No, he isn't, lovie,' Mrs Drew cut in. ''Twas his brothers did it. I was there cleaning the kitchen silver when Mr Jago told 'em to go and do it.'

'Oh,' Emma said. 'I'm glad it wasn't you after all. It won't get me my things back, though, will it – knowing that? But they're gone and that's all there is to it. I won't keep you any longer. Thanks for bringing me here. A few nights' good rest and I'll be on my way again.'

'Oh, Emma,' Mrs Drew said, 'I can give you a bite to eat, and some to take with you for later. But my ol' man will be home drunk as a skunk later and he ain't a pretty sight. And besides, I've got my Mary's little ones stopping for a bit. Then there's my Edward who needs a room to hisself. I'm sorry, lovie, but I haven't got a spare yard of mattress for you to sleep on.'

Seth pushed open the drawing-room door without knocking.

'Pa,' he said as his father looked up, hastily stuffing papers back in the desk and locking the drawer. 'I …'

'Knock before you come in here,' Reuben Jago bawled.

Seth chose not to comment. His brothers never had to knock and he didn't see why he should have to. He had something to say to his pa and he was going to say it. He walked on into the room, closed the door behind him.

'You can take the rent for Shingle Cottage out of my wages, Pa. Emma Le Goff deserves a bit of time to …'

'Emma Le Goff deserves nothing.' Reuben Jago leapt from his chair, knocking it over in his haste.

Seth thought he might be about to be hit, and stiffened himself ready for the punch. But the punch didn't come.

'She deserves some compassion for her circumstances, if nothing else, Pa.'

'You heard the way she spoke to me, or did you turn a deaf ear?'

'I heard,' Seth said. And you were deserving of everything she said, he thought, but didn't say.

'I'll say it again – that mouthy madam deserves nothing. Nothing! Like mother, like daughter, no doubt. She'll be just as tight-arsed …'

'I don't want to listen to this. No amend that – I *refuse* to listen to this.'

Seth made to leave – he'd obviously chosen a bad time and had interrupted his father doing something and he was irked about it. But his father grabbed him by the elbow.

'You'll listen. She's a fiery little wordy madam just like her mother was. You'll do yourself a favour, Seth, if you forget all about Emma Le Goff. She'll soon sink into selling that lovely little body of hers to earn enough to get by and then you wouldn't want her, would you?'

'That would be for me to choose. But she won't go down that route, Pa. Not Emma. I ...'

'Forget her.'

Then his father pushed Seth towards the door, grabbed the scruff of his neck with one hand and with the other yanked the door open. He pushed him into the hallway, then slammed shut the door behind him.

Forget Emma Le Goff? Seth would no sooner be able to forget her than he could forget to breathe.

Emma slipped into the alley that went along behind the back gardens of the cottages. Shingle Cottage was the middle one. Filled with a good portion of Mrs Drew's steak-and-kidney pudding, and a bowl of stewed apples and custard, Emma was feeling stronger now. Bolder. Her papa had built an outhouse out of bits of wood washed up on the tide. The outhouse was never locked. She could sleep there. For tonight at least. Whoever the crewman was who was coming up from Slapton and who was going to be the new tenant of Shingle Cottage, need never know she was there. And then in the morning she'd go and see the bank manager about getting her money.

Letting herself in through the back gate, she crept towards the blackened remains of the bonfire. She lifted a piece of fabric that had once been part of her mother's Sunday dress – navy blue grosgrain with lighter blue butterflies embroidered around the neckline – then let it fall again. Closing her eyes she could see her mother in the dress, bending to Johnnie to show him the place in the hymn book – Johnnie had been a slow reader, always a word or two behind the rest of the congregation. How she'd chided him for it, and how she wished now that she hadn't.

The book she'd seen – the one with the ripped-off spine – was still lying on the ground. She picked it up, turned to the first page. *Persuasion*. Jane Austen. She hadn't even begun reading it. Slapping shut the book she threw it hard towards the back gate.

'Hey!' someone said from behind her. 'That's no way to treat a book.'

Emma's blood seemed to freeze in her veins. The new tenant. He must have arrived and it was nowhere near nightfall, although the sun was beginning to slide down the sky now. And it seemed to be getting chillier by the minute.

She tried to run towards the gate but her legs didn't seem to want to move. She began to shake. She listened hard for footfalls in case the new tenant was walking towards her, but she couldn't hear any. Taking a deep breath Emma moved one foot forwards, then the other. But it was as though she was walking in slow motion.

Slowly she turned her head to see who it was she was trying to run away from – who it was that was going to sleep in a bed that had been her parents'. Who it was who was making her homeless.

Emma blinked. The new tenant was younger than she'd imagined he would be. But not as young as Seth. He was about thirty at a guess. And he was taller than Seth – who was a good six foot – too. His hair was somewhere between fair and ginger – and long; it reached his shoulders almost. He was standing on the doorstep, his hands in the pockets of a pair of black trousers, looking at her. His blue-and-white striped shirt was only half done up, as though he'd been having a wash and she'd disturbed him when she'd thrown the book at the gate and he'd come hurrying out to see what the noise was.

'It's my book,' Emma mumbled under her breath. 'I can throw it if I want.'

But he must have heard her.

Frozen to the spot with fright, Emma could only watch as he walked past her and picked up the book. 'And you are?' he said, returning to where Emma stood, shivering now with nerves.

'Emma Le Goff. This used to be my home.'

'Ah,' he said. 'All is becoming clear. I'm Matthew Caunter. I'd shake your hand but I'm not sure you'd want to shake mine in return. At a guess I'd say you aren't thrilled not to be living here any more.'

'You guess right,' Emma said.

'Take it. I've no use for books.'

Matthew Caunter thrust the book at her and Emma snatched it from him, clasped it to her chest. She couldn't imagine how a life would be that had no space in it for books. She could read in both English and French, thanks to her papa. And she knew a bit of Breton, too, although only to speak it, not to read it or write it.

But if she kept the book, what would she do with it? She'd have no lamplight to read by in the outhouse, would she? And then she realised she wouldn't be able to sleep there now because this man knew she was here.

'Sorry to have bothered you,' Emma said. 'I'll go now.'

'Your decision, Miss Le Goff. But I was just about to make a pot of tea. You're welcome to join me. You know the way.'

Matthew strode towards the back door and despite her misgivings that this could be the worst decision she would ever make, Emma slowly followed. From the open doorway Emma saw him take two cups – neither of which Emma recognised as having been her mama's – from hooks on the dresser. She licked her lips. Her mouth was as dry as ash from thirst and nerves. Matthew Caunter was seriously tempting her by his action with the cups.

'And I've got some scones here I bought from Callard's Bakery,' he called out to her. 'I'm sure I could spare you one.'

'No, thanks,' Emma said. 'Mrs Drew fed me up handsome.'

She patted her stomach as though to show this man how full Mrs Drew's good food had made her.

'Just the tea, then?' he said. 'You're in luck because I drew water from the pump at the end of the lane earlier.'

Emma licked her lips again. Yes, she could drink a cup of tea. When might she get the next one if she didn't?

Chapter Three

Emma woke with a start. Where was she? Slowly her eyes became used to the darkness. A stub of candle flickered in a holder on the windowsill.

And she was lying down. On a bed. The bed that had been her mama's and her papa's. She turned her head into the pillow, now without a pillowcase on it, and caught the scent of the tobacco her papa had smoked, and she was suddenly suffused with gratitude that Reuben Jago had at least left this, even if he had only left it for the next tenant to have somewhere to lay his head.

Hardly daring to look in case she saw something – or someone – she didn't want to see, Emma peered around the room. But the bed was the only thing in it, apart from the candle in its holder. No remembered dresser with her mother's tortoiseshell brushes on it, or her scent bottles – not that there was ever very much scent in them. And her papa's trousers weren't hanging from the handle of the wardrobe, because that wasn't there, either. Nor the chair in the corner where she'd sat reading to her mama after yet another miscarriage.

How had she got here? She remembered drinking tea with ... with Matthew. Matthew Caunter. Yes, that was what he'd said his name was. But where was he?

Emma pulled herself to a sitting position, then slid from the bed, the floor cold to her stockinged feet. There was a bowl on the floor and a jug of water – neither had been her mother's. She carried both towards the candle and could just make out that the water was clean enough. How dirty she felt, how soiled. But she would give herself a lick-and-promise-for-a-better-one-tomorrow wash and then slip from the house.

She listened out for Matthew Caunter moving about somewhere but couldn't hear him. She heard the clank of a chain on the harbour wall; a sound she'd heard many times – a sound that told her it might be the fishing boat with her father on board that had just reached harbour. Except it never would be Guillaume Le Goff ever again.

She tried to judge the time but it was impossible with the candle flickering against a dark sky outside. So she snuffed it; waited for her eyes to become used to a different darkness.

Almost morning. Emma could see the sky lightening on the horizon now. Slowly, and as noiselessly as she could, Emma padded down the wooden stairs that rose up from the right-hand side of the fireplace. To her horror, Matthew Caunter was asleep in a chair. The fire still glowed red in the grate. Had he been there all night? Had he given up the only bed that had bedding on it for her? Emma was certain now that he had and she knew that manners decreed she should thank him. Whether he heard her or not didn't matter – she would do what her parents would have expected of her.

'Thank you for looking after me,' Emma whispered into the silence of the room.

There – that would do. Emma yawned then, her mouth drier than the ash that had fallen from the fire onto the slabs of the hearth. What would she give for a cup of tea.

Tea. Yes, she remembered now. Matthew Caunter had made a pot of tea and poured Emma's into a cup decorated with brightly coloured birds. The tea had been hot and strong, sweetened with a spoonful of honey. She'd felt warm, drowsy almost. She remembered eating a mouthful or two of scone and then placing her arms on the table and leaning onto them. And then nothing. She must have fallen asleep.

Emma licked her lips at the memory of that tea.

'Ah, you're up.'

Emma jumped, startled. Matthew was awake and uncurling

his huge form from the chair. He stood up, stretched. He was so tall that as he did so he had to extend his arms out sideways and his head almost reached the ceiling.

'I am,' Emma said, 'and I'm going now. Thank you for looking after me.'

She began to walk towards the door. But Matthew loped after her, grabbed her wrist. 'Let me go!'

Matthew loosened his grip but didn't let go. 'I'm not going to hurt you. I promise. This was your home, you say?'

Emma nodded.

'I heard a crewman had been lost to the sea. It's your late father's old place on the Jago boats that I'm filling, isn't it?'

'Yes,' Emma whispered.

How odd the expression 'your late father' sounded. As though he'd forgotten the time and was later getting back than expected, but that he'd be home any moment. Which he wouldn't be ever again.

'It's a cruel life,' Matthew said. 'But that's how tied cottages work. My guess is you haven't got a ma?'

'Not any more. Six weeks after I buried my papa, I buried my mama and my brother, Johnnie.' Emma delivered the information in a voice that she knew sounded dead and flat and without emotion. It was the easiest way. Certainly, she didn't want this man's pity.

'I'm sorry. Truly sorry. But what to do with you?'

'You can let go of my wrist for a start. I can't stay here,' Emma said. She wriggled her wrist, and Matthew released her, took a step away from her. She was less frightened of Matthew now, but only a little. 'People will talk.'

'You'll more than likely find your reputation is already tarnished, I'm afraid.'

Emma drew her breath in sharply. What might he have done to her up there in the bedroom? She felt the blood drain from her face. Her clothes had all been in place, but …

'I didn't take advantage of you if that's what you're thinking,' Matthew said.

Emma pressed her lips together and nodded. She hoped and prayed he was telling the truth about that. 'Thank you,' she said, 'for letting me stop. I've been ill. I was lodging with a neighbour – Mrs Phipps – but she didn't feed me very well and I've got thin and weak. As you see.'

Emma looked down over her now almost non-existent bosoms – bosoms she'd been pleased had been forming so nicely and rounded before she'd been orphaned and become ill – and could see right down to her feet. How scuffed her mama's Sunday best shoes had become in so short a time.

'You certainly look like you need feeding up. But am I right in saying you're not lodging with the *good* Mrs Phipps any more?'

'No. I'd rather die.'

'A very dramatic answer, if I may say so.'

'It's the truth. Mrs Phipps only pretended to take care of me. She appropriated the food the doctor had sent round for me.'

'So, you haven't got anywhere to go?'

'No, but I'll find somewhere.'

'Not before you've had a cup of tea and a bite to eat. I've got bacon.'

'Bacon?' Emma said. How long had it been since she'd eaten bacon? On Sundays, if he wasn't out fishing, her papa had cooked a breakfast of bacon and eggs for the whole family; the one English meal he could see the point of, he'd always said.

'So, you'll stop?'

'Best not,' Emma said. 'The longer I'm here the worse my reputation will get no doubt. All it would take would be for Mrs Phipps to know I'm here and I'll be being talked about over every table between here and Plymouth and up to Exeter.'

35

'Oh, I expect I could buy off Mrs Phipps if you just tell me which one she is. There aren't many women averse to my charms.'

'That would be your opinion,' Emma said. Honestly, the audacity of the man. Although she had to admit there was something attractive about him.

'But not charming you, eh? Well, you know where the door is. Avoid Mrs Phipps at all costs when you go. And close the door behind you or I'll have every cat in the neighbourhood in here after my bacon, because I, for one, can't hold off eating a moment longer. It wasn't the most comfortable night's sleep I've ever had in that chair.'

'I didn't ask you to sleep in it,' Emma said.

'And my alternative was?' Matthew laughed heartily, then walked into the kitchen. To follow or not? She heard Matthew bang a pan down heavily on the range. He began to sing as though he didn't have a care in the world – which he probably didn't compared with her.

Emma crept towards the kitchen. Maybe just a sniff of cooking bacon would be enough – make her feel less hungry?

But Matthew must have heard her because he turned to Emma and smiled, although he said nothing. He put the bacon on. Took two plates from the rack on the wall that had once housed Emma's mother's best Sunday china, but which now held a collection of mismatched plates and bowls. Threw a faggot of wood into the range and raked it to stir the flames, raise the heat. Took two knives and two forks from a wooden box on the draining board. And grinned at Emma. 'Mr Jago must have assumed I'd have company. There's two of everything.'

'I'd rather you didn't talk about him if you don't mind.'

'Ah, yes. He's a thorn in the flesh to you, no doubt. I'll try to keep him out of the conversation from now on.'

'I'm going,' Emma said, her mouth watering as she

watched Matthew turn the bacon, crack four eggs into the pan. Four eggs. Would he eat that many himself if she didn't stop to share it? 'You can talk about him as much as you like to anyone else.'

'Fried bread?' Matthew said, sawing a thick slice from a loaf.

'No, thank you. Just the eggs and bacon will be fine.'

Gosh, had she really said that?

Evidently she had because Matthew lifted crispy bacon onto two plates. But just as soon as that bacon and eggs – and maybe a cup of tea – were down her throat she'd be off.

What would be expected of her now? Some small talk? Around her parents' table there had always been conversation. Matthew was humming something to himself as he pressed a slice of bread into the bacon fat in the pan.

'Why did you leave Slapton?' Emma asked.

'That's for me to know and you to wonder,' Matthew told her, spinning round. And he winked.

'I'd have thought there was plenty of fishing in Slapton,' Emma said, doing her best to ignore that wink. Her mama had warned her about men with seductive grins and fancy words.

'Then you think right. But it wasn't the fishing that forced the issue.'

Matthew wasn't smiling quite so broadly now.

'A woman then?' Emma said, then clapped a hand to her mouth. She'd been thinking the words and somehow they'd slipped out over her tongue as easy as honey off a spoon, when she ought to have bitten them back.

'I've known lots of women, Emma.' Matthew added two perfectly fried eggs to Emma's plate. 'Now get that down you and then you can go and if you're as bright as I think you are then you'll know to keep to yourself what's just been discussed in this kitchen.'

'Of course,' Emma said. 'And I'm sorry for being so outspoken. My papa always said my mouth would hang me.'

'Did he then?' Matthew said. The kettle came to the boil and he poured water onto the tea leaves, stirred vigorously. 'And for the record, I don't think there's a lot wrong in speaking your mind. I expect there's lots you would like to say to me considering I'm in the home that was yours.'

'It's not your fault you are,' Emma said. She sliced angrily at a rasher of bacon. 'But Mr Jago shouldn't have sold my parents' things without telling me. Or burned what he couldn't sell.'

Matthew's face darkened. 'No,' he said. 'He shouldn't have. But there's not a lot I can do about that now.'

'All I've got left is a book,' Emma said, willing the tears that puddled her eyes not to fall. 'And a broken book at that.'

'How old are you, Emma?'

'Fifteen. Sixteen come Michaelmas.'

'Too young to marry at the moment.'

'Marry?' Emma thought she was going to explode. Did he really think she would have to marry to get out of her predicament?

'It's a great institution – when it works.'

'It was for my mama and my papa,' Emma said. 'I wouldn't settle for anything less than they had. And I certainly wouldn't marry for convenience.'

'Shame,' Matthew said, the grin back on his face again. 'I could use a woman around the house. Not that I'm suggesting I marry you. But I do need someone to cook, someone to ...'

'I hope you're teasing me. But if you're not then I have to tell you I won't be that someone,' Emma said. She crammed food – very inelegantly, she knew – into her mouth and chewed and swallowed quickly until it was all gone. 'But thank you very much for my breakfast and for looking after me last night. I'll be on my way now.'

Emma retrieved her shawl from the back of a chair and slung it around her shoulders, knotting it firmly at her waist.

'Nice to meet you,' Matthew said. 'And any time you're down on your luck, you'll be welcome to come back. I ...'

'Oh, I couldn't do that,' Emma said. 'It wouldn't be right. Last night was an ... an ...'

'Emergency, Emma. I'm glad I was able to help. But before you go, I've got something of yours you might like.' He strode into the sitting-room and came back with Emma's book. 'I've mended the spine. The leather's a different colour, but it's well stuck down and it will stop the pages from falling out.'

He held out the book towards Emma and she took it, hugged it to her. Her mama had bought her that book, saving a halfpenny a week until she'd had enough to pay for it in Bastin's. And Matthew had mended it for her.

'Thank you,' she said. She regretted being so sharp with him now.

'My pleasure.' Matthew placed a hand under Emma's elbow and guided her towards the front door. 'And for what it's worth, you'll be a fine young woman once your sharp edges are rounded off.'

'How, how ...' Emma began, all ready to be outraged and sharp with Matthew all over again. Then she laughed. He seemed to know her better than she knew herself.

'Ah,' Matthew said, reaching into a box beside the front door, 'and another thing. You might as well have this. My old landlady must have dropped it in the box as a heavy hint. Fisherman can smell a bit sometimes.' He laughed and held his nose and Emma couldn't help but smile.

He handed her a small block of soap. Unused. Pale pink. Emma put it to her nose and it smelled of roses.

'I haven't got much use for flowery soaps, Emma. Can you imagine the comments of the rest of the crew if I went on board smelling of roses?'

'I certainly can.' Emma laughed. She opened her carpet bag and added the soap to its meagre contents, along with her mended copy of *Persuasion*.

'And one thing more,' Matthew said, smiling at her.

'Oh, I can't accept anything else, Mr Caunter. You've already given me enough.'

'Nothing to eat, drink or make yourself pretty with, Emma. But if you can't find anywhere else, then I could give you the offer of a bed for the night …'

'I can't. I …'

But Matthew put a finger to her lips. 'You might not have other choices. It'll be hard for a girl as young as you, and on your own.' His voice was grave and his look stern. 'But mind you don't get into bad ways. Some women …'

'I'm not "*some women*". I'm Emma Le Goff.'

Matthew patted her shoulder. 'There, there, don't get on your high horse. It can be a long way down coming off.'

Then he opened the door and ushered Emma outside. The sun was up now and it was going to be a warm day, she was sure of it. But what she was going to do and where she was going to go she had no idea. However, there was food in her belly and she'd been shown kindness by a stranger.

'Good luck,' Matthew called out as she reached the gate.

Emma turned to wave and then she saw her – Mrs Phipps. And the old harridan was grinning, storing up the picture before her no doubt, ready to embellish it and milk the gossip for all it was worth.

'Hmm, like mother like daughter,' Mrs Phipps said.

Emma was doing her best to ignore every single thing

Mrs Phipps was saying as they walked side by side towards the harbour. Emma was walking as fast as she possibly could, given she'd been so ill for so long, but Mrs Phipps was keeping pace with her easily enough for such a large woman.

'What's that supposed to mean?'

'Ah, found your voice, have you?'

'I never lost it. I just asked you a question, Mrs Phipps. What do you mean by the reference to my mother?'

'Ah, well, when you were in the school, Rachel Le Goff – for all her fancy name – had visitors. After your pa died, that is.'

'Visitors?' Her mama had never been one for having the neighbours in for tea and cake and to trade gossip, mainly because she never had much money to spare for such frivolities, but mostly because her mama didn't say anything bad about anyone, or want to hear it either.

'That's what I said.'

'What sort of visitors? The doctor's wife used to pass on her son's outgrown clothes for Johnnie sometimes. Or maybe ...'

'Gentlemen visitors,' Mrs Phipps said. She had a sneer of a grin on her face, her lips pulled back so that Emma had a full view of a mouthful of rotting teeth. It made her want to retch.

'The vicar then, or the doctor. I'm well aware both called on my mother after Papa was drowned. Now if that's all you've got to say, I'll be on my way.'

Emma made to change direction, walk anywhere as long as it was away from Mrs Phipps, but the older woman grabbed at her shawl, pulling it from Emma's shoulder. 'It's not all I've got to say. Like I said, it's a case of like mother like daughter here – you stopping all night with that fisherman up from Slapton.'

'I didn't have any choice about where I stopped last night, Mrs Phipps. I must have passed out. Mr Caunter threw a blanket over me and let me sleep. On the chair by the fire.' Behind her back, Emma crossed her fingers that she wouldn't go to hell for telling a lie. 'And no one stopped the night with my mama after Papa died, Mrs Phipps. Ever. Understand?'

'Not the night, no. But the daytime was a bit different. Came round the back alley and in the gate, brazen as you like, many a time. I could see 'n from the end of my garden, when I was up the you-know-what, doing my business.'

Emma took a moment or two to digest this unsavoury information. Yes, Mrs Phipps' cottage was on the contour above Shingle Cottage and she could easily see down into the Le Goff garden. But she must have made a special effort to do so because to Emma's knowledge none of the privies in Cliff Terrace had windows.

'Who did?'

'Mr Reuben Jago. And sometimes his son, Carter. Walked up the path bold as brass they did.'

Just the sound of Reuben Jago's name made Emma's bile rise – it felt sharp as vinegar in her throat. And Mrs Phipps was suggesting there was something untoward about him calling on her mother, wasn't she? And Carter Jago, too.

'I've been told my mama was a bit behind with the rent after my papa died,' Emma said softly. She was almost too ashamed to say the words. But if it would defend her mother's reputation then she'd say them. 'I expect Mr Jago called to ask for it, that's all. And sent his son to ask when he couldn't call himself.'

'Oh yes? And how do you think your *mama* paid it off? Weren't with pence and pounds, were it? Unless it were the pounds of her body ...'

'You ... you ... foul-mouthed, bitter old woman,' Emma

yelled. She didn't care who heard her. 'And you're a liar with it.'

She snatched at the catch of her carpet bag and thrust her hand in, searching out the bar of soap Matthew Caunter had just given her. 'Here, take this. Wash your filthy mouth out.'

She threw it at Mrs Phipps, then turned on her heel and ran. She skirted round people she knew, who averted their eyes when they saw her coming. The heels of her shoes clacked on the cobbles outside the homes of school friends where once she would have been welcome, but now as she passed she saw curtains hastily pulled across and doors closed at her approach. Why? Why? What had she done that was making people turn against her so?

Wasn't there anyone who would take her in? The vicar? Dr Shaw, perhaps? Just until she could find a job of work and preferably one that provided a bed to sleep in, too.

Her mama had always been adamant that no daughter of hers was going to go into service and that was why she'd been saving for Emma's teacher-training, taking in sewing jobs to make a bit extra. Pin money, quite literally, her mama had always said, laughing as she said it. But perhaps going into service was going to be Emma's only way to survive. It would be her last resort, though – there had to be something else she could do. Emma's head throbbed with thinking about it all, and her calves ached from hurrying faster than her body was ready for yet.

She *would* call on Dr Shaw. Perhaps he'd have a position for her in his own house. Or in the surgery on the reception desk – yes, that would be a better job. She could learn to do that easily enough, couldn't she? There was a shortcut – an alley between two inns; it was steep but it would save her a longer walk round and up the hill. Emma slowed her pace and slipped into the alley. It was darker between the high walls but not so dark she couldn't see the shape of a person lying on the ground. A woman. To turn around and go back and pretend she hadn't noticed, or to go on and see if the woman was all right?

Emma knew what she had to do. She crept forward, a slow step at a time. She recognised the flame red hair. Sophie Ellison. Sophie had been in the year above Emma at school. Had got in with a bad crowd. But she'd been at the funeral for her mama and Johnnie, and Emma would always be grateful to her for that.

The hem of Sophie's skirt was pulled up, twisted round, over the top of her thighs. Her legs had a bluish tinge, and Emma shivered looking at them. She leaned down and tried to pull Sophie's skirt down to cover her legs, give her some decency here in this alley that smelled of stale beer and urine and fish.

Then she crouched down beside the curled form of Sophie. Was she drunk? 'Sophie?' Emma said. 'It's me, Emma Le Goff. Are you hurt?' She touched the back of Sophie's hand. It was cold. Like alabaster.

'Sophie, speak to me,' Emma said, frightened now. 'Please, speak to me.'

And then she noticed the blood – a burgundy pool of it under Sophie's chest already beginning to congeal – and Emma knew that Sophie was never going to speak to her again because Sophie was dead.

''Morning, Seth,' Mrs Phipps said.

Seth puffed out his cheeks, let the air escape slowly. The last person he wanted to see. She was forever offering him the services of her over-large and probably under-washed body.

'Good morning, Mrs Phipps.' Seth made to hurry past. He was on his way to the harbour, but was late – held up by his father asking if he'd come to his senses yet over Emma. In Seth's opinion he'd never lost his senses. He rubbed his eyes, dry and itchy through lack of sleep, thinking about Emma and how he might help her.

'Not so fast.' Mrs Phipps grabbed his forearm. 'You can spare me a few minutes.'

'Not for what you're about to suggest.'

Mrs Phipps cackled. 'Got to get rid of that ol' virginity of yours some time. Might as well be with someone who can learn you a thing or two. But that's not what I'm meaning.' She leaned in to whisper. 'Your pa done right throwing Emma Le Goff out of Shingle Cottage. 'Cept from what I saw, she's got herself back in. Only spent the night there with the new tenant, didn't she? Looked all cosy on the doorstep they did earlier. Presents and all going in that bag of hers.'

Seth made a tight line of his lips. Anger was boiling in him, making his heart beat faster. He didn't know which was the worst of the evils – Mrs Phipps for spreading gossip, or Emma for spending the night with his pa's new crewman, or himself for believing any of it.

'I hesitate to call you a liar, Mrs Phipps …'

'I ain't no liar. Saw her with me own eyes, did'n I? Right little harlot she is.'

'You're a right one to be calling anyone a harlot, Mrs Phipps,' Seth hissed.

'You'd not be likely to know, would yer? Seeing as you'm not like your brothers and are as pure as the good Lord made yer …'

'Out of my way,' Seth said. 'Or my pa's boats will miss the tide.' Then he pushed her hand away from his arm as though it were fire, and turned on his heel and left.

Had his pa been right when he'd said it would be best if Seth forgot all about Emma? Had he? But where else could Emma have gone for the night? Mrs Drew had had no space, and from what he'd heard, she'd been shunned by old friends who believed Rachel Goff had been a suicide. It had been a cold night and Seth shivered, thinking Emma might have fallen asleep from fatigue and hunger under a hedge somewhere and died of the cold.

He hurried on. If he had to keep seeing Emma he'd never be able to stop thinking about her, or be able to avoid hearing all sorts of tales – true or not – about her. His Uncle Silas fished out of Vancouver on the west coast of Canada – it wouldn't hurt to write and ask if his offer of a job running the shipping office for him still stood, although he'd like to get the truth about what had really happened to his ma and that fall down the cellar steps before he made a firm decision to go.

But he had a feeling even Canada wouldn't be far enough to forget the lovely Emma.

Chapter Four

'Dr Shaw! Dr Shaw!' Emma yelled, but the yelling made her cough. She turned the huge brass door knob and stumbled into the doctor's waiting room. Three surprised patients stared at her. No glared – but Emma had no time to challenge them about that now. She ran on and banged on the surgery door.

'Dr Shaw. Open up. You've got to come.'

Behind her she heard someone say, 'Get that trollop out of here. Taints the place.'

Emma turned and recognised Mrs Phipps' next-door neighbour. What lies had *she* been spreading about her?

And then someone else said, 'Wouldn't want the good doctor touching me after he's touched *her*.'

And then the door opened and a startled Dr Shaw said, 'Emma? Whatever is the matter, child?'

'You've got to come, Doctor,' Emma said, 'you've got to. It's Sophie Ellison. She's … she's hurt bad. Down the alley.'

'Hurt? In what way? There's lots of drinking …'

'Blood, Doctor. There's lots of blood. And she isn't moving. I don't think she's …' Emma couldn't say the word 'breathing'. And that she was certain Sophie was dead.

'Did you touch her?'

'No. Well, yes. But only her hand. It felt colder than marble, Doctor.'

'And did she speak to you?'

'No.'

'Then we're wasting time. I'll get my bag. Wait here.'

So Emma waited, no more than a few seconds but it felt like years as the waiting patients tutted and whispered to one another behind their hands. About her no doubt, but Emma couldn't care.

Dr Shaw closed his surgery door behind him, placed his free hand under Emma's elbow and guided her towards the front door.

'Well, if that's the lie of the land, there's more than one doctor in this town so I'll be seeing Dr Green from now on,' someone said as they walked past.

'Standards are definitely dropping if the likes of *her* can come in here and jump the queue.' Another person joined the debate.

'Do as you think fit,' the doctor called out. 'All of you. At the moment Emma's case is more pressing. Come, Emma, lead the way.'

He smiled kindly at Emma and his smile brought tears to her eyes. She had someone on her side.

Emma sat, shivering inside a blanket Dr Shaw's wife had placed around her shoulders, her chair pulled up close to the range in the kitchen. Florrie, the doctor's maid, handed Emma a mug of steaming cocoa. 'Get that down you, girl,' she said.

'Thank you.' Emma took the mug, clasping her hands around it for warmth.

She knew she shouldn't have looked as the doctor turned Sophie Ellison over, but she hadn't been able to stop herself. There had been a huge, open wound where Sophie's heart was, her clothes ripped from her so that Emma had been able to see the white mounds of her breasts bared to the world. The doctor had removed his jacket and placed it carefully over Sophie, covering her wound and her nakedness and her face.

And now she was in shock from the sight of it. Dr Shaw had banged on the back door of the inn and asked for someone to go for the constable and the undertaker. When they arrived, Emma had stood with hands over her eyes, not wanting to see Sophie Ellison being heaved about like a sheep's carcass onto a wooden trolley. She'd answered the constable's questions as best she could, her head aching with the pressure of having to remember every little detail. Then Dr Shaw said that Emma needed treatment herself so she'd better come back to the house with him. He'd given her brandy and checked her pulse and her breathing and listened to her heart and said she could stop in his kitchen until she felt stronger. Emma wondered if she could delay feeling stronger until the morning at least because it was warm in the kitchen. And she could smell meat being cooked, and there was a pan of potatoes all peeled and ready to be put to the heat.

'You saw it *all*, Emma,' Florrie said, with something like awe in her voice. 'Was she murdered?'

'Yes,' Emma said, still shivering. She didn't want to talk about it really. Sophie *had* been murdered and the murderer could still be around somewhere.

'Were her eyes open? My brother saw a dead man once and his eyes were open. Staring they were …'

'I don't want to talk about it.'

Sophie's eyes *had* been open, and Emma didn't think she'd ever be able to forget the terror in those eyes. And Sophie had smelled of drink when the doctor had turned her over. Stank of it. Beer and stronger things, like brandy. If there was a lesson never to go down bad roads then the state of Sophie Ellison had been that lesson.

'Oh, go on,' Florrie said. 'I won't tell.'

'There's not a lot to tell,' Emma said. 'Sophie's dead and the constable is looking for who did it.'

'Hah. He'll be on a boat already and gone, that's for sure. There was a coal barge in earlier from Wales. Like little ferrets the Welsh are, their tongues never still and their hands neither once they've had a drink or two.'

'The murderer could have been a *her*,' Emma said.

Florrie cackled raucously. 'You're a rum 'un, Emma Le Goff, with your fancy name and your fancy ideas. Whoever heard of a woman murdering anyone? Bound to have been a man. Someone she didn't want to offer her favours to, I 'spect.'

Emma shrugged. Let Florrie have her theories, but in a way she hoped the girl was right and the murderer was on his way. Because soon she would have to leave the warmth of this kitchen and the safety of this house. She'd asked the doctor if he knew anyone who could give her a job – in a shop, or a boarding house, or a hotel – but he'd said he didn't know of anyone needing help right now. Although he did say once he'd seen to his afternoon patients he'd give it some thought.

And then, as though just thinking of him had summoned his presence, Dr Shaw came into the kitchen. 'And how are you feeling now, Emma?' he asked kindly. 'Wrist, please.'

Emma slid an arm out from under the blanket and held it out for him to take her pulse. 'I feel a bit better, Doctor,' she said. 'But not a lot.' She tried not to let her gaze rest on the pan of potatoes but it did. And by the way the doctor smiled at her she knew he was reading her thoughts.

'Hmm,' he said. He put the ear pieces of his stethoscope to his ears. 'Florrie, leave us for a moment, will you?'

'But the tatties, Doctor – I've got to put them on.'

'What's that? Can't hear you with these things in my ears. Go, girl, when I tell you to.' He pointed – a stern expression on his face – towards the door.

Florrie went.

'And now I can listen to your chest, without Florrie's nose poking in your business,' Dr Shaw said to Emma. 'Open your blouse a couple of buttons, child.'

The listening over, Dr Shaw removed his stethoscope and

pronounced Emma in reasonable health, given she'd been so ill when she'd stopped with Mrs Phipps, as she'd feared he would. No supper for Emma, then?

But she took a deep breath and said, 'I could help Florrie with the supper. And if there was bit left over …'

'I was just going to suggest that very thing. And my wife has discovered some clothes my daughter Sarah has outgrown which she thinks will fit you. A pair of boots, too. And a warm coat. My wife has packed it all neatly for you, but I fear it'll be too heavy for you to carry after your terrible shock of earlier, so I've arranged for Seth Jago to come and collect you.'

'Seth?' Emma said. 'Him? Where's he going to take me?'

'Oh, I'm jumping ahead of myself, aren't I? I called on Mr Jago after seeing to the arrangements for poor Sophie, and I put it to him that as it was he who had made you homeless, the least he could do was offer you refuge in that enormous villa of his. He just happens to have a vacancy for a housemaid now that poor Sophie is dead. He said he'd send Seth to fetch you.'

'Sophie worked for Mr Jago?'

'Yes. Apparently she slipped out of her room last night and never came back. Didn't you know she'd worked for him?'

'No. And I can't work for him, either. I don't want to be a housemaid. My mama was saving for me to train as a teacher when I'm old enough. She …'

'And do you want to be a teacher?' Dr Shaw interrupted.

Emma thought for a moment. No, she didn't really. She didn't like having to chastise the children for shrieking with laughter in the playground when all they were doing was being little children – and heaven only knew most of them had little to laugh about. And then there was the fact a woman teacher had to leave if she married. The thought of being an elderly, spinster teacher filled her with dread. She'd gone along with it because her mama had wanted a better life for her so much. But at this moment, it was as though the doctor was seeing into her mind, her soul.

'Not really,' she said. 'But for Mama's memory I would.'

'Very commendable. But I think the moment has come for you to give some thought to your future and what you want for yourself. Time spent in the Jago household could give you that.'

'But not in service. I don't want to be a servant. I won't be!'

'It doesn't have to be forever, Emma.'

'It can't be at all, Doctor.'

'Now, now, child – it never does to make decisions in haste. Or after a shock the like of which you've had today. Some good food inside you and maybe a small glass of porter and you'll see it all differently.'

'I know what you mean, Doctor,' Emma said, 'and I'm grateful to you for asking on my behalf, but ...' Emma tried to swallow but couldn't. She gulped and gulped trying, until she coughed suddenly, felt whoozy with the effort of it all.

'What is it, Emma?' Dr Shaw touched her arm lightly, smiled. 'Whatever it is that's bothering you, you can tell me.'

'I've got a little money saved but it probably won't be enough to pay your bill,' Emma said. 'I could do some jobs for you to pay for your services if you've got anything I could do. I ...'

'It might surprise you to know I don't charge everyone who comes to see me.'

Should she tell him? The real reason she didn't want to stop under the Jago roof. A doctor was like a priest, wasn't he? Bound by some sort of oath not to divulge what a patient had told him, unless the law had been broken. She knew the doctor had seen her mama without her drawers on after the miscarriages. To tell him what Mrs Phipps had been saying about her mama and Mr Jago couldn't be any worse, could it?

'Mrs Phipps said Mr Jago and his son Carter had been visiting my mama. And ... and ...'

'And Mrs Phipps intimated it wasn't the rent they were calling for?'

Dr Shaw knelt in front of Emma, held her hands in his, narrowed the gap between them

'Yes,' Emma said. She hung her head. Images of Mr Jago and Carter even touching her mother were making her feel sick.

The doctor placed a hand under Emma's chin and raised it so she was forced to look at him. 'I think we can both discount anything that Mrs Phipps says, don't you?'

'I want to, Doctor, but ...'

'Then you *must*. I regret now agreeing the woman could take you in after you collapsed. Sadly, no one else offered, and I had no bed spare here at the time. But rest assured, I'm sure whatever it is Mrs Phipps has told you is all make belief.

'Now, I can hear Florrie pacing up and down the hall which tells me she's keen to get the potatoes on.' The doctor rose, stiffly.

'That's not the only reason,' Emma said quickly, not wanting him to go. She had to persuade him somehow that she couldn't go to the Jago's. 'I went to see Mr Jago because he sold – or burned – all my things. I told him in no uncertain terms what I thought of him. He threw me out. He's not going to want me back.'

'Ah, yes. Mr Jago did mention it. But he's accepted it as having been said in the heat of the moment.'

'Heat of the moment ...' Emma began. But her words died on her lips. If she had to tell Mr Jago the same thing a million times, she would.

'Yes, my dear – heat of the moment. Now, I must get on. And so must Florrie. Seth Jago will be here with the pony and trap to collect you at nine.'

The second Seth stepped into the hall Carter raced towards him. 'Oh, there you are, baby brother,' he said. 'Where've you been?'

Seth decided to ignore the 'baby brother' insult. 'At the police station, as you well know. Answering questions, same as you were earlier. About Sophie, and if I …'

'What did you say?'

'That I had no idea she'd left the house.'

'And you were all tucked up in bed and wouldn't have heard her going out anyway?'

'Something along those lines, yes.'

'I heard that slut Emma Le Goff found her …'

'Emma's *not* a slut.'

'Tried it on with her, did you? Got slapped for your pains?'

Carter was blocking Seth's path, arms folded.

'No. Let me pass.'

'Need a few lessons in seduction, you do. Loosen 'em up with gin first. She'll be in Sophie's old room tonight. She'll be a bit of practice for you.'

Seth didn't want to practise with anyone. He didn't want a different woman each night the way his brothers did.

'Emma's coming here?'

'You heard. Dr Shaw was round here earlier, pleading the slut's case …'

'Call Emma that one more time and I'll thump you.' Seth balled his fists. He and Carter had had a scrap or two as children, the way brothers do. But as they'd grown, Seth had learned to avoid being in his brother's company if at all possible – Carter had a foul temper and was far too quick to settle things with his fists, in Seth's opinion. Carter had moved far beyond boyhood scraps – keeping out of his way as much as possible was Seth's best option.

'How gallant,' Carter sneered. He jutted his chin towards Seth, taunting him. 'Go on. Hit me. Bet you wouldn't dare.'

'Then you lose the bet.'

Seth brought his right fist up and it smacked against Carter's chin, sending him crashing against the wall. A picture was knocked to the floor, the glass shattering loudly in the cavernous hallway.

Without waiting to see what damage he might have caused his brother, Seth strode away to see his father – find out what it was all about. He couldn't imagine that his father had had a voluntary change of heart about Emma.

But his father must have heard the commotion because the drawing-room door opened and he bellowed, 'What the hell is going on here, boys?'

Seth turned to see Carter struggling to his feet.

'You tell him, big boy,' Carter said.

'In here,' Reuben said, pushing Seth none too gently into the drawing-room.

'Carter was making derogatory remarks about Emma Le Goff. Who, he tells me, is going to be coming here.'

'He told you right. She is. But I'm not happy about it. She's a nest of vipers, that girl.'

'So, why is she coming, then?' Seth asked.

'Because we now have an empty room following Sophie Ellison's demise, and Dr Shaw knows it. The good doctor seems to think I'm the cause of Miss Le Goff's distress. A load of rubbish, of course, but ...'

'You are. You should ...'

'Don't interrupt when I'm speaking.'

'Go on,' Seth said.

'I will – not that I need your permission. In case Carter didn't get around to telling you before you socked him one, you're to fetch the little madam. I've arranged for you to collect her in the pony and trap at nine.'

'Why me?'

'Because I'm telling you to, perhaps? You've already given me grief by bringing her here ...'

'I didn't bring her. She was coming here of her own accord. I merely followed with her bag.'

'How gallant.'

Gallant? Emma was hardly likely to see it as that. But now he was thinking about it, Emma would be safer with him than she would be if one of his brothers was fetching her. 'That's as maybe. But I'm ashamed to be a Jago at the moment, and that's the truth. If Dr Shaw hadn't asked you to take Emma in, you wouldn't have volunteered, would you? You'd rather have seen her die of starvation and cold than take her in.'

Reuben Jago laughed loudly, pushing his face close to Seth's so that Seth could smell the stench of none-too-fresh breath. He backed away. 'I could still change my mind, son. Now you have ten seconds to leave this room and do as you're bid.'

Seth left. He would never forgive himself if Emma starved and died of cold with nowhere else but Hilltop House to go to.

'Have I got to sleep in Sophie's bed?' Emma asked Seth as the pony plodded up the hill, struggling with the incline and an extra passenger and her carpet bag now full of clothes and a pair of boots that Emma wished she hadn't been given because it would make leaving Reuben Jago's house more difficult.

'Yes, but Mrs Drew changed the sheets and gave it all a good clean. She says she's sorry she can't take you in.' Seth loosed a rein and patted the blanket covering Emma's knees.

The pony skidded on the cobbles and Seth jiggled the reins to steady it. 'She wasn't asked to do it, Emma. Pa said she wasn't to, when she suggested it. But being Mrs Drew she did it anyway when his back was turned.'

'I must remember to thank her,' Emma said. She hunched her shoulders, squashed herself in as small as she could. She was finding it unsettling being so close to Seth in the pony trap. She cast a sideways look at him. Strong profile, a hint of a seven o'clock shadow on his chin.

They travelled on in silence. It wasn't a long journey and Emma felt her heart plummet as they reached the Jago villa.

Seth guided the pony and trap in through the gateway, talking soothingly to the animal. 'Easy, Ned, easy,' he said, and they came to a standstill outside the front door.

Almost immediately the door was flung wide and Reuben Jago filled the space. 'Around the back, Seth,' he yelled.

Emma stared up at him, glaring down at her from the top of a short but wide flight of steps. He looked like some sort of angry god – Zeus perhaps.

'No, Pa,' Seth said – not angrily, but there was confidence in his voice; a confidence he didn't feel, Emma, could tell, because his leg shook beside her in the trap. 'The doctor said Emma has to take it easy for a couple of days. There are too many steps at the back.'

'Oh yes, the good doctor. But that's as maybe,' Reuben snapped. 'Servants use the rear entrance. Now do as you're told, son.'

'I'm not going to be a servant, Seth,' Emma whispered, leaning into him. The emotion of the moment was making her feel weak. She needed support. 'I won't be.'

'You won't be doing anything for a few days. You've got to get your strength back first,' Seth whispered back. He reached under the blanket for Emma's hand and held it firmly.

'Stop muttering like a pair of lovesick pigeons,' Reuben Jago bawled. 'I said, round the back, Seth. Now get to it!'

'No, Pa,' Seth said. He jumped down from the trap and ran round in front of the pony to help Emma down. He held out a hand towards her, but Emma kept her hands tightly clasped under the blanket.

'Take me around the back, Seth,' she whispered. 'I don't want you to get into trouble with your father on my account. Besides, I won't be stopping long.'

'Well, for as long as you're here you'll come in and out of the front door. And harm will come to you in this house over my dead body.'

It was Seth himself who showed Emma to her room up in the attic. The gardener and Mrs Drew came in daily, and only the cook and one maid ever slept in he told her – and the cook had retired to her room immediately supper had been served and cleared away – so there was no one else around to do it.

No need to remind Emma that the maid who'd slept in had been Sophie Ellison. Poor, dead, Sophie Ellison.

Seth's brothers – Miles and Carter – goaded him mercilessly, walking up the flights of stairs behind her and Seth, making ribald comments about him being a virgin and did he know what he had it for and he might as well practise on the servants.

'If you mean me,' Emma said, turning to look back at them, 'I'm not a servant. Dr Shaw has arranged for me to stay here for a little while. Until I'm stronger. Seeing as your pa has made me homeless, through no fault of my own.'

'Ooh, she's a mouthy one, Seth,' Miles said. 'Got something you could stick in her gob to shut her up?'

'I've got something I'll stick in yours in a minute,' Seth said. 'My fist.'

'And your puny fist is going to frighten me?' Miles taunted. 'No one comes into this house unless Pa's got a use for them, Seth, and you know it.'

'Shut up, Miles,' Seth bellowed at his brother. 'Emma's right – she's not a servant. At the moment she's a guest.'

'Servant? Guest? What's the difference? Nice tight little spirited one for you to practise on there, Seth,' Carter commented. 'Remember my tip about the gin.'

'I don't drink gin,' Emma snapped. 'Or any other spirits for that matter.'

'Ignore them,' Seth said. He placed a hand under Emma's elbow to urge her onwards.

But Emma was going nowhere for the moment. Seth's brothers needed reminding of their manners, and tired as she was, Emma was going to do just that. Afraid she might be dizzy if she moved too quickly, Emma slowly turned around to face them. 'Didn't you two hear your brother?'

'What? What?' the brothers said, cupping their hands to their ears, giggling like schoolgirls and not the twenty-something men they were.

'Obviously not,' Emma said. 'So, I'll say it again – I'm not here to be a servant although I might give Mrs Drew a hand with some jobs to help pay for my keep if she needs me to. And nobody's going to do anything to me against my wishes. I hope you two understand the plain English of that.'

'Not quite,' Carter said. 'Explain some more. Your bosom heaves up and down quite deliciously when you're cross.'

Emma sucked in her breath. She had no bosom to speak of really. But she folded her arms across her chest anyway. 'I'll say it in French if you'll understand it better. *Je ne suis pas …*'

'Come on, Emma,' Seth said. 'It's only making them worse, standing up to them.'

He put a protective arm around her then squeezed her

shoulder, and Emma had a niggle of a suspicion that he might be trying to get his way with her by gentler, more subtle means. But she stayed within the protective curve of his arm. In the room, he laid Emma's carpet bag on the bed. Then he drew thick woollen curtains together at the windows, before checking there was water in the jug for her to wash in the morning.

'There's water in taps downstairs,' he said, 'but not up here.'

'That's all right,' Emma said. 'I'm used to a jug and a bowl.'

'You're worth more than that, Emma,' Seth said quietly. 'And I'm sorry for the way my pa has treated you over Shingle Cottage, really I am.'

Emma shrugged. What could she say? And if she did speak she had a feeling she might cry and no way did she want Seth Jago feeling sorry for her. She was surprised when he drew a small bar of chocolate from the pocket of his trousers.

'I thought you might like this,' he said.

Emma had eaten chocolate once before and had found it bitter. But Seth was offering her a gift, and she would accept it with good grace. 'Thank you.' She took the chocolate, sniffed it. It smelled of almonds. And then she noticed the wording on it and her heart lifted. 'Oh, it's French! Where did you get this?'

Eagerly she read the words, not needing to translate them into English, but understanding them for themselves. How good it felt. How close to her papa she felt reading them. Maybe she could buy more for herself somewhere close by when she had the funds.

And then she realised Seth hadn't answered her question.

'Well, Seth?' she asked. 'Where did you get it? When I've got some pennies saved I think I'd like to buy some for myself if only you'll tell me where I can. I haven't seen any chocolate like this in Mrs Minifie's sweet shop.'

Seth mumbled something Emma didn't catch.

'It's not smuggled goods, is it?' Emma said, all ready to hand it straight back to him if it was.

'It came in on one of our boats, I can't deny that. Our boats have to pull into French ports sometimes, Emma, if the weather turns and they're too far from home to come back safely. They can be there for days sometimes. And they go ashore. Buy things.'

'Is that the truth about this chocolate?'

'I paid my brother, Miles, for it. Does that make it better for you? A more honest answer would be that I have my suspicions, but no real proof about what goes in and comes out of my pa's boats.'

'You mean smuggling, don't you?' Emma said.

'Leave it, Emma. Best you get to sleep now. And you'd be wise to take my advice and pull a chair up to the door and ram the back of it under the handle.'

And then he was gone. And Emma was left alone in the cold attic room and wondering if her papa had discovered something was going on – something he didn't want to be part of; some sort of contraband goods racket. A sudden chill enveloped Emma that maybe Reuben Jago had left her papa to drown so he couldn't go to the authorities. Would it serve any purpose to try and get the truth from Reuben Jago? She thought not.

But she did as Seth had told her and placed the back of a chair under the door handle.

Chapter Five

'Emma! It's me, Beattie Drew. Are you awake, lovie?'

The door knob rattled and Beattie Drew knocked again. Emma rubbed sleep from her eyes – surprisingly, she'd slept well. As she shot bolt upright in the bed the thought hit her that seeing as Seth had suggested she put the chair against the door handle he had had no intention of foisting his attentions on her in the night. And that thought made her smile. She liked Seth. But maybe it would be better if she squashed down those feelings. He was a Jago, after all. And although she was now under the Jago roof, it hadn't been her choice. No, she had nothing much to thank any of the Jagos for, did she?

Beattie knocked again. 'Emma, lovie, open the door.'

Emma thought there was something approaching fear in Mrs Drew's voice. Anxiety, at the very least. 'I'm coming, I'm coming.'

She slid out of bed and grabbed the coat Dr Shaw's wife had given her, and covered her near-nakededness. She'd had to sleep in her chemise and drawers, but she'd been warm enough – surprised to find a heated brick in her bed. Had Seth done that for her? She had a feeling he had.

'Come on then, lovie, I've got work to do.'

Emma dragged the chair away from the door. The legs scraping against the bare boards setting her teeth on edge, the way chalk had on a blackboard when she was at school.

'Well, what a sight you are, and there's no mistake.' Beattie Drew bustled into the room, pulled back the curtains.

Emma put a hand over her eyes to block out the low, bright, sunlight. What time was it?

'I've brought a jug of hot water, lovie. It's on the landing.'

Mrs Drew scuttled out again, came back in holding the jug carefully as though it were a newborn. 'What a to-do there is going on about that trollop, Sophie. Got no worse than she deserved. I ...'

'No one deserves to be murdered, Mrs Drew.'

'I know. I know. And the devil take me for even thinking it. It's the shock of it all making me say these things. I was only talking to her yesterday and now ...' Mrs Drew bit on her bottom lip. 'Now, it won't be doing any good to shed tears for Sophie, 'cos she didn't worry about anyone else, that's for sure. But better you get yourself washed while this water's hot. Had to do it when Mr Jago weren't looking, didn't I? He don't hold with lesser mortals having *hot* water. Oh no ...'

'Don't get yourself in trouble on my account, Mrs Drew.'

'And you think old Beattie Drew can't get herself out of a bit of trouble?' The older woman chuckled, put a finger to her lips intimating that they weren't to make too much noise.

'Mr Jago's still around?'

'He is, but he should be on his way soon. If he isn't then he'll miss the tide and he'll have to pay off the crews and no fish to show for it to pay their wages.'

Still feeling weak after her illness and no doubt all the trauma of the previous days' events, Emma walked slowly over to the dressing-table. There was a set of silver-backed brushes and a comb neatly laid out like the rays of the sun in a child's drawing. Were they Sophie's? Had she used them before going out to her death? Emma bent to inspect the brushes. She couldn't see any long, flame-red hairs that might have been Sophie's. But still she didn't want to use them just in case.

'Get yourself tidied up, lovie. You can use them brushes you'm looking at like they're going to bite. They weren't

Sophie's, if that's what you're thinking. Seth got them from somewhere. His ma's, I expect, God rest her soul. I was up here changing the bed and he came in and asked if there was anything else you might need. So I said you wouldn't want to use the filthy brushes Sophie left behind. And off he went, came back with those.'

'Oh,' Emma said. For a fleeting moment she wondered if the brushes might be contraband, as the chocolate she hadn't yet eaten more than likely was, but she dismissed the thought from her mind. She wasn't going to let the Jago family make her suspicious of everything and everyone.

'He's a changeling that Seth, right and all he is,' Beattie Drew said. She opened the bottom drawer of the dressing-table and pulled out a large towel – navy and beige stripes that Emma thought might once have been white. And a smaller coffee-coloured towel with a flower-sprigged trim. And a flannel. 'Now, get that lovely hair of yours freshened up a bit.'

She took a bar of soap from the pocket of her apron and handed it to Emma. Pink soap. It looked suspiciously like the very same pink soap that Emma had thrown at Mrs Phipps.

'Just lather it up a little and finger a few suds over the top of your hair, rinse it off again with the flannel. There ain't enough water here for you to wash the lot. You've got that much of it.'

Emma put her hands behind her back.

'Now come on, lovie, take it.'

'Where did you get it?'

Had Mrs Phipps given – or sold – it to Beattie Drew? And if it was either of those things then had she said that Emma had spent the night in Shingle Cottage with Matthew Caunter?

'Found it. Down by the harbour. It had a bit of sand on it but I picked it off, gave it a bit of a wash. Beggars can't be choosers, lovie.'

'No,' Emma said, 'no, they can't. Thank you. I'll just use a little bit to wash and then I'll leave it to dry off on the windowsill and you can have the rest of it back.'

'No you won't. You'll keep it. And if you take my advice you'll leave this place just as fast as you can. Good job you had that chair under the door knob, lovie, or those Jago boys ...'

'Seth told me to put it there,' Emma said.

Mrs Drew raised an eyebrow. 'Did he then? I've still seen evidence of Jagos having been in that bed many a time, though, haven't I? I'm not saying it were with poor dead Sophie Ellison, but there's been maids here before her.'

Emma didn't know that she really needed to know all this. 'Thank you for the hot water, but I won't keep you from your work any longer.'

'And that's me dismissed, is it?'

Emma felt herself blush. 'I didn't mean ...'

''Course you didn't. And I haven't taken offence.' Beattie Drew shook out the largest towel and laid it over the back of the chair. 'Now get yourself tidied up.'

'Mrs Drew,' Emma said, 'I don't know what's expected of me here. Dr Shaw said I was coming here to get my strength up. When I do, I'll look for a job and somewhere to live. But Carter and Miles called me a servant, and I don't want to be ...'

'There's lots we don't want to be, but have to when circumstances dictate, lovie. You don't suppose I want to be poor and have to wash out chamberpots to earn a crust 'cos my old man drinks most of what he earns at the quarry, do you?'

'Well, no.'

'There you are then. But you'm doing nowt for a few days. The good doctor's orders. He's left money for your keep until circumstances change. Reuben Jago can well afford to keep you and after what he's done to you, making you homeless and all, I think it's his duty. But he's taken the doctor's money all the same, the greedy bugger.'

Emma let Beattie Drew prattle on, glad of the company if she was honest, but she couldn't think of a single thing to say in return. She walked towards the window and stood staring at Nase Head House on the horizon, the far side of the harbour. It looked newly painted – the low morning sun striking the white paint almost blinding her. She knew Captain Godfrey had lived at Nase Head House alone since his wife had died. And his son, Arthur, before her – killed in the Boer War somewhere. Rumour had it that Captain Godfrey hadn't been right in the head since. And rumour also had it that Arthur Godfrey had preferred men in his bed to women. But Emma knew what rumours were like – not a grain of truth in most of them.

'There's been some changes to Nase Head House since I last saw it. Not that I ever saw it much because I had no call to go up that side of town. And I've never seen it from here before,' Emma said at last. 'It's been all painted up.'

'I'll say. Inside as well as out. You could go and work there, lovie – clever girl like you.'

Emma shuddered. She didn't fancy working for an elderly widower who was losing his marbles. And an ex-serviceman at that. He was bound to be particular. And old people smelled a bit, no matter how rich they were. There always seemed to be the smell of death hovering around old people – dust and decay. 'No,' she said. 'I don't think I could work for Captain Godfrey.'

'Well, not now you can't. He's dead. Happened about the same time your pa … oh, I'm sorry, lovie. I …' Beattie Drew's voice trailed away.

'It's all right. You can say it.'

Beattie Drew came over and placed an arm around Emma's

shoulder. 'And your ma's gone, too. She was beautiful, your ma was. And you'm going to be just as lovely.'

'Don't be nice to me, Mrs Drew,' Emma said, swallowing back tears, 'or I might cry.'

Mrs Drew's hold on Emma's shoulder tightened.

'Seems Captain Godfrey didn't *own* Nase Head House. It belonged to his late wife's brother. A fellow called Smythe. Rich as Croesus, he was, this Smythe fellow. Well, he went and died as well and it were left to his son up in London where he owns God knows what else as well – coffee houses, or fancy French cafés or summat like that. Anyway, this Mr Smythe – goes by the handle of Rupert, so I've heard – 'ev moved down here for the better air, so rumour has it. I ...'

'How do you know all these sort of things?' Emma interrupted.

Mrs Drew tapped the side of her nose. 'No point cleaning for folks if you don't find out a thing or two, is there? Eavesdropping some might call it but I call it keeping meself informed. I heard Mr Jago and Carter talking about it, didn't I? Anyway, what I was saying before I got interrupted was, that this Mr Smythe is turning Nase Head House into a hotel, that's what. About a dozen bedrooms and there's no way I'd want to clean that lot. Going to be chandeliers and everything. And dancing with a band open to the public. And fancy cooking. Builders have almost done.'

'Chandeliers?' Emma said. 'Dancing?'

'Didn't I just say? Now I'd better go or I'll be looking for a job there an' all.'

Emma stood staring over at Nase Head House long after Mrs Drew had left the room. The sun was catching the windows on the upper storey and they sparkled like so many diamonds. The view from those windows had to better even than the one she had right at that moment. Maybe on a fine day you'd be able to see France. Roscoff. Her papa had come from Roscoff. Maybe she'd visit it one day.

But for that she'd need money. Emma knew nothing about cleaning chandeliers or dancing, although she did know a little bit about cooking. But a hotel that size would surely need someone to organise everything, and run the reception desk. There was a big hotel in Torquay – The Grand – and Emma had glimpsed inside it once and seen a man standing behind a huge desk that looked like it must have taken a whole tree to make. She *could* start at the bottom doing cleaning – anything – and work her way up if it was going to be a means to an end, couldn't she?

'You can do that, Emma Le Goff,' she whispered, her breath furring up on the glass of the window so that it looked as if she was seeing Nase Head House through a fine mist. 'You can do that.'

'And where do you think *you're* going?' Reuben Jago barked at Emma as she headed across the black-and-white tiles of the hallway towards the front door.

'Out,' Emma said.

'Not through that door you're not.'

'But …' Emma began, but was halted by someone clanging the door bell loudly.

Mr Jago called for Beattie Drew to open the door, but Beattie didn't respond.

'You can open it,' he told Emma.

And I'll be out of it as soon as I have, Emma thought. She walked towards the door, turned the knob.

Matthew Caunter. He stood before her, a huge grin on his face, and a bundle of papers tied with string in his hands. A cloth bag dangled from the crook of his arm.

'Just the girl I came to see,' Matthew said.

'Good morning, Caunter,' Mr Jago said. 'And I might

remind you, seeing as you are in my employ, that the back door is your point of entrance to this house.'

'My apologies,' Matthew said, looking at Emma as he spoke.

She had a feeling he wasn't sorry at all.

'State your business,' Reuben Jago said.

'I already have … Sir,' Matthew said – just a little hesitation between the 'have' and the 'Sir'. 'I've come to see Miss Le Goff.'

'Then you can see her around the back of the house. I was just pointing out to her, her place of entry and exit of my house. The servants' entrance.'

'Oh, I can see her well enough from where I stand, Mr Jago.' Matthew turned towards Emma, held out the bundle of papers. 'I found these in the outhouse when I was …'

'Outhouse?' Reuben Jago interrupted. 'I thought I'd ordered that to be cleared.'

'Seems those orders weren't obeyed then, doesn't it?' Matthew said. 'There wasn't much in there anyway, beyond this and some tools and some half-used packets of seeds. Perhaps whoever it was you gave your orders to didn't think it worth his effort clearing it.'

'Could you continue this conversation elsewhere?' Reuben Jago said.

Emma could see he was discomfited and that Matthew was enjoying being the instigator of that discomfort.

Matthew removed the bag from the crook of his arm and placed it on top of the papers. 'This, too, is rightly yours.'

But still Emma didn't take it from him.

'Enough!' Reuben Jago said. 'Take it all to your room, Emma. And you can forget about going anywhere today. You can stay here and help Mrs Drew.'

'I can't,' Emma said. 'Dr Shaw said I wasn't to do physical work for a few days and he's paid you so I don't have to.'

Emma heard Matthew laugh, and Mr Jago clear his throat as though he had something to say and plenty of it.

'You've got a boat going out I understand, Mr Jago, Sir,' Matthew said, taking advantage, no doubt, of Reuben Jago's disconcertion. 'And as pleasant as it is looking at the lovely Miss Le Goff, we'll miss the tide if we don't move quickly. Sir.'

'Don't you tell me how to run my fleet,' Mr Jago said.

'Again, my apologies,' Matthew said. 'Your papers, Miss Le Goff. And some things which I think might have been your mother's.'

He held the papers and the bag towards Emma and this time she took them. A look passed between them and Emma had the feeling there was more to Matthew Caunter than met the eye. The way he spoke for a start – the way she did, not with a dropped 'h' the way most locals spoke.

'Don't get into trouble on account of me, Mr Caunter,' she whispered.

'I have no intention of it,' Matthew whispered back. Then he turned his full attention to Mr Jago. 'I'd best be off to see to my duties, Sir.'

'We'd both best be off,' Reuben Jago said. 'You've wasted enough of my time already.'

Emma watched the men go. At the gate Matthew turned to look back at her.

'Enjoy your walk,' he called.

And Emma felt a smile spread through her – Matthew, at least, had got her mettle.

Emma didn't want to be in the house a moment longer. It was another glorious, unseasonably warm, April morning. The vision of Seth with his shirt off painting Shingle Cottage came to her mind. How unfair life was sometimes. Men could bare their chests and no one minded, but when women went out they had to wear their blouses buttoned to the neck, and their skirts to their ankles, and a hat at all times. Sometimes Emma wished she'd been born in Regency times when the women wore their dresses practically off their bosoms showing the creamy flesh of their necks that men dropped kisses on.

'And that's enough of drifting off into flights of romantic fancy,' Emma said into fresh air.

She held the bundle of things Matthew had given her in one hand and with the other rammed the blue felt hat that Dr Shaw's wife had given her on her head, and marched down the front steps of Hilltop House.

It was a long climb up the narrow streets until she got to Nase Head House. She had to stop to get her breath back many times. But she was sure the sun was doing her good. It made her feel better anyway, just being out in it.

Mrs Drew had been right. The builders had been busy. Paintwork gleamed and windows sparkled. Flower borders had been dug around the edges of what Emma remembered had only ever been a lawn before, and plants had been placed at regular intervals, some in flower, some about to be. How pretty it all looked. Imagine having enough money to spend on frivolities like flowers. The only time Emma had ever seen flowers in Shingle Cottage had been when her mama had picked wild ones. And the ones the florist had delivered for her papa's funeral, paid for after a collection by the neighbours.

A pair of wrought-iron gates were open so Emma walked in, made her way along the drive that led to the front door. She bent to touch the petals of a red flower she didn't know the name of.

'Oi! What're you doing, girl?'

Emma jumped to a standing position, turned round.

The sudden action made her giddy for a moment. A gardener with a hoe in his hand was glaring at her.

'I'm admiring the flowers,' she said. 'You must have worked hard to transform this place.'

'I have an' all that,' the gardener said, and Emma was relieved to see that her soft words had brought a smile to the man's face.

'I'm thinking of working here myself,' Emma said. 'Who do I see?'

The gardener raised his eyebrows in surprise. 'Mr Rupert Smythe. Not that it'll be any use you seeing 'im. All the inside staff's bin brought down from London. An' a right po-faced lot they are an' all.'

Emma laughed. 'You don't think I'm po-faced, then?'

'Stop fishing for compliments.'

The word 'fishing' brought Emma up short. Would she ever get used to hearing it and not instantly thinking of her papa and how he'd lost his life fishing? 'I'm not,' she said. 'Up those steps over there to the front door, is it?'

'Yes. An' don't forget to wipe your boots.'

'I won't,' Emma said, and scuttled away.

Emma counted the steps. Eleven of them. They made the double oak doors seem more imposing somehow. One door was slightly open so Emma peeped around it. Now she was here nerves had overtaken her bravado.

And then it was as though she were being pulled by an invisible thread. She inched around the edge of the door, slipped inside. She was in an octagonal reception area with a tiled floor. Black and white. Not the black-and-white rigid lines of the Jago house, but black and white in a pattern – some of the tiles cut diamond-shaped, some circular. Emma stretched out the toe of one of her newly acquired, hand-me-down boots and traced the pattern directly in front of her. Her toe glided easily across the surface. She imagined how it would feel to wear shoes with heels like her mama had worn to church on Sundays. Shoes with a little strap across the instep and a pearl button on the side.

No one seemed to be about so Emma crossed the floor, the heels of her boots clicking noisily. Someone would hear her in a minute. But before they did she'd have a good look around.

Beattie Drew had been right. There *were* chandeliers. Two of them hanging from the ceiling, long droppers of crystal like stalagtites. And lit by electricity. She could see the round switches on the walls, and wires. Emma gazed in awe at the chandeliers, first one then the other, until her neck ached.

There was a central, circular, seat that Emma guessed could accommodate at least a dozen people. She walked forward and ran a hand across the seat. Leather. Red leather – red the colour of hawthorn berries.

There was a wooden desk against one wall and it had a bell on it. *Please ring* was written on a card in a fancy script.

Emma rang.

The sound echoed around the cavernous reception area. But it seemed ages before anyone came to see who might be ringing the bell and there seemed to be a whole meadow of butterflies fluttering in Emma's stomach as she waited.

'And you might be?'

Emma looked up. A man was standing at the top of one of the two staircases, a hand on the rail, staring down at her. 'Emma Le Goff. I've come about a position. Here. If you have one, which I hope you will have. Please.'

Emma's heart rate had increased rapidly now. She could feel her pulse in her neck. She just had to be here – work her way up until it was her standing behind that desk answering the ring of the bell.

The man walked slowly down the stairs towards her.

'Have you now?' he said. 'You've come to the right man. I'm Rupert Smythe.'

Emma readied to shake his hand, but no hand was offered. 'This is a beautiful place,' she said. 'I *would* like a job if you have one. Preferably living in.'

'Living in?' Mr Smythe said.

'Yes, please.'

'And how old are you, Miss Le Goff?'

Miss Le Goff? No one had ever called her that before, except Matthew earlier, and her guess was that he'd been formal and not called her Emma so Mr Jago wouldn't know they'd already met. Hearing Mr Smythe say it made her feel older somehow. She pulled herself up taller, looked Mr Smythe in the eye. 'I'll be sixteen soon. At Michaelmas.'

'You look younger.'

To tell him she'd been ill, or not? He might not want someone who wasn't strong enough to hold down a job. 'If that's a compliment then I thank you kindly,' Emma said.

Mr Smythe laughed. Laughing *at* her, Emma thought. He had blue eyes – like a winter sky on a sunny day. Rather cold. But he did hold the key to her future – Emma was sure of it. She smiled back at him, willing the smile to reach her eyes. But she had a feeling it fell far short of that.

'You're bright enough, Miss Le Goff, I can see that. Pretty, too. But I've got all the staff I need for the moment. You could ask again in, say, six months. But I must point out girls have to be well dressed to work for me, do you understand?'

'I do. But this is all I've got for the moment.'

Emma glanced down over the skirt that Mrs Phipps had given her. Glanced at the boots that had once been the doctor's daughter's. Those boots pinched a bit even though they did still have all their buttons. The clothes the doctor's wife had given her were good quality but a bit too tight across the bust. She wished with all her heart now she'd taken the time to let the darts out before coming here.

Mr Smythe began to walk away. He reached a door, opened it, and Emma could see lots of tables covered in white linen cloths.

She'd been dismissed, hadn't she?

'I hope to get better things before too long, Mr Smythe,' she called after him.

But he ignored her.

Emma lowered her voice to a whisper. 'And when I do, I'll be back. You just watch if I don't.'

Seth looked up from checking the sails and ropes as his father approached with the new crewman, Matthew Caunter. So, that's what he looked like – long, pale, gingery sort of hair tied back with a shoelace. Tall. Older than Seth had expected him to be. Certainly too old for Emma in his opinion. Seth felt a stab of something that could only be jealousy pierce him between the breastbones.

'Caunter will be in Carter's crew today, Seth. Make sure everything's in order.'

'I always do, Pa.'

'This is your son?' Matthew said, sounding surprised – as though he had expected an introduction.

'The youngest.'

'And are you joining us on this boat, Seth, or are you skippering one of your father's other boats?'

'Ha!' Reuben said, before Seth got a chance to speak. 'Put to sea? Him? Gets sicker than a babe on pork fat, he does. Legs like a girl's for the water.'

There was an uncomfortable silence between the three men for a few moments. Seth moved a crab pot from one place to another, quite unnecessarily, just for something to do.

'So, if you don't put to sea what do you do, Seth?'

'Make and mend the crab and lobster pots. Load them. Do repairs on Pa's boats. Always something to do in that line.'

'And will you be here to unload when the boats get back?'

'No,' Seth said. 'My brothers do that.'

'Is that so, Mr Jago?' Matthew asked, turning to Reuben.

Reuben nodded. 'Seth might fall short as a son in many ways but he doesn't lie.'

And Seth knew why he used those words – fall short as a son. Carter and Miles would do everything their father told them to do, however illegal – contraband goods, or over-fishing. Although Seth was yet to find any hard evidence of it, he knew in his bones it was going on. And if he found that hard evidence then he'd go to the authorities – father or not. And his pa knew it which was why, Seth suspected, his pa and brothers were careful to keep underhand dealings well-hidden from him. Certainly, there weren't piles of brandy or other goods hidden at Hilltop House as far as he'd been able to see, although there was often a bottle of brandy in the kitchen for culinary purposes. But if there were …

'Enough talk,' Reuben Jago snapped. 'Or we'll miss the tide.'

'I'll double-check the sails, Pa, first.'

'Then be quick about it.'

Seth turned to the task.

'So, how well do you know the Le Goff girl?' Seth heard his father ask Matthew.

'Probably rather less than you do,' Matthew replied.

Seth's pa laughed raucously.

Seth wanted to retch. Had his Pa laid his filthy paws on Emma? Was that what Matthew Caunter was implying?

'I get your meaning. But if you think you can hide anything from me – anything at all – think again, Caunter.

I've got my spies everywhere.' He tapped the side of his nose in a knowing way.

'Is that so?' Caunter said. He bent to stow his kit bag under a plank.

'Stopped the night with you, so I understand?' Seth's pa obviously wasn't going to let the issue of Emma stopping the night at Shingle Cottage go. 'All cosied up. Tight ...'

Caunter put up a hand. 'I did offer Miss Le Goff refuge, yes. And no doubt Mrs, er, Phipps, isn't it? has spread some gossip. But as I'm sure you'll know, Sir, a gentleman never talks about the women he goes with.'

Caunter straightened, pulled himself to his full height. He towered over Seth's pa.

'As you wish. But we'll get one thing straight – if Emma Le Goff shares your bed again ...'

'She did *not* share my bed. Or I, hers.'

Seth had heard enough. Feeling sick right through that this stranger had been able to offer Emma refuge when he hadn't been, he abandoned the double-checking of the sails and left.

Chapter Six

Hugging the precious bundles that Matthew Caunter had given her closely against her chest, Emma scurried through the fish market. She'd loved the smell of fish once, but didn't care much for it now.

Her mama had had a way of cooking scallops with herbs picked from the garden, and cream fresh from the dairy that tasted as close to heaven as Emma thought she would get without actually being there, and Emma had learned to cook it well enough herself.

'Emma!'

Emma slowed. It was Florrie. Dr Shaw's maid. No doubt she wanted more gory details about Sophie Ellison's body. Details Emma didn't want to give. The sooner she could put the whole tragic scenario out of her mind the better.

'Emma, you've got to get back. The constable is looking for you. He …' Florrie skidded to a halt, bent over and grasped her side to stop a stitch.

'The constable? What does he want me for?'

Florrie gulped in air. Stood up. 'I don't know, do I? All I'm saying is he came to Dr Shaw and they were in the study talking for ages. All that talking made lunch late and the parsley sauce was all dried up. And it was the best …'

Emma thought Florrie was about to cry. Poor Florrie, who was never likely to progress in life beyond working in someone else's house.

'I'm sure Dr Shaw and his wife would understand why the sauce wasn't perfect, Florrie.'

'Oh, they did an' all,' Florrie said. 'Now, I've been out long enough. I'm supposed to be going to Foale's for a rib of beef for supper and I've spent at least fifteen minutes talking to my sister who was coming out of the dairy. I'll be in trouble if I'm out much longer. The constable, mind. You'd best go back to the Jagos' place because I know the constable was going there after he left Dr Shaw.'

Emma pressed her lips together. She'd rather go anywhere than back to Hilltop House and the Jagos. But her carpet bag was there and the clothes Dr Shaw's wife had given her. And now she had a bundle of things that Matthew Caunter had brought round that morning and which she hadn't looked at yet.

She could do that in the privacy of her room – the back of the chair rammed under the door handle for safety.

'Thanks for telling me, Florrie,' Emma said. 'Go careful on those cobbles. They're more slippery than usual.'

'I will,' Florrie said. 'Looks like someone didn't clear up proper after the fish auction, don't it? Anyway, I'll be off. I hope they don't lock you up or anything.'

Florrie giggled, then ran off.

Now why, Emma wondered, had Florrie said that? Had she overheard the constable and Dr Shaw in the study? Probably – Florrie was more than capable of a bit of eavesdropping.

Dragging her feet, skirting seaweed here and there, Emma made the distance between the fish quay and Hilltop House take as long as she possibly could to cover.

'The necklace, Miss,' Constable Jeffery said the second Emma stepped into the kitchen. Emma knew who he was – it was he who'd come to tell her that Mama and Johnnie had fallen to their deaths.

'What necklace? I don't have a necklace. What's more, I'm sure you know enough about me to know I was left with nothing. Nothing at all.'

'Got a lot to say for herself, hasn't she?' The constable turned to Reuben Jago and smirked.

'I warned you,' Reuben Jago said.

'The necklace in question is the one that was around Sophie Ellison's neck when she was last seen in The Port Light.' Constable Jeffery spoke as though he considered Emma an irritating insect of some sort, and a slow-thinking one at that.

Emma shrugged. She didn't have a clue what he was talking about – Sophie hadn't had a necklace on when she'd found her.

'Don't you want to know what sort of a necklace it is?'

'Not particularly. I don't have a lot of use for necklaces. Not at the moment.'

But I will one day, Emma thought. When I've been working at Nase Head House and earned lots of money. I'll be able to buy as many necklaces as I want then.

'You'll make things easier for yourself if you co-operate with me, Missy.'

'Miss Le Goff, not Missy.'

'Oh, Miss Le Goff, is it? That's what comes of letting furriners in, I suppose. All hoity-toity are we, with a fancy name?'

'It's the only name I've got, Constable Jeffery,' Emma said as firmly as she could. Inside she was shaking.

'Well then, Miss Le Goff, I'll just take a look at that stuff there you're clutching to you like a baby, shall I?'

'No! I was only given it this morning and I haven't looked at it myself yet.'

'We'll do it together.' The constable made to take the bundle of papers and the bag from Emma.

'We won't,' Emma said.

She didn't want anyone else touching her mama's things. That Matthew Caunter might have fingered them when he'd found them in the outhouse was enough. She slid the papers onto the table, turned each one over. Her parents' marriage lines. Hers and Johnnie's baptism certificates. Letters – the envelopes written in her papa's hand. Emma wondered for a moment why her mama had put them in the outhouse. Had she been hiding them for some reason? From someone? Emma gulped back tears – with her mama in her grave she'd never know now, would she? Then she opened the bag. Tipped the contents carefully onto the table.

And that's when she almost stopped breathing. The gold links of the chain caught the light from the lamp on the table. Glistened. The large piece of highly polished amethyst in a gold casing shone. It had been her papa's gift to her mama on their wedding day. Emma remembered sitting on her mama's knee and reaching up to place the palm of her hot and sticky hand against the coolness of the amethyst.

'My mama's,' Emma said, her voice the barest of whispers. How thrilled and yet how horrified she was to see it lying there.

'Oh, what a consummate little actress you are. You knew it was there all along.'

'I didn't, Constable. I've only just opened this parcel. I told you that. Why shouldn't I have it if it was found with all these other things?'

'Because I don't think it was found with those other things for one minute. I've been making enquiries, Miss Le Goff,' the constable told her. 'Seems Sophie Ellison was trying to sell it in the inn to pay for gin and the like – and there are plenty of witnesses to testify she was – but no one would give her the price she wanted.'

'So someone murdered her and stole it,' Emma said. 'But it wasn't me. I could never do such a thing. Murder or steal.'

'So how did you acquire it?' Reuben Jago asked.

'I ...' Emma began then stopped.

Matthew Caunter had given her the bag of her mama's belongings with the necklace in it. Things that were hers by rights. But if he hadn't found the necklace in the outhouse with the other things, then how had he come by it? Had *he* murdered Sophie Ellison?

A thousand thoughts were fighting for space in Emma's mind. She felt faint with the weight of them. She didn't think Matthew Caunter was capable of murder. After all, he'd been kind to her, letting her sleep in the bed while he slept in a chair. And he'd mended her book. Given her soap as a present, even if he had no use for it himself.

'Did you take that necklace from around Sophie Ellison's neck before you called on Dr Shaw?'

'No, Constable.'

'Did Dr Shaw remove it and give it to you?'

'No.'

Emma trembled, afraid her legs were going to go from under her. She was telling the truth – but would the constable believe her?

He began rifling amongst the things Emma had tipped from the bag – a nightdress of her mama's, the hem embroidered with purple irises; a photograph of her parents on their wedding day; three gold sovereigns in a soft leather pouch; a copy of the *Book of Common Prayer*, well thumbed. And a key with a plaited length of black embroidery thread hanging from it. Emma herself had plaited that thread. Made it as a present for her Papa to hang his key from the hook inside the back door. The back-door key to Shingle Cottage. Had Matthew put that in the bag? So that she could go to Shingle Cottage if she had nowhere else to go? He *had* said she could come back if she needed to.

Emma felt sick to her stomach watching the constable's fat and rather grubby fingers pawing at her possessions. If only she'd looked in the bag earlier. Three sovereigns sounded like a fortune to her now. If the constable didn't arrest her for stealing the amethyst necklace from around Sophie's neck then she'd have enough to stop in a hotel for a night or two.

Constable Jeffery laid a hand on the necklace and slid it across the table towards Reuben Jago. 'Is this the same necklace stolen from your bureau, Sir?'

'It is.'

'*I* didn't steal it!' Emma shouted. 'I haven't been in this house a day yet. I only know where my room and the kitchen are. I don't know what room your bureau is in. And I didn't take it from around Sophie Ellison's neck, either. I ...'

'Quiet, Miss,' Constable Jeffery ordered. 'Neither of us has suggested you took it from anywhere, have we?'

'Well, no ...'

'My question was directed at Mr Jago and whether this is the necklace taken from his bureau.'

'By Sophie?' Emma said. 'If she was seen wearing it ...'

'I'll say it one more time, Miss. Quiet. I'm conducting this enquiry, not you.'

'But I want to know how Mr Jago got my mama's necklace.' Emma felt hot and clammy and fired up with anger. She wasn't sure she wanted the truth, but she had to have it.

'Answer her Mr Jago, Sir,' the constable said.

'It was given me by your dear mother's own fair hand. In lieu of rent ...'

'I don't believe you. She'd never have given away my papa's necklace.'

'Be that as it may,' Reuben Jago said. 'That's how I came by it.'

'Your word against mine,' Emma snapped. She knew with every word she said she was probably digging herself into a hole, but if she didn't stand up for herself and her mama's reputation, who would?

'Enough, Miss,' the constable said

'Well, Emma,' Reuben Jago said, 'we both know, you and I, who gave you those things, don't we?'

'Yes,' Emma said.

'Then tell the constable who it was.'

'Mr Caunter,' Emma said. She felt like a traitor – she just couldn't believe he was capable of murder.

'Time to speak to Caunter, then, don't you think, Mr Jago?' the constable asked.

'You'll have to wait. He'll be at sea three days.'

'I'm a patient man,' Constable Jeffery said. And then he picked up the amethyst necklace and handed it to Reuben Jago. 'Yours I think, Sir.'

'It is ...' Emma began, but the constable put up a hand to stop her flow of words.

'I'll leave you to deal with this feisty little piece, Sir.'

And then Constable Jeffery made his farewells and left.

The second he was out of the house Emma squared up to Reuben Jago. 'That necklace is by rights mine, Mr Jago. And I want it back.'

'I'm sure you do. And you can want on. But I'll tell you one thing, I want you out of this house. Now. You're more trouble than you're worth.' He leaned towards her, his face almost touching hers. 'You've got ten minutes to collect your things from your room and go, Emma. I'm going into the drawing-room and I don't want to see you here when I come back out again.'

'I'm going,' Emma said, and ran from the room.

But three days? Emma's heart began to lift from somewhere around her boots to its rightful place. Matthew Caunter was going to be away for three days and she had a key to Shingle Cottage.

She'd use one of the sovereigns to buy food on the way so she wouldn't have to go in and out and risk being seen until Matthew came back. Three days would give her time to get a bit of strength back. And the minute Matthew returned, she'd be gone again – he wouldn't even know she'd been there.

But first, she'd go to the cemetery and speak to her mama.

'I'm sorry I'm making such a mess of things, Mama,' Emma said. 'Trouble seems to be courting me at the moment. I might have to move away to find work and somewhere to live, although I don't want to. And I'll get your amethyst necklace back one day, you just see if I don't.'

It gave Emma comfort to say her thoughts out loud – she could imagine her mama really was listening. She sat on the damp grass beside the grave hugging her knees, her carpet bag now bulging with things beside her. She felt sad about not telling Beattie Drew she was leaving, but even though Emma had called her name on the landing and looked in the kitchen, she'd been nowhere to be seen. Thank goodness Carter and Miles hadn't been around. She'd have liked to have been able to say goodbye to Seth, though. But he hadn't been in the house, either.

And where the cook was, Emma had had no idea. Out marketing like Florrie had been perhaps.

'And when I've got enough money I'll get a headstone for you and Johnnie. And one for Papa, too. And I'll make you proud of me one day.'

Emma hung her head and said a prayer. She wished with all her heart that it had been possible for her mama and Johnnie to have been buried in the same grave as her papa, but it just hadn't been – something to do with earth that hadn't settled properly in her papa's grave, seeing as he'd only been buried six weeks before her mama and Johnnie.

Emma raised her head from her prayer and her thoughts and looked around for something to put the flowers in she'd picked from the lane – some primroses and a few dog violets and some green stuff that was glossy that she thought would turn into arums later on.

Ah, a metal pot lying abandoned. She'd use that. The water tap wasn't far.

It was as she was walking back with the pot full of water, her flowers loosely arranged, that she saw Seth. The click of the gate had made her look up and there he was – looking directly towards her.

'Emma.' Seth raised a hand in greeting, smiled shyly, and began walking towards her. He had a bunch of narcissi wrapped in brown paper hanging from his other hand. As though he was embarrassed to be carrying flowers.

'They're for my mother,' Seth said, bringing the flowers to waist height in front of him. A barrier between them. 'I expect you're on the same mission.'

'Yes. Only I couldn't afford to buy flowers, so I've taken mine from the hedgerow.'

A lie. She had three sovereigns in her bag, didn't she?

'They're just as lovely, Emma,' Seth said. 'It's not the cost of the flowers, but the reason behind bringing them, that matters.'

'I suppose,' Emma said. She began to walk towards her mama's and Johnnie's grave, hoping that Seth would go away. But he didn't – he followed her.

'And I'm going to get a headstone carved when I've earned enough money, Seth. And one for my papa over there.' She pointed to where her papa's grave was sighted, crammed in with the relatives of other people who couldn't afford headstones either – they were just mounds of grass, cut three times a year by old Harry Truscott, and only then if he wasn't drunk.

Emma bent to place her pot of flowers, some of the water spilling onto the grass. 'Don't let me keep you,' she said.

'You're not. But you're running away, aren't you?' With the toe of his boot, Seth tapped Emma's carpet bag.

'Don't you kick my bag.'

'I'm not kicking it,' Seth said, reasonably enough. 'I was merely noticing that you seem to have your bag with you and it's a lot fuller than it was a few days ago when you left it outside Shingle Cottage and went to bawl my father out.'

'And he deserved the bawling, Seth.'

'I agree.'

'You do?'

'Yes. I think he's treated you abominably. As he treats most people. I'm ashamed to be his son sometimes. But you *are* running away, aren't you?'

'I've left Hilltop House, yes,' Emma said. 'There's the evidence. You've seen it for yourself.' She pointed to her bag. Seth didn't need telling his pa had thrown her out, he'd find out soon enough. Just thinking about Mr Jago with her mama's amethyst necklace in his hand was making her feel sick – the less she said the better, and the sooner she could get back to Shingle Cottage was more to the better, too.

'Where will you go?'

'I haven't decided yet,' Emma said, praying Seth wouldn't detect a lie. 'But before I do go, I want to say thank you for suggesting I put the back of the chair against the door handle. I did hear it rattle a couple of times before I fell asleep.'

Seth shrugged, said nothing.

'And it was you who put a hot brick in my bed to warm it, wasn't it?'

Seth nodded. 'It can be cold at the top of the house,' he said. 'But you didn't have to leave. I would have looked out for you. Kept you safe from my brothers I mean. Because I don't have a skinful of ale most of the time, I'm faster, more accurate in a fight, if it should come to that.'

Was Seth saying he would have fought his brothers for her? Seth had been looking right into her eyes as he spoke. The way he looked at her was making Emma's stomach flip. Not nerves – something else she couldn't put a name to.

'I still couldn't stay, Seth,' Emma said.

'Well, I wish you weren't going,' Seth said. 'You were the best thing to come into our house for a long time.'

'Oh, Seth,' Emma said, her eyes beginning to puddle with tears. 'That's a lovely thing to say. But I've got to go. You do understand?'

Seth nodded. 'I'll miss you,' he said. 'Where will you go? I could come and see you sometimes perhaps …'

'No, Seth. You'll always be a Jago and I'll always be a Le Goff and, and …'

And then Emma couldn't say any more. She couldn't tell him she was going to let herself in to Shingle Cottage now she knew Matthew Caunter wouldn't be there for a few days, could she?

'If you think my pa would object to me seeing you, then I'll stand up to him.'

'And he'd throw you out for doing it,' Emma said.

'I'd face that if it came to it, Emma. But you could let me carry that bag to the station. If that's where you're going?'

'No! I'm not going to the station.'

'Where, then?'

There was a lump in Emma's throat that was becoming increasingly difficult to swallow. Seth was standing before her, the flowers still held in front of him, telling her he'd miss her, that he'd stand up to his father over her, and she had just realised that she would miss his kindness and his gentleness, too.

'I'll bring flowers for my parents and Johnnie sometimes,'

she said. 'So, if you're here bringing flowers for your mother then maybe I'll see you here?'

Emma had to look away from Seth as she spoke because there was such sadness in his eyes and all she wanted to do was kiss those eyes and kiss the sadness away. And how very inappropriate that would be in a cemetery.

'Here, Emma, take these,' Seth said, thrusting the narcissi towards her. 'I can buy some more for my mother.'

'No, I ...' Emma began as she caught the sweet scent of the flowers.

'Please, Emma. I want you to have them. Take them with you wherever it is you are going. God only knows you deserve pretty things. Who else is there to spoil you, except me?'

'Seth!'

Olly. Olly Underwood. Seth didn't really want to see Olly at this moment, even though they'd been best friends since school days, with never a falling out. He was still burning with anger at his father for throwing Emma out – and all over a necklace his pa had that had belonged to Rachel Le Goff. Given in lieu of rent, his pa had said. A likely story. No doubt it had been taken along with other things from Shingle Cottage when his pa had ordered it to be cleared. Something pretty he could hang, some day, around the neck of some girl young enough to be his daughter, that he hadn't had to pay for. But thank goodness Emma had been believed when she'd denied stealing it. Poor Emma. The very least he could do was make sure she had some money so she could get a room somewhere for a night or two. *If* he could find her.

Seth turned to greet Olly, shake his hand.

'Where are you off to at such a pace?' Olly asked.

Seth shrugged.

Olly tapped the side of his nose. 'Ah, an assignation?'

'Not the sort you're thinking of.'

'Well, whatever it is, it's fired you up. I had the Devil's own job catching up with you.'

'I don't suppose,' Seth said, 'you've seen Emma Le Goff about, have you?'

'Emma the orphan?'

'You make that sound like an affliction. Being an orphan isn't a nice position to be in, I shouldn't think.'

'Oooh, am I detecting a tender heart in that direction?'

'Give over, Olly,' Seth said, well aware he was wearing his heart on his sleeve. 'Dr Shaw got Pa to take her in but now he's thrown her out.'

'And you wish he hadn't?'

'Selfishly so, yes. But for her own safety with my brothers being as they are …'

'She's better off out of there,' Olly finished for him. 'Where do you think she might have gone?'

'I couldn't hazard a guess,' Seth said. 'I'm on the way to the station to see if the stationmaster or the guard or anyone saw her get on a train, and if so where she might have got a ticket to.'

'Then I won't keep you. But before you go … I don't suppose you'd come and work for me, Seth? Percy Adams has gone down with consumption. Not likely to get better, either. I thought I'd ask you first before putting word about I need a hand. I know fishing's not engraved on your heart the way it is on your pa's and your brothers'.'

'How well you know me,' Seth said. He would much prefer to work for Olly in his boatbuilding business but knew his loyalty – for the time being – had to be to his pa. 'And I'm sorry about Percy Adams. But to answer your question – no, not at the moment, but thanks for asking.'

'Let me know if ever you change your mind. A pint in The Crabshell later?'

Seth hesitated.

Olly seized on the hesitation. 'You might have other fish to fry? If you find Emma?'

Seth gave Olly a friendly slap on the shoulder and went on his way.

'You're sure?' Seth asked – rather out of breath from the swift walk up the very steep hill.

'Certain,' the ticket clerk told him. 'Been here all the time and no one came in here yesterday answering that description and carrying a carpet bag.'

'Today then? I'll make it worth your while to tell.'

Seth dug deep in his pocket and found a half-crown. He slapped it down on the counter. He'd already been to see the carrier and Emma hadn't booked a space on his cart, either.

'Can't take that under false pretences. I don't lie. It's the Le Goff girl you're talking about, isn't it?' Before Seth could admit it was, or deny otherwise, the ticket clerk went on. 'Rumours spread faster in the pubs around here than fire does through a hayrick. Your pa threw Emma Le Goff off his property, and now she's gone you're all lovesick for her. Am I right?'

'What makes you think that?' Seth snapped.

''Cos you look like you've lost a £5 note and found a farthing. Why else would you be asking for her if you're not sweet on her?'

'I just want to know she's all right.'

'That *and* lovesick, lad,' the ticket clerk said. 'Good riddance to her, though, I'd say. Who wants a daughter of a suicide about the place? If I ...'

Seth reached across the counter and grabbed the man's collar. Not tight enough to make the man cough and splutter but firmly enough to let him know that Seth wasn't liking what he'd just heard.

'That's gossip. Women's talk. And I don't want to hear another word.'

The ticket clerk grappled to free himself from Seth's grasp. 'Take that bliddy half-crown and go and get yourself a skinful of ale and forget all about her. She'll likely break your heart, that one. Too beautiful for her own good. Too tainted, too. Spent the night with that new fisherman your pa's hired, so I've heard.'

'Well, *un*-hear it,' Seth yelled at him. 'Like I said, talk like that is women's talk. Do you understand me?'

The ticket clerk had the decency to blush.

'I won't tell what I *know*,' Seth said, 'if you don't repeat the lies you *think* you've heard. Are we clear?' It was fairly common knowledge that it wasn't women's bodies the clerk was after in the bars around the town.

'Perfectly,' the ticket clerk said. 'Will that be all? Going now, are you?'

Seth slid his hand over the half-crown, curled his fingers around it. And went.

Chapter Seven

Emma had slept two nights in the bed that had been hers when she'd lived in Shingle Cottage with her family. How small that bed seemed to her now. There'd been no sheets or blankets on it so she'd used the nightdress of her mama's, that Matthew Caunter had given her, to sleep in and pulled her shawl over her. She'd been warm enough.

The narcissi Seth had given her were scenting the room so powerfully in the old jam jar Emma had found to put them in that it almost took her breath away. There was a lot of life in them yet and she didn't think that Matthew would want them. Perhaps she would take them to the cemetery and add them to the pot of wild flowers she'd picked for her mama and Johnnie – her mama would have appreciated the scent of narcissi more than her papa would.

The trawler Matthew was on was due in today and once she'd warned Matthew the constable was looking for him, she'd have to leave. She knew Carter and Miles Jago always unloaded the boats, so she hoped Matthew would be able to come ashore quickly and get back to Shingle Cottage before the constable got to him. Where she was going to go after that she had no idea.

Emma dressed quickly and stuffed every last thing of hers into her carpet bag. She shook the water from the stems of the narcissi and re-wrapped them in the brown paper Seth had presented them to her in. Then she lifted the window sash just a crack so she could tip the water over the sill into the back garden.

But with lightning speed, and as noiselessly as she could, Emma pulled the sash back down. A constable was coming along the narrow back alley. He was swiftly followed by a second policeman. And Emma was surprised to see Reuben Jago bringing up the rear. She held her breath waiting to see where they would go. But she'd half guessed they'd turn in through the back gate of Shingle Cottage. They strode purposefully down the back path.

Emma tiptoed through to the bedroom that had been her mama's and her papa's and which was very obviously the one Matthew Caunter was using now, because his clothes were strewn all over the place. There was a tea chest in the corner that looked full to the brim he hadn't even unpacked yet. How right he'd been that he needed a woman about the place to tidy up after him.

Emma wouldn't be able to escape from the back door without being seen. And as she knew she'd left the kitchen door open she knew they would be able to see her if she tried to make her escape through the front door.

'Emma Le Goff ...'

Emma heard Reuben Jago say her name as the back door creaked open. Were they coming for *her*? Had Mrs Phipps seen her slipping in and out to the privy and gossiped about it?

Then came the sound of footsteps across the bare boards of the kitchen. There was a lot of mumbling between the men but Emma couldn't pick out a single, clear, word of it. She crept out onto the landing so she might hear better what was being said.

'No need to wait Mr Jago, Sir.'

Constable Jeffery – how well Emma remembered *his* voice and his condescending way of speaking. It *was* better here – sound drifted upwards.

'I'll stay,' Reuben Jago said.

'We can deal with Mr Caunter, Sir.'

A different voice this time.

'I said I'll stay,' Mr Jago replied. 'This is my property.'

With a sigh Constable Jeffery suggested making tea. Emma salivated at his words. She'd been as neat as a pin in the kitchen. Washing the teapot and the cups the second she'd finished using them, replacing them in the exact positions Matthew Caunter had left them in. She'd fetched water at night so as not to be seen, being careful not to be wasteful so it would last until she could get more. But how she could drink a cup of tea now.

She heard the back door open as someone went to draw water from the pump. And then she heard it close again as whoever had done the task returned. Then there was a clatter of cups and someone banging the kettle down on the range. The range. She'd had to light it because Matthew had let it go out when he'd gone to sea. She waited to hear if someone would remark on the fact that the range was warm, despite Matthew Caunter not being at home. But no one did, as far as she was able to hear.

Certainly no one bothered to come upstairs – she heard the scraping of chairs on the wooden floor of the kitchen, and the sound of bodies dropping heavily onto them. She crept back into the front bedroom. She peeped around the edge of the curtain at the window. Could she somehow warn Mr Caunter that the constables and Mr Jago were waiting for him?

But she was too late. Matthew Caunter was kicking open the front gate, his arms full with the bag he had taken to sea with a change of clothes should he get wet, and food supplies. Emma's papa had had such a bag. And often it had come back with more in it than when he'd left – a fish, or a crab, or a handful of prawns. And sometimes, if the boat had had to pull into a French harbour somewhere because of bad weather, there would be a lace handkerchief for her mama and maybe some sweet treat or a toy for her and Johnnie.

Emma wondered what it was that might be in the heavy bag that Matthew Caunter was carrying. She crept back out onto the landing. Matthew would have a clear view up the stairs towards her. Should she make 'go back' gestures at him?

'What the hell?' Matthew Caunter's deep voice – very loud and obviously outraged – echoed through the house. He didn't look up towards where Emma was standing, her back splayed against the wall, and barely breathing from fright. She could see the top of Matthew's sandy hair now, but no one else.

'A few questions, Mr Caunter. I'm Sergeant Emms. My colleague, Constable Jeffery, and Mr Jago you know, of course.'

Emma sucked her breath in. A sergeant, not a constable. This had to be serious, didn't it? They'd come to accuse Matthew of murdering Sophie, hadn't they?

'Ask away. I've nothing to hide.'

Emma heard the sergeant clear his throat.

'I shall be asking the questions. Constable Jeffery will make notes.' He halted, and Emma heard the rustle of paper. 'You called at Mr Jago's property on Wednesday last with some papers and a bundle of possessions belonging, so you said, to the late mother of Miss Emma Le Goff?'

'I *assumed* that was who they belonged to seeing as she had lived here. Mr Jago was there when I called.'

'And did you know what was in the bundle?'

'Some photos. A book of some sort. Item of clothing. Three sovereign coins I put there myself, in case someone is accusing Emma of stealing them. God only knows the girl's going to find it hard to survive. I thought a bit of cash would help. Oh, and a necklace. Purple stone. Amethyst perhaps?'

'And where did the necklace come from?'

'I found it.'

Emma pressed her lips together to stop the sound of her shock escaping.

She didn't want to even think that Matthew Caunter had murdered Sophie, taken the necklace from her bloodied neck and then given it to her. She didn't think a man who had been so kind to her, so respectful in not forcing his attentions on her, could murder a woman.

'Where did you *find* it, Mr Caunter?' the sergeant asked.

'I *found* it,' Matthew said, 'outside Mr Jago's own front gate.'

'I don't believe that for a minute.' Mr Jago's voice dripped anger.

'I don't lie, Mr Jago. To you or anyone.'

'Enough,' the sergeant said. 'We'll hear Mr Caunter out. You found it – so you say – outside Mr Jago's gate. When?'

'When I was on the way to deliver the other things to Miss Le Goff. I knew she was stopping at Hilltop House because I'd asked a neighbour if she knew where I would be able to find her and she told me the doctor had arranged lodgings with Mr Jago. I thought the necklace such a pretty thing, and in my experience women like pretty things. It was a bit muddy, so I ran it through the damp leaves of Mr Jago's hedge to wash it off a bit. Came up handsome it did, and …'

'Thank you, Mr Caunter. We only want a statement, not a novel.'

'Well, you won't be getting one from me. Can't write nor read, can I?'

He couldn't read? Emma knew there were plenty who couldn't, but Matthew Caunter seemed so learned somehow. And so confident in his replies to the sergeant.

There was a low murmuring of voices then that Emma didn't catch a single word of.

Then Matthew spoke again – impatience in his voice. 'Will that be all?'

'It most certainly will not,' Mr Jago said. 'I like to know the measure of any man I employ.'

'Leave this to me, Mr Jago, Sir,' the sergeant said.

'Very well, but you'd better get to the bottom of it.'

'We will. Now, Mr Caunter, you tell me that you found this necklace outside Mr Jago's house ...'

'If I said I did, then I did, Sergeant.'

'That's as maybe. But I have another question for you, Mr Caunter. Where were you on the evening of Monday last?'

'I'd like to know why you are asking,' Matthew said.

'Answer my question first and I'll tell you.'

Matthew sighed heavily. 'Very well. I was here. I'd arrived from Slapton, asked the neighbour on the left for a spoonful of sugar because I'd forgotten to bring any with me and the shops were closed. I lit the range, cooked a bit of supper. Sat by the fire later.'

'Alone, Mr Caunter, or did you have company?'

Emma swallowed. Would he say that she'd been with him? If he did then Mr Jago was sure to tell Seth. And what would Seth think of her then?

'I had company.'

'Male or female?'

'Female.'

'Anyone we can reliably call upon as witness?'

'No one I'd want you to question, Sergeant. And now that I've answered your questions I'd like to know what this is all about. I've been at sea, as Mr Jago well knows, and I'm in dire need of a good scrub in the sink.'

'Miss Sophie Ellison?' the sergeant said. 'Know her?'

'No. Why?'

'She was found stabbed and with her clothes in disarray in the alley behind The Port Light. A necklace she'd been trying to sell in the inn earlier was missing from her body. An amethyst necklace on a gold chain.'

'Probably got what she deserved,' Matthew said.

All the men began talking at once. Emma was still holding her breath – it was making her feel giddy.

She heard Reuben Jago tell Matthew that Sophie had worked for him, and Matthew reply that he ought to keep a tighter control on his servants, then – not allow them time to go ripping men off in inns for the price of a drink and other things done in dark alleys for money.

There was more general shouting. Then Emma heard the thump of a hand on the table.

'No!' Matthew said. 'I did not go to The Port Light. Neither did I meet Miss Sophie Ellison. I told the truth about finding the necklace. And now I am going to have to ask you all to …'

'Not so fast, Mr Caunter,' the sergeant interrupted. 'Unless you can supply me with the name of your, er, companion on Monday evening last, then I shall have to ask you to accompany me to the station for further questioning.'

'Then we'd better go,' Matthew said. 'I have no intention of dragging an innocent young woman into this. But I'll say the same things at the station that I've said here.'

'That's as maybe. Now, have you made a note, Constable, of everything Mr Caunter has said?' the sergeant asked.

'I have. Not looking good for him is it, Sergeant?'

'The cuffs, Constable.'

Emma felt her blood chill in her veins. They were arresting Matthew Caunter for the murder of Sophie Ellison. She knew he couldn't have done it because he'd given her a cup of tea and a buttered scone. It had grown quite dark outside. Then he must have put her to bed when she'd fallen asleep, mended her book – and that would have taken ages to do. Matthew wouldn't have had time to go to The Port Light, drink, murder Sophie Ellison outside, *and* mend her book.

Emma heard the snap of the cuffs being fixed to Matthew's wrists. She unpeeled herself from the wall, her back sticky with nervous sweat. She took a step forward to the top of the stairs so that if anyone looked up she'd be in full view.

'Wait!' she cried. 'I was here with Mr Caunter on that evening. All night, too. Mrs Phipps saw me leaving the next morning.'

Three faces looked up at her. Reuben Jago's eyes were hard as flint, and flashed anger. The sergeant and the constable looked totally surprised and not a little confused.

And Matthew Caunter? After a huge sigh, he looked up at her, too.

And winked.

All eyes were on her, but it was Matthew who spoke first. 'Seeing as these cuffs are on you may as well take me to the station, Sergeant. I'll answer your questions there. But not in present company.'

Emma saw him tip his head slightly towards Reuben Jago.

'You and Miss Le Goff both, then,' Sergeant Emms said.

Slowly Emma descended the stairs. What was going to happen now?

'Seth. In here.' Reuben Jago bellowed at Seth from the drawing-room.

What did he want now?

'Yes, Pa?'

'I suppose *you* let her in?'

'Who?'

'The Le Goff bitch.'

'A bitch is a female dog. Emma's not a bitch.'

'I can think of worse words. She was found in Shingle Cottage. Did you give her a key? There was a key in the bundle of things Caunter brought, but that's not to say it was a Shingle Cottage key or that he put it there.'

So *that* was where she had gone. Seth couldn't stop a smile lifting the corners of his mouth now he knew that she hadn't left the area. And then he remembered Matthew Caunter was living in Shingle Cottage and his smile dropped.

'No. I didn't give her a key. Where is she now?'

'Still with Caunter. I've been reliably informed by Sergeant Emms not half-an-hour ago that Caunter couldn't possibly have murdered Sophie Ellison so I'll have to take his word for it. And as Caunter's a good crewman – strong and hard-working, and I won't be able to find a replacement for him easily – I've said he can stay. He stopped by on his way back from the police station. He says he feels bad the bitch has been thrown out of her home and wants to take her on as housekeeper.' He leered, implying they both knew what that meant.

Seth felt sick at the implication. He knew his father wouldn't have agreed to let Emma stay if there wasn't something in it for him. He'd agreed to the arrangement because Caunter was going to be smuggling for his father, wasn't he? There could be no other reason, could there?

'Don't put her in any danger, Pa. If Caunter is bringing in contraband stuff …'

'Contraband? Whatever makes you think my boats are bringing in contraband?' His father curled his lip at him.

Seth shrugged his shoulders. Perhaps he was wrong? Certainly, there'd been nothing there shouldn't have been in the cellar of Hilltop or in any of the netting lofts when he'd looked. 'I'm just saying that *if* there is smuggling going on, then my decision would be made for me.'

'Your decision to do what? Get hooked up with the Le Goff piece?'

'Her name is Emma, but that's not what I meant. I'm thinking of going over to Canada. Uncle Silas has always said in his letters that I could work for him. He …'

'Your Uncle *Silas*? Your mother's pure-as-the-driven-snow brother?'

'I only have the one Uncle Silas,' Seth said.

Who, Seth knew, wouldn't get involved in smuggling. He owed it to his mother's memory not to live on the fringes of criminality – or get up to his neck in it as his pa and brothers more than likely were – even if only by association. The second he found any hard evidence of smuggling through his pa's boats he'd be off. Or would he? Perhaps not yet – not with Emma in danger as she would be if Caunter was going to be smuggling.

'Is that all you wanted me for, Pa – to know if I'd given Emma the key?'

'No. Not quite all.' To Seth's surprise his pa laid a hand on his shoulder – a gentle touch and not the rough push or a thump he usually got. 'I'm pleased it wasn't you who gave her the key after all.'

But I would have done if I'd been here and heard you tell her to leave, Seth thought.

'What else?' he said.

His father's hand on his shoulder, his fingers digging in a little now, was making Seth feel how he imagined a cat's prey might – trapped, totally trapped.

'I want to make a deal with you, son. You're not your brothers, I'll admit, but you more than earn your keep here. You've a good head for figures. And your education was better than mine was for letter-writing. You write the entries in the books neater than I ever could. I need you here, Seth, not in Canada with your Uncle Silas. I ...'

'Get on with it, Pa. That's the longest sentence you've spoken to me in a long time. But just so you know, if your "deal" has anything illegal about it ...'

'Just like your ma,' his father interrupted him. 'She was high on her moral horse most of the time.'

'There's no need to bring Ma into this,' Seth snapped. 'Just tell me about the deal.'

'Not so unlike me, son.' His father beamed at him, squeezing his shoulder. 'Wanting to know every last detail. You've reached your majority and I consider it high time I make over the properties I own to your name. Many businessmen do it. A sort of insurance against hard times.'

'Hard times?' Seth said.

'Do I need to explain it to you chapter and verse, son? You know as well as I do that there are good years and bad years for fishing. Times when prices are good and times when we wouldn't be able to give fish away. Debts can pile up in a minute in hard times. D'you get my meaning now?'

'I'm beginning to. And signing your properties over to me so they couldn't be sold to offset any debts would be legal?'

'It will be perfectly legal, son.'

'Carter and Miles aren't going to like it, though.'

'They're not going to know. Neither you nor I are going to tell them, understand?'

Seth nodded.

'Good. I've made an appointment at a solicitor's office in Exeter for tomorrow afternoon. For us both.'

Seth had never thought of himself as calculating or of being capable of using anyone. But his ma had brought a great deal of money to the marriage – her father's money. If Carter and Miles were to get their hands on it they'd only fritter it away on women and high living. No, the properties were safer with him.

'And the books, son,' his father said. 'You write them up, so I think it's high time you signed them, too. What do you think?'

Sign them? Seth was already concerned sums weren't quite adding up. His pa was depositing more money than the profits of the fishing fleet showed. He was up to something and Seth had no intention of being part of it. He'd have questions of his own about the exchange of property deeds when he met the solicitor. Besides, if he signed obviously false accounts it might affect his entitlement to the properties – something his pa seemed not to have realised – and he was not going to give them up.

'No need to mention to the solicitor about signing the books. That's a different matter.'

Seth shivered. It was as though his pa was reading his mind. And he *was* up to something – Seth was certain of it now. So, there was no way on this earth he was going to put his signature to anything other than the exchange of property deeds.

'I can see you're thinking about it,' Reuben laughed. 'I nearly nodded off there for a moment. Circumstances change, son. They change people.'

'Don't they just,' Seth said.

As always, Seth's thoughts turned to Emma. For a moment in the cemetery he'd felt deeply towards her, had felt those feelings reciprocated. But if she was going to be Caunter's housekeeper Emma's feelings might change. Caunter was a good-looking man, after all. Kind, too, to have given her refuge when she needed it.

Damn and blast it, Seth thought, that I'm a Jago. But he wasn't going to give up on winning Emma's heart – it might just take a little longer than he'd been hoping for, that was all.

'What did you say to Mr Jago?' Emma asked. 'Why won't you tell me?'

She and Matthew were back at Shingle Cottage now. They'd walked via Hilltop House and Emma had been told to stay outside while Matthew went in to speak to Mr Jago – not that she was ever going to go in there again. All the way home she'd been asking what had been said but Matthew wouldn't tell her.

At the police station Emma had been questioned first – alone. She'd nearly died of embarrassment when she'd been asked if Matthew had taken her to his bed, and she'd said – no, shouted – that she was underage for that sort of thing and anyway she wasn't *that* sort of girl. And then Matthew had gone in and she'd had to wait almost an hour before he came back out again.

'Patience, Emma, is a virtue you'd be wise to learn. I wasn't going to tell you anything out in the street where I might be overheard. Tea?'

Matthew banged a kettle of water down on the range.

Did she have time for a cup of tea? She'd have to find somewhere else to stay before nightfall and already the sun was going down. 'I don't have time,' Emma said. 'I'll collect my bag and then …'

'No need,' Matthew said.

'I don't understand.'

Honestly, Matthew was talking in riddles.

'You can stay here. And you'll have an official title – housekeeper. Nothing wrong in a man having a housekeeper if there's no wife around to keep house for him. Mr Jago will spread it about that that's all you are. It's the best I can do to stop the gossip on your behalf.'

'I don't know that Mr Jago ever does anyone a favour. Certainly he didn't do me any. He'll be getting more out of this than you or I will,' Emma said. 'He'd never make an offer like that if there was nothing in it for him. He …'

Matthew held up a hand to stop her.

'Neither of us can read Mr Jago's mind or know what his intentions are, can we?'

'I suppose not.'

'But I'll tell you what's in mine. I think Jago has treated

you despicably. You've been orphaned such a short time and I think he might have shown more compassion. And I told him so. So, my housekeeper – how does that suit? Remembering, of course, you have nowhere to lay your head tonight. I'm not forcing you to stay, of course. You're free to go.' Matthew waved an arm towards the door.

Emma wanted to say there was no way on this earth she was going to be anybody's housekeeper. But something stopped her and it wasn't only that the kettle had boiled and Matthew had taken biscuits from a tin and put some on a plate. Where *would* she go if she didn't stay here?

'I can see you're mulling the idea over, Emma. Yes?'

'Yes,' Emma said. 'But it's making me feel like some tool a neighbour borrows like a saw to lop off tree branches or something. And in return gets offered the loan of boots for his children to go to school …'

'I don't want you to feel that way. It's not how I see it.'

Emma heaved her shoulders up to her ears and let them drop heavily. She sighed.

'And now *I* want to make deal with you, Emma.'

Emma folded her arms across her chest. If he was going to ask for the favours of her body then she'd be out of that door faster than a rat up a drainpipe. She was underage for goodness' sake. It would be against the law.

'What deal?'

'If you stay, I promise not to enter your bedroom, as long as you promise not to enter mine. Is it a deal?'

'*That* part goes without saying,' Emma said. 'But what *will* I be expected to do? I've got the money you told the sergeant you put in my bag, and I could use that for rent and food.'

'No need. I'll pay the rent, and give you money to shop for food. You keep house. And you cook.'

'Cook? For you?'

Matthew put a hand to his forehead and pretend-scanned

the room. 'No one else seems to be here. So yes, you get to cook for me. You *can* cook?'

'Yes. My mama was a good cook. And although he didn't like anyone knowing he could – or that he did – so was my papa. He showed me how to make *tarte aux pommes* ...'

Emma's mind wandered off to the times she'd spent helping her papa cut the apples so thinly she could have read the newspaper through them. And then the bit she loved best when the tart came out of the oven and she glazed the top with melted apricot jam. She licked her lips. She could almost taste it.

'And what would that be when it's at home?'

'It's French. A sort of apple tart, but with pastry only on the bottom. Served with cream.'

'Sounds good to me.'

'But I hope I won't be cooking for you for long ...'

'Don't be in any rush, Emma. I admire you for the way you came to my defence against Jago and the rozzers. My way of saying thanks – to put a roof over your head for the time being.'

'But people will talk about me, and ...'

'Let them. Small minds. You and I will know the truth of what goes on inside these walls. Hold your head high and ignore the lot of them.'

'I'm getting good at that. Holding my head high – well as high as I can – because there's lots here still think my mother was a suicide, even though the Coroner ...' Emma pressed her lips together. Couldn't go on. She would love to be able to clear her mama's name once and for all, but didn't know how. And she wasn't going to ask anyone to help, least of all Matthew Caunter.

'The truth will out, Emma,' he said. 'It almost always does.'

Matthew began emptying the contents of the bag he'd

taken to sea. He hung wet clothes over a line strung across the kitchen ceiling. Emma watched him, wondering if she should suggest he wash them in soapflakes first. If they were to share the cottage then she didn't think she'd be able to live with the stinking smell of mouldy clothes.

'I wonder who did kill Sophie Ellison?' Emma said. She shivered – the sight of poor Sophie and the mess she was in when the doctor turned her over was still very fresh in her mind.

'I wonder,' Matthew said. 'But don't you worry. You're safe with me. And that necklace that's caused all this brouhaha … I'll get that back for you as well one day. You can be certain of that.'

Chapter Eight

Seth ran his hand over the counterpane that Emma had slept under not that long ago. The pillow, he noticed, still bore the indent of her head.

Any minute now Mrs Drew would be up to change the bed-linen. A new maid was arriving after lunch – a new plaything for his brothers probably. Well, there was no way whoever it was, was going to be using his ma's silver-backed brushes. He hadn't minded Emma using them – had wanted her to. He picked up the brushes and held them to him – they smelled of roses; Emma must have washed her hair in rose-scented soap.

'You're sweet on her, aren't you, Seth?' Mrs Drew startled him, even though her usually loud voice was gentle.

Seth twitched his shoulders.

'You can't deny it, lad. But …'

'But she's living back at Shingle Cottage with Caunter.'

'She's *working* for him. And trust me it won't be easy work looking after a man. But all that don't mean she's sweet on him, though, do it?'

Seth gave another, small shrug. 'No, I suppose not.'

Mrs Drew laid a hand on Seth's shoulder. 'She's a free spirit, that one. Neither you nor Matthew Caunter will be able to clip her wings until she's ready. She's only young – not sixteen yet. Born at Michaelmas and don't I know it 'cos it were me holding her ma's hand while she screamed the place down. A lot's happened to that poor maid in a short space of time. 'Er needs time to adjust. Let her fly a little first, Seth. And you do the same, lad. Away from this house if you've got any sense. And that's all I'm saying on the matter.'

Mrs Drew dragged the counterpane from the bed, began to strip sheets.

'I'll let you get on.'

'You do that. And take those brushes with you. If I were a betting woman – which I'm not – I'd say you'll get to give them to your lady love one day.'

'A florin on it,' Seth said, smiling. 'But you're not a betting woman ...'

'Oh, I could be prepared to bend my own rule.'

Seth and Mrs Drew shook on the deal ... a florin wasn't a lot to lose but he was prepared to lose it if Emma could be his one day.

Although she would never have admitted it, Emma was enjoying cooking for herself and Matthew. So much so that weeks had passed since she'd even thought about looking for another job. She could hardly believe it was almost the end of May. Well, Emma thought, as she ladled soup into two bowls, she could in reality because the nights were much lighter now and she could cook well into the evening without having to light an oil lamp to do it by. She placed a bowl of soup in front of Matthew.

'Thank you,' Matthew said, as he always did when she served him food. But no other conversation seemed to be forthcoming. It was as though he had something on his mind and Emma was learning not to pry.

She sat down opposite him, stirred her soup six times to the left, six times to the right to cool it – an old habit of her mama's that just wouldn't die.

Emma looked up at Matthew but his head was bent over his bowl, hungrily eating now. She returned to her thoughts.

Her savings towards some good clothes and shoes in which she would return to Nase Head House and ask for a position were growing, because if Matthew particularly liked something Emma had cooked, then he'd slip her a shilling, or even a florin. She'd been to the bank and had been issued with a replacement bank book seeing as the original was one of the things Mr Jago had consigned to the bonfire for some reason best known to himself – not that Emma was going to ask. The bank manager had, though, when he'd written to Mr Jago to see if he had it or if he could confirm it had been destroyed. It was hugely satisfying to Emma, now, to see the balance creeping up, if slowly, in her new bank book.

On the days Matthew was away at sea Emma dreamed of the clothes and the shoes she would buy – jewellery even. And she saw to the house – cleaning it, moving furniture around to get a better look – while she dreamed. And flowers – as spring flowers were replaced with early summer ones, Emma walked the lanes and picked dog roses judiciously from the hedgerows; just enough to lift her spirits, but not too many as to leave little for other people to look at and enjoy.

And Matthew had been true to his word – she was safe with him. He had fixed a bolt to her bedroom door, although she rarely used it. Just the fixing of it for her was enough to tell her he had no intention of violating her body against her will.

But Matthew was seeing *someone*, getting to know *her* body because he often went out, returning late and smelling of perfume. 'A man has needs, Emma,' was all he said when she commented on the sweet smell of violets about him. And Emma had learned not to comment again. And not to mind being alone while he was out enjoying female company. She read her book by lamplight, making the words last, reading the same paragraph over and over – drowning, almost, in Jane Austen's prose. And sometimes, on a warm evening, Matthew sat on the back doorstep whittling a piece of wood – turning it into a squirrel or a mouse or some other small animal while she read. At times like that Emma felt almost happy again.

'You know, Emma, this soup is delicious,' Matthew said, breaking into her thoughts like a cavalry charge. 'Never tasted the like anywhere.'

'My papa taught me how to make it. The stock you make it with is important. He said that. You have to boil the prawn shells and the fish bones to make the stock. His mother taught him how, and no doubt her mother before her and back through the generations in Roscoff.'

'Roscoff?'

'It's in Brittany. It's a fishing town, too – like this place only not as big. And no fleet owners like the Jagos – just one boat per family, so my papa said.'

'So how come your papa, as you call him …'

'He was my papa! That's how the French say daddy.'

'Keep your shirt on, Miss. But I'm intrigued to know how he ended up here.'

'A storm blew him in, so Mama always said. And she kept him.'

'Ah,' Matthew said, slurping down another spoonful of soup. 'It's an ill wind that does nobody any good.'

'That's what Mama used to say. She was helping in the Seamen's Mission – you know the place where seamen can go if their boats sink or get damaged and they're far from their own harbour, as Papa was.'

'I know,' Matthew said. 'Every seaman needs to know where the nearest one is. Mr Jago pointed it out to me.'

'Oh, him.'

Emma shrugged. She was sick of the sound of the Jago name. Even Seth. She'd thought he was beginning to like her – not bothered by the fact she was an orphan and able to ignore the rumours that her mama had committed suicide. But every time she saw him now, he pretended he hadn't seen her coming and turned and walked off in the opposite direction. Perhaps she'd misread his feelings in the cemetery when they'd met accidentally? Although she hoped, very much, that she hadn't.

She hoped with all her heart that Seth didn't think she wouldn't want anything to do with him because his pa had her mama's necklace. If only she could see him she could ask if that was the reason and assure him it didn't alter her feelings about *him* one little bit.

Emma swallowed back her sadness at not seeing Seth as much as she would like to. But still there was an ache somewhere around her breast bone that wouldn't go away – like a nagging toothache, but something no dentist could put right.

'Mr Jago's not a nice man, Matthew. Nor are his sons, Carter and Miles.'

'So I'm fast finding out. What do you think about Seth?' Matthew asked.

'He's not like the other Jagos,' Emma said. 'We were friends, me and Seth.'

'Were?'

Emma shrugged. If she didn't think of the times she and Seth had walked together, talked together, laughed together, then maybe she wouldn't miss them too much.

'I expect it's because I'm living here. With you, and …' Perhaps his father hadn't bothered to tell Seth what her position with Matthew was exactly?

'I didn't have Seth Jago down as small-minded,' Matthew said.

'Neither did I.'

Emma sipped her fish soup. She wished she'd had some dill to go in it but it was too early in the growing season. She broke off a piece of bread from the basket on the table – a habit she'd taken on from her papa which her mama had happily applied to her own way of doing things. As she tore the bread into bite-sized pieces her thoughts strayed to Seth – as they often did – even though she tried her hardest to banish those thoughts.

'Is it true that Mr Jago smuggles things?'

Matthew stilled his spoon on its way to his mouth. 'Smuggle? What makes you say that?'

'Oh, just something someone said,' Emma said with a shrug.

'But you're not going to tell me who that someone was?'

'No.'

Matthew allowed his spoonful of soup to continue its journey. Laid the spoon back in the bowl. He wiped the corners of his mouth with the back of his hand.

'Emma Le Goff – didn't you tell me yourself your pa said your tongue would hang you? I'm going to tell you the same thing. I can read you like a book. Seth Jago told you that, didn't he? And in confidence, if it was him.'

'I'm not saying. And I only mentioned it because if you're going to be in with the smuggling then I don't want to stay here.'

'Very commendable,' Matthew said. 'I'm going to ask you something and I want an honest answer. Has Seth Jago ever given you something you suspect was smuggled goods?'

'Chocolate. Seth gave me some chocolate once. He said he'd bought it off his brother, Miles. It's got a French wrapper. I haven't eaten it yet.'

'Any particular reason?'

'The French writing reminds me of my papa – makes me feel close to him. I don't want to spoil the perfectness of it by opening it. And another is that I don't want to be a party to smuggling which I would be if I ate it – *if* Miles Jago got it by that route before he sold it to Seth. I know my papa would never have been party to smuggling. He only ever brought home a crab or some dabs from the boats. And things he bought for Mama in Roscoff when they landed a catch there, which they had to do sometimes if the sea got rough in the Channel and they couldn't make it back to Devon. I remember my mama complaining she had to buy brandy for the Christmas puddings and why couldn't she have some like other fishermen's wives did? So, does Mr Jago smuggle things in, and ...'

'I don't know what I'm going to do with you. You don't listen to a word of advice. All I'll say on the matter is that there's barely a fisherman who doesn't come off a boat with a bit of something they covet – like your papa with the crabs and dabs. What do you miss most, Emma, of the things your father brought home off the boats?'

'That's easy,' Emma said. 'Coffee. French coffee. Even though he didn't bring it very often I've never forgotten the taste.'

'So,' Matthew said, 'if I were to be anywhere near Roscoff and could get my hands on some French coffee, would you like some?'

Emma inhaled deeply – her memory was playing tricks on her. She *could* smell the coffee her mama used to make with the beans her papa had brought home, grinding them up with a pestle and mortar. The aroma was in her nostrils now. Oh, how she'd love to drink a cup of it again.

'Only if it's honestly come by.'

'It will be. But it comes with a deal on your part, too. Some coffee in exchange for that delicious crab tart you made for me last week, times six.'

'Six?'

'Same as the *one* you made me, but multiplied by six. You *can* do multiplication?'

Matthew smiled widely at her. Winked. Emma was getting used to that wink. She wondered if he did it to win the favours of the lady – or ladies – he was seeing who was satisfying his needs. She knew what *needs* meant. Knew the facts of life. But there was no way she wanted to apply that knowledge to her own body just yet. She didn't want to get with child as more than a few in the year or two above her at school had done. She didn't want to know what making love did to her body in case she liked it and she couldn't get enough of it and ended up dead in a back alley like Sophie Ellison had done.

'Times tables, Emma – you do know them?' Matthew teased her when she was slow to reply.

'Of course I do. And I can say them in French.'

'French? Can you write in French, too?'

'And read it.'

'Well, well – what a dark little filly you are. Even better.'

'Even better what?'

'I've got an idea. But first I will need those six crab tarts. Obviously I'll supply the crabs and I'll give you the money to get more tins to bake them in. And whatever other ingredients you'll need for the tarts. Eggs?'

'Of course, eggs. But why do you want six? They'll go off.'

'Not if they're eaten right away they won't.'

'Tell me!'

'No. Not yet.'

Matthew took a sovereign from his back pocket and handed it to Emma. 'Take it,' he said. 'Buy yourself something – ribbons perhaps for that beautiful hair of yours – with the change. But now I've got the night tide to catch.'

He patted Emma on the top of the head. 'If I ever have a daughter, I'd want her to be like you,' he said.

Which very neatly puts me in my place, Emma thought, on the off chance I might be harbouring romantic notions about him.

'And as the saying "Time and tide waits for no man" has more than a grain of truth in it, I'll be off.'

Emma had no idea when Matthew would be back. She'd forgotten to ask and he hadn't said. He'd seemed in a terrible hurry. And what was all that talk about making six crab tarts? They'd hardly fit in the oven. She wouldn't be able to buy the eggs and the cream for tarts just yet, but she could buy the tins in readiness.

She pushed open the door of Annings, the ironmongers.

'I'm afraid we're closed.'

Mrs Anning stood behind the counter, arms folded.

'Thirza, dear ...' her husband began, but Mrs Anning put up a hand to stop him.

'Closed. You do understand the word, Miss Le Goff. *Fermé* in French, in case you don't.'

Emma replied in a torrent of French – calling Mrs Anning a bigoted old goat – praying she wouldn't understand.

Her puzzled expression told Emma that she didn't.

'I understand what *fermé* means, Mrs Anning. And I also understand you are a retail outlet,' Emma said. 'Which means you sell things. To the public. I'm here on an errand for a friend.'

'Doesn't go by the name of Caunter, does he, by any chance?' Mrs Anning said. She tucked her hands underneath her armpits, squashing her very substantial bosom in the process. Emma wanted to laugh – it looked as though she'd put too much suet pastry on top of a pie and in the steaming it had pushed up everywhere it shouldn't.

'I won't ask you the names of your friends, Mrs Anning,' Emma said, 'as long as you don't ask me the names of mine.'

'Well!' Mrs Anning's multiple chins wobbled.

Emma heard Mr Anning begin to laugh, then to clear his throat. A strangled sort of choking sound came out.

Mrs Anning looked at her husband in alarm. And Emma took advantage of the diversion.

'I've been asked to purchase five baking tins. With narrow edges. Round ones.'

Emma took the sovereign that Matthew had given her from her purse and slapped it on the counter in front of Mrs Anning.

As always, money talked. The shopkeeper scurried off to find the tins.

'Why are you avoiding me, Seth?'

Emma stopped – some dog roses she'd gathered for her parents' graves in her hands – on the path between the rows of headstones.

Seth had just straightened up after laying pale yellow tulips on his mother's grave.

Slowly he turned to face her. 'You're another man's now.'

'Who told you that? I'm nothing of the sort. I'm Mr Caunter's housekeeper. Nothing more than that.'

'That's not what my pa said.'

'Then your pa's a liar. And he's broken his agreement with Mr Caunter. He agreed he would let everyone – everyone Seth, know that's all I am.'

'Ssh, Emma. This is a consecrated place. It's not the place for arguments.'

Emma lowered her voice. 'You could have asked *me*,' she said and fingered the two posies of flowers she'd made. Her mama had taught her how to pull a few strands of hair from her own head and plait them to make a sort of rope to hold the flower stems tight. Emma had pulled six long hairs, plaited three together for each posy.

'I *should* have asked you, Emma. I'm sorry now I didn't.'

'But you believe me? About being Mr Caunter's housekeeper and nothing more.'

'I do now.'

Even though part of her was cross with Seth for being so weak as to take notice of anything his father said, she could understand his reason for it – Reuben Jago was not a man to be crossed. Emma had often wondered why Seth's pa didn't *make* him go to sea, especially if one of his boats was a crewman short as they sometimes were if there was an epidemic of the influenza – her papa had often complained he was doing three men's work at such times. Perhaps Seth had had a near-drowning and was fearful of it happening again? How little I know about him really, Emma thought. Well, if she didn't ask, she'd never know, would she?

'Can I ask you something, Seth?' Emma said. 'Something that's been on my mind?'

'Ask away.'

'What's the real reason you don't go to sea?'

'I get seasick, if you want to know. Every time.' He didn't meet Emma's eye.

'Seasick?' she said. 'Or is there something going on, on your pa's boats, you don't want to see?'

Seth shrugged again.

'Things like brandy being fished up instead of mackerel? And French chocolate?'

'Forget you've even thought that, Emma. But this isn't the place to talk about things like that. My ma ...' Seth kissed the tips of his fingers then touched his mother's name on her headstone – his back to Emma. 'Sorry, Ma.'

'How did your ma die, Seth?'

Seth wheeled round then, eyes wide with surprise – shocked she'd asked, no doubt. Emma wanted to bite back the insensitive words, but it was too late now.

'I shouldn't have asked, but ...'

'She fell down the cellar steps late one night. My father said the candles were burning low and for her to get more ...'

'Why didn't he go?'

'He and my brothers had had a skinful, as usual.'

'Oh. So she fell?'

'That's what I was told. Being the youngest, I'd been sent to bed earlier. I was asleep. It was two whole days before I was told Ma had died. And then it was left to the maid to tell me.' There were tears in Seth's eyes as he spoke.

'Oh, Seth, I'm sorry,' Emma said. She laid a hand on Seth's arm. Squeezed.

'No one talks about her any more.'

'You can talk to me.'

Emma knew how lonely it felt not having anyone to talk to about times past – happy times, funny times. And sad times too, because everyone had those.

'Not here,' Seth said.

'Where then?'

'Shouldn't you be getting back to …'

'Mr Caunter's at sea as you well know. He didn't say when he'd be back. But let's not talk about Matthew Caunter,' Emma said. 'We could go down to Crystal Cove. It'll be quiet there. You can talk. And if you get upset it won't matter. There'll only be me and a few oyster catchers as witness.'

'Men aren't supposed to show their feelings, but I can't help it sometimes.'

'I don't see why they shouldn't. My papa used to cry. When Mama lost her babies, he cried after every one.'

Emma swallowed hard – tears were threatening again like they did whenever she let her mind dwell too long on her parents.

'I think we both need to talk,' Seth said.

Emma nodded.

'So, if you're sure Mr Caunter won't mind, we could …'

'Why would he mind? I'm his housekeeper. For the

moment. Until I'm older and can fend for myself better. And,' Emma said, embarrassed to even be mentioning it, but she had to set the record straight, 'Mr Caunter doesn't think of me in that sort of way. He sees me as a daughter.'

'I'm glad of that,' Seth said. He laid his hands on Emma's shoulders and leant in to kiss her cheek.

A bubble of pure joy bubbled up inside her. A new feeling. A good feeling. A feeling that had no place in a cemetery.

'I'd better lay these flowers,' she said.

'We'll do it together,' Seth said.

But as they approached her mama's and Johnnie's grave, Emma could see something was wrong. The grass had been torn up and there was a pile of horse droppings where the grass had been. And sticking out of the droppings was a sailor doll with the head ripped off – the head lying face down in the mud.

Who could have done such a thing? And why? Poor, innocent little Johnnie. And her beautiful, gentle mother who'd never said a bad word about anyone.

Emma felt her blood cool in her veins – turn to ice almost. She went rigid with shock. And anger. A cold, hard anger.

'Someone still thinks my mama was a suicide. My mama didn't jump, Seth,' she said. She felt his hand rest on her shoulder, and didn't resist when he pulled her close to him. 'I'm sure she didn't. She'd never have willingly left me.'

'And neither did my mother fall down those cellar steps.' Seth gently held her away from him. 'Now come on. I'll help you get this mess put to rights.'

'So you don't think it was an accident,' Emma said. 'That your ma fell down the steps. If the candle had gone out …' Emma let her words trail away when she saw the pain in Seth's eyes as he remembered his mother and what *might* have happened to her.

She sat beside him on the sand, her hands clasped over her knees. It was warm in the shelter of the cliff, and Emma had removed the jacket Matthew had brought back for her. He said he'd found it on a bench in the park, but Emma had suspected otherwise. She didn't have many clothes and Matthew had noticed that and bought it for her, hadn't he? Or it had been a cast-off from one of his lady friends. Oh well, beggars couldn't be choosers. And it *was* a nice jacket – fine wool, the colour of heather.

For quite a while neither Emma nor Seth had had much to say beyond what a beautiful day it was for May and was summer going to be hot this year, and how busy the oyster catchers were. Then Emma reverted to their interrupted conversation.

'I'm almost certain she was pushed,' Seth said now, in response to her comment. 'I remember there were often arguments between my parents late at night. I remember hearing doors slam. And there were many mornings when my ma didn't get up for breakfast, and when I asked the maid where she was I was told that Ma was "indisposed".'

'Do you think your pa might have hit your ma?' Emma asked. Although her own papa had never been anything less than gentle and kind to her mama she knew that there were plenty in the cottages around theirs who used their wives as punchbags after a bellyful of ale – and those wives had the bruises on their faces for weeks sometimes to prove it.

'Did your pa knock your ma about?'

'No,' Emma said. 'Never. And I wouldn't stand for it, either.'

'I think my ma was trapped because of me being so much younger than my brothers,' Seth said. 'Where would she have gone if she'd left? She could have gone to my Uncle Silas in Canada, I suppose, but she'd never have left me and my brothers. Never.'

Where indeed? Emma thought. She was finding it hard enough herself to keep a roof over her head and she didn't have the responsibility of a child as well, did she? She gulped back tears – tears that were for herself and also for Seth in his sorrow over his ma.

Seth reached for Emma's hand and she placed hers in it. How good it felt – the touch. The caring. The mutual understanding.

'It's as if we can't let the deaths of our mothers be an end of them, isn't it?' Emma said. 'We can't get on with our lives – not really – because we've both got unanswered questions.'

Seth lifted Emma's hand to his lips and kissed the back of it.

'It's all I can offer you for now, Emma. Beautiful Emma.' Seth lifted her hand and kissed it again. 'A chaste kiss. You know that. And besides, you're so recently bereaved.'

'And you're still grieving for your ma,' Emma said.

She hugged that Seth had called her beautiful to her the way she hugged her copy of *Persuasion* to her as she fell asleep each night, knowing her mama had bought it for her, touched it.

They fell silent then, both with their own memories.

But then, because all sorts of thoughts were rushing through her mind the way a March wind rushes through the trees and under doors and in the cracks of windows, she said, 'Do you know if the police have found anyone for Sophie Ellison's murder yet?'

'Not as far as I know. They've questioned Pa and Carter because they weren't at sea that night, although Miles was. Pa laughed them off the premises – said it was more than likely a passing chancer. Someone Sophie didn't want to offer her favours to the way she offered them to my brothers. And me, I might add.'

Emma's mouth seemed to go wide and round of its own volition. 'You? Did you ...'

'Of course not! I thought you knew me better than that.'

'I do. But ... did all that go on in the room I slept in? Did your brothers visit her there?'

'I can't say with conviction that Sophie let them into her room. But others did. Yes. Some resisted, but they soon left after Carter and Miles accused them, falsely, of some misdeed. It's why I told you to put the back of the chair under the door handle.'

'I know that's why. I might be young but I'm not ignorant of the ways of men like your brothers and your pa.'

'I'm relieved to hear it.' Seth smiled at her and Emma leaned in to his shoulder.

'You always seem to be looking out for me,' Emma said. 'That day when I came home to Shingle Cottage after I'd been ill and stopping with Mrs Phipps, only it wasn't my home any more. You followed me and kept me safe from Margaret Phipps and her gang, and took me to Mrs Drew's ...'

'It's gone, Emma. All those horrid times have gone. You have to look forward. We both have. However hard it's going to be. Will you move away from here, do you think?'

Would she? Now Seth had planted the seed in her mind, why end her ambition by working at Nase Head House, when there was London and Bristol and even Paris to explore?

'Will *you*? Move away from here, I mean.'

'I might. I've got an uncle in Canada, fishing out of Vancouver.'

'Canada? But that's an ocean away. The Atlantic's so big and you get seasick!'

'There's that,' Seth laughed. 'Anyone would think you didn't want me to go ...'

'I don't know that I do,' Emma said quickly.

She knew in her heart Matthew Caunter wouldn't be

around forever to take care of her, and Seth was the only other person in the whole town – apart from Mrs Drew and Dr Shaw – who spoke a kindly word to her.

'You can relax,' Seth said, but a shadow seemed to pass across his mind. 'I won't be going just yet.'

'Your ma? And if she fell or ...'

'Yes. I've got unfinished business here. I won't be going anywhere until I find out what really happened to her.'

'I can't leave Mama and Papa yet, either. Or Johnnie. And ... and,' Emma leaned over and kissed Seth on the cheek, 'I'd miss *you* if I went away.'

There – she couldn't make it plainer that she liked him, and liked him very much, could she?

Chapter Nine

Five days had passed and still Matthew Caunter hadn't returned. Emma had been down to the quay, counted Reuben Jago's bigger boats – the trawlers, the ones that went as far as France – and there was one still out. She rather hoped that the boat *had* put into a French port and that Matthew had got the coffee he'd promised her and that it hadn't got a soaking from a rough sea.

She wondered now, as she washed her clothes at the sink, if she should try and see Seth and ask if he knew when the boat would be back. Since the afternoon on the beach she'd only seen him once when he'd been in a hurry to go to the bank for his father before it closed. He'd promised to call at Shingle Cottage but so far hadn't – unless he'd come when she was out.

Emma reached under the sink for extra soapflakes, her hand brushing against the bag with the tart tins Matthew had insisted she buy. Why had he been so insistent that she did? Who was going to want six crab tarts all at once? She hoped, when she eventually got to cook them, the oven in the range wouldn't play up and burn the pastry or leave the filling unset.

Matthew had to be back soon. The longest her papa had ever been at sea had been four days. The boat didn't have room to carry provisions for longer than that, and already Matthew had been away for a day longer. Ought she to buy in the eggs and the butter and the cheese for the tarts? No, the weather was getting warmer by the day – she left the windows open most of the day now to air the place out. Best get the things that would go off once Matthew was back with the crabs.

Emma rinsed her washing in cold water. She was about to throw out the water it had been washed in, still warm and frothy with soapflakes, when she changed her mind.

Matthew hadn't given her any clothes to wash before he left. He liked a clean shirt to wear on the evenings he did go out. There were always shirts of his to wash and dry. And iron. Goodness, what hard work that was – heating the flat iron just enough so it didn't scorch the cloth, but after a few sweeps of it across a shirt it cooled down and she had to start the whole heating-up process over again on the range.

If she went into his room and ignored everything but whatever dirty linen Matthew had left lying around she wouldn't be reneging on her promise never to enter it – not really. She'd be selective in where she looked and what she touched. And he wouldn't mind if she broke her promise when he got a bundle of clean laundry in exchange, would he?

Emma ran up the stairs before the soapy water lost its heat altogether. But the second she opened the door she forgot her promise to herself not to look at things she perhaps ought not to.

Matthew's bed was strewn with maps and sea charts. She knew what they were because her papa had owned sea charts. He'd told Emma he needed to be able to read them in case the skipper took ill and he had to take charge – for his own safety as much as anything. A notebook lay open on Matthew's pillow. And there were books piled up on a little table beside the bed. And pens. So many pens and bottles of ink. Pencils, too.

Slowly, Emma crept towards the notebook. The writing in it was large and well-formed, artistic-looking even, with curls and long tails to the 'p's and the 'g's and the 'y's.

But Matthew had said he couldn't write. She'd heard him

tell the sergeant when he'd come to question Matthew about Sophie Ellison. So why had he lied?

Emma picked up the book from the top of the pile. *The Principles of Marine Law*. She opened it. Matthew's name was written in black ink on the inside – the same writing as in the notebook.

'He's lied to me,' Emma said, just so she could hear the words, know they were true.

What was going on? What was he doing here really?

Grabbing a blue-and-white striped shirt that was half on and half off Matthew's bed, Emma ran from the room. Back in the kitchen she threw the shirt in the bowl of suds and scrubbed with all her might, trying to scrub away her anger that Matthew had lied to her.

'I've bought the tart tins,' Emma snapped later that day when Matthew eventually returned home.

'And hello to you, too.' Matthew laughed. He threw his canvas bag down on the floor inside the front door. 'I can see you are just *thrilled* to see me. A rabid dog would probably have had a better welcome.'

'Hello,' Emma said, staring down at her toes.

'What's wrong?'

'Nothing's wrong,' Emma said. She dug her hands into the pocket of her apron.

'Women's troubles?'

Emma looked up then. Girls just didn't talk to men about things like that.

'I've got a bit of a headache,' she lied.

'And no doubt that's because you've been dreaming up all sorts of scenarios about why I asked you to get tart tins?'

'I did wonder, yes. But I haven't been addling my brain dreaming up scenarios, as you put it,' Emma said. 'But why *did* you ask me to get them?'

'Nase Head House? Know it?'

'Yes.'

Of course she knew it. She was saving hard to be able to buy nice things of her own, so she didn't have to rely on people's kindness and wear hand-me-downs. Then she'd be smart as Mr Smythe had said girls had to be to work for him and she could get a job there. Live there.

'Good. Well, I happen to know that business is picking up well. And seeing as the rail company has added more passenger carriages to its rolling stock there'll be people coming down from London. People used to fancy food. Mr Smythe ...'

'How do you know Mr Smythe?' Emma interrupted.

Was Mr Smythe into smuggling, too?

Matthew didn't answer for what seemed ages. He just looked at Emma, as though staring right inside her head. As though he could read all her thoughts. And those thoughts were rushing around in her head the way a swallow does when it flies into a room through a window and can't find the way back out again.

'You're a very clever young lady, Emma, if I'm not mistaken. But wisdom you are going to have to learn. The wisdom to accept things as they're presented to you and not ask questions is a trait you'd do well to try and master. It's my belief that if a body has the money to go somewhere and buy things then they have every right to be in that place or have those things. I've eaten at Nase Head House and – in my opinion – what was being presented is nowhere near as good as your cooking. I told Mr Smythe ...'

'You never did?'

'Tiresome, tiresome girl,' Matthew said, with a theatrical sigh. 'Wisdom, Emma. Have the wisdom to listen to the end of an explanation.'

'Go on, then,' Emma said. She was itching to know what

was coming next, really. And she also wanted to ask if Matthew had taken his lady friend there to eat. If he had then she had to be someone special to him. But now wasn't the time to ask, was it?

'Mr Smythe has agreed to pay you …'

'He hasn't tasted my cooking yet.'

Matthew laughed. 'Not doubting your abilities, are you?'

'No, but …'

'I sang your praises high enough. I'm surprised your ears weren't burning.'

'Oh, thank you, thank you,' Emma said. 'How much is he going to pay me?'

'We didn't discuss that. But you could ask for, say, a shilling a tart?'

A shilling a tart? Six shillings for six tarts. Rapidly, Emma began to calculate how much the ingredients would cost. Assuming Matthew would give her the crabs she'd have to buy flour and butter and eggs and cream. And cheese. If eggs cost a shilling a dozen, and cream was …

'Ha ha!' Matthew said. 'I can almost see the numbers going around in your head.'

Emma grinned at him. She still had two of the sovereigns Matthew had put in the bag with her mother's things. She could use them to start up a little business providing tarts for Nase Head House. And with the money earned from that she'd be a lot nearer being able to buy a good dress and good shoes and a well-cut coat so she could work at Nase Head House all the time.

'I'll get the crabs in, shall I?'

'Please,' Emma said.

The words spilling out of her, Emma followed Matthew to the front door as she told him about her dream to work at Nase Head House and dance in the room with chandeliers.

'Out the back with these, I think,' Matthew said, as he

hefted a Hessian sack wriggling with live crabs. 'I see there's an old boiler in your pa's outhouse. You can boil them in that.'

'And in the morning I'll go to the market and get all the other things while they're boiling,' Emma said.

'Good girl. I had a hunch you learned fast. I ...'

But the second Matthew threw wide the back door and dropped the bag of crabs onto the path, Emma's heart sank. The shirt she'd taken from his room was flapping in the breeze. Matthew had seen it, she knew he had. He'd known in a heartbeat that she'd been in his room. He'd stopped walking, stopped talking.

He ran back to the house, slammed shut the door again and spun round to face her. 'But you don't learn fast enough. That shirt, Emma Le Goff, was on the bed in my room. And ...'

'I don't want to be party to smuggling, even if I am an innocent party.'

'Who said anything about smuggling?'

'You ... you said you couldn't read or write, but you can and you've got sea charts. Smugglers need to know where they can safely drop contraband. And Mr Jago ...'

'I can't speak for Mr Jago, Emma. And I think you know that. But answer me one question – if you don't stop here, where will you find a roof over your head?'

'Tonight?' Emma's heart skipped a beat. Was he going to throw her out right now?

Matthew raised his eyebrows and shrugged. The man was complex. Emma had never met anyone like him. He seemed ruthless and kind in equal measure.

'I'll forget about anything I saw in your room, if you'll forget I went in there. I need to be able to make those crab tarts, Matthew, because I know I can't stay here forever.'

Matthew sighed loudly. 'Women! They'll be the death of me.

Now run and get some water on to boil before I'm up before the beak for murder.'

Emma ran.

'And this is Emma Le Goff.' Matthew placed a hand under Emma's elbow and guided her forward.

'We've met before,' Rupert Smythe said. And this time, Emma was pleased to see, he extended a hand for her to shake. A little part of her was glad that he had remembered her, too. Perhaps she *would* be able to work here some day. And, with luck, soon. 'Pleased to see you again, Miss Le Goff.'

Emma gazed around the foyer. She hadn't wanted to come to Nase Head House because she knew her clothes weren't fine enough for such a place. But Matthew had insisted. Her clothes were clean and honestly come by, he'd argued, and with some polish on her shoes and a smile on her face she'd more than pass muster.

And now here she was and glad to be. Everything was even lovelier than she'd remembered. The chandeliers seemed to sparkle more brilliantly, and the leather carousel seat seemed more lustrous, the wooden desk more highly polished. And the floor tiles were so clean and bright she could see her reflection in them.

She wondered if Mr Smythe was waiting for her to speak, to say how glad she was to meet him again.

She felt Matthew squeeze her elbow before letting go. 'The crab tarts, Mr Smythe,' he said. 'In the box here. Emma has made them and I thought it only right that she see first hand how pleased you will be with them.'

'Yes, yes,' Rupert Smythe said. 'Quite right.'

He rang the bell on the desk and an elderly man in some sort of black uniform with a high starched collar came in, and Rupert Smythe instructed him to escort Emma and her tarts to the kitchen.

'And stay there, Emma,' Matthew said. 'Please.'

'Wisdom?' she mouthed to him.

Matthew nodded. Winked. How well they were beginning to understand one another. But just what was going on between Matthew and Mr Smythe?

Emma was escorted into a vast kitchen that had a long trestle table in the middle of it. A lad scrubbing pans at the sink looked up but didn't speak. Emma wondered if she ought to talk to him – say good morning at the very least – but decided not to. Instead she looked around. On the walls hung rows of copper-bottomed pots. And ladles of all shapes and sizes. She stared around in wonder at it all and giggled – she'd had a game of it cooking six crab tarts in one small oven, swapping them top to bottom, half-cooked, in and out, so that they were all more or less cooked at the same temperature. But they'd all turned out perfect in the end. Matthew had lifted her from her feet and twirled and twirled her around the kitchen, pleased with her handiwork.

'And who might you be laughing in my kitchen?'

She turned to see a man of about forty years old. Fat. Balding head. He had a white apron tied, not very neatly, around his middle. And it was smeared with grease.

'Emma Le Goff.'

Emma held out her hand but the man merely sniffed and turned his back on her. He hauled a sack of potatoes from under a bench and thrust a potato peeler towards Emma.

'If you're the new skivvy then you can get yourself to peeling these.'

'I'm not the new skivvy. I've come with Mr Caunter, who's gone somewhere with Mr Smythe. I've been told to wait here.'

'Smythe's bit of interest, are you?'

'Interest? I don't understand.'

'Oh, don't come the innocent with me. Comely girl like

yourself. It's common knowledge Mr Smythe will be needing female company. What with his wife still up in London and all. And …'

'Well, I'm not it,' Emma said. She knew what this odious man was meaning now. 'I was asked to make some crab tarts and Mr Caunter insisted I come with him when he delivered them.'

'Crab tarts? What are they when they're at home?'

'A pastry case with an egg-and-milk mixture, cooked crab, and grated cheese. My papa taught me how to make them.'

'Le Goff you say? Wouldn't be fancy French tarts now, would they?'

'Yes.'

'Well you can take them back where they belong. Is that them over there?'

He pointed to the cardboard box containing the tarts Emma had placed on a side table. She raced towards it and placed her hands protectively on the lid which Matthew had secured with string and lots of fancy knots.

'Yes. And don't you dare touch them.'

'And I won't be eating them, either. My cooking was good enough for the Smythes when they lived in London. Ate out most of the time, they did, him and his wife. But for everyday stuff – roasts and the like – there were no complaints.'

Emma wondered why Mr Smythe's wife was in London and who might be cooking for her if this man wasn't. But then she remembered it was none of her business and Matthew had instructed her to learn wisdom. She'd start practising that right now.

'And I'm sure that still holds,' Emma said. 'But Mr Caunter said there's more and more trains coming down from London with visitors for this hotel, and they'll be wanting London restaurant sort of food.'

'And a slip of a girl like you is going to provide it?'

One day, Emma thought, one day. And if she ever got to work in this kitchen she'd make sure it was cleaner than it was now. She could see a dollop of fat on top of the draining board. And the tea-towel hanging from a bar by the range was none too pristine, either. Didn't Mr Smythe ever come in here to see these things?

'No,' she said. 'The tarts are by way of an experiment.'

Emma picked up the box of tarts and sat on a chair at the centre working table. She'd sit there and hold them tight on her lap for as long as it took before Matthew and Mr Smythe came back. What happened to them after that was no concern of hers, but she wasn't going to let this man wreck what might be her way of making a living for herself.

'I didn't expect Mr Smythe to eat half a tart!' Emma said.

'One bite wasn't enough. Ye of so little faith – I told you they were good.'

'And he wants six every other day.'

'That'll keep you out of mischief.'

'I don't look for it,' Emma said. 'It just sort of finds me sometimes. Anyway, why are we waiting here?' She patted the red leather of the carousel seat they were sitting on.

'Mr Smythe wants to show off his new motor. He's gone to the garage to fetch it. He's going to bring it to the front steps shortly. And who better to show it to than the maker of the most divine-tasting crab tarts a man is likely ever to eat?'

'Me?'

'And me.'

Emma clapped her hands together excitedly. Riding in a motor car – who'd have thought it.

'Would you like to work here if there was an opening, Emma?' Matthew grinned at her. Winked.

What did all that mean? Had Matthew been talking to Mr Smythe to ask if he would take Emma on in the hotel? Just so he could get her out from under his own roof? So she wouldn't blab to anyone – however accidental that blab might be – if contraband goods came in to Shingle Cottage?

'You know I would. But I need to practise my cooking a lot more first. And learn other things like book-keeping. Or, I suppose I could learn on the job, couldn't I?'

'I don't doubt you could,' Matthew laughed. 'But now, if memory serves me well, you said you wanted to dance on this floor under these chandeliers. Yes?' Matthew stood up, held out his hands towards Emma. 'There's no one here at the moment to see us. Now's your chance.'

'Yes, but ... but, I don't know how to dance.'

'Then I shall teach you. I'm sure we'll be able to affect a fairly passable waltz.'

A waltz?

'I've never known a fisherman who could dance before,' Emma said. 'Except for country dancing. And I don't know that it's proper. Won't Mr Smythe mind?'

'Some fishermen, Emma – as I'm sure you'll know from your father – are fairly well-educated. Not all of them are illiterate. And I'm sure Mr Smythe won't mind us having a little dance on his shiny floor after eating your crab tart. Now ...'

Matthew pulled her from her seat.

As though she was a puppet he moved her arms into the correct position to dance. Then he began to sing softly. He had a good voice. A tenor voice. He sang about birds and trees and roses and love.

'Take a small step back with your left foot, then move your right foot to the side, then bring your left foot to join your right.'

Too shocked at the nearness of Matthew to do anything

136

else, Emma did as she was told. She'd never been this close to Seth – so close she could feel his heartbeat.

'Then step back with the right and repeat the process. Good girl. Let me guide you,' he said in between the words of the song.

And then he didn't have to give her instructions any more because it was as though Emma was welded to Matthew; as if they were one person. Round and round the central island seat they danced, as though they had been dancing together all their lives.

Emma wondered just why and where Matthew had learned to dance so beautifully.

But then Matthew surprised her even further. He stopped dancing, drew her closer towards him and kissed the top of her head. A chaste kiss, but a kiss that thrilled Emma all the same.

'Thank you,' Emma whispered, 'for the dance. And for the kiss. I'll never forget either.'

Matthew cleared his throat. 'Another of life's skills, dancing, which I hope you've stored away in that clever mind of yours, Emma. Now, I can hear that motor outside. Time to go.'

'I said you should have got in first,' Seth's brother Miles said – he had a sickening grin on his face that Seth wanted to remove for him with his fist.

'What are you talking about? And make your answer quick. I've got work to do.'

He had the accounts book to get up to date for his father. Although there was no way he was going to put his signature to it. The solicitor had assured Seth that an exchange of deeds was perfectly legal. When they'd left the office his pa had treated him to a steak pie in The White Horse, and a pint of ale. Thanks, his father had said, for not embarrassing him by bringing up mention of signing the books.

Yes, his pa was definitely up to something. He'd have a fight on his hand refusing to sign, but it was a fight he was prepared to take on.

'The Le Goff tight-arsed bitch isn't quite so tight-arsed now. Saw her arm-in-arm with Caunter, didn't I?'

'I don't know. Did you?' Seth struggled to affect indifference.

'Coming out of Nase Head House, they were. Walking down the steps to Smythe's car as cosy as you like.'

Seth wondered what one of his father's crew was doing in an expensive place like Nase Head House. And why Emma was with him for that matter.

'If you say so. Now if that's all you've got to say I've got work to be getting on with.'

'Ha! You don't fool me.' Miles jabbed a finger repeatedly at Seth, stopping just short of his nose each time. 'You're like a dog around a bitch in heat with the Le Goff girl. You were seen walking with her over Crystal Cove way. Likes it outdoors, does she?'

'Shut your dirty mouth! And get your filthy hands away from me.'

'Or you'll do what exactly?' Miles sneered.

Seth balled his fists. The thought of Matthew Caunter being anywhere near Emma, never mind touching her, was making him white hot with a jealous rage he knew he had no right to have. So much for her understanding and tenderness to him over his mother when they'd been down on Crystal Cove. Just because he'd been too busy lately to call on her, she'd switched her allegiance.

'Shove off, Miles,' Seth said.

'And if I don't?'

Miles was being a complete pain in the rear end. Both Carter and Miles had used Seth as a punchbag when he was younger, often leaving him black and blue. He'd already shown Carter he wasn't going to be used as a punchbag anymore. And if Miles didn't shut up he'd find that out, too.

'Mummy's boy too lily-livered to fight?' Miles goaded. He shoved Seth with his shoulder. Cuffed Seth's ear.

That did it.

Seth turned, and rammed his right fist against Miles' chin, heard the crack of bone on bone. Saw his brother's eyes go wide with shock before he thudded to the floor.

His work could wait. Seth left the room before he gave in to the urge to kick his brother where he lay.

Chapter Ten

'Emma, I ought to have told you before. And I'm sorry now I didn't. I'm a married man,' Matthew said, the second they were back at Shingle Cottage.

'Married?'

'You heard.' Matthew smiled at Emma – a shy smile she thought. The swagger of him had gone for the moment. 'That dance was a mistake, Emma. And the kiss. I'm a dangerous man to know. Can you forget it happened?'

'I won't tell anyone about it, if that's what you mean. But you can't make me forget it if I don't want to.'

'I wouldn't dare try.' Matthew laughed. 'It would take a stronger man than me to take you on.'

'Is that an insult or a compliment?'

'Take your pick,' Matthew said.

Emma mulled it over for a moment – did it matter which? 'Does your wife know where you are?' she said suddenly.

'Yes.'

'Then why didn't she come with you?'

'She doesn't approve of what I do.'

'Fishing?'

'That's just part of it. The less you know of what I'm doing here, the better it will be for us both. But I will be eternally grateful to you over the issue of the necklace. My cover could have been blown and ...'

'I'm not going to ask what cover,' Emma said. Although my guess is you're working undercover for some authority she thought, but didn't add. 'But I would like my mama's necklace back. Reuben Jago said Mama gave it to him in lieu of rent, but I don't believe him.'

'Hmm,' Matthew said. 'I'm not sure I believe him either.

But one thing I am sure about, Emma, is that I'll get that necklace back for you. Come hell or high water.'

'Thank you,' Emma said. 'But I don't want anyone hurt in the getting of it.'

'They won't be,' Matthew said. 'Now if you've got no more questions ...'

'I have. Just one,' Emma said. 'Does your wife know I'm staying under your roof?'

'Yes.'

'And is it her you've been going to see, coming back smelling of violets?'

'That's two questions. But yes, again. Slapton's not far to go of a night.'

'By road or by sea?'

'You're like a dog with a bone when you have something in your head, Emma. But to answer your *third* question – by sea.'

Matthew sighed, letting his breath out noisily.

'No more questions. Wisdom, Emma – define the word, please.'

'In this instance you mean the wisdom to keep my thoughts, about what you might also have been doing when you go to see your wife, to myself.'

'Exactly. So do.'

'Thank you for the dance,' Emma said. 'And the kiss. They were both lovely. I'll never forget them.'

And then before Matthew could chastise her, yet again, she ran up the stairs to her room.

June passed in a flurry of tart making and July was now nearing its end, too. Nase Head House was gaining such a good reputation that the hotel was almost always fully booked and Emma was making her tarts every day. Best strike while the iron was hot was what Matthew said,

141

because trade was bound to fall off a bit once autumn came and went and winter spread out its icy claws, freezing railway lines and making the roads too dangerous for cars and carriages.

On 25th July a Frenchman – Louis Blériot – had flown in an aeroplane from Calais to Dover and Emma had joked to Matthew that her feet wouldn't touch the ground she'd be that busy making tarts when people could come by aeroplane to Devon. In her heart, Emma was glad it was a Frenchman who had been the first to make a flight. How exciting it all was. The world was changing, and on days like that Emma was glad she was part of that world.

When there wasn't any crab available Emma improvised and used bacon, or trout, or prawns – whatever Matthew could provide or she could buy in the market. Mr Smythe wrote her a note to say how pleased he was with everything she made. Emma guessed that the cook was less pleased. But she didn't care – her savings were mounting up now.

Today's tarts were ready for collection but Emma had some left-over pastry. She added a handful of sugar and worked it in. Then she made a sugar syrup and peeled apples to make a tarte tatin. She could hear her papa's voice in her head as she worked, telling her how one of the best recipes ever had come about because two French sisters had made a mistake in their patisserie in Paris, rescuing that mistake with a unique combination of pastry and apples and sugar.

It was ready to take from the oven just as Matthew returned from wherever it was he had been. Not out fishing today, Emma was certain of that because he'd gone out wearing his best clothes, not his working ones – although he had been carrying the canvas bag he took out fishing with him. What was in that bag Emma wondered? But she was learning not to think too much about what might be in the bag or to ask.

'Mmm, but that smells good,' Matthew said. He licked his lips.

'Tarte tatin,' Emma said.

'And what's that in good, plain English?'

'There isn't really a translation. It's just what it is. But I suppose the nearest in English would be a very syrupy, fancy, upside-down apple tart.'

'Do we have to eat it?'

Emma laughed. 'What other plan would you have for it? Door stop? Bookend?'

'Selling it.'

'To Mr Smythe?'

'Who else?'

Emma felt her eyes widen with sudden realisation – a seed of something had just been planted in her mind; something that could grow and grow and grow given the right environment. And a bit of luck.

There must be other hotels which might take what I cook.

Emma placed the palms of her hands down on the table to steady herself – her head was suddenly full of ideas and they were making her giddy. Yes. Why have only the one outlet for her cooking? If Mr Smythe should change his mind about taking her tarts, or the cook learned how to make them just as well – although she doubted the oaf she'd seen ever would – then her income could be lost overnight.

Matthew would be moving on somewhere soon, she was sure of it – just as soon as he had accomplished whatever it was he had come here to do. Where would *she* go when he left? There was an empty shed down on the quay – could that be put to good use?

'Emma, you're an open book,' Matthew said. 'Am I reading you correctly?'

'I expect so,' Emma said. 'How many hotels are there in this area, do you think?'

'How would I know? Lots, I should think. I've heard the rail journey along the coast to get here is one of the loveliest in the country. The town's a lot busier now, I've noticed, so no doubt that bit of information has been passed on by word of mouth. And more and more cars are appearing on the roads.'

'And aeroplanes!' Emma said. 'Oh, I can't wait to see one going over. Just think, people from all over the world could be coming here and ...'

'It was a *very* small aeroplane from what I read in the papers. Don't try to run before you can walk, Emma.'

'I'm not. But don't try and hold me back.'

'I wouldn't dare,' Matthew laughed. 'But trust me a little longer. I'm going to have to leave soon, and I want to make sure you'll be secure when I do. I owe you that. Do you understand?'

'Not completely,' Emma said. 'And I don't want you to leave ...'

'But we both know I must.'

'Yes,' she said.

'Good. Now get that fancy apple tart ready to go. I'll be passing Nase Head House later so I can deliver it – even though I think I could eat the whole thing in one sitting.'

'I'll make you another,' Emma said, tears in her eyes.

She was going to miss Matthew more than she'd thought she ever would.

But Matthew had seen her tears. He took a handkerchief from his pocket and wiped the tear that was escaping down Emma's hot cheek. 'That tart could be your passport to better things, Emma. So, when you've packed it I want you to go into town and spend one of those sovereigns I gave you to buy yourself something pretty to wear. Something with lace, which my wife assures me, and on which she's spent no small part of my fortune, is the latest thing.

You and I are going to be eating at Nase Head House not very many hours from now.'

'We are?'

Matthew reached out to touch Emma's left ear, and then her right. 'Ears not working? Didn't I just say we were?'

'But the likes of us don't eat in places like that.'

'Do you learn nothing, girl? Didn't I tell you that if a man's got the money to be somewhere or to buy something then he can?'

'Or a woman,' Emma said.

'Or a woman,' Matthew laughed. 'Goodness, but the man you end up with will have a challenge on his hands. But you're not quite a woman yet.'

I nearly am, though, Emma thought. Come Michaelmas.

'Why are we going to Nase Head House?' she asked. 'Isn't what I cook good enough for you?'

'You *know* it's good enough for me. But I fancy a change. Nothing wrong with that, is there?'

Emma could see what Matthew said was sound. And also that he was tiring of her persistence.

'It'll be expensive, though, won't it?'

'More than a cup of tea, yes.' Matthew laughed.

'Well, I can't afford it. It would take all my savings, and …'

'A man doesn't ask a woman to dine with him and then expect her to pay, Emma. You'll have to get used to that.'

'I will?'

'Pretty girl like you, yes. There'll more than likely be a queue of men after me inviting you to dine in the future. Now, are you accepting my invitation or not?'

'Oh, I am. Thank you. Thank you.'

A bubble of something that was a mixture of excitement and apprehension fizzed inside Emma – she thought she might burst with it. Gladwyn's had some pretty blouses in the window. A silk, apple-green one with a froth of lace running down the front – the buttons almost disappearing in its loveliness – had caught her eye. She'd go and see how much it was. But first she'd go up to the cemetery and tell Mama and Papa and Johnnie her news.

'Oh!'

Emma stared at her papa's grave in disbelief. There was a simple stone tablet at the head of his grave – *Guillaume Le Goff. Lost his life to the sea. 15th January 1909.*

Who could have put it there? Who had paid for it? Who had had the kindness to do it? Matthew? She'd told him about her mother's grave being covered in horse droppings and the grass ripped up and flowers strewn everywhere. But as far as she knew he didn't know the exact locations of either of the graves.

Only Seth knew that. Yes, it had to be Seth. She rushed over to her mama's and Johnnie's grave and there was an engraved tablet there, too. *Rachel Le Goff and her son, Johnnie Le Goff. Cruelly taken from us. 1st March 1909.*

Emma ran a finger in the grooves of the engraved letters, felt every single one. Then she kissed her fingertips and touched the top of the tablet.

'Whoever's done this I'm glad, Mama,' she whispered. 'And I've kept Shingle Cottage neat and tidy just the way you did. But I'm going to have to leave soon. I'm going to start a business. Can you believe that?'

Emma shivered. She could hardly believe it herself. She still hankered after working – and living – at Nase Head House but only if she could continue to cook. But would Nase Head House want two cooks?

However, before she could work out the feasibility of such a situation she would go and see Seth, certain now it was he who had had the tablets made. She could wait a little longer to buy her new clothes.

She ran from the cemetery, up the steep alleys that led to the Jago household. She hadn't been there since the time she'd opened the bag of her mama's things that Matthew had given her and found the amethyst necklace. And she wasn't at all sure she wanted to be going there now, but if Seth wasn't in then she would leave a message to say she wanted to see him. Ask for him to meet her at Crystal Cove so she could thank him in person. She hadn't seen him in ages, and she missed him

Emma slowed her step, took a deep breath and – head held high – she walked up the front drive of Hilltop House and knocked on the door.

Beattie Drew answered. 'Well, if it isn't our Emma, turned up like a bad penny. You'm not wanting to come back, I hope, lovie.'

'No, no,' Emma said – perish the thought. 'I'd like to see Seth. Is he in?'

'He's not. And even if he was you couldn't see him. Not here, that is, though you can see him any other place you like. The thing is, lovie, Mr Jago Senior said you were never to darken his door again, see. And it would be more than my life's worth to …'

'Who is it Mrs Drew?' Carter Jago came striding down the hall.

'Emma Le Goff. Come to see Seth,' Mrs Drew said. She stood between Carter and Emma as though sensing trouble. But Carter Jago was all smiles.

'Is it now? I can't think why she would want to see my baby brother, but she'd better come in. Step aside, Mrs Drew.'

'But Mr Jago said …' Mrs Drew began.

'My father isn't here. And what he doesn't see can't hurt him. Now step aside, Mrs Drew.'

Mrs Drew did as she was told, and Carter Jago extended a hand towards Emma, beckoning her in.

147

'In the drawing-room, I think.'

'Oh, I don't think so. I …'

'Nonsense. You can tell me whatever it is you want to tell my *baby* brother and I'll pass the message on. I promise.'

'I could come back,' Emma said, bridling at the derogatory way Carter was speaking about Seth. She wasn't at all sure now she should be alone with Carter Jago. But if Mrs Drew was there?

'And would you be prepared to risk my father's wrath if he's here when you return?'

'No,' Emma said.

Carter gestured for Emma to follow him. So she did, relieved to see Mrs Drew bringing up the rear as they walked across the hallway. But when the older woman went to follow them on into the drawing-room, Carter barred her way.

'Your cleaning duties don't extend to chaperoning Miss Le Goff,' he said.

'I don't need a chaperone, Mr Jago,' Emma told him, although in her heart she was glad of Mrs Drew's presence.

'Possibly not. Mr Caunter has, no doubt, absolved you of *that* need.'

'You, you …' Emma began, but words escaped her.

Carter Jago laughed at her confusion. He placed a hand under Emma's elbow and held it tightly.

'The kitchen, Mrs Drew. I'll ring when I need you to show Miss Le Goff out.'

'You lay one hand on her, Carter Jago …'

'And you'll do what exactly, Mrs Drew? You'll lose your job if you accuse me of anything, make no mistake about that. But I'll be the perfect gentleman, never fear. Or I'll have Seth to answer to, won't I?'

Neither of the women answered. Carter let go of Emma's elbow, then in a very swift movement he more or less pushed

Mrs Drew through the doorway and closed the door behind her. Turned the key in the lock.

He walked towards Emma, loomed over her. Not touching. Threatening. Emma froze.

'Now then, my pretty, seeing as you are giving so freely of your favours to Caunter, I think it's only fair you give them to me.'

'Mr Caunter asks nothing of me,' Emma said. She wasn't feeling frozen now – boiling more like. 'And I offer him nothing either. I'm his housekeeper. We have a room each. I …'

'I don't believe a word of it.' He grabbed Emma by the shoulders. She twisted to try and get away from him but he held her fast. He pushed his face towards her as though to kiss her and Emma could smell stale coffee and bacon on his breath. She felt like retching, but knew she had to keep her head.

Should she scream? If she did, Mrs Drew would race to her rescue, she knew it, but she wouldn't be able to get into the drawing-room because the door was locked.

'Your father isn't going to be pleased to find me here,' Emma said, desperately trying to buy time. 'I've been banned from the house. Mrs Drew said.'

'My father is away on business.'

Carter released his hold on one of Emma's shoulders and with his free hand he brushed against her breast.

'Don't touch me!' Emma yelled.

'Shut up,' Carter hissed. He pulled Emma roughly to him and pressed his wet lips against hers, his teeth crashing up against her own. She thought she really would be sick now.

He tried to force his tongue between Emma's teeth while she squirmed in his arms, resisting for all she was worth. And then the need to breathe overtook her resistance and her teeth parted and Carter Jago flicked his tongue around the inside of her mouth, like a snake seeking its prey.

And that's when Emma bit him. Hard. Instantly she tasted his blood in the back of her throat. Her breath was coming in fast, short gasps now. And her heart rate seemed to be increasing, keeping to the same rhythm.

'You bitch!' Carter yelled, his hand to his mouth.

He pushed Emma from him, but not before grabbing her left breast. The suddenness of Carter's actions caught Emma off-balance and she stumbled, falling sideways into an ornate dresser, catching her forehead on the corner. She felt the crack of it inside her head and knew she'd have a bruise even if the skin hadn't broken.

Stay upright, she told herself, stay upright. If she were to fall what might Carter do to her?

Carter made a lunge for her, but he was a big man and Emma, shorter and slimmer, was more nimble. She kicked him hard in the shins while at the same time she drew her nails down his cheeks. Carter went rigid with anger and probably shock as well, but Emma wasn't going to stay around to ask which. She dodged out from under his arm, tore towards the door, turned the key in the lock and wrenched it open.

'Mrs Drew,' she yelled. 'I'm going.' Making as much noise as she could she knocked the dinner gong from the side table in the hall, sent a glass-based lamp crashing to the floor.

She ran for the front door, which mercifully was unlocked. And then she was breathing clean, fresh, salt-laden air – like nectar after the staleness of Carter Jago's breath and his sweaty body odour.

She'd have to send Seth a note asking him to meet her at Crystal Cove now, because there was no way on this earth she was ever going to set foot over the doorstep of Hilltop House again.

'Does it look a bit better?' Emma asked.

Matthew had given her witch hazel to put on her forehead

to bring out the bruise. He'd also cleaned her wound and put a piece of gauze across the cut to keep germs out while it formed a scab.

'It looks like what it is, Emma – evidence that you somehow court trouble.'

'I don't!'

'What happened?'

Emma shrugged.

'I want the truth, Emma, or there's the door. No pretty things to wear to dinner ...'

Emma had a sudden vision of dancing again under the chandeliers at Nase Head House. With Matthew. She'd bought the blouse she'd so admired in Gladwyn's after she'd left Hilltop House. The assistant had commented on the cut on Emma's forehead but she said she'd tripped in the street, hit her head against a wall, and they'd both laughed – if a little nervously – at Emma's *carelessness* in tripping. The assistant had suggested a crêpe de chine skirt in deep sage to wear with the blouse. The skirt was selling at a discount price because a bit of the hem had come undone. Well, with a mama who had been a dressmaker, stitching up a hem was no trouble to Emma at all – and even if she hadn't learnt from her mama, Miss Holgate had made sure Emma and all the others girls in her class knew how to sew.

She didn't want not to be able to go out to dinner with Matthew wearing her new blouse and skirt. So she told him the truth. Although not everything – not the bit about having her breast grabbed. Or about biting Carter Jago's tongue. Or about what he had said – that Matthew had absolved her of any need for a chaperone.

'And did he touch you? Other than forcing unwanted kisses on you?'

Although Matthew was asking her in a concerned way, his eyes told Emma that he still wanted the truth, or else.

'Yes.'

'Where?'

Emma tapped her breast with an index finger. 'Twice,' she said. 'Once just a brushing past of his hand, but I knew he meant to do it and the other time he grabbed me.'

'The bastard!' Matthew said.

'I bit his tongue. Drew blood.'

'Retribution if ever there was any,' Matthew said. Emma thought he looked pleased that she had done what she did. 'But he's not going to be best pleased, you know that?'

'Of course I do.'

'Anyway, why did you go to Hilltop House in the first place?'

'To try and see Seth. There are headstones – just small tablets, but they're lovely – on my papa's grave, and on Mama's and Johnnie's. Seth must have had them done because I've only shown him where the graves are. I wanted to thank him.'

'An easy conclusion to jump to but is there anyone else who could have had them put there?'

'Well, there were quite a lot of people in the church for the funerals, but most were poorer than Papa and Mama were. And …'

Emma was suddenly overwhelmed with sadness that she was now an orphan. And lonely. Apart from Seth – when she did see him – she was still being cold-shouldered by almost everyone. Especially the girls she'd gone to school with. She had a feeling the fact she was sharing Shingle Cottage with Matthew had something to do with that. She could imagine what their mothers might say – 'don't talk to that harlot', or 'she'll come to no good' and other things of that ilk.

Emma would so love to have a friend. Someone to talk to about her hopes and dreams. Apart from Matthew and Seth, she'd never had anyone to share them with. Emma gulped, swallowing back tears and told Matthew all this.

'There's a price that comes of being as beautiful as you are, Emma,' Matthew said. 'People are jealous. Or as you found out just now with Carter Jago, they assume things that aren't true and think they can take liberties. What did he say exactly?'

To tell him or not? The last thing she wanted was for Matthew to go around to Hilltop and have it out with Carter Jago on her account. She'd fight her own battles, thank you very much.

'Well, Emma, I'm waiting,' Matthew said. 'And can wait for as long as it takes for you to tell me.'

'Well,' Emma said, knowing there was no escape now, 'it was when Mrs Drew said she'd come in the room with me – he said I'd been absolved of the need for a chaperone now I was living with you. Something along those lines anyway. He assumed ...'

'It's all right,' Matthew said. He touched her shoulder lightly. 'We both know what it is he assumed.'

'He's not the only one,' Emma said. 'There's more than a few walk straight past me in the street like I'm not breathing air.'

'I'm sorry. Coping with all that is making you lonely, isn't it? That's the price.'

Emma nodded. Too full up now to speak. Because despite the prospect of earning a living with her cooking and going to dinner with Matthew all dressed up, she *was* lonely, achingly so.

Would the ache ever go?

'You did what?' Carter said.

'The thump Emma gave you dulled your wits? I've just told you.'

Seth couldn't help smiling. Carter had a bruise breaking on his chin and deep scratch marks on his cheeks that looked at odds with his immaculate evening dress. Good for you, Emma, he thought, even though he realised it was because of him she'd been at the mercy of Carter's clutches.

'Headstones, for God's sake! For a bloody Frenchie and his tight-arsed wife and brat? Does Pa know?'

'There's no need for him to know. My – legally-earned – money paid for it. I can spend my money on anything I want.'

'Then you're wasting it on the Le Goff bitch.'

'Call her that one more time and you'll get a repeat performance of what Emma gave you.'

'Only probably not as hard,' Carter sneered.

'Don't tempt me.' Seth refused to be riled. He had bigger things on his mind – like challenging his pa about the book-keeping records.

'Maybe if I'm too tough for you, you could practise on Caunter.'

'Any reason why I should?'

'He'll be up at Nase Head House tonight, so I've heard. He'll be wining and dining *Mademoiselle* Le Goff.'

Carter had made the word 'mademoiselle' sound like the contents of a cess pit, and Seth realised it was only to get a reaction from him. Well, he wasn't going to give his brother the satisfaction of providing one.

'If you say so.'

'Got my spies everywhere, I have.'

Seth pressed his lips together. He ought to have tried to see Emma more, and he regretted he hadn't now. Matthew Caunter was obviously turning her head if she'd accepted an invitation to dine with him.

'You're going green, Seth,' Carter laughed. 'An unbecoming shade of jealousy green.'

'Shut up.'

'In my own time. Anyway, pity you're not invited.'

'I wouldn't go if I was.'

Seth didn't think he'd be able to bear seeing Emma with Matthew Caunter.

'Pa, Miles and I have ourselves some lovely ladies …'

'Whores more like.'

Carter roared with laughter.

'Yeah. A man can learn a thing or two from a whore. Although our ladies for tonight are no worse whores than *Mademoiselle* Le Goff.

'I'll ask you a question, Carter. Do you ever think how Ma would feel to know how you speak? How you behave?'

Carter didn't flinch. 'Never. The dead don't talk.'

Before he did something to his brother he might regret – like kill him – Seth left the room. He had things he needed to discuss with his father and he knew the conversation wasn't going to be any more pleasant than the one he'd just had with his brother.

He found his father coming out of his dressing-room, forcing cufflinks through the holes of his shirt as he came.

'Pa, we need to talk.'

'Not now, Seth. I'm in a hurry, as you can see.'

'It won't wait.' And then, because he knew to try and reason with his father would be a total waste of his time and his energy, he said, 'I'm not signing the accounts.'

'Don't be a damned fool. Of course you are. And what's more I'll make sure you do.'

He grabbed Seth by the shoulder, knocking him off-balance slightly, and forced him down the stairs and into the drawing-room.

'Get them,' his father said, pointing to the desk.

Seth did as he was told.

'There's too much falsification, Pa,' Seth said as he laid the papers on the table. 'The amount of fish being landed and the prices we get for it at auction don't tally with the deposits you've made in the company account. Either you're landing fish elsewhere and not declaring payment for it or something else is being landed here that shouldn't be. Am I right?'

'That's for me to know. Now sign.'

His father thrust a pen and a bottle of ink at Seth, but he shook his head, refusing to take them.

'I'm in a hurry, son. And you know I don't like to be late. And what I like even less than being late is being disobeyed by my sons. Sign!'

'Over my dead body.'

'It might come to that yet.'

God, what did he do now? Seth knew his father was capable of anything. But he'd started standing up to him and he wasn't ready to back down yet.

'You wouldn't dare.'

Seth unscrewed the top of the ink bottle, dipped the nib of the pen in the ebony ink.

'Don't tempt me. But I see you've come to your senses.'

'I have. Whatever happens from this moment on I'm no longer going to be doing your bidding.' Seth handed the pen to his father. To his amazement, his father took it. Shock, probably, that Seth was getting the master of him.

'I, too, am going out, Pa. I might be late back. In fact I might not even be back tonight. And those accounts have to be with Easterbrooks by close of business today. I'm sure you know how important it is that they are there. You can take a detour there on your way to Nase Head House, can't you?'

And without waiting for a response, Seth marched from the room. At the door he turned to look back at his father. There was a startled expression on his face. But to Seth's immense relief he saw his father put his signature to the accounts.

Chapter Eleven

'Who's going to be sitting here?' Emma asked. 'There are three chairs and only two of us.'

'Mr Smythe said he'd join us later. If he has a spare moment.'

'Why?'

'Questions, questions, Emma. Why so many questions? Now – the menu.' Matthew handed her an ornately decorated card.

'Oh, this is so wonderful!' She put the menu down on the table and clapped her hands together. Twice.

'Sssh. Keep your voice down a bit.' Matthew smiled at her. 'What with the gash on your head – disguised as it is, slightly, with the contents of the flour bin mixed with rouge – you're getting enough attention as it is.'

Emma giggled. What fun she'd had making up the mixture to hide her bruises and the beginnings of a scab.

She glanced around the dining-room, but no one seemed to be looking her way at the moment. Two waiters, in black trousers and stiffly starched white shirts, were busily polishing glasses before putting them in their places on the only table still vacant. A table for six. It had a *Reserved* card on it.

Everyone was dressed in their finery. Some of the women had ornaments in their hair – feathers and jewels and pieces of organza. Emma had to pinch herself to believe she was really here and not dreaming. And she was so grateful to Matthew for suggesting she buy something special to wear.

'That and my beauty,' Emma laughed back. 'Or so you're always telling me.'

When Emma had walked down the stairs towards Matthew dressed in her new clothes and with her hair piled on top of her head secured with pins bought at Gladwyn's on a whim when she'd bought the blouse and skirt, he'd breathed in deeply, as though in shock. But when he'd recovered he'd still only been able to say one word – beautiful. And that over and over and over.

'Compliments could go to your head, my lady. Much as that drink is.'

'I've only had a few sips. But it *is* nice, sort of bubbly.'

'Champagne usually does have bubbles, Emma.'

'Well, I know that. I've just never had it before, that's all.'

'Then have some more and then maybe you'll have recovered your memory a bit and you'll be able to tell me what's so wonderful about the menu.'

'It's in French.' Emma turned the menu over. 'Oh, and in English on the other side.'

Matthew laughed. 'That's taken the wind out of your sails. You don't think there's many local residents who can speak French, do you? Although visitors from London probably can. All those people sitting over there in their fancy finery, for instance.'

'I know,' Emma said. 'I've already seen them. But they probably don't speak French as well as I do.'

'Don't brag,' Matthew laughed.

'I'm not. I'm just saying.'

Being able to understand the French side of the menu had given Emma's spirits a lift – made her forget all about Carter and what he'd tried to do to her for a moment. She picked up the menu and read it again, in her head. In the doing of it she could almost hear her papa correcting her pronunciation. How close she felt to him, still, in that moment.

'Penny for them,' Matthew said. He tapped his forehead.

'Worth a lot more than that,' Emma told him, a lump in her throat. 'I expect Mr Smythe has his own reasons for having the menu in the two languages.'

'I expect he does,' Matthew said.

Emma clasped her hands together. A table by the window was being served. Small plates with ... with slices of her crab tart on them. How exciting that felt.

'They're eating my tart,' Emma whispered, clutching at Matthew's sleeve.

Gently he prised her hand away. 'And why wouldn't they be? Ah, here's the waiter. Time to choose something from that menu. In whichever language you choose to do it.'

The waiter hovered beside Emma, a pad and a pencil in his hand. She ordered in French.

'Sorry, Miss,' the waiter said. 'I didn't understand a word of that.'

'Well, you should. If the menu is in French then you ought to expect people to ask for things in French.'

'Emma, for goodness' sake,' Matthew said.

'Sorry. It's the champagne, I think it *is* going to my head.'

Emma turned to the waiter and ordered – in English – the crab tart. Matthew said he'd have the same. For the main course Emma chose the roast lamb – how long it had been since she'd tasted lamb. Matthew elected to have jugged hare. They'd already agreed to order tarte tatin for dessert.

'I wonder who's going to be eating there.'

Emma pointed to the vacant table. There was a branch of candles in the centre, not lit yet. And there were two low bowls of flowers – the palest of pale pink carnations – at either end of the table. Crisp linen cloths stood like mini mountains at each place-setting.

Emma considered just how much her meal was going to cost. The prices weren't on the menu she'd been given. Perhaps in a place like this it was assumed one could afford anything and everything that was on the menu?

'I wonder,' Matthew said, just as the waiter arrived with their first course.

Emma and Matthew ate without talking, Emma listening hard to try and hear what diners at tables nearby were saying. Something about the train being late, one woman was saying, but the room she was stopping in making up for it because it was so well-appointed.

Emma wondered what it would be like to stay in a place like this. Own something like this. Maybe Mr Smythe would take her on in some capacity if she couldn't rent the shed down on the quay and sell her tarts further afield. When Matthew left she'd have to find some work. Which she knew in her heart he would be doing soon – she could tell. He'd begun packing things in boxes – things he said he didn't need much now autumn was coming; his thin cotton shirts and singlets. Autumn? It wouldn't be August until three days' time. And everyone knew August could be hot and sultry. Yes, he was preparing to leave, and Emma knew it.

'Tuppence for them this time?' Matthew said.

'Oh, they're going to be worth far more than that some day. I'd love to *own* a hotel like this, never mind work in one.'

Matthew raised his eyebrows.

'You're surprised? Don't you think I can do it?' Emma asked.

'I know you can, and I sincerely hope you do. We all have to have a dream.'

'And that's mine,' Emma said. There was a loud bang then as a champagne bottle was opened and Emma looked towards the noise. 'Oh!' She clapped a hand to her mouth.

Her lovely dream was rapidly turning into a nightmare.

Reuben Jago had entered the dining-room as though he owned it. A young woman, young enough to be his daughter, if not his granddaughter, was hanging onto his arm, gazing up adoringly at him.

And round her neck was Emma's mama's amethyst necklace.

'Matthew ...'

But Matthew stopped her, putting a hand on her arm, and raising a finger to his lips.

'I've seen. I'll deal with it later. Here's our main course.'

'I'm not hungry any more.'

'I thought you had more spirit than that. More backbone. You can't let the likes of him,' and at that Matthew jerked his head towards Reuben Jago who hadn't noticed them yet, 'manipulate your feelings or your life.'

'Easy for you to say. It's not your necklace.'

'Food, Emma,' Matthew said.

Emma thanked the waiter as he placed her plate in front of her. She cut off a tiny corner of lamb and popped it in her mouth. Eating was the only way to stop her talking, stop her saying what she wanted to say. Stop her going right over to Reuben Jago to ask what he thought he was doing letting that trollop wear her mama's necklace.

'Don't look up and don't react, Emma,' Matthew said. He placed a hand on her arm. 'Carter Jago and his brother Miles have just joined their father. Complete with floosies of their own.'

Emma struggled to comply with Matthew's order, but couldn't resist peeping out from lowered lashes. Carter was walking towards her, but not looking at her. She could see the pink vertical marks on his cheeks where she'd caught him with her nails. Obviously she hadn't scratched him nearly hard enough. She wondered what lie he might have told the woman he was with as to how he came by the scratches.

'Seth's not with them,' Emma whispered. And thank heaven for that, she thought.

'I didn't expect him to be for one moment,' Matthew whispered back.

It was on the tip of Emma's tongue to ask if Matthew had been expecting Reuben Jago and Carter and Miles, but she was learning wisdom, wasn't she? Slowly, but surely, she *was* learning it.

'I feel like I want to go and scratch Carter Jago's eyes out for what he did to me,' Emma whispered, a hand over her mouth to silence her words further.

'Sssh, don't court trouble.'

'Me?' Emma cried, and the second the word was out of her mouth she knew it had come out too loud because practically the whole dining-room looked her way. And Carter Jago in particular.

He excused himself from his companion, leaving his brother to show her to her seat and came striding over to their table. He had a false smile on his face as he did so.

Completely ignoring Emma, Carter dropped onto the spare chair at their table and glared at Matthew.

The hubbub of conversation of the other diners resumed, and Emma was thankful for that.

'Who said the likes of you can eat in a place like this, Caunter?'

Emma gasped, but Matthew shot her a look that told her she was to keep quiet – already she'd said too much though, hadn't she?

'I don't need anyone's permission to eat anywhere, Mr Jago,' Matthew said. He reached for Emma's hand, touched it briefly. 'With whomsoever I choose.' Carter cleared his throat ready to speak, but Matthew held up a hand to silence him. 'And if ever you lay a hand on Miss Le Goff again you'll have me to answer to.'

'You're welcome to the little bitch.'

Emma gasped again as Carter made to stand, but Matthew put a hand to his shoulder to restrain him. 'You'll take that back,' he said, his voice low, controlled, but Emma could tell there was anger in his eyes.

'Or what? I told Seth he was wasting his money having

headstones made for *her*. Pity he's not here to see how she's dolled herself up for someone else.'

'I'm dressed for *me*, thank you very much,' Emma said. Although she was angry with Carter she was heartened that it *had* been Seth who'd had the headstones made for her parents and Johnnie.

'Hush, Emma,' Matthew said. 'I'll deal with this. As for you, Carter, I think you owe Miss Le Goff an apology.'

'I owe her nothing!' Carter said.

'Keep your voice down, man. We're in a public place. If you won't apologise now, then I'll expect one later. Outside.'

'You'll have to catch me first,' Carter said. 'And you can count your days as numbered working for the Jagos. I'll be having a word with my father.'

'Then don't let me keep you from him. Or your, er, companion.'

Carter Jago made a snorting sound, stood up, and walked back to his table.

'If you'll excuse me a moment, Emma,' Matthew said. 'I have a phone call to make. I won't be long. The Jagos won't make trouble for you, don't worry. Look at them swigging the wine back – they've forgotten we exist already.'

'I hope so,' Emma said.

But a phone call? Why now in the middle of a meal? Emma wondered. And to whom?

But Emma was learning wisdom.

'Of course,' she said. 'Take as long as you like.'

The dining-room emptied table by table, until there were only Emma and Matthew seated at their corner table, and the Jagos sitting around the table in the bay window left – and everyone on the Jago table red-faced from too much wine and champagne.

Mr Smythe had joined Emma and Matthew for dessert,

saying very complimentary things about Emma's tarte tatin and asking if it was possible to make it with other fruits. Emma said she should think so although she'd never tried.

'Then try,' Mr Smythe had said.

Matthew had joked that he would tie Emma's ankle to the leg of the table in the kitchen to make sure she did. He had a fancy to taste it made with blackberries, he said.

But now both men were talking, heads together, so quietly Emma couldn't catch all of what they were saying. But she did hear Mr Smythe say that his wife's time was almost due and that she would be joining him from London as soon as she was able. He regretted having to leave her behind but business matters had come to a head forcing the issue of his move to Devon.

As the two men continued talking, Emma sat as still as she could, dreamily thinking about her future, making grandiose plans in her head. Who was to know if she might not achieve them? Sitting and thinking was easier than looking across the room to Reuben Jago's dining companion and seeing her wearing the amethyst necklace that should be around Emma's neck. She wondered when she might get back to Shingle Cottage.

And then Reuben Jago left his table, knocking his chair onto the floor as he got up.

'Wait there, boys,' he shouted to his sons. 'Don't move until I tell you.'

Carter and Miles Jago laughed, and returned to nuzzling the necks of their companions.

'I want a word with you,' Reuben Jago said, coming to loom over Matthew.

'I dare say you do. But not in present company,' Matthew replied. He turned to Mr Smythe. 'Is there a room available?'

Mr Smythe nodded.

'What's this about?' Reuben Jago snapped, although

Emma couldn't help noticing he had a wary look in his eye. 'We talk here or we don't talk at all. Understand?'

'And I'll thank you to remember you're on my property,' Mr Smythe said. 'And we have a minor here.' He touched Emma lightly on the shoulder.

'Slut, more like. More trouble than she's worth, that one. I should never have agreed she could stop on at Shingle Cottage, Caunter.'

'You'll take that slur back, Mr Jago,' Matthew said. His voice was low and deep, but Emma could see he wouldn't take no for an answer. 'Even though I'll concede it's the alcohol talking here as well as yourself.'

'It *is* not and I *will* not. Have you seen what she did to Carter?'

'Do you see what your son did to me?' Emma spat on her fingers and rubbed at the flour and rouge mixture covering her cut and the bruises. Matthew gripped her wrist.

'Keep out of this, Emma.'

'No! It's me he's talking about.'

'Yes, and like mother, like daughter,' Reuben Jago snarled. 'Tight-arsed madam your mother was, too. She'd probably still be alive today if only she'd been a bit more accommodating.'

Was she hearing right? Was Mr Jago saying it was he who'd pushed her mama and Johnnie off the cliff because she'd refused his advances? Was he?

'I know she'd never have jumped – that someone must have pushed her. Was it you? Mrs Phipps told me you came calling, but I know my mama wouldn't have done the things with you Mrs Phipps said she did.'

'I'm admitting to nothing. What I said was pure speculation,' Reuben Jago said. 'You can't pin anything on me, now or any time.'

'Enough!' Matthew grabbed Reuben Jago by the arm. 'And that's where you're wrong.' With his free hand,

Matthew drew some papers from the inside of his jacket. 'His Majesty's Customs.'

Reuben Jago struggled to free himself, but Matthew was younger and stronger, and not pickled with drink.

'Boys!' Reuben yelled.

But neither Carter nor Miles moved – it was as though they were transfixed with shock. Or fear.

Four men Emma had never seen in her life came rushing in then – she guessed they were colleagues of Matthew's.

'He's all yours,' Matthew said, releasing his hold on Reuben Jago, pushing him towards the newcomers. Within seconds Reuben Jago had been apprehended.

'I'm sorry you've had to witness this, Emma. But Mr Smythe has a room you can go to,' Matthew said. 'I'd like you to go there and stay there. Understand? If you know what's good for you, you won't go anywhere near Shingle Cottage. Or Hilltop House. There could be reprisals once any of the crew who are implicated in all this find out, and they might want to take revenge, I …'

'But my clothes. My book. My family papers. I've had things of mine burned once. I couldn't bear for it to happen again. I …'

'It won't.'

'And Seth. I'm worried about *him*. He …'

'Seth isn't going to be accused of anything I know he's completely innocent of, Emma. Trust me on that.'

'Come, Emma,' Mr Smythe said. 'Matthew has things to do.'

'Yes. I have to go now. And I won't be around for a while, Emma. Things to do, as Mr Smythe says,' Matthew said. 'I'll be in touch when I can. But …'

One of the men – who'd been joined now by Sergeant Emms – yelled Matthew's name and he sped across the room to confer wth them.

Emma was escorted upstairs by Mr Smythe, a hand under her elbow. How bony and hard that hand was. But she knew it would be rude to extricate herself from his grasp. Besides, where else would she go?

Mr Smythe took her to a tower room at the top of the house. A very small room with little floor space although there were windows on three sides looking out to sea. A telescope on a stand pointed towards a window. There were lots of papers on the table with writing on – Matthew's hand. A narrow bed, made up, against the only wall that didn't have a window in it. A cheval glass stood in a corner.

'Matthew's been spying from here, hasn't he?' Emma said.

'Best if I don't answer that, Emma, and best if you don't mention what you think has been going on here to anyone. Anyone at all,' Mr Smythe said. 'Do you understand?'

'Yes,' Emma said. 'Thank you. Thank you for letting me stay.'

'Pleased to be of help. Now I must go. You should be comfortable enough here for the moment.'

Yes, she'd be comfortable – more than. She'd dreamed of being at Nase Head House one day, but by her own endeavours – not like this.

'Seth?'

Mrs Drew was sitting on a chair in the hall as he let himself in. A candle guttered in its holder on the side table. No matter how many times he told Mrs Drew she could leave the lights on, she didn't – she said she was afraid the new-fangled electricity would leak out if no one was around to keep an eye on it.

'You shouldn't be here,' Seth said. He wondered why she was.

'And don't I know it. But Cook took to her bed this afternoon with a migraine, so I stayed on in case Mr Reuben or your brothers needed anything when they came back home.'

'Thank you,' Seth said. 'But I'm sure they can all rise to cutting a slice of bread and a hunk of cheese if they want it.'

Seth stifled a yawn. He'd only had a couple of pints with Olly, but the alcohol seemed to have gone straight to his head. The sooner he could get to bed the better. He ought to escort Mrs Drew home safely before he did, though.

'I'll see you to your cottage, Mrs Drew.'

'Not yet. You haven't heard, have you?'

'Heard what?'

'Police and Customs and God knows who else – and He won't tell – have been here. Cook got out of bed fast enough when 'er heard the commotion, didn't 'er? Nearly fainted and all. 'Er ran off down the road to get that useless lump of a gardener your pa employs, Tom, out of bed and they came back here. By that time, the maid came down wanting to know what the din was about. After the Customs people, or whoever they were, had gone they began bellowing for their money. Well, I didn't know anything about that, did I? So they took some silver apiece in lieu of wages they don't think they're going to get and buggered off. Excuse my French, but I didn't want you to think we'd all left ...'

Seth stopped listening, went on through to the drawing-room, flicked on the light and saw that indeed some silver was missing from the dresser. Drawers had been opened and papers rifled through. What hadn't been taken away was lying on the floor or on chairs and tables. Mrs Drew came scurrying in.

'They've been down the cellar and up the attic, too, poking their noses into everything. There weren't nothing there they was after, though. I tried to stop them, Seth, honest I did.' Mrs Drew sniffed back tears.

'I'm sure you did.'

'They said they had authority. Waved a bit of paper at me. I couldn't argue with that. I had to stand by and watch 'em. I didn't make them no tea, though.'

Seth couldn't stop a smile from coming. Mrs Drew was fighting his corner, as always. He put an arm around her – she'd tried, in her way, to take the place of his ma and he loved her for that.

'And none of them's come back yet – your Pa, nor your brothers, I mean. I expect they've been arrested or summat.'

'Seems like it,' Seth said. Thank God he'd refused to sign the accounts.

'Will they come for you, Seth?' Mrs Drew said.

Seth saw real fear in her eyes that they might.

'No doubt I'll be asked a lot of questions but I would think if they wanted me then someone would have been posted outside to wait for my return.'

'That's a mercy, then. 'Ere, I've had a thought. D'you think Emma's had a hand in this? I know Carter tried, you know, to kiss her and that. Or worse ...'

'Can you forget you know that, Mrs Drew?'

He didn't think Emma would have reported the attack – and if she had, who would have believed her? – but he didn't want her name said in the same sentence as his pa's and his brothers'.

'Forgotten already, ain't I? Now, we could both be doing with a mug of hot chocolate, I'd say. With a tot of brandy in it, seeing as there won't be any more coming in, looks like.' Mrs Drew smiled warily at Seth. 'I suppose we're all guilty if we've ate things and drunk things if they'm dishonestly come by?'

'But we don't *know* they were,' Seth said, smiling. 'So make that two tots of brandy apiece in the chocolate. We're going to need it.'

Where was Emma at this moment? Seth knew in his gut

that Matthew Caunter had a hand in whatever had been going on up at Nase Head House. He was far too sure of himself, and obviously better educated than any of the other fishermen his father had ever employed. And if what Carter had said was true, Emma would be up there with him. His brothers could turn nasty in a fight. Miles had a gun. A pistol. Seth had come across him cleaning it outside the back door.

'I think I ought to go up to Nase Head House and see what's going on. Make sure Emma's not in danger.'

'No. Don't, Seth. You won't help the cause. I might only be a cleaner what left school at twelve years old but I'm bright enough to know that the more you're out of whatever it is your pa and brothers have been up to, the better it'll be for you. And Emma, I'd say.'

'Yes,' Seth said. 'And Emma.'

Emma? Would she ever be his now? After this.

Emma woke groggily after a deep and amazingly untroubled sleep, given what had happened the night before. The sun, low and dazzling, streamed in through un-curtained windows. She'd slept in the tower room, warm and comfortable enough because Mr Smythe had given her an eiderdown to put on top of the blankets – the softest thing Emma had ever seen, ever touched. And the pillows. Well …

Someone knocked at the door.

'Come in,' Emma said, pulling the eiderdown up tight around her neck.

The door opened and a young girl peeped around the edge of it. 'Mr Smythe says to tell you breakfast finishes in half-an-hour, Miss Le Goff. Oh, and Mr Caunter has seen to it that yer things have been delivered. Jimmy Dunn will bring 'em up later.'

'Oh,' Emma said. 'Who's Jimmy Dunn?'

'He's a porter, Miss. Carries the guests' cases to their rooms and that.'

'Oh,' Emma said again. 'A porter.'

'Yes, Miss. It's why 'e'll be bringing yer things up.'

Was she going to be staying here now? If her things were being brought to this room then it looked as though she would be, for the time being. It was a wonderful room even if it was small. She pinched herself so she'd know she wasn't dreaming.

'Ouch,' she said, when the pinch was a bit too hard.

The girl came rushing over. 'What's the matter? Are you ill?'

'No,' Emma laughed. She let her gaze wander around the room, over wallpaper that was decorated with huge purple irises, and a chest of drawers that gleamed with polish against one wall. She glanced upwards as sunlight bounced off the glass bowl of a lampshade hanging from the ceiling – it seemed over-large in the small space but wonderful all the same. Oh, Mama, if you could see me now, she thought. 'I pinched myself so I'd know I wasn't dreaming, being here in this lovely room.'

The girl laughed. 'That's all right, then. But best you get out of that bed and go and get some breakfast down you. That was a right old ding-dong went on 'ere last night. You were involved in it, so I 'eard.'

'I was,' Emma said. 'But I don't want to talk about it. What time is it?'

''Alf-past nine, just gone.'

'Oh, my Lord ...'

Emma leapt from under the eiderdown.

'I've brought you a jug of water. There'll be a basin in 'ere someday soon I 'spect, like there is in all the other rooms, but it's a jug for you today, Miss Le Goff. Mr Smythe's given orders for curtains to be put up in 'ere this afternoon, and all.

Not that there's anyone to spy on you from outside this high up, Miss Le Goff.'

'Call me Emma.'

'Oh, I can't, Miss. You'm a guest and I'm staff.'

'I'm not a guest. So in this room you can call me Emma. What's *your* name?'

'I'm Ruby. Ruby Chubb.'

'Pleased to meet you, Ruby Chubb.' Emma extended her hand.

'Oh, I'm not to shake hands with guests.'

'I've told you – I'm not a guest,' Emma told her.

'Not what I heard,' Ruby said. 'If you need brushes and the like there's some in the top drawer of that chest over there. Then you'd best get your clothes on or Stephen Bailey will die of a heart attack at the sight of your bosoms in that thin chemise at the breakfast table.'

'Stephen Bailey?' Emma laughed. 'Who's he?'

'One of the waiters. The other one's 'Arry Webber. Only 'e's doing other duties now seeing as we're a bit short-staffed here. Brought most of the staff from London, did Mr Smythe, but not many of 'em like it down here so they've scarpered back again.'

'You're not from London?' Emma said.

'With an accent like this?' Ruby laughed. 'Where've you been living, Miss? Under a stone?'

'That's what I meant.' Emma giggled. 'You're local.'

'From Galmpton. Just a couple of miles away. And proud of it.'

'So, what do you do here, Ruby?'

'Chambermaid. Well, that's the official title. Eve Grainger's the other chambermaid but 'er's always off sick. Like today. So it means I clean the rooms and make the beds and make sure there's towels and the likes by the basins in all twelve bedrooms today instead of just six of 'em. But seeing as the staff seem to be leaving faster than flies leave an abattoir when it stops trading, I do a bit of everything else as well. Laundry – eurgh, I hate doing laundry. All they dirty sheets from guests who've been doing goodness knows what. And talking of which, there's a mountain of it waiting for me downstairs, so I'd better get on. You won't tell old Frosty Drawers I've been up here yacking, will you?'

'Frosty Drawers?' Emma said.

'Mr Bell. On the reception desk. Thinks he owns the place, especially when he's in charge those times Mr Smythe goes back to London to see his wife. Never smiles.'

'Hence Frosty Drawers?'

'Yes. But don't say I told you.'

Ruby grinned and ran from the room. And Emma knew if she was going to be stopping here then she'd like Ruby for a friend.

Chapter Twelve

Emma knew she had to see Seth and soon. After she'd eaten porridge and toast for breakfast – served, to her amusement, by a blushing Stephen Bailey who couldn't get his words in the right order when he spoke to her – Emma was told she had the morning free to do as she wished. But – Mr Smythe had been firm about this – she was not to go to Shingle Cottage or to the Jago household as Matthew had said she shouldn't. And she certainly wasn't to say anything to anyone about what had gone on in the hotel the night before, should anyone ask for a first-hand account of it. She was to be back by 2 o'clock at the very latest. After lunch, he had said, he would think what he was going to do with her, but before that he had to meet Matthew Caunter at the courthouse.

Emma had asked if a note could be sent to Seth at Hilltop House and when she was told it could, she hastily scribbled a request that he meet her at Crystal Cove.

And now she was sitting at the bottom of the steps, glancing anxiously up them, willing Seth to arrive soon. She prayed he hadn't been arrested because, to her alarm, there had been lots of activity in the harbour – most of it on board Jago fishing vessels of one sort or another, although some of the sheds on the harbourside that were kept for storage had also had their doors forced open and had been searched. Sergeant Emms and Constable Jeffery, who had come to Shingle Cottage to talk to Matthew, were in attendance along with at least a dozen other men who seemed to be there in an official capacity although they weren't in a uniform of any sort – Customs Officers perhaps? She had even glimpsed Matthew before he'd disappeared below deck.

Would Seth want to see her? Would he think she had had a part in what had happened at Nase Head House the night before?

But then, before she could torture herself further, Seth appeared at the top of the steps. Waved. He walked slowly towards her.

Emma leapt to her feet, ran up the steps to meet him. He looked serious, troubled – which wasn't unexpected in the circumstances. But Emma couldn't stop smiling – she was just so pleased to see him. No, more than pleased – overjoyed.

'Thank you for your letter, Emma,' Seth said.

'I had to thank you for getting the tablets engraved for my parents and Johnnie. I wanted you to know how grateful I am in case you ... you were arrested.'

'As you see, I haven't been.'

'I'm glad. And I want you to know, from my own lips, that I had nothing to do with what happened last night. To your pa, I mean.'

It was obvious Matthew had been involved but Emma didn't think it sensible to bring his name into the conversation at this moment.

'I didn't think that for a moment,' Seth said.

'As to the tablets, I'll pay you back just as soon ...'

'I don't want paying for anything, Emma,' Seth said, his face grave. He reached a hand towards Emma's forehead, now washed clean of its flour-and-rouge cover-up, but didn't actually touch her. Her bruise had begun to fade to a dirty yellow, and the cut had formed a crust.

'Carter did *that* to you?'

'You heard?'

'He told me. You packed a mighty punch ...'

'He deserved it. Thank goodness Mrs Drew was around, though, or ...'

'I'd have killed him if he'd, you know ...'

Emma nodded. They both knew the word Seth was needing to say but wouldn't was 'rape'.

'Or possibly I'd have killed him first. Oh, I know he's your brother and all, but he's more like an animal. I'm sorry to have to say it.'

'And you aren't afraid to be here – alone – with me?'

'Of course not. Why would I be?'

Seth shrugged, and Emma thought the whole world's sadness was in that shrug.

'Let's sit down.' Seth took Emma by the elbow and guided her a little way down the beach. He took off his jacket and laid it down on the sand.

Poor Seth. It couldn't have been pleasant discovering his father and brothers arrested. And now his pa's boats were crawling with police the way maggots crawl over a bit of rotting meat.

'It's not your fault Carter tried to ...'

'But he didn't?'

Seth indicated for Emma to sit, waited while she did so. Then he dropped heavily onto the sand beside her. A cloud of fine sand rose and fell.

'No, he didn't, you know ... touch me. Honestly,' Emma lied. Telling Seth the truth wouldn't help him and it certainly wouldn't alter things. 'I scratched his face before he could ...'

'I saw. You should have gouged his eyes out.'

'Seth!'

'Well, you should. I'm ashamed to be a Jago at the moment.'

'Don't be,' Emma said. 'But you're not caught up in the smuggling, are you?'

'No. But when your beef is seared with contraband brandy, Emma, and you eat it – suspecting the brandy was illegally come by – then I think that could be said to make you party to the act.'

'How could you *not* eat what your cook prepared for you?'

'Exactly.'

'Mmm,' Emma said. Deep in thought. She still had the chocolate Seth had given her – in fact she had it in the pocket of her jacket at that moment. For some reason she just couldn't fathom she'd taken it with her to Nase Head House the night before. She was glad she had, now. She hadn't eaten so much as a tiny corner of it, though. She took the chocolate from her pocket and placed it on the sand between them.

'You didn't eat it,' Seth said, his voice achingly sad.

'No. It's contraband, isn't it?'

'I honestly can't say it is, just as I can't say it isn't. But why didn't you eat it?'

'It's the first thing you ever gave me. I kept it for sentimental reasons, I suppose. I still don't know that I should eat it, though. If it's contraband.'

Emma unwrapped the chocolate. She read the French on the paper wrapper over and over. She would have to get some books in French soon or she'd forget how to read in the language, write in it. She would read out loud so she didn't forget how to speak it.

'*Fabriqué en* …' Emma began to read the wrapping before her throat closed over with sadness.

She screwed the wrapping into a ball and stuffed it back into her jacket pocket. And then she got up and walked to the sea, snapped the chocolate into tiny pieces and threw it fragment by fragment into the small waves that flopped like sinking meringues onto the shoreline.

She stood for a while staring out across the water. Would she ever get to the land that was her father's? Would she ever walk into a hotel and ask for a *café au lait* and a *crocque monsieur*? And if she did, who would she be there with?

If she squinted hard Emma could imagine that was France she could see across the water although she knew in her heart – because she'd been good at geography in school – that it wasn't; it was just a large vessel of some sort far out on the horizon.

Suddenly she felt a hand on her shoulder.

'Don't be sad, Emma,' Seth said. 'I'll get you some more chocolate, and I'll guarantee it will be honestly come by.'

Emma tried to speak but all that came out was a sob. So Seth turned her to face him, took her in his arms. He smelled of fish a little, but it didn't bother Emma – quite the reverse. It was a smell from her past, a comforting smell. But she couldn't always live there, could she? – in the past.

'What will you do?' she said between sobs into Seth's knitted jumper. The rough fibres in it were tickling her cheek but she couldn't pull away. Not yet.

'About what?'

'The boats. They were crawling with men when I went past earlier.'

Seth didn't answer right away. Instead, he smoothed her hair with his hand, and she was glad Ruby had told her where the brushes were now. She hoped her hair didn't smell of cooking, though.

Loath as she was to move, Emma was forced to wriggle in Seth's grasp because her feet were sinking into the soft, damp sand. Seth released his hold on her, but reached for her hand. And Emma placed hers in it. They began to walk.

'There are men with families to consider,' Seth said. 'And they're my responsibility now. I've been told at least one of the trawlers will be impounded to offset the cost of taxes unpaid on contraband goods if there's a guilty verdict. The crabbers will still be able to be put to sea. I'll make sure that they do. Thank goodness I've never wasted money. Pa always paid me well enough and I've saved most of it. So

I've got adequate funds to pay the crew for a few weeks, at least.'

They'd reached the place on the sand where they'd been sitting previously and Seth lowered Emma back down onto his jacket.

'Won't Carter and Miles continue to run things?'

'Carter and Miles?' Seth said, as though the names were alien to him.

'Your brothers,' Emma said, although she knew it was superfluous to say so.

'Didn't you see anything of what went on last night?'

'Not much,' Emma said. 'I saw your pa arrested, but then Mr Smythe took me to a room where I spent the night.'

'My brothers, Emma,' Seth interrupted, 'are both locked in cells at the police station. Miles is more than implicated in smuggling, and ...'

Seth dropped onto the sand beside Emma. He ran a finger gently over her scab and her bruises. Then he kissed her injuries. Very gently, a feather-light touch – as though a butterfly had thought about stopping and then changed its mind.

'And Carter?' Emma prompted.

She felt Seth stiffen at his brother's name.

'Carter,' he said, 'is in it up to his neck, too.'

Seth had never even seen a gaol before and now he was *in* one – seated on the opposite side of a small, dirty table to his father. A uniformed warder stood in the corner, arms folded. Listening – Seth knew the warder was listening.

'Bail's been refused. Can you believe that?' Reuben Jago said, jutting his chin towards Seth.

Seth leaned back, away from his father. 'So I've been told.'

'Come closer, I don't want *him* hearing.' Reuben Jago flicked his eyes in the direction of the warder.

'I'll hear you from here if it's all the same to you.'

'Hah!' Reuben Jago hissed. 'You always were difficult.'

Seth pressed his lips together. If *difficult* meant not so malleable to his pa's orders as his brothes were, then so be it.

'Get on with it, Pa, what is it you don't want the warder to hear?'

'Thank God you had the sense to sign the transfer of deeds when I told you to,' Reuben Jago hissed, *sotto voce*, at Seth.

'And thank God I didn't sign accounts I suspected you'd falsified,' Seth said, only louder. Let the warder hear *that*.

'What falsified accounts, son?' his father said, speaking louder himself now. 'News to me, falsified accounts. Who's been at 'em? Lots of lies being bandied about here, that's for sure.'

'You know well enough what accounts I'm talking about, Pa. The ones I refused to sign.'

'Be that as it may, I'll be out of here soon, once that damn fool solicitor of mine does his job properly. Carter and Miles, too. Nothing's proved yet – innocent until proven otherwise.'

Seth scratched the back of his left calf. This place was giving him the creeps, with its peeling paint and where it wasn't peeling, thick with dirt. It was making him feel lousy. He'd picked up a flea already, hadn't he? He wasn't going to visit again unless he really had to.

'Plenty have talked once money came their way to loosen their tongues, so I've heard. People you and Carter and Miles did the dirty on.'

'Hold your tongue! Have you no respect?'

'Not a lot.'

'Oh, you think you can say what you like to me now, don't you? Safe in the knowledge I can't lay a finger on you with *him*,' Reuben Jago jerked a thumb towards the warder, 'hovering.' He lowered his voice. 'But you just wait until I get out. And when I do there'll be the little matter of transferring the deeds back into my name. Your attitude to all this – ' he went on, pointing to each wall in turn – 'hasn't pleased me one bit.'

'You're here by your own doing as far as I can tell. And as for transferring the deeds back into your name, we'll see …'

Reuben leapt to his feet. 'Damned right we will!'

'Sit, prisoner,' the warder yelled.

'I will not.'

'Then I'll help you.' The warder raced forward, pushed Reuben back onto the chair.

It was as if all the bravado went out of Seth's pa. He looked a broken man, not one who usually did the pushing around and the bullying.

'Did you push Ma down the cellar steps?' Seth asked, surprising himself that he felt no anger, no hatred, just a cold indifference to his father.

'Hold your tongue.' Reuben leapt to his feet again, but again the warder pushed him back into his seat.

'Going deaf, prisoner? I told you to sit. Didn't you hear me?'

'I heard.' Reuben Jago spat a gobbet of phlegm onto the floor.

'Time's up, visitor,' the warder said.

Seth nodded. Rose from his seat. 'For all your money, Pa, and your fine food, and your big house – mine now, of course,' Seth said, 'you're nothing but a bully of a peasant.'

And then Seth allowed himself to be escorted out the door, heard the key lock behind him. He'd had the last word for once. It was a good feeling and as he walked along the corridor behind the warder he experienced a strange sense of emotional freedom. He couldn't wait to get back home.

All the talk among the staff at Nase Head House was about the Jagos. Jimmy Dunn had come in with the news

– goodness only knows where he'd got it from – that the Crown was keen to get a quick conviction so that the Jagos were taken out of their illegal operation as soon as possible.

And they were talking about her, too, behind her back – Emma knew it – because more than a few times when she'd come into a room conversation that had been going on had died. The gardener must have spread the gossip that he'd been asked to take a letter from Emma to Seth Jago because word had got round that Emma and Seth were friends. Emma had been quizzed more than a few times about what she knew about the smuggling. But she always denied knowing anything – which was the truth. And she said little about Seth beyond, yes she and Seth *were* friends and that she knew nothing about what his father and brothers had been up to. And that was the truth of it because she hadn't seen Seth since that time on Crystal Cove when she'd thrown the chocolate he'd given her in the sea – a good fortnight ago – because he was busy now, running the Jago fishing fleet.

One or two had asked how she'd come to be linked with a Customs Officer but Emma always gave the same answer – she hadn't known he was at the time.

'What're you looking at then, Emma Le Goff?' Ruby said. 'Lovesick doesn't come into it the way you gawp out that window hoping for a glimpse of that Seth Jago.'

Emma laughed. 'As if I could see him from here. Anyway, who says I'm gawping at Seth?'

'I says. You only ever look in the direction of the harbour. Even though there's lovely things to see in other directions. Am I right?'

'You are.'

There was no denying it. Emma turned from the window of the dining-room where she was supposed to be helping Ruby lay the tables for lunch. Bored with nothing much to do, once the tarts Mr Smythe asked her to make each day were done, Emma was always more than happy to help her new friend. She'd asked Mr Smythe – at least three times – what her position in the hotel was and he had said each time that he was honouring his promise to Matthew to keep a roof over her head. He was, he told her, considering his options as regards a position for her and that he'd let her know when he'd come to a decision. Whatever that meant. Emma lived on tenterhooks, though, waiting for the moment when Mr Smythe might decide that one of those options was for her to leave. Or that he would tell her she'd have to get into a chambermaid's uniform.

She'd rather leave than wear such a frumpy uniform. Even though the thought of an uncertain future terrified her.

For the moment, though, Emma's way of ensuring she wasn't asked to leave just yet was to make the best job she could of the crab tarts. The cook didn't like it much, and he huffed and puffed and grumbled non-stop when she was in *his* kitchen. But there was nothing she could do about that – she had to do as she was asked by Mr Smythe. And the tartes tatin Mr Smythe loved so much – she made sure those were glistening and succulent and oozing with sweetness, thereby increasing her chances of being taken on as a cook. She hoped.

The cook hated her for doing it, though – jealous, no doubt, that Mr Smythe had particularly asked her to make them. Well, she had to do *something* to make herself useful, didn't she? The other chambermaid – Eve Grainger – glared at Emma as though she was a bit of dog dirt she'd found on the bottom of her shoe every time they met in passing. Emma had no idea why because she always smiled at the girl warmly enough. Jealousy, probably – because hadn't her mama always said that the only reason a person is horrible to another is because they're jealous? But with Ruby as her friend, Emma could ignore Eve Grainger.

'Hey, Miss Daydream. Are you in 'ere with me, or in some flowery bower inside your 'ead with Seth Jago?' Ruby laughed.

'Is it that obvious?' Emma asked, laughing with her. 'To everyone here I mean? That I'm looking out for Seth? Not that I can be certain which tiny ant-like figure is him down there on the quayside.'

Emma laid down a knife, straightened it. She closed her eyes for a second. In her mind's eye she could see him exactly as he'd been the last time she'd seen him at Crystal Cove, feel his arms about her, and his kiss against her hair.

'Probably it's me more 'an most what notices, seeing as we're together most,' Ruby said. 'Are you going to marry him?'

'Marry him? I'm not sixteen yet.'

'Two of my sisters got married at sixteen. With a babe apiece by their seventeenth birthdays. Married to older men the pair of 'em, and happy enough.'

'Seth's not old.'

'Ha! My hunch is right. You're mighty quick to his defence. You *do* want to marry him.'

'I didn't say that, Ruby,' Emma snapped. 'I said Seth's … oh, forget it.' Emma knew she was digging herself into a hole by continuing the conversation.

'Well, my money's on 'im asking you the second that day comes. Sending you a present an' all. I'd marry a man like that tomorrow.'

Yes, Seth had sent a parcel to Nase Head House for her: chocolate – honestly come by with English writing on it this time – and a set of hair brushes. New ones. He'd put a note in with the brushes saying he was sorry he didn't have time to meet her at the moment and that he was sure Emma understood how things were for him. And he ended the note by saying that she was in his thoughts and he hoped she was comfortable at Nase Head House.

Emma understood, of course she did. And he was in her thoughts as well. But marry? Did Emma want to marry? Yes, she knew she did one day. She wanted children of her own and her first son she would call Johnnie after her brother. But not yet. She needed to know what she was capable of, and to have a bit of money behind her before she married; have the safety net of savings. And possibly a place to call her own, not one small room in a hotel that Matthew Caunter had arranged for her to be in.

'Just think of it, Em,' Ruby said, her voice all dreamy. 'Hilltop House.' Ruby pointed out across the harbour to the hill on the other side. 'You could live up there and be a lady ...'

'No!' Emma said, leaping between Ruby and the window. 'I am never, ever going to live in that house.'

Ruby jumped back, startled at the vehemence of Emma's words.

'Well, best you get on and buff up that silver or lunch will be late and we'll be thrown out, you and me both, for making it so. And then where would you go?'

Where indeed? Emma wondered, as she gave each knife a brisk rub with a tea-towel before setting it in its precise position on the pristine damask cloth.

'Emma! Emma!' Ruby came rushing into Emma's room in the tower. Her chubby face was troubled – her cheeks bright pink – and her eyes glistened with what Emma thought might be tears. 'You've got to come. Mr Smythe ...'

'What's happened?' Emma said. Please, dear God, don't let anything have happened to Seth. Or to Matthew. There was no one else in her life that Emma cared for – apart from Ruby and she was standing right in front of her, obviously alarmed about something, but well. She didn't think she'd be able to bear it if something had happened to Seth or Matthew.

'I'm not to say. Mr Smythe's going to tell you. I was walking past the desk in the foyer, a load of clean sheets in my arms, when he took the call. I couldn't help but realise what was wrong. Mr Smythe flopped onto the chair by the desk and I thought he was going to pass out. He's in his office waiting for you. Oh, Emma ...'

'We're wasting time, Ruby,' Emma said.

She ran a hand through her thick, wavy hair in a vague attempt to tidy it. No time to use one of the brushes Seth had sent her. Then she twisted her hair at the nape of her neck and secured it with a clasp as best she could. It would have to do for now. If Mr Smythe was in the kind of distress Ruby had said he was, then he was hardly likely to notice the state of her hair, was he? Then she checked the front of her blouse for stains and to see if the buttons were done up properly. They were.

She ran from the room. She took the stairs two at a time, sliding her hand down the handrail as she went, even though she'd been told off for doing the same thing more than once. Not ladylike, Mr Smythe had said. Well, she wasn't a lady yet. Still a girl.

Skidding to a halt outside Mr Smythe's office, Emma took a couple of deep breaths. Her heart was racing, wondering what it was Mr Smythe was going to tell her. She knocked lightly on the door, and it was opened at once by Mr Smythe himself.

'Ah, Emma.'

Mr Smythe always called her by her Christian name – something the rest of the staff didn't go much on because they were always addressed by their surnames. But when she mentioned it to him he had said she was still a minor and he would address her as he saw fit.

'You wanted me?' Emma said.

'Yes, yes. Come in.'

He closed the door behind them.

'Is it Seth? Matthew?' Emma asked. She felt herself go cold, then instantly heat coursed through her veins again. The palms of her hands felt damp, clammy. As surreptitiously as she could she wiped them on the sides of her skirt.

'Neither, Emma,' Mr Smythe said. 'It's my wife, Claudine. She died this morning. Our baby came a little early a month ago and my wife was slow to recover. She took an infection in her ... in her ...' Mr Smythe seemed unable to go on. He looked at Emma as though he wasn't sure who she was or why she was there.

'I'm sorry,' Emma said, not knowing what else to say. But her voice seemed to have brought him back to the present.

'I should have gone back to our London home more. Two weekends wasn't enough. I planned to. I telephoned, of course. I thought to be nursed at home would be a safer place for her than a hospital where she might have picked up all sorts of diseases, and now ...'

So that was why Mrs Smythe was still in London and not here.

'I'm truly sorry,' Emma said. 'What can I do?' And why are you telling me, she wanted to know. Why had she been chosen when, perhaps, Mr Bell on reception might have been a better recipient of such news, especially as he had come from London and might have known Mrs Smythe.

'Claudine was ...' Mr Smythe's voice was hoarse now and he cleared his throat, but seemed unable to go on.

'Claudine?' Emma said.

Mr Smythe nodded, then dropped into a chair beside the window, put his head in his hands. His shoulders heaved up and down but he made no sound.

To go to him or not?

Slowly she walked towards the window. She reached out to touch Mr Smythe on the shoulder. How thin he seemed beneath his jacket. As though the sudden shock had made him smaller somehow.

'I know what it's like to lose someone you love,' Emma said.

Mr Smythe turned to look at her then, his eyes red-rimmed from crying. 'Forgive me for my weakness.'

'It's not weak to feel emotion. I might have thought less of you had you not shown any.'

Emma knew she was saying the right thing but it was painful to watch Mr Smythe in his terrible grief. She had enough of that of her own. It wrapped itself around her like the Liberty bodice her mama had made her wear when she was younger, itching and scratching and making her skin raw.

Emma's hand was still on Mr Smythe's shoulder, and gently she removed it.

'I expect you're wondering why I'm telling you, possibly, rather more than you might be expecting to hear. And why I've sent for you.'

'There must be other, older ...'

'There are, but you're the only one here who speaks French.'

'French?' Emma said. And then it came to her that Mr Smythe had called his wife Claudine – a French name. 'Your wife is ... was ... French?'

'Yes. And the twins, Sidney and Archie, are – were – being brought up by-lingual. And the baby ...'

Mr Smythe put his head in his hands again, turned away from Emma back towards the window.

'Has the baby died, too?' Emma said, a lump in her throat that it might have.

'No. Thank the Lord.' Mr Smythe stood up, took a handkerchief from the breast pocket of his jacket and wiped his eyes. 'And that's where I need your help, Emma.

My daughter won't know her mother – they've been separated almost since the birth because of Claudine's infection – but I'll do my best that she will know her mother's language and her culture. Do you think, Emma, that you could tutor my sons in French, and be nursemaid to Isabelle on the nanny's day off? I'll pay you, of course.'

'Yes,' Emma said. How could she have said anything else? At the same time, she wondered just how much of her own life she might have written away with that single word.

Mr Smythe had found a position for her, hadn't he? – even if it probably wasn't one of the options he'd been considering.

Chapter Thirteen

Emma sat on the rug in the centre of the drawing-room in Mr Smythe's private quarters, surrounded by books. Boxes and boxes of them had come down by train, and been delivered by the carrier's cart to Nase Head House. It had taken two men well over an hour to bring them all into the house and up the two flights of stairs to where Emma now sat poring over them.

Alexandre Dumas. Georges Sand, Guy de Maupassant. She drank in the French names on the covers, opened them and devoured the language she'd so loved to speak with her papa.

Mr Smythe had asked her to put them on shelves he'd had hastily built along one wall. There were some children's books which Emma thought perhaps Sidney and Archie might be able to read themselves at six years old. She put those to one side. Then she arranged the books in alphabetical order. Her guess was that Claudine Smythe had bought some of the books – the adventure story ones by Alexandre Dumas in particular – for the boys to read when they were older.

Further along the corridor the nanny was settling the children into their rooms. Emma had had only a glimpse of two, small identical boys, their heads bowed, being led by their father up the steps from his car. And she hadn't really seen Isabelle at all, because she'd been swaddled in layers and layers of fine wool with a bonnet pulled down almost over her eyes and held tightly in the nanny's arms when she'd arrived. And she'd been asleep. A month old, and small for a baby of that age because she'd been premature, and no mama – it made Emma gulp back tears to think of it.

Emma stood – her legs stiff from sitting on them for

so long. She began to read out loud the titles of all the books. Something fizzed up inside her, like dandelion-and-burdock cordial, at the joys she had to come reading all those books. Until now, the only book she had to read was her Jane Austen, mended for her by Matthew.

Emma had her back to the door when she heard it being flung open.

'Well, I'm off.'

Emma turned to see the nanny, hat on, bag clasped in her hand.

'But you can't go,' Emma said.

'Who says?'

'Well ...' Emma began. She'd thought the nanny would be staying to have the main care of Isabelle and that she was going to be responsible for French tuition with the twins when they were home from school. Would she be expected to care for Isabelle full time if the nanny left?

'Well yourself, Miss.'

The nanny was still staring at her as though challenging her. Emma took a deep breath. 'Does Mr Smythe know you're leaving?'

'He's not here. I've left a note. Nothing, but nothing, is going to keep me in this backwater. Besides, I've already secured another position.'

'But won't Sidney and Archie miss you? Couldn't you lessen the time you spend with them each day until ...'

'Look, Miss. I don't know who you are, and I care less, but I don't have to explain myself to you, do I?'

'But the baby? Where is she?'

'Where babies usually are – sleeping in her crib.'

'You can't just leave her!'

'I can and I am. Gave her a good feed, didn't I? She'll be all right for an hour or two.'

'But Archie and Sidney? Where are they?'

'Outside, giving the gardener the run-around. I've told him to keep an eye on them 'til their father gets back. Now I'm off.'

And with that she turned on her heel and left, slamming shut the door behind her.

'And just as well, I'd say,' Emma said. 'Those poor children need more care and concern for their welfare than that.'

But was she the person to provide it?

Emma looked in on the sleeping Isabelle. She hoped and prayed she would be all right for an hour or two because Emma had a tarte tatin to make.

When Mr Smythe got back from wherever it was he'd gone then no doubt she'd find out just what her duties would be from now on.

Mr Smythe came into the kitchen where Emma had just finished mixing the pastry for the tarte tatin. She laid the dough on a marble slab to keep it cool.

'Leave that, Emma,' Mr Smythe said. 'I'm sure Cook knows how to make those now. He must have watched you do it dozens of times.'

'Cook's not here,' Emma said. She began to peel an apple, cutting slices into a bowl of water so they didn't brown. 'He sent Ruby to the dairy for cheese but then he noticed the plaice was off. So he's gone down to the harbour to the fishmonger. He ...'

'Off?' Mr Smythe said.

'Stank a bit,' Emma said. 'Cook said he couldn't serve that to your guests.'

Mr Smythe shook his head, as though trying to rid it of a spider's web he'd just walked into. He looked puzzled.

'If he says so. Now leave that and come with me.'

'It won't take a minute to finish it off.' Emma listened

hard for Isabelle crying but there was no baby's wail of a cry. She had a hunch Mr Smythe had already found the note the nanny had left but knew better than to ask if he had. 'Besides, Cook said I was to keep an eye on the ... oh, here's Ruby with the cheese now. Perhaps she can do that?'

Ruby came rushing into the kitchen with a lump of cheese the size of a house brick wrapped in greaseproof paper. She skidded to a halt when she saw Mr Smythe. Ruby was a little afraid of her boss – she'd told Emma so.

'I said leave it, Emma,' Mr Smythe yelled at her. 'I've just discovered the nanny has left and I don't need you disobeying orders. Do you understand?'

Emma glanced towards Ruby, who was cowering now, a hand to her mouth. Her eyes were wide and round and terrified.

'It's all right, Ruby,' Emma said. 'Mr Smythe isn't shouting at you. And he's only shouting at me because of the tragic circumstances he's found himself in.'

Ruby nodded, her curls wobbling.

'Emma ...' Mr Smythe began.

'I'm coming. I'm truly sorry for your plight, but I'll thank you not to shout at me like that.'

Emma knew she was risking being thrown out on the street for her cheek in standing up to Mr Smythe, but if she didn't stand up for herself, who was there to do it for her?

It was Mr Smythe's turn now to have eyes that were wide and round – if not exactly terrified – at Emma's outburst.

Emma waited for him to tell her she could pack her bags and follow the nanny to the station, but he didn't. A smile played at the corners of his mouth.

'You, my dear,' he said, 'remind me of my dear, late, wife. Perhaps it's because you are – and she was – French.'

'Half French,' Emma corrected him.

'Which it is, is of no consequence. But there's no escaping

the forwardness. Now I suggest you show Ruby how to finish off that tart and then come upstairs to my drawing-room.'

And then he was gone.

'Did he really say that?' Ruby said, jumping up and down on the spot.

'Say what?'

'That I'm to make your fancy apple tart?'

'Amongst other things he did, yes. So, get your hands washed and that apron on and I'll show you how.'

Dr Shaw was called to Nase Head House to examine the baby. Emma stood beside the table the doctor had laid the naked child on and watched. Isabelle was so tiny – still smaller than many newborns the doctor said. She had a lot of hair, though – loose dark brown wisps that curled around her ears – although she had no discernable eyelashes yet. Her eyes were blue – although the doctor said the colour might change as she got older.

Isabelle screwed her face up, went red, and bawled.

'Sssh, sssh,' the doctor said. He turned to Emma. 'Now, if you would like to have a go at dressing this young miss ...'

'Now?' Emma said. There seemed to be a mountain of things piled on a chair. She knew they'd come off Isabelle because she'd seen the doctor undress her. However, it had been such a long time since she'd dressed a baby she'd completely forgotten how to put them all back on again and in which order.

'We'll do it together, shall we?' the doctor said. He had to raise his voice so he could be heard over the wail of a screaming baby.

'Yes, please,' Emma said. 'I'm a bit out of practice at this and I think Isabelle knows it, Doctor. I helped Mama with Johnnie a few times but really she was so pleased to have another baby she wanted to keep him to herself, mostly. Do everything for him.'

'I expect she did,' Dr Shaw said kindly. 'And it's bringing back memories, being asked to do that task now?'

Emma pressed her lips together for a moment before answering. 'Yes. But it's not just that. I like cooking. Mr Smythe likes my crab tart and he adores my tarte tatin, which he asks me to make most days. Only a few weeks ago I was full of plans to start a business selling my tarts to hotels and restaurants in the area. And I dream of having a little cottage to live in someday, all paid for by my endeavours. But now ...'

The doctor laid a hand on Emma's arm.

'I understand. A lot has happened to you in a very short space of time – and not much of it pleasant. But sometimes, life isn't about planning, or wishes and dreams – it's about making the best of the situations we find ourselves in. Do you understand?'

'I think so, Doctor.'

'Good, now let's get this young lady dressed before she catches a chill and I have to revise my diagnosis of her excellent health.'

'There's nothing wrong with her lungs, Doctor,' Emma said.

The baby, at that moment, sounded like a siren going off.

Emma slid a tiny vest – like an envelope – over the baby's head, but still she cried. Then the doctor watched as Emma put a nappy on a very tiny bottom and secured the pins so they didn't pierce infant flesh. In no time the doctor and Emma had Isabelle dressed between them, and the doctor placed the baby in Emma's arms.

'My wife will call to talk to you further about the care of small babies. And little boys. Sidney and Archie, you'll be pleased to know, are also in fine health. If lively.' The doctor chuckled as he re-packed his Gladstone bag. And then he was gone.

Emma stood, the baby still crying in her arms, not knowing what to do next. '*Sois sage, ma petite*,' Emma said. Be good little one. It seemed more natural to talk to her in French than it did in English. And it seemed to do the trick. The baby gulped and swallowed and her eyes – slightly boss-eyed, Emma thought – struggled to focus on Emma's.

Emma began to sing.

'*A la claire fontaine, m'en allant promener. J'ai trouvée l'eau si claire, que je m'y suis baigné …*'

She had this job for now. Good food and a warm room to sleep in. She would try and live by the doctor's wise words, to make the best of the situation.

When Mr Smythe returned from London and his wife's funeral she would have a talk with him about her duties. But, in the meantime, goodness knows what Seth was going to say when she told him it was going to be harder for them to meet than ever. She'd write to him tonight to tell him how her circumstances had changed.

As summer wore on, Emma lost count of the weeks before she was able to get a free hour to see Seth.

'Of *course* I understand, Emma,' he said.

His face was serious and Emma had a feeling that while he understood he didn't much like it.

'It won't be forever,' Emma said. 'My Smythe has put an advertisement in *The Times* for a nanny. I told him I can't be speaking French with the twins *and* seeing to Isabelle at the same time. I think the poor mite knows her mama's dead because she cries all the time. Only Ruby can soothe her when I'm not there, but she has to split her duties now between chambermaiding and the kitchen, and …'

'I said I understand,' Seth said. 'You don't have to explain it to me chapter and verse.'

Seth glared at Emma then turned his head to look out to sea.

'And you don't have to be quite so sharp with me, Seth,' Emma said quietly.

The sudden change in Seth's mood from when he'd hugged her and kissed her on the cheek when they'd met in their usual spot at Crystal Cove to the hard-faced young man he was now, frightened Emma.

'Well, I'm a bit sick of hearing how wonderful your life is turning out living up at Nase Head House with …'

'I didn't say it was wonderful. I'm making the best of the situation I've found myself in. That's not the same thing.'

Seth shrugged. 'Mr Smythe – no doubt – will be wanting not just a nanny or a nursemaid but a wife.'

'Oh, that's it, is it, Seth Jago? You don't like it that I'm living at Nase Head House. But you don't have to be jealous of Mr Smythe if that's your issue. He speaks to me occasionally about the children, but that's all.'

'Don't put words in my mouth, Emma. I didn't say I was jealous.'

'But you implied it,' Emma said.

'He's too old for you, Emma.'

'I'll be the judge of that – if it comes to it. And anyway, he can't be much older than thirty or thereabouts.'

'You know nothing about him, Emma. He's turned up here with his money and his fine ideas …'

'And he could have as evil a family as you …' Emma clapped her hand to her mouth. 'Oh, Seth. I'm sorry. I shouldn't have said that.'

Emma was filled with the most awful guilt – it hung heavy about her like a head cold – because Seth had never been anything but kind to her. How could she have even thought what she had, never mind have said it?

She kissed the tips of her fingers and laid them against Seth's cheek. She felt him stiffen beside her.

'I'm sorry.'

'I'm sorry, too. But evil was the right word to choose. Although, that said, Pa had one saving grace. He swore on the Bible that I'd been kept ignorant of the smuggling racket. Mr Caunter spoke up for me, too. But the upshot is, Pa's got three years and my brothers, two. They were sentenced yesterday.'

'Oh. Was it in this morning's paper? I haven't had time to read it yet. I don't know what to say. I can't say I'm sorry, can I? They've got what they deserve, everyone knows it.'

'You *could* say sorry,' Seth said. 'If it was *me* you're sorry for.'

'I'm sorry,' Emma said. 'For you. Truly I am.'

She shivered – and not because she was cold. While it was sunny, there was a brisk wind coming in off the sea and it was colder than it usually was in early September, but she'd wrapped up warm against it. No, her chill was nothing to do with the weather – there was an emotional distance between them now, and Emma wasn't liking it one little bit.

When Seth didn't respond, Emma said, 'You do believe me, don't you? That I am truly sorry for all you're having to cope with at the moment.'

'I believe you, Emma. And I'm sorry if I'm not my usual self.' Seth put his head in his hands.

Not knowing what to say, Emma acted on reflex and put her arm around his shoulders.

They sat then for some time, Emma's arm still about Seth's shoulder. From time to time Seth looked up, turned to Emma and smiled sadly. Other times they both looked out to sea, each thinking their own thoughts.

'This should be *our* time, Emma,' Seth said, breaking the silence between them. 'We're young and we should be able to fall in love and be happy. Not have all this ... this unwanted stuff to be carrying about with us.'

'You, because of your pa and brothers, and me because there are still people around here who think Mama shouldn't be buried at St. Mary's.'

And, no doubt, there were still those who thought it improper she'd been living alone with Matthew at Shingle Cottage, she thought, but didn't add. Saying that would only add to Seth's distress, wouldn't it?

'The easy option would be to go away,' Seth said. 'Where no one would know us.'

'I've never been away anywhere,' Emma said. 'I've never had a holiday.'

'I've only had one. Pa took us all to London. It was hot and dirty and noisy. I won't mind if I never have to go again.'

'Oh, Seth. Maybe we could go to other places one day. Nicer places.'

'I like to think we will, Emma.'

'But not now,' Emma said. 'We can't let other people's small minds force us from the place that's always been our home.'

'No,' Seth said. 'Anyway – time we went. I've got a boat due in soon and crew to pay off. Fish to get on ice and ready for market.'

Emma slid her hand from Seth's shoulder, started to stand. But Seth leapt to his feet and pulled her up. Pulled her towards him. Then he kissed her on the lips. Just a gentle kiss.

A comforting warmth, like the first warm rays of a summer sun, spread through Emma. But the heat was soon shot through with a spear-like shiver of fear. She didn't think Seth would want to take advantage of her, but ...

'What's the matter, Emma? Didn't you like me kissing you?'

'I did.'

'Then can I kiss you again?'

For answer Emma lifted her face to his.

But before he kissed her Seth said, 'You'll be sixteen at the end of the month. Old enough to marry.'

Marry? Was Seth asking her to marry him? And if he was, was that what she wanted? In time, perhaps, but did she want that now? If she were to marry Seth she could be certain of a roof over her head, and good food in her belly, nice clothes.

'I don't know that I want to marry you, Seth. Not yet. I'm too young ...'

'I don't remember asking you to,' Seth said.

His voice had resumed its sharpness of earlier. Emma backed away from him slightly.

'But ...'

'I'm trying to warn you, Emma. I'm not saying that I wouldn't want to marry you, but I'm not the only man who might want to.'

Seth turned and began to walk towards the steps that led up from the cove.

'Are we back to talking about Mr Smythe again?' Emma said, hurrying after him.

'Yes!' Seth shouted, striding forward, not bothering to turn around to look Emma in the face as he spoke. 'He's a widower with three children. A good catch. He'll be wanting a wife again, and soon. And one who speaks French, as you do, would be a considerable advantage to him. Think about it.'

He took the steps two at a time. At the top he turned to wait for Emma to catch up with him.

'I don't want to be Mr Smythe's wife,' Emma said, struggling for breath after her quick ascent of the very steep steps.

'Any other girl in this town would be glad enough to marry him.' Seth stuck his hands down hard into the pockets of his trousers, turned on his heel and rushed off.

'Seth!' Emma yelled. 'I'm not any other girl. I'm me. Come back. What's happening to you? To us? I thought we were friends? Seth, come back!'

But Seth didn't come back. And Emma didn't get her second kiss. She thought she might die from the longing for it.

'Do you think five years is too big a gap between a man and a woman, Mrs Drew?'

'And who might we be talking about? If it's you and Emma, I've told you once and I'll tell you again, Seth Jago, she's been through a lot. Let her spread her wings for a while. She'll find out which side her bread's buttered best by herself. And you've got enough on your plate to be worrying about, too, what with all those men with families to support to be kept in jobs. You haven't got time to lope about the place like a lovesick swain from the story books.'

'Perhaps you're right.'

He knew he'd been too sharp with Emma because of everything that was happening with his pa and his brothers, and trying to do his best by the boat crews – and now he was beginning to regret his sharpness.

'Now if that's all you want me for, I've got the dining-room to sweep and polish. I've got a roast in the oven and …'

'You're not regretting moving here, I hope,' Seth said, smiling.

Just weeks after his pa and brothers were arrested, Mrs Drew – along with her son, Edward – had come to live in at Hilltop when her husband had been killed in an accident at the quarry where he'd worked.

''Course not, you daft 'apporth. But I want to get it all done because the solicitor's coming. You haven't forgotten?'

'No, no,' Seth said quickly.

But he *had* forgotten. Being with Emma made him forget time and responsibilities. He put his fingers to his lips – he could still feel the softness of her lips when he'd kissed them.

He'd make it up to her for rushing off so childishly. He was a man, for goodness' sake. He should have stopped and talked things through with her. He would write her a note and apologise the minute the business with the solicitor was over – he had a Will to make now he was a man of property.

It would be Emma's birthday soon. When the solicitor left he'd go into town and look for something special for her. Surprise her. Mend the rift he'd so stupidly created between them.

Chapter Fourteen

'There's a man wanting you down in the foyer, Emma.' Ruby burst into the room, eyes wide, a huge grin on her face that Emma had a gentleman caller.

Emma struggled to fix a smile on her own face and hoped her irritation at the interruption didn't show. Sidney and Archie had just left the schoolroom, where she'd been testing them on their times-tables in French. Isabelle was asleep in the nursery. And Emma had thought to write again to Seth now that she had a few minutes to spare.

He had written to her to apologise for his bad manners down in Crystal Cove, and Emma had replied to say his apology was accepted – she understood how things must be for him over his father and his brothers.

'A man?'

Seth knew the date of her birthday. Had he come to surprise her with a present? Flowers, perhaps?

'Didn't I just say, Emma Le Goff?'

'Do you know who it is? Has he got black hair?'

'No and no.'

'What colour, then?'

'I'm not saying. You'll have to go and find out.'

Emma almost didn't want to go downstairs, even though she thought Ruby might be teasing her. She didn't want to find out that her visitor wasn't Seth with a present for her. She wasn't likely to get one from any other source, although Mr Smythe would know it was her birthday today if he looked at his staff records. And she hadn't told Ruby because it might look as though she was asking for a present, and she knew Ruby didn't have a spare halfpenny piece to buy anything.

What would her mama and papa have bought her for her birthday had they been alive, she wondered.

'I've seen him here before a time or two,' Ruby said, 'and that's all I'm saying. But I don't know his name. And neither will you if you don't go down and see what he wants, because he'll get bored of waiting.'

'Bossy boots,' Emma said, smiling.

She gave Ruby a playful punch on the shoulder. She liked the girl – she was her only friend in the whole wide world at the moment. All the girls she'd known at school still shunned her when they saw her in the town – jealous, perhaps, at her good fortune in living at Nase Head House, albeit as an employee. And some of them had their own – wrong in this case – opinions on what exactly had gone on when Emma had lived under the same roof as Matthew Caunter. Well, she didn't think she wanted to know any of them any more, anyway, if they were that small-minded. But to have only one friend?

Isabelle began to cry then.

'Oh, no,' Emma said. 'I can't go now. Mr Smythe hates it when the baby cries. He says it upsets the guests. They come here for peace and quiet and they don't want a bawling baby.'

'I'll see to the baby,' Ruby said. 'I've seen to babies often enough with the half-dozen my ma had after me.'

'Would you?'

'Didn't I just say? You're a one for not believing things folk tell you, Emma Le Goff. Eve Grainger will 'ave to help me out today for a change and do a room or two for me while I'm with little Belle, seeing as I'm always doing 'er job for 'er when she goes sick. Now run a brush through your hair and go down and see what the tall, handsome man in the foyer wants of you.'

And with that Ruby marched off towards the crying

Isabelle and Emma was left with no alternative but to go down to the foyer.

'Matthew?' she said, surprised that it was him.

'The very same,' Matthew said, grinning at her

Emma hurried towards him. 'How did you know I was still here?'

'I have my ways of knowing.' Matthew laughed. 'But to answer your question – and without giving away all my secrets – let's just say that I've needed to contact Mr Smythe from time to time. I suggested to him you could be useful here and he assures me you are.'

'Oh,' Emma said. 'He's never said.'

'And make that pretty little head of yours bigger?' Matthew teased.

Emma wished he wouldn't. He looked so different now from the man who had pretended to be a rough fisherman, always in clothes that stank of the sea and stale saltwater, barely taking time to shave or wash his hair. How smart he looked today, with a cravat at his neck and a handkerchief in the top pocket of his jacket.

She stopped in front of him, unsure as to what to do next. Shake hands? What was the form with married men one had once shared a home with? – even if she hadn't known he was married when she'd first moved in with him.

Matthew had a broad grin on his face, his delight in seeing her obvious. 'Give me a smile,' he said. 'Anyone would think you're not pleased to see me.'

'Oh, I am. I am,' Emma said.

'Good.' Matthew clasped both her hands in his, then raised them to his lips, before letting go again.

'This life is suiting you, Emma,' he said. 'You've filled out. You look well. Your hair shines.'

'It does and it doesn't suit.'

'No one to dance with around this highly polished floor?'

'Not since you, no,' Emma said. She kept her voice as low as she could. Some guests were booking out at the desk with Mr Bell. Other guests were leaving the dining-room after breakfast, and Stephen Bailey hurried across the foyer to clear the tables. 'But I didn't mean the dancing. I meant it was suiting me fine until Mrs Smythe died. Now I'm looking after Isabelle until Mr Smythe can hire a nanny, but no one seems to want the position. And I hardly get any time to cook now.'

'And you miss it?'

'Yes.'

'And I don't suppose anyone here knows it's your birthday today?'

'No. No one. I'm surprised you remembered.'

'I'm paid to remember things, Emma,' Matthew said. 'You did say when I asked how old you were that you'd be sixteen come Michaelmas and it's Michaelmas today – 29th September.'

'You've got a good memory.'

'Got to have. It's why I'm good at the job I do.'

'Putting the Jagos behind bars. Seth told me they've been sentenced.'

'Yes. It's why I'm back. There are a few things to be cleared up ...'

'Nothing to do with coming to see me on my birthday, then?' Emma said, trying to make a joke of it, desperate to get off the subject of the Jagos.

'Shall I go back out and come in again? Maybe you'll be pleased to see me a second time, seeing as I'm here bearing gifts and no one else seems to be?'

'I'm sorry. It's just ...'

'I'm not the man you'd hoped to see?'

'I'm glad to see you, of course I am.'

'But I'm not Seth Jago?'

'How did ... oh.' Emma stopped speaking as Matthew tapped the side of his nose. He was still working undercover, wasn't he? Perhaps he'd even seen her and Seth going down to Crystal Cove? Seen them kiss?

'Seth Jago's got a lot on his plate and on his mind at the moment. Be patient, Emma,' Matthew said. 'Not your finest virtue, I know …'

'Have you come here to insult me?' Emma said, suddenly bridling.

Matthew laughed. 'You've not lost your spark, I see. But no, I didn't come here to insult you. I've brought you something.'

He walked over to the desk, on which sat a small parcel wrapped in red paper all tied up with a wide silver ribbon.

He picked it up and held it out towards Emma. 'Happy birthday.'

Emma took the parcel and hurriedly tore off the wrapping. Inside was a small wooden box, the lid exquisitely carved with a spray of roses and tiny leaves. In one corner was the letter E.

'You made this?' Emma asked. She knew Matthew was clever with his hands. But to have made something just for her.

'I did.'

'Why?'

'Does there have to be a reason?'

'I think so,' Emma said. 'Married men shouldn't be making things for young girls.'

Matthew shrugged. 'I've got a lot to thank you for,' he said. 'You walked into my life like a whirlwind and I thought my cover would be blown as a Customs Officer, but it was quite the opposite. The immediate neighbours and the Jago crews were far more interested in what I might have been getting up to with you in Shingle Cottage than they were in wondering what exactly I *was* doing here.'

'We were mutually useful,' Emma said. 'Even though I didn't realise that at the time.'

'So you understand?'

'I do now,' Emma said. She hugged the box to her. 'Thank you for this.'

'Aren't you going to open it?'

'There's something else?'

Slowly Emma opened the box. She felt her throat close over and tears sprang to her eyes. Her mama's necklace. Her mama's amethyst necklace. The one that had been taken from around the neck of poor dead Sophie Ellison and which had been dangling in the cleavage of Reuben Jago's floosie not so long ago. But still she was thrilled to have it.

Carefully, Emma took it from the box, let the fine chain slip through her fingers until only the amethyst was in the palm of her hand, hard and cool and precious against her skin. 'How did you get it back?'

'Let's just say I called in a few favours with various legal bodies,' Matthew said.

'Then I'm glad you did,' Emma said. 'Thank you.'

'My pleasure. And now perhaps you could get your coat and anything else you might need because we are going out.'

'Out?' Emma said.

'Still doubting what people tell you, I see,' Matthew said, smiling, his eyes holding hers, challenging. 'But yes, out. I'm treating you to lunch – for your birthday. We'll be out for most of the day.'

'Oh, but I can't. There's baby Isabelle. I've left her with Ruby and ...'

Matthew's gaze had strayed from Emma's. He raised a hand in greeting, and Emma turned and saw that it was Mr Smythe coming down the west staircase.

Emma had run out of words now. Mr Smythe was never going to let her just go out for the day when there was his daughter to care for.

'Matthew,' Mr Smythe said. He hurried down the last few steps and strode across the tiled floor. The two men shook hands.

'Thank you for my present, Matthew,' Emma said. 'Really. It's the best present I could ever have.' She turned to Mr Smythe. 'I'll get back to Isabelle now. I've left her with Ruby.'

'Then she can stay with Ruby,' Mr Smythe said. 'Now go and spend your birthday with Matthew as we've arranged.'

'Arranged?' Emma said.

'Why else do you think he is here?' Mr Smythe asked.

Emma didn't know what to say. She looked to Matthew for guidance, but he said nothing. The kindness in his eyes was almost more than Emma could bear – she guessed now that he had arranged this, her first birthday without her parents and Johnnie, especially so she would feel their loss a little less.

Mr Smythe put a hand inside the jacket of his suit and pulled out a leather wallet; dark leather the colour of ebony almost, but with ginger tints in it. It seemed to be bulging with notes. Emma had never seen leather like it – she wondered what it might be, but now wasn't the time to ask.

Mr Smythe took out two white £5 notes and held them out towards Emma. 'A thank you for stepping into the breach, caring for Isabelle, keeping the boys up to scratch with their French ...'

His voice trailed away. He sounded and looked so sad. Broken almost. It was on the tip of Emma's tongue to say she couldn't possibly accept all that money, and she knew Matthew had read her mind because he put a finger to his lips – don't say a word, Emma, the gesture said.

'Take it,' Mr Smythe said. He waggled the notes at Emma. She did as she was told.

'Thank you. I'll look for something nice and bring you the

change,' she said. How crisp and new the notes felt between her fingers.

'You won't,' Mr Smythe said, looking up. 'You will spend it all. I know I've been sharp with you when I shouldn't have been and I apologise for that ...'

'You don't have to,' Emma said. She looked into Mr Smythe's handsome but tired face, and saw that his eyes were glistening with tears. 'I understand. I know what it's like to be sharp when you don't mean to because you're so sad and ...'

'Emma,' Matthew interrupted. 'Your coat. And anything else you need. Mr Smythe knew I was coming and it's all agreed.'

'Someone might ...' Emma began.

She was going to say 'have told *me*' but thought better of it. Hadn't Dr Shaw told her that we can't always plan things for ourselves and have hopes and dreams, and that sometimes it's better to make the best of the situations we find ourselves in? She had two £5 notes in her hand, and Matthew – who she liked very much – wanting to spoil her on her birthday. And a few hours without a squalling and often very smelly baby to look after would be bliss.

'Two minutes,' Emma said, starting to run to her room to fetch her things. She stopped, turned back to Matthew. 'No, make that five minutes. I'll need to change from these work things if I'm going out. Don't go without me.' Then she sped towards the bottom of the stairs.

And the last thing she heard as she scooted along the landing towards the next flight of stairs was Matthew saying, 'That girl,' and his deep, booming laugh.

'Torquay?' Emma said as Matthew took her arm and led her along the quayside to the small ferry that plied across the bay. Mostly it took fish and cabbages to the shops and restaurants, but in the summer months the skipper had started to capitalise on the burgeoning tourist trade and took fare-paying passengers, too.

Like Rome, Torquay was said to be built on seven hills. And her father had once said that gazing at it across the water, Torquay looked to him like Monte Carlo – only more green.

'More potential for you to spend your money in Torquay,' Matthew said. 'More shops.'

'I don't know that I do want to spend it,' Emma said as they reached the ferry. She glanced at Matthew and saw him raise his eyebrows in surprise, and a little smile began to form at the corner of his mouth. Emma thought how lucky his wife was to be married to him. And if his wife knew he was taking her to Torquay, spending the day with her, maybe flirting with her a little.

The skipper greeted Matthew like an old friend. 'Matthew Caunter, you old dog. What brings you here this time?'

'Adam,' Matthew said, shaking the ferryman's hand.

'And who might the lovely young lady be?' Adam asked.

'A friend of mine. Miss Emma Le Goff.'

'Then any friend of Caunter's is a friend of mine.'

The ferryman extended a hand and Emma took it, allowed him to help her into the boat. Red sails hung like wet washing against the mast.

'For a fisherman's daughter I'm a novice sailor,' Emma said. 'I hope I won't be sick.'

'Today?' Adam said. 'It's like a mirror out there. We're going to have to row out a few hundred yards to pick up any breeze at all to sail. But we'll need to move quick, or we'll miss the tide.'

And with that Matthew leapt aboard, too. Emma settled herself on a seat and glanced at the handful of passengers. All seemed very well-dressed. None made eye contact and one couple spoke to one another in whispers behind their hands.

'Were they talking about her? Emma didn't care if they were. She was feeling happy – something she hadn't felt in quite a while now. Even the sadness of not seeing Seth today couldn't dent that happiness – well, not much. As the ferry went through the harbour entrance Emma looked around to see if she could see him on one of the Jago boats, but couldn't. She felt something like relief flood through her that Seth hadn't seen her with Matthew and her shoulders dropped from somewhere around her ears.

The last thing she wanted to do was hurt Seth in some way, what with all he had on his mind at the moment.

'We're meeting my wife at The Lanterns for lunch,' Matthew said.

The ferry had been tied to a bollard, the other passengers had gone ashore and were already hurrying along the quay to whatever it was they were going to do to fill their day.

Emma gazed up towards the villas at the top of the hill – they were huge and imposing. A narrow path zigzagged its way up the hill amongst palm trees. There were more cars here than she'd ever seen in one place at a time before. Smarter carriages, too. More well-groomed horses. This was a rich man's resort indeed. And now *she* was here. How very exciting.

'Did you say we're meeting your wife?'

Emma felt her little bubble of excitement deflate a little.

'Are you hard of hearing or something, Emma Le Goff?' Matthew quipped. 'I always have to say everything twice to you. Yes. My wife. She's called Annie.'

'Why didn't she come to Nase Head House with you, then?'

'You and your questions.' Matthew wagged a finger at her, but jokingly. 'She had some things she wanted to shop for alone. Don't ask me what – shopping's a woman's prerogative.' He laughed. 'She came up with me from Slapton on the carrier's cart. But she came on here by rail. She doesn't like being on the water.'

Matthew jumped onto the landing steps and held out a hand to Emma to help her ashore. Then he looked back towards Adam who touched a finger to the side of his nose. And in that instant Emma knew why Matthew had called for her and brought her to Torquay by ferry. Without his wife.

'You were spying on something. Or someone. Weren't you?' she whispered. 'If you're using me again, Matthew Caunter, I'll …'

'I'm not using you. Trust me. You trusted me enough to stay in Shingle Cottage alone with me, so trust me now. You're sixteen now, Emma, not a child. Please stop acting like one.'

Matthew seemed to have taken on the role of her father without anyone asking him to and Emma was itching to tell him so. But then she fingered the amethyst at her throat. It came to her then that maybe he might have put himself and his professional reputation at risk in getting it back for her.

Emma nodded. 'I'll try.'

'And just in case you think I'm coming the heavy-handed father with you, I'm not. As I told you once – and it was the truth – had you been older and we'd met in different circumstances then …'

'Then you'd better forget you even thought that if we're meeting your wife for lunch.'

Torquay was laid out before her, ready for her to explore, and she was going to do her best to enjoy it all.

'It's been a lovely day,' Emma said.

Much to her surprise she'd liked Matthew's wife, Annie, very much. Annie was much younger than Emma had thought she would be – nearer her own age than Matthew's.

And the two women had giggled their way through the racks of clothes in Rockheys and Williams & Cox, and Bobby's.

Annie had picked out a dress for Emma in the prettiest of greens – chartreuse. It had a self-coloured belt and tiny pearly buttons running from throat to waist. And it flared out deliciously around Emma's ankles, feeling wonderful where it swished against her calves as she spun round for Annie to admire it some more. And then they'd cooed over shoes in shop windows until Emma had seen a pair she really loved and Annie had insisted she go in and try them on. And buy them. And a bag to match. And then some earrings – pearls – had been bought in Hadleighs, only *the* most expensive jeweller in the whole of Torquay.

Lunch had been eaten in the restaurant of The Lanterns hotel. Lobster soup and chicken poached in white wine followed by a pudding Emma hadn't gone much on – too heavy and doughy and not at all right after such a delicate main course.

She'd shocked Matthew and Annie by asking to speak to the manager. Then asking him if he would be interested in French pastries and tarts, the pastry crumble-soft and butter-scented.

'At a later date,' Emma had finished. 'My business is only a fledgling one at the moment.'

And she and Annie had giggled together at Matthew's discomfiture. But it had sown more seeds in Emma's mind about what she really wanted to do with her life. She could see herself with a small hotel that served only the best of everything. Sometime. Sometime in the future.

'Annie enjoyed it, too,' Matthew said.

They'd all come back together on the train. Annie had declined the short, but very steep, climb up to Nase Head House from the station. Her feet really ached, she said, from all the walking around the shops and she'd wait for

Matthew to deliver Emma safely to the hotel. She would sit in the Ladies Waiting Room at the station until his return.

'You can leave me here,' Emma said when they reached the gateway to Nase Head House. 'You'd best get back to Annie. No harm's going to come to me between here and the front door.'

'I hope not,' Matthew said. 'But I'll see you inside. I promised Rupert I'd deliver you back safe and sound.'

He slipped a hand under Emma's elbow and guided her up the steep drive. At the top of the steps Emma turned towards him and said, 'Annie's lovely. Don't upset her any more by taking on dangerous covert jobs.'

'I won't, bossy boots. In fact this could well be the last time we see one another – you and me. Today, I was finalising one last job. Annie and I are leaving for America soon.'

Matthew pushed open the double doors and ushered Emma inside, all Emma's carriers of purchases dangling from his other hand.

'At the risk of you thinking I'm deaf or disbelieving, I have to ask – America?'

'Yes. So, this is probably goodbye, Emma.'

Goodbye? For one silly moment Emma had harboured thoughts of doubling up her list of friends to include Annie. But it wasn't going to be.

On impulse she turned to face Matthew, put her arms around his neck and kissed his cheek. 'Thank you, thank you for a wonderful day, and well … for everything.'

It was thanks to Matthew she had the roof of Nase Head House over her head. She was sad that she probably wouldn't see him ever again, of course she was. But she would never forget him.

Matthew kissed her on the forehead. Put his free hand to the back of her head.

And that's when she saw Seth.

He was sitting on the leather seat in the centre of the foyer. He had a bunch of roses in one hand and a large parcel wrapped in pink paper in the other. He seemed to freeze on the spot. Their eyes met – hers and Seth's – and even with a good few yards distance between them Emma could see the pain and hurt and loss in Seth's eyes. Seth stood up and, without looking at her, marched straight past and out through the double doors, his gifts hanging one in each hand at his sides.

Oh, if only she'd insisted Matthew leave her outside the hotel. She had a feeling that as well as this being the last time she would see Matthew, it would probably be a very, very long time before she would see Seth again, either.

'You're not the only woman around!' Seth yelled across the inky water of the harbour. A gull, head tucked down in sleep, fluttered on the rim of a rowing boat, startled momentarily by Seth's shout, but settled down again.

He looked back up towards Nase Head House where lights were still on. He shook his head to try and banish the picture he had in it of Emma kissing Matthew Caunter, but couldn't. And then that kiss Matthew had given Emma so tenderly on her forehead. They were probably still in there, arms entwined, and he'd been forgotten by them both.

Seth considered taking a boat out in the darkness – letting it drift with him in it – even though after only a few minutes he felt sick whenever he was on the water. Well, he was feeling pretty sick about things anyway at the moment – what difference could a bit of motion sickness make? He'd have a pint or two in The Blue Anchor. And some female company. There'd be plenty of women in there who, for the exchange of a few florins, would permit him their favours if he was so inclined as to accept them. It looked as though his brothers had been right about him wasting his time on

Emma after all, didn't it? But that didn't mean he had to behave like them.

Emma had looked so happy and glowing coming back with Caunter that he thought he might explode with rage and thump the living daylights out of the man. But what good would that have done? It would only have set him fairly and squarely in the same camp as his brothers and his pa, wouldn't it?

Seth turned, kicked a discarded beer bottle into the water, and headed for the inn. If his future was going to be without Emma Le Goff, then so be it.

Chapter Fifteen

Seth had wined and dined a few women in the nine months that had passed since the night of Emma's birthday.

There had been a few weeks in May when the country was mourning the death of King Edward VII, when everyone had worn black and no one had dared to consider enjoying themselves, but that time had passed now. All the talk was of the Coronation of King George V to come, and for the women, what they were going to wear to the parties that were being organised for the occasion.

He was meeting one such woman now. Caroline Prentiss. Whilst she was the daughter of the most successful builder in the area – Charles Maunder – she was also a widow, older than Seth by a good ten years. He was meeting Caroline for the fifth time, feeling anxious but excited, too. She'd intimated that she would be happy to welcome Seth into her bed as long as he was discreet and didn't boast about it to his friends. And Seth had to admit that the offer appealed to him, although he hadn't taken her up on it yet. Might tonight be the night? Caroline was pretty enough – her blonde hair piled on top of her head and almost always fixed with a diamanté clip, exposing a long, creamy neck that only a cadaver wouldn't be tempted to kiss. The exact opposite of Emma in looks, if truth be told. Why did he still persist in comparing every woman to Emma? It would have to stop.

Seth walked on towards Church Road where Caroline lived. Her late husband – a solicitor – had left her not only with a fine house but with substantial savings, so rumour had it. There had been no children of the marriage, for which Caroline had told Seth she was grateful.

'You're late, Seth,' Caroline said, when the maid showed

him into the drawing-room. 'You may go, Giles,' she said, turning to her maid. 'Weren't you telling me your mother has been ill and you're anxious to see her?'

'Yes, Ma'am.'

'Then, go to her. Stay the night.'

'Thank you, Ma'am.'

The maid scurried off as though she was afraid Caroline might change her mind.

Caroline returned her attention to Seth. 'As I said, you're late. But I could forgive you.' She ran the tip of her tongue along the edge of her top lip.

Seth raised his hands towards Caroline in supplication. He *was* late, there was no denying it. He'd walked the long way round to Church Street – via Nase Head House in fact, a route he took often in the hope he'd have the courage to walk up the steps, ask for Emma, apologise for his silence. The longer the rift went on, the harder it was going to be to heal. He'd been stupid to be jealous of Caunter because the man had long left for America, so he'd heard. The kiss he'd seen Emma give him, and the one she'd been given in return, had been goodbye kisses, that was all.

'Paperwork,' Seth lied. With a businessman father, Caroline would know how much paperwork was involved in running a business. He could hardly tell her he was late because he'd strolled, oh so slowly, past Nase Head House in the hope of seeing Emma Le Goff, could he? 'My apologies.'

'Accepted,' Caroline said, stretching out a long, slim arm towards Seth, inviting him to kiss her hand.

Seth complied. Caroline's hand felt icy and he jerked his shoulders.

'I know. I'm cold, aren't I? Cold waiting for you,' Caroline said.

'I'm sorry.'

'So you said.'

'You'll soon warm up with some good food inside you. I've booked a table at The Grand …'

'I don't know that I want to go out, Seth,' Caroline purred. 'I'm too tired for the trek to Torquay. You can ring and cancel.' She waved an arm in the direction of her telephone. 'I'd rather stay in. You can warm me up. Warm us both up.'

Seth knew exactly what she meant by that remark.

'Giles knows I'm here,' he said, playing for time, not at all sure that he wanted to be Caroline's 'secret' any longer. While they'd dined in hotel restaurants out of the town, where they were unlikely to be seen, it could only be a matter of time before someone spotted them. The whole thing – the subterfuge – made him feel second rate. And yet …

'And I asked Giles to leave out some cold cuts and pickles. Enough for two. The table's all set in the dining-room. I pay her enough to forget she was asked to do that and to know that you're here.'

Caroline fingered a gold locket dangling on a chain in her cleavage. Seth struggled not to look, but it was impossible. Caroline Prentiss was a fine woman, a very fine woman indeed. She took a deep breath and her breasts rose, pointing themselves at Seth almost, and he felt a stirring inside him. Lust.

Seth knew in that moment that tonight would be the night he took up Caroline's offer to share her bed.

''Ere, Emma,' Ruby said. 'Have you heard?'

'Heard what?' Emma said. Ruby was forever asking her things she couldn't possibly answer. 'Tell me. I'm not a mind reader.'

'Oh, sorry. I forgot you're not 100% genius, Miss Le Goff,' Ruby giggled. 'What with the French you're spouting all the time. Those boys were yattering away to one another yesterday on your half day, and they could have been saying I was an old witch for all I know.'

Emma laughed. 'You'll never know, will you?'

'And you won't tell.' Ruby stuck her tongue out playfully at Emma.

'Of course not. Anyway, what was it I may or may not have heard?'

'Only that there's rumours doing the rounds that Carter Jago's name is being mentioned in the same sentence as the murder of that poor girl ...'

'Sophie Ellison,' Emma said, a sudden flashback to the day she'd found Sophie's body making her feel nauseous. She swallowed the feeling away.

'Her,' Ruby said. 'That was the name I heard being bandied about. Seems the police have been in and out of all the inns asking questions. And it seems there are lots willing to tell what Carter Jago did to 'em against their wills for the sight of a shiny sixpence from those asking the questions.'

'If it's only rumours, then you can discount them,' Emma said. She doubted very much that the police would be handing out shiny sixpences in return for answers to their questions. Didn't she know, firsthand, that rumours were almost always only that?

'Rape, Emma,' Ruby whispered. 'Can you imagine a more horrible thing?'

A ripple of fear snaked its way up Emma's spine.

'Let's not talk of such things,' she said. 'I've work to do. Those children need to be washed and dressed and ready for their papa to take on a drive in half-an-hour. I'll need to jump to it.'

'That's me dismissed, then.' Ruby laughed, and scuttled off.

Emma hurried towards the nursery, a stone on her heart that someone might come to question her at some stage about the night Carter Jago tried to assault her. If Seth was asked if he knew anything, then he might tell that his brother had assaulted her. Mightn't he? Or Matthew – who as far as Emma knew was still in America. He knew because she'd told him and he'd dressed her cut forehead.

She wished with all her heart she hadn't said a single thing about it to anyone now – although, of course, Matthew had had to know.

Emma lived on tenterhooks for weeks. But no one came to Nase Head House to question her, and she began to breathe a little easier. She was settling down at the hotel, grateful to have a good roof over her head and food in her belly. And, now she was used to it, caring for Isabelle wasn't as arduous as she'd thought it would be. When the child slept in the day, she was able to go to the kitchen and make tarte tatin or a savoury tart for Mr Smythe and the children.

Today was her half day and with nothing to do and no one to do it with, Emma decided to take some flowers and put them on the graves of her parents and Johnnie. She'd been bold and asked Mr Smythe if she might have some roses from the border in front of the dining-room – the bushes were groaning with them; deep peach roses with a heavenly scent. And Mr Smythe had smiled and said that yes, of course she could. And why didn't she take some for her room while she was about it? 'You're becoming invaluable to me, Emma,' was what Mr Smythe had said, and Emma had shivered at his words – she didn't want to become invaluable to him, that was the last thing she needed. But she knew which side her bread was buttered for the moment, thanked him, and took the flowers.

And now, as Emma made her way through the lych-gate into the graveyard of St. Mary's she was on tenterhooks again. Might Seth be there laying flowers on his mother's grave?

A part of her hoped he would be, but another part hoped he wouldn't because, while she'd written to him at least a dozen times, he'd only replied once – and that rather stiffly, if politely, wishing her well, saying he was very busy and he regretted he wouldn't have time to see her for a while.

Emma had clung onto that phrase – *for a while*. There was hope in that phrase, she thought.

Emma fetched fresh water from the tap in the corner and filled the tin vase that was set into the tablet of the memorial stone Seth had paid for on her mama's and Johnnie's grave. She began to set the roses in, one by one, turning them this way and that for the best presentation.

'Emma?'

No need to guess who the speaker might be. She knew. Didn't she hear his voice every night in her head as she went to sleep?

'Hello, Seth,' she said, standing up, turning to face him. She took a deep breath. She was laying her heart on the line and she knew it. 'I hoped you might be here. It's been ages since I've seen you. I've missed you.'

'Mmm,' Seth said, lips pressed together.

Emma waited for him to say he'd missed her, too, but he didn't. He didn't think anything of her any more, did he? He didn't have any flowers with him, though, did he? Unless he'd already placed them on his ma's grave? Emma resisted the urge to look and see if he had.

'I expect you've heard about Carter,' Seth said.

'Only rumours.'

'They're not rumours any more. Evidence is piling up and Carter will be in Court again at some stage, charged with Sophie Ellison's murder. I saw you walking this way, so I followed you. I didn't want to write to you about it in case the letter got into the wrong hands and you were questioned. But in case you hadn't heard ...'

'I hadn't. Not that bit. The bit about him having to go to Court again, I mean,' Emma said. She twisted her hands over and over, anxious that she might be questioned, that the police would call at Nase Head House. She could well imagine the alarm that would cause – and the rumours that would go with it.

'Don't worry,' Seth said. He patted Emma's hand lightly before taking it away again. 'I haven't told anyone what Carter tried to do to you, Emma. Even though I was asked if there was anything I knew that could be held against my brother.'

'Thank you,' Emma said. 'I don't think I would be able to bear it if I had to go to Court, swear on the Bible, face Carter across a courtroom.'

'It's why I kept quiet,' Seth said.

'Thank you,' Emma said again. Seth still cared about her if he was trying to save her from that ordeal, didn't he? 'And I'm sorry, truly sorry, that the Jago name will be all over the newspapers again, on everyone's lips in the inns and ...'

'I can cope well enough with that,' Seth said. 'I don't think there's anything about my pa's and brothers' behaviour that can shock me now. Let's change the subject, shall we?'

Please, Emma thought, please – yes, let's change the subject. Ask me to walk down to Crystal Cove with you so we can pick up where we left off. Hold me in your arms again, give me that second kiss I've been waiting so very long for.

'It's my half day,' Emma said, smiling up at him. 'We could ...'

'I'm sorry, Emma, I can't do what I think you're about to suggest. I've been seeing someone,' Seth interrupted.

Well, of course he had. A handsome man like Seth. She was stupid not to have thought of that before laying her soul bare before him.

'Who?' Emma said, knowing she was looking even more stupid now by asking.

'I'd rather not say.'

'Someone with more money to spend on finer clothes and shoes and hats than I have, no doubt. Is she rich?'

Emma only had two hats. Her navy blue felt for winter – the hand-me-down from the doctor's wife – and the straw one she'd bought for pence and was wearing now against the hot July sunshine. At the moment, her straw was trimmed with a green ribbon the colour of a Granny Smith apple – no doubt her face was the same shade she was so jealous.

'I can't tell you that either.'

Seth took a watch from the pocket of his jacket, glanced at it and replaced it.

'Then don't let me keep you from her,' Emma said, trying to salvage what dignity she had left. 'Whoever she is.'

'You're not. But I wanted you to know about Carter before ...'

'Does *she* know?' Emma knew she'd made the word 'she' sound like something best left in the gutter, and she hadn't meant to. It just came out.

'Yes. She reads the newspapers, Emma. Although I have, of course, spoken to her about it.'

'Oh,' Emma responded, not knowing what else to say. Seth was someone else's now.

'I'm sorry,' Seth said, 'that things turned out between us the way they did. I ...'

'Don't apologise,' Emma said.

'But I must. There's nothing I'd like more at this moment than to spend your half day with you, but it would be discourteous. In the circumstances.'

'So don't,' Emma said.

She turned her back on Seth then, bent down to finish arranging the roses for her mama and Johnnie, fully aware

225

that it was Seth who had provided the tablet with their names on, and the tin vase. 'Thank you for letting me know about, about …'

'Carter,' Seth finished for her.

He knew she was struggling even to say the name, didn't he? He still cared. Dared she hope he might finish with whoever it was he was being so secretive about and ask her out instead?

She stood up and turned to face him. Smiled. Willed him to give her some sign that he might.

'I'd better go,' Seth said.

He was looking at her the same way he'd looked at her just moments before he'd kissed her down at Crystal Cove – it seemed so long ago now, and yet only yesterday at the same time.

'Before you kiss me again?' Emma whispered, shredding every last ounce of decency and dignity.

'Yes,' Seth said.

He kissed his fingertips and blew the kiss towards Emma, before turning on his heel and rushing back down the path.

Emma threw herself into her work at Nase Head House and tried to forget all about Seth – or rather she waited for Seth to contact her and tell her he was no longer seeing anyone at all and that he would like her, Emma, to walk out with him instead.

But Seth made no contact with her, beyond two brief notes to tell her that the enquiries into Carter Jago were still ongoing – there seemed to be no end to it, he said. He signed his notes 'Yours, Seth' – except he wasn't hers, was he?

So, on her half days, instead of going into town to shop or to go to the bank to deposit her wages, where she might bump into Seth, she stayed close to the hotel. If the weather was fine then she took Isabelle out in the perambulator that Mr Smythe had bought at huge expense from a catalogue.

It had wheels almost as big as cart wheels, Emma thought, but it was easy enough to wheel over the rutted paths of the lanes behind the hotel with Isabelle laughing and smiling at everything. She would do just that today. And while she was there she'd see if there were enough blackberries to go with the apples for a tarte tatin.

Almost before she knew it, July had given way to a busy August, the hotel full with visitors. Emma had been fully occupied with the twins in their holiday from school, happy that they were becoming almost fluent in French. And now September had come around once again.

'Letter for you,' Mr Bell said, as Emma made her way to the boot room to fetch the perambulator. She'd done her best to walk quietly so that Mr Bell, who seemed to be getting more hard of hearing by the day and should be pensioned off in Emma's opinion, wouldn't hear her. But he had.

Another letter? From Seth? Her heart hoped it was the letter she'd been dreaming and wishing for, but her head told her it more than likely wasn't.

'Thank you,' Emma said, taking the proffered letter.

No, not a letter. It was too stiff for that. A card. A birthday card? It was her seventeenth birthday and she'd been doing her level best to forget it was. There'd been no £5 notes from Mr Smythe this morning, as there had been on her sixteenth birthday when Matthew Caunter had called to take her out for the day.

Perhaps the card was from Matthew?

She hurried on her way to the boot room, where she would be able to open her card in privacy.

It was from Seth. A birthday card. A simple drawing of some roses. Peach roses like the ones she'd been placing on her mama's and Johnnie's graves when last she'd seen him. The choice of card told Emma that he was still thinking of her.

Did that mean he'd finished with whoever it was he'd been seeing and would call on her soon?

Chapter Sixteen

'Don't be stupid, Seth,' Olly said. 'Of course you're going to be there. You're a client as well as a friend.'

'I know that. But I'm still *not* going,' Seth said.

Olly was inviting him to a dinner he was giving for his clients at Nase Head House, and he wasn't going there – especially as Caroline was also going to be there. She'd told him as much. It wouldn't be fair to Emma – he knew how she felt about him, and Caroline was bound to speak to him at some stage during the evening, wasn't she? Discreetly, or under the cover of other people present. But Emma might see, and he didn't want to hurt her anymore than he already had.

'One excellent reason why not,' Olly said. He called for the barman to pour another pint of ale into his and Seth's tankards.

Seth was glad of the lull in the conversation – it gave him time to formulate his reply.

'Because,' Seth said, resuming their talk as the barman went to serve another customer and they were alone again with no one within earshot, 'and this is strictly between you and me, I know you've invited Caroline Prentiss ...'

'I'm not sure I follow? I have invited her, yes, because I've built a boat for her father, and ...'

'Olly, stop. I've been seeing Caroline Prentiss. Discreetly.'

'You should have said before. Older woman. Experienced. You dog. But for your information, I've done the seating plan now. And as it happens I've already seated you together. My thinking was you're a single man, she's a widow, so pure chance on my part ...'

'Well, undo it. I want to end things with Caroline.'

'Ooooh, feathers will fly. I bet you've enjoyed the bits under the bedcovers, though?' Olly laughed. He gave Seth a playful punch on the arm.

Seth shrugged. He didn't have to answer that.

'Anyway, like I said, the seating plan has gone to the hotel now. Couldn't you do me a favour and turn up? It's a bit late in the day for me to find a single male to sit beside the charming-the-pants-off-you Mrs Prentiss.'

'I don't know ...'

'You could tell her you want to end things, *sotto voce,* over the dessert,' Olly said.

'She's going to love that,' Seth said, unable to stop a smile from turning up the corners of his mouth.

'So you'll come. Good. Now, how about some mutton stew to go with this beer?'

'Why not?' Seth said, although he didn't think he'd be able to swallow a mouthful. He only had himself to blame for the situation he was in, didn't he? And therefore, he was the only one who could get himself out of it.

'I don't know I should be showing you this,' Ruby said, rushing into Emma's room. 'And I'm certain you ain't going to want to know. An' if I gets caught up here instead of doing me work then I'm for the chop. Only I knows you're sweet ...'

'What, Ruby?' Honestly, Ruby could be so irritating at times. 'What's that you've got to show me?'

'A card, Em,' Ruby said. 'Me and Stephen Bailey've been set to laying the place settings for Mr Underwood's dinner ...'

'Why you? That's Harry's job.'

'He's gone sick, hasn't he? The influenza. It's all over town like a rash of measles. Well, up this side of the harbour it is. If Harry's got it then we might all go down with it, and ...'

'Don't be so dramatic, Ruby,' Emma said, although inside she was terrified the influenza might rip through the hotel. She wasn't fearful for herself so much, but for Isabelle – she was a baby still. 'The card?'

Emma held out her hand, and with a sigh, Ruby placed the card on it.

Emma turned it over.

Fishcombe Marine Celebratory Dinner
Saturday, 10th December, 1910
Mr Seth Jago

'But that's not all, Em. Oh, I was so pleased at first to find it. I thought maybe you could be about and speak to him. But his card was right next to one with Mrs Caroline Prentiss' name on it. Why is Seth sitting next to her? She's a widow, so Stephen said, God only knows how he knows. I didn't stop to ask.' Ruby took a deep breath and prattled on. 'Oh, Em, you like Seth, don't you? I know you haven't had a minute, not even on your half day, to see him, have you? Well, I'm guessing you haven't 'cos you ain't spoken to me much about him in a while. Is Seth seeing Mrs Prentiss now?'

Ruby seemed to have run out of things to say – or breath, or both.

So that was who Seth was seeing? Why would he have been seated next to Mrs Prentiss otherwise?

'By the look on your face, if you didn't know before you do now. And you don't much like it. What's he doing with her? She's ancient.'

'Ancient?'

'At least thirty, I'd say. And Seth's …'

'I know how old Seth is, thank you.'

'So did you know?'

'I knew he was seeing someone,' Emma said. She handed the place-setting card back to Ruby. 'You'd better put this back where it belongs before someone notices it's gone missing and comes looking for it. Now, run.'

Ruby ran.

And Emma put her head in her hands and let the tears come. It was going to be too much to see Seth with Mrs Prentiss.

'Please, God,' she sniffed, 'if you're listening, let me have a touch of Harry's influenza by tonight. Just enough to be indisposed so I have to stay in my room. But not enough to kill me.'

God hadn't been listening.

Or if He had, He'd given the influenza to the wrong person. Mr Bell. Emma had seen him being escorted to his room, coughing and spluttering and looking very poorly indeed, by Stephen Bailey.

When Mr Smythe came into Isabelle's bedroom where Emma was settling the child for the night, she felt her stomach plummet to somewhere around her knees. She was dreading what Mr Smythe was going to say.

'We must hope Isabelle falls asleep quickly, and stays sleeping,' he said. 'You see …'

'Why?' Emma said.

'If you'd let me finish … Mr Bell is indisposed. I will need you to take his place this evening. I can't ask you to wait at table because you haven't been taught how. But you'll be able to manage taking the coats easily enough, I'm sure. We have an important dinner. Clients of Fishcombe Marine.'

Emma already knew about that – Ruby had shown her the card, hadn't she? Besides, she'd overheard two of the waiters debating how much they were likely to get in tips.

But on reception? The worst place she could possibly be.

Everyone would come to the desk with their coats and she'd have to hand them a ticket then hang their coats in the cloakroom for them. Seth would be there.

'Couldn't Ruby do that and I'll take over …'

'No, she can't, Emma. She isn't the right sort of person to be on the reception desk. Besides, Cook tells me he needs her to help him today. I've already asked Grainger to keep an eye on the children. Get yourself down to reception. And be sharp about it.'

Emma thought about saying Isabelle wouldn't be happy if she woke up hungry or wet or just needing a cuddle to find it wasn't her or Ruby doing the cuddling, because Ruby had been detailed to be in the kitchen, but thought better of it. It wasn't her place to sort the running of the hotel and Mr Smythe's domestic arrangements.

Emma left the room – but sharpish it most certainly wasn't. And she wouldn't be rushing down to reception, either. The dinner guests wouldn't be arriving for another hour. She had time to make herself look as good as she possibly could – let Seth see just what he was letting pass him by.

'Mr Jago,' Caroline said, sidling up to him, but not touching – her voice a purr. 'I had no idea *you*'d be here.'

Seth had watched her weave her way through the throng of Olly's guests, making her way to him. But subtly – she'd stopped to pass a word with this one and that. But now she was here.

And she didn't sound in the least put out that he hadn't told her he'd be attending Olly's function. But Mr Jago indeed. In case anyone was to overhear, obviously.

'Olly invited me. We're friends. And he does repairs to my boats.'

'I don't need your reasons for being here chapter and verse. But seeing as you *are* here, you can make yourself useful,' Caroline said. 'You can take my fur to reception. I hate queueing for things. I see my parents are deep in conversation with some boor already.' She turned sideways on to Seth and slipped her fox fur cape from one shoulder – the better for him to admire her milky flesh, no doubt.

Anxiously, Seth searched the doorways where staff were standing waiting to be called to do some task or other, looking for Emma, but couldn't see her. He breathed a little more easily.

'My fur.' Caroline leaned towards him. 'I don't bite,' she whispered. 'At least, not in public.'

She made little gnawing gestures with her teeth that Seth hoped and prayed no one else had seen. He was regretting every second he'd spent with Caroline now.

'Of course,' Seth said. 'Your fur. I'll take it to reception. Ah, there's your father. He's walking this way with your mother. I'd better ...'

'Golly, Mr Jago, anyone would think you were nervous about a little dinner given by a carpenter.'

'Boatbuilder,' Seth corrected her. 'Olly's a boatbuilder. A master craftsman, in fact. You should know that, seeing as he's so recently finished building a boat for your father.'

'I stand corrected. Oh, there's the waiter with the drinks. If you could just relieve me of my fur, I'll go and stand over there and wait for him to glide by. I hope it's *good* champagne,' Caroline giggled, slipping her other shoulder from her cape. Seth took it, careful not to touch her. She seemed, Seth thought, to be totally unconcerned that people might think, from her action, they were well acquainted.

'It will be,' Seth said to Caroline's retreating back. Olly might like a drink or two in the pubs, like many his age did, but he was an astute businessman as well.

He made his way across the foyer towards the reception desk and almost stopped breathing. Emma was behind the desk dealing with the coats. He hadn't expected her to be there. How beautiful she looked. Wonderful even. He thought, in that moment, that his heart might burst with love for her, while at the same time wishing he was anywhere but waiting his turn. But his wishes would go unanswered.

'Mr Jago,' Emma said, holding out her hands towards him to take his coat and Caroline's fur wrap when his turn came. 'May I take those for you?'

Mr Jago? Well, of course she would have had to call him by his surname, but it still felt alien to him coming from Emma's lips. How glorious and so very desirable, she looked – even in a plain white blouse and a black skirt. Her hair was shining under the lamp over the desk. Her skin glowed with health, and how good *that* was to see after all she'd been through. Her eyes glistened and he hoped that wasn't with tears; that he wasn't the cause of any distress. Did she know he was here with Caroline?

Stupid thought – he had two garments in his arms and one of them a woman's. She'd know he was here with someone.

'Thank you,' Seth said.

Their hands touched for the briefest of moments as he handed over the coats.

'You look beautiful,' Seth said, *sotto voce*, when Emma turned around to face him again, and was heartened when a flush came to her cheeks and she put a hand to her left one. She tore two tickets from a small book and handed them to him.

'You can return to Mrs Prentiss now,' Emma said, coldly. 'There are others waiting behind you.'

So she *did* know who he'd been seeing. She'd probably seen the seating plan Olly had handed in and put two and two together.

'Of course,' Seth said. He lowered his voice. 'Might I speak to you later?'

He would tell her that this was a duty dinner for Olly. Tell her that this was definitely the last time he would be in Caroline's company. Just seeing Emma told him where his heart really lay.

But Emma shook her head. 'No,' she said. 'You may not. Please don't ask me again.'

She stepped sideways behind the desk, turned her smile on the next guest. He'd been dismissed.

Chapter Seventeen

'Mr Smythe,' Emma said, 'I want to ask you something.'

She'd been asked to cover on reception because Mr Bell was still ill. Thank goodness Ruby had finished her morning chores quickly and was able to see to Isabelle.

'Then make it quick,' Mr Smythe said. 'I have to be at the bank for one-thirty.'

'Of course. It's just that I wonder if you might consider having a Christmas tree for the children?'

Emma had long given up hoping he might spend more time with his children than merely kissing them goodnight, or chastising them with a strap across their hands if they were naughty, as the twins often were. But Christmas was fast approaching and he'd made no arrangements, as far as she could tell, for any sort of celebration for them. Or presents.

'A Christmas tree?'

'Yes. I thought the children might like to make decorations for it. I understand that last Christmas was too soon after …'

'Yes, yes. We both know why a thing like that was out of the question last year. Get a Christmas tree if you must. I suppose we must be grateful to Prince Albert for introducing that little bit of jollity into our lives.' He tapped the desk between them. 'Take the money from petty cash. And while you're at it take some money and buy some presents for my children. Make up stockings. My wife always took on that sort of thing, although it was a shoe by the hearth in the French fashion.'

'Then that's what I'll do for them,' Emma said, glad to see the man had a heart after all.

She smiled at him, and was surprised when he smiled back.

'I've had another thought, Emma. Perhaps we might go into town together and you can show me what it is you think my children might want from Rossiter's.'

'Oh, I don't …I mean, it's not appropriate. I …'

'It will be perfectly appropriate, Emma. As you are my sons' French tutor and have the care of my daughter it will be perfectly in order for us to be seen together on an errand for them.'

'Oh,' Emma said. That was the last thing she had expected him to say. She wished she hadn't mentioned the tree now.

'Mr Bell assures me he will be fit for duty the day after tomorrow. We will go then, you and I. And while I have Christmas on my mind, I wonder if I might put on a little something for the staff. You all work so hard.'

And then, not waiting for Emma to respond he went on his way.

Goodness, Emma thought, whatever had got into him?

'Good morning, Giles,' Seth said when Caroline's front door was opened. 'May I see Mrs Prentiss?'

'I'll ask, Sir,' Giles said.

But as the maid turned to fetch her mistress, Caroline came rushing down the hallway. 'Seth,' she said. 'I hope no one saw you …'

'Not that I know of.'

'Good. Daddy's been asking me if you and I are better acquainted than we ought to be, given your father and brothers are in prison.'

'What did you tell him?'

'What do you think? Your attentions to me at Mr Underwood's dinner were only those of a gentleman to an unattached lady. But be that as it may, this is still a lovely surprise to see you.'

A surprise, probably, Seth thought, but it was doubtful

she'd consider it a lovely one. Giles stood looking dumbstruck at the conversation going on in front of her – did Caroline think her maid was deaf? In that moment Seth felt unutterably sad for the poor young woman – it was as though she didn't exist.

'May I come in? For a moment?'

'Of course.' Caroline turned to Giles and told her to go to the kitchen and begin preparation for lunch. And to stay there until she was called.

The maid scuttled off and Caroline led the way to her drawing-room. She sat on a couch and indicated for Seth to sit beside her.

'I won't be stopping,' he said. 'I've come to apologise for not returning your telephone calls. Mrs Drew gave me the messages and I ought to have acknowledged them. That was very bad-mannered of me.'

While installing a telephone so he could be kept abreast of developments concerning his father and brothers in Court had its advantages, it also had its disadvantage – copious phone calls from Caroline being one of them. Not to mention the fact Mrs Drew now also knew he had been seeing her.

'I understand. You've been busy with the boats. Daddy said that whenever he sees you, you always seem to be seeing a boat off, or unloading one. But you're forgiven. Now, do come and sit beside me.'

Caroline patted the seat beside her.

'No. I have something else to say. And that couldn't be said over the telephone. It needs to be said in person. I can't say I haven't enjoyed times spent in your company because you are a very lovely woman. But I can't give you my heart, and for a relationship ...'

'I wasn't asking for your heart,' Caroline snapped. 'And I wasn't stupid enough to think I had it. There was always part of you that was detached, if you get my meaning.'

'I do,' Seth said. Always his head and his heart were with Emma, even if his body had been with Caroline. 'And I apologise for that.'

'Whoever she is, I hope she makes you happy. That body of yours will go to waste if she doesn't. I'll get Giles to see you out.'

And that, Seth thought as Giles ushered him from the front door, is me dismissed – but thankfully with no bad feelings, it seemed.

He hurried on into town. He had Christmas presents to buy for Mrs Drew and Edward. And for his pa and brothers, even though he felt less charitable towards them than he should, given Christmas was a festival of giving.

And Emma. He wanted to buy something for Emma. Some perfume, perhaps? His ma had always loved scent, as she called it. Or a pretty scarf. Something frivolous she might not need but which she would love.

His head – and his heart – was full of Emma. He knew that although she'd been frosty towards him the night of Olly's dinner, and had said that no, she didn't want to speak to him or for him to ask her again, she had reason for it. He had respected her wishes and given her time. But the Emma he'd met laying roses on her mama's grave in the churchyard was the real Emma – her feelings for him had been there in her eyes then, right enough. He just hoped she would realise it soon, too. His Christmas present to her would surely tell her how he felt about her.

With the happy prospect of having her back in his life soon, now that he had broken things off quite conclusively with Caroline, Seth approached Rossiter's. The window was decorated lavishly for the festivities with bows and swags and tails and he stopped to look at the displays of clothes and china and glass, and clocks. There were three cars parked outside. Three. The town would be over-run

239

with cars soon. He'd even considered getting one himself, once he built up a healthier – legal – profit from the fishing. How wonderful it would be to be able to drive Emma somewhere – the moors perhaps? Or even as far as Cornwall. He had a fancy to see Padstow, see how the fishing fleets operated there. They made greater profits than he did, so he'd heard.

Deep in thought, Seth approached the door of Rossiter's. The door was being held wide for someone coming out.

Emma. She had an armful of parcels and was laughing. She had a felt hat on her head – midnight blue, with feathers nodding in the breeze. Who was she buying the presents for? He made to walk towards her when his question was answered for him.

Mr Smythe from Nase Head House was with her. He was as close to Emma as he could be without touching her. And he was laughing, too, looking down at Emma. Happy in her company. Neither had noticed him in the throng of other shoppers going in and out.

So, that was the lie of the land. That was why Emma had been frosty to him when she'd taken his and Caroline's coats. It was nothing to do with her having been jealous he was with Caroline. Emma had her feet well and truly under the table at Nase Head House, didn't she?

Seth turned on his heel. He didn't feel in the least bit like buying presents now. Or being charitable.

'A clothes allowance?' Emma said, after she'd settled two very excited little boys and a very tired baby girl for the night. 'You want to give me that as a clothes allowance?'

Mr Smythe was dangling a £5 note between thumb and forefinger. He'd given a small present to every single member of staff, and treated them to a lavish Christmas lunch with wine and brandy, but she was certain she was the only one being given a clothes allowance. She didn't know that she wanted it.

All she wanted at this moment was to get back to her room, because she was tired, too.

'You do understand what a clothes allowance is, Emma?'

'Of course I do. It's for clothes to wear here, in the hotel. But I've got my black skirt and white blouses to wear with it ...'

'This is for occasions when you might be with the children. Outside the hotel. Occasions when I might also be with you.'

Emma wanted to talk to him about that – about the children. Isabelle was taking up more and more of her time now that she was walking. And beginning to talk. She could no longer put her in her cot, certain she'd lie down and go to sleep while she got on with something else. No, the child hollered for all she was worth if Emma did that these days.

'I'd like to ask you something, Mr Smythe,' Emma said.

'Please do.'

'Have there been any applicants for the postion of nanny? Someone who's qualified for the post? You said you were advertising ...'

'None suitable,' Mr Smythe interrupted.

He looked away from Emma as he spoke and she had a feeling he wasn't being entirely truthful with her.

Perhaps it was time for her to look for somewhere else to work, which would force the issue of Mr Smythe engaging a trained nanny. Somewhere far away from Nase Head House. It had hurt her too much to see Seth with Caroline Prentiss – which she had done. They'd been sitting side by side at Mr Underwood's dinner, chatting and laughing, and while Emma wished now she hadn't spied on them through a crack in the door, she had, and so she knew. Often she wanted to wind back time. But no one could do that, could they?

However rich they were, however important, and whatever dreadful thing had happened to them.

'The money, Emma,' Mr Smythe prompted.

Still Emma kept her hands clenched by her side.

If she took Mr Smythe's £5 note then it would be like a shackle. More and more would be expected of her. More than she wanted to give. But to refuse him now, at Christmas, when he'd been so unexpectedly generous to everyone, would be churlish.

'Would it hurt you so very much to take it?' Mr Smythe asked.

Emma took a deep breath. Swallowed.

'I'll bring you the receipts,' she said. 'So you can see what I've spent your money on.'

And in the saying of it she felt the metaphorical shackle lock around her ankle. It looked like she was going to be here for some time yet.

Chapter Eighteen

For the Coronation of King George V, Mr Smythe threw a grand party, opening Nase Head House to the people of the town. Extra staff were taken on to bake scones and cakes. Anyone who had a spare idle moment between duties was put to making bunting from red, white and blue crêpe paper. Crockery was washed and cutlery polished to a high sheen. Timed tickets were issued to anyone who wanted one so that everyone didn't come at once and a three-piece band had been hired.

Emma had never been so busy. Certainly, she'd never seen the hotel so full of visitors. In the six months between Christmas, when she'd been given her surprise clothes allowance, and June, many of Mr Smythe's London friends had been coming down to Devon for long weekends, glad to be away from the hustle and the bustle of the city, but they were all back there now – some of them, no doubt, had lined the streets to see the new King and his Queen ride by in their golden coach.

Ruby, in particular, had been excited about the Coronation party. Over-excited almost. Especially when staff were told they could forego their uniforms for the day and wear their best clothes – jewels too, if they wanted to.

'Seeing as we can't get to Westminster Abbey, seems it's come to us. I can't wait for the morning papers to see all the photographs,' Ruby had said.

'Just don't get your grubby hands on 'em 'til the guests have finished reading 'em,' Harry Webber had told her.

But now it was all over. The dishes had been washed and dried and put away, the trestle tables returned to the cellar. Only the bunting remained and Mr Smythe had said it could remain for the weekend, keep everyone in the high spirits they'd enjoyed all day.

Emma had hoped that Seth might come to the Coronation party. But he hadn't – not unless he'd come when she was upstairs giving the children their tea, or putting them to bed.

She'd glimpsed him a time or two in recent weeks when she'd been on errands for Mr Smythe – clothes and shoes for the twins mostly, because they were growing faster than nettles did in spring. Seth had changed. He seemed taller and broader, and he wore his hair longer – she liked how he looked now, more than ever. Each time she'd seen Seth in the town he'd been on his own, never with Caroline Prentiss – but that didn't mean he wasn't still seeing her. And as Seth hadn't been in touch with her, then she feared he might be.

'What was it Dr Shaw told you, Miss?' she said now to her reflection in the cheval glass as she stepped out of her skirt. 'Sometimes life's not about wishes and dreams but about making the most of the situations we find ourselves in.'

'You're changing, girl,' she said. She'd taken off her blouse and stockings and was down to just her drawers and chemise; her very thin chemise, made of the finest lawn. That was one invoice Emma hadn't given Mr Smythe to show how she'd spent his money.

For a start she was taller, and more rounded. She had breasts now – they were pushing out the front of her chemise in little mounds the size of the sugary doughnuts they sold in Callard's Bakery.

What would it feel like to have Seth cup her breasts in his hands? Goodness, what thoughts she was having, these days. It was all part of growing up, she knew. But still …

The only downside of the Coronation party had been that she'd heard a few people mention Carter Jago's name – how his trial for the murder of Sophie Ellison had started, although it could take weeks to hear all the evidence and reach a verdict.

Emma shuddered, remembering how she'd been touched by a suspected murderer.

She took a swig of milk from the glass she'd brought up to bed with her. She hoped it might help her go to sleep more quickly. But her head was full of the chattering voices of all the people at the party and the sound of the music that the three-piece band had played almost non-stop all day.

And Seth – her last thought of all before sleep overcame her was of Seth.

As always.

'Did you go, Seth?' Olly asked, when Seth called on him with a present of a basket of fish for him and his mother.

'Go where?'

'Smythe's shindig for the King and Queen?'

'No. Did you?'

'I took my ma. She's not been the same since Pa died. She's forever telling me I don't run the business as well as Pa did, even though we both know he died four years ago and I doubled the profits the first year.' Olly laughed. 'I thought it might let me off the hook a bit if I took her up there to sit about under Smythe's chandeliers and eat his fancy cakes. I thought it might cheer her up.'

'And did it?' Seth asked.

He bit on his bottom lip so as not to ask Olly what he really wanted to ask, which was, had he seen Emma – seen Emma on the arm of Rupert Smythe perhaps.

'For the time she was there, yes. But it was soon back to the old refrain – "Your pa this, your pa that".'

Seth couldn't think of a thing to say. How he would have loved to have his ma tell him he wasn't running the fishing fleet as well as his pa had. Which he knew he wasn't, at the moment. His father's smuggling racket must have been bigger than he'd ever imagined because it was the devil's own job to turn in the same sort of profit by his own, legal, means. The only blessing in his ma's death, as far as Seth could see, was that she wasn't alive to see Carter on trial for murder.

'D'you know, Seth Jago, it's often what a man doesn't say rather than what he does that matters?'

'Sorry. Thinking. About Carter.'

'Ah, him. Let me know if there's anything you want me to do.'

'Do?'

'Do – like tighten the rope,' Olly said.

'You'd have to beat me to it,' Seth said, if awkwardly.

He'd be left forever with the legacy of his brother's misdeeds, wouldn't he? – however much his brother would deserve to hang for his sins if found guilty.

'I know. We can joke about it but it must be hard for you. However, it wasn't Carter I meant. You went very pale when I mentioned Nase Head House. Nice little piece by the name of Emma Le Goff works there …'

'Shut it, Olly,' Seth said.

'Touchy, touchy,' Olly said. 'And for the record, I wasn't being disparaging of Miss Le Goff at all. She *is* a nice little piece. Feisty. Beautiful. She's blooming, I'd say, up there. I saw you talking to her on reception the night of the dinner I gave. For rather longer than it takes to deposit a coat in the cloakroom.' Olly tapped the side of his nose.

'So did lots of others, I expect. It's a public place. But if you must know, she gave me the brush off.'

'Ah, sorry about that. I can't imagine sitting you next to Caroline Prentiss helped. Talking of whom …'

'I'd rather we didn't. I ended things with her months ago.'

'Then if you'll take the advice of an older man –' Olly

laughed because he was all of three months older than Seth – 'I think it's high time you went and rescued Emma Le Goff from Smythe's clutches.'

'How d'you mean?'

Olly sucked his breath in through his teeth.

'This isn't going to be an easy one. Let's just say she was far better dressed than any of the other staff, even though they weren't in uniform for the shindig. Quality. Better quality than a girl her age working in a hotel would be able to afford. Ma said as much to me. Smythe stopped and spoke to Emma a few times – and Ma didn't miss that either. Rather more than the giving of orders one might expect a boss to give to his staff ...'

'I don't want to hear any more ...'

'You'll hear me out,' Olly said. 'I don't for one minute think she's sharing Smythe's bed. That's not what I'm saying. Emma wasn't flirting with him. In fact, she took a step back from him, putting a bit of distance between them, I think, every time he stopped to speak to her. But it's been known before – a widower with children being generous with his money, making a girl feel special, and before she knows what's happening, and why, she gets used to all the fine clothes and the jewels and then it's a short step up the aisle to become Mrs Whoever Number Two. Especially a girl like Emma Le Goff, who hasn't got any parents, any family at all, to warn her of the trap she's being set.'

I warned her, Seth thought, but didn't say. And she hadn't much liked hearing his misgivings, had she?

'Are you listening to me at all?' Olly said.

'I don't have a choice, do I?' Seth said. 'Thank you for your insights.'

He struggled to banish the picture from his mind of Emma coming out of the door of Rossiter's, laughing, with Rupert Smythe, her arms full of parcels.

'My pleasure. As your older and *wiser* best friend, Seth Jago,' Olly said – and it touched Seth to see the genuine care and concern in his friend's eyes – 'I felt it my duty. Don't say I didn't warn you.'

'I don't think Smythe's going to take kindly to me butting in on his life. They looked happy enough Christmas shopping together.'

'Christmas shopping? That was months ago. And besides, would you know what to buy your children if you had any?'

'I ...'

'I haven't finished yet. A man like Smythe, used to servants and staff, wouldn't have the first idea about buying presents, I shouldn't think. That's a woman's preserve, and you know it. Which is more than likely why he asked for Emma's help. And you, Seth Jago, have got a bigger chip on your shoulder than what comes off an eighteen-foot length of teak.'

'If you say so. God only knows it's been hard enough to hold up my head in this town, what with ...'

'Calm down.' Olly put a hand on Seth's shoulder. 'There's new respect for you around here of late, for the way you've kept local men in work, kept the fleet going. For heaven's sake, Seth, you know as well as I do that if you hadn't, then the tied cottages would have gone and there would have been families homeless. So, stop giving yourself a hard time. But my guess is, you're more than sweet on Emma Le Goff, and if it's her you want, then you'd better be doing something about it. And soon.'

'Anything else?' Seth asked as Olly took his hand from his shoulder.

But soon? Might he already have left it too late?

Emma thought, afterwards, that she would always remember the date – 16th July 1911. Not only because it would have been her mother's birthday and she would have been forty-one-years old that day had she been alive, but because of what happened.

'I've got a surprise for you,' Mr Smythe said. 'A thank you for all your hard work in the hotel and your care of my children.'

'Oh, I don't need surprises. Or thanks,' Emma said. 'You pay me well enough.'

'I'm pleased to hear you're satisfied with your remuneration,' Mr Smythe said, one side of his mouth turning up in the beginnings of a smile – as though he found Emma amusing. 'But all the same, I want the children dressed in their best clothes by 10 o'clock. You, too. We're going out.'

Emma glanced at the clock in Isabelle's nursery. It was already a quarter-past nine. 'Out?' she said.

Mr Smythe smiled again – a wry sort of smile this time, Emma thought.

'You do understand the word, Emma? It means the opposite of being in, as in this hotel.'

'Of course,' Emma said. She wasn't sure she liked surprises – most of the ones she'd had so far she'd have been better off not having.

'Warm coats for the children, Emma,' Mr Smythe said. 'It can be cold up on Dartmoor, even at this time of year.' And then he was gone, to prepare himself for the journey, no doubt.

But he'd given Emma a clue as to where they were going. She was excited and terrified in equal measure – she'd be going on a journey with Mr Smythe, sitting beside him in the car possibly.

Emma went to the window. Dartmoor could be seen in the distance. She loved to look out towards it in the early morning when the hills and tors seemed to be draped with grey silk, and then again, before sunset when they were a bluish shade – blue running into purple, but not quite as dark as indigo. And then as the sun set they became black and hard against the crimson sky. Emma had longed to go there – she'd heard there were wild ponies and sheep everywhere and lots of bright yellow gorse and lilac-coloured heather. And cows roaming loose.

And now she was. She couldn't wait to tell Ruby.

Emma – with Isabelle in tow – found Ruby in the kitchen. She blurted out her good news.

'The boys will be down in a minute. I've left them excitedly getting ready.'

'I wish *I* could come,' Ruby said. She rolled the pastry far harder than it needed to be rolled, banging the rolling pin down as she turned the dough.

'I wish you could, too. But you're murdering the life out of that piece of dough.'

'Am I so?' Ruby said. 'I'm not supposed to be here. But wouldn't you know, the kitchen boy's gone sick again and Cook wants a hand with these tarts. And talking of murder – have you 'eard the verdict on Carter Jago's due any day?'

'No,' Emma said. 'I haven't heard.'

'It's in the paper. Yesterday's *Western Morning News*. 'Arry read it to me,' Ruby snapped.

Emma made a mental note to ask Ruby if she wanted her to help her with her reading. Now wasn't the time to ask, though – Ruby was already put out about having to be in the kitchen and now about not going on a trip, no doubt.

'I wouldn't have told you about the trip if I'd known it was going to make you so grumpy.'

'Who says I'm grumpy?' Ruby demanded. 'Oh, gawd, 'ere's the little varmints come looking for yer.'

Archie and Sidney came bounding into the kitchen.

'We're going to Dartmoor. We're going to Dartmoor,' Archie squealed.

'And we're going to have a pony. A pony.' Sidney joined in the excitement.

'Quieten down, boys,' Emma said. 'And couldn't either of you find a comb?'

The boys looked at one another and giggled.

With Isabelle perched precariously on one hip, Emma licked her fingers and made a passable attempt at tidying Archie's unruly hair, then set to work on Sidney's.

What they looked like every day at prep school she had no idea. Although Lupton House was only a mile away, the twins boarded in the week.

Ruby wiped her floury hands down the sides of her apron.

'You have a good time, Belle, my lovely,' she said, plonking a noisy, wet kiss on the baby's forehead.

'*Isa*belle. Mr Smythe doesn't like her being called Belle.'

'Well, he's hardly ever around to hear me call her anything the times I'm with her, is he? I wonder if he's her pa sometimes.'

'Don't think such things, Ruby,' Emma said. She turned to the twins.

'Boys, wait outside in the foyer for me, will you, please?'

They scarpered off happily.

'Don't talk about their father in front of the children, Ruby, please,' Emma said. 'This little one's talking more and more each day, understanding more, and very soon will be able to tell Mr Smythe what you say in two languages.'

'Well, it seems to me that the less time 'e spends with the children the better it is for Mr Smythe. When you were down on reception when Mr Bell were sick, I asked Mr Smythe if 'e wanted to hold little *Isa*belle because I thought she ought to know the feel of being in her pa's arms seeing as her ma isn't around to touch her – although I didn't tell 'im that –

but 'e said his suit had just been pressed. What sort of an excuse is that to ignore your own daughter, Emma?'

'None at all,' Emma said. 'But Mr Smythe has a hotel to run. He's busy. He ...'

'I *knew* you'd stand up for 'im. It's all right for *you* going off in cars and being Mr Smythe's favourite. *I've* got to help that useless lump of lard of a new chambermaid, Maisie Bellamy, to turn mattresses while you're out once I've finished this pastry. God only knows where Cook's got to, and He won't tell. Perhaps, Miss Hoity-Toity, you could tell Mr Smythe what a liability Maisie is ...'

'Hoity-Toity?' Emma interrupted. 'I'm not Hoity-Toity am I, Ruby?'

'Sometimes,' Ruby said. 'Someone had to tell yer and that someone was me. But best you get going, eh? Bring me a sprig of heather. It's lucky, is heather, or so they say. And mind the piskies.'

Ruby kissed Emma's cheek.

'I will,' Emma said, returning the kiss.

They were still friends – thank goodness for that.

Emma sat in the seat beside Mr Smythe, Isabelle on her lap, and barely spoke a word all the way to Dartmoor. The lanes seemed to get narrower and narrower. A cow ambled onto the road in front of the car, and Emma jumped in her seat, startling Isabelle. It made the child cry.

'For goodness' sake, Emma, it's only a cow. And a small one at that. We're quite safe in here. Don't frighten the children.' Mr Smythe didn't exactly snap at Emma, but the tone of his voice was admonishing all the same.

'*We*'re not scared, Papa,' Archie said.

'Oh, look – ponies,' Sidney shouted. 'I want the black-and-white one.'

'Pipe down, boys,' Mr Smythe said.

The road seemed to be winding higher and higher and all Emma could see in front of her was grass and sky. And then they rounded a bend, and Mr Smythe turned sharply to the left.

'What's that, Papa?' Sidney shouted.

'Mine workings. Tin, I expect. Now pipe down.'

Sidney did as he was told, fascinated by the pumps going up and down. But Emma hated them – they seemed like horrible scars on an otherwise beautiful landscape to her.

'Enjoying the views, Emma?' Mr Smythe asked, taking his eyes from the road in front of him to look at her.

She glanced at him briefly. 'Yes, thank you,' she said, then looked away again.

She'd never been alone with Mr Smythe for this length of time before. She wondered if she ought to open up some topic of conversation, but what could she talk about? The hotel was the only thing they had in common and she was glad to be out of it for a little while.

But the truth was Emma didn't know what was expected of her. Was she still an employee or was she now a friend?

'Will you marry again, Mr Smythe?' she asked on a sudden impulse, and the way Mr Smythe snapped his head round to stare at her wide-eyed, she wished she hadn't.

'Whatever made you ask that?' he asked.

He looked, Emma thought, amused rather than cross.

'My mouth races ahead of my mind sometimes. I ought not to have said it. I apologise.'

'No need, my dear, no need. Your outspokenness reminds me of my dear Claudine. But to answer your question – yes, I am thinking of marrying again. No one could fully replace my darling Claudine, but the children do need a mother. And I need a wife. To stop the predatory widows who come to the hotel and make a play for me when they learn I'm a widower, if nothing else.'

Nothing to do with loving someone new then – whoever she was – Emma thought. But since she'd opened up this particular topic of conversation she felt she had to continue with it.

'I hope you'll be very happy,' she said.

And she honestly meant that. Rupert Smythe had been a good guardian to her, which was what he had become when Matthew had asked if she could stop at the hotel.

'And the children,' Emma added, her voice a whisper, wondering just how much of this conversation the boys would understand. 'I hope they will like your new wife.'

'I'm sure they will,' Mr Smythe said. He smiled warmly at Emma and it disconcerted her because when he smiled he became a different man altogether – more handsome, less hard about the eyes and the mouth. Attractive, even.

Emma's conversational thread seemed to snap then. If Mr Smythe wanted to tell her who his new wife was to be then she would wait until he did so. She wasn't going to ask – it might sound as if she was jealous and she certainly wasn't that.

Isabelle had gone to sleep, and Emma's arm ached holding the child. She was feeling nervous now, alone with Mr Smythe – well, apart from the children. She wondered what his future wife would think of him taking an employee out in his car. Perhaps he was about to tell her that her services were no longer going to be required.

'Ah, here we are,' Mr Smythe said. He braked and brought the car to a halt in front of a farm gate hung between two very substantial stone pillars.

Emma could see a two-storey house with a thatched roof at the end of a very long drive. From where she sat it looked like a dolls' house. Smoke rose from the chimney. Who lived here, she wondered – Mr Smythe's future wife? Was she going to be introduced to her as Isabelle's nursemaid? The boys' French tutor?

'I'll open the gate,' he said, opening the car door, unfolding his long legs onto the grassy track.

'We're here. We're here,' Archie said, bouncing up and down on the back seat.

'We're going to have a pony. A pony!' Sidney joined in, bouncing more than his twin, if that were possible.

'Sssh, boys,' Emma said. 'Your papa won't want you damaging the leather on the seats.' But she smiled as she said it, glad to see them being proper little boys again. Just a few seconds without their father and Archie and Sidney were able to be their usual exuberant selves. And they obviously knew more than she did about what was going on because Sidney had said they were going to have a pony more than once.

But here? In this isolated spot? Emma had noticed a handful of cottages a mile or so back, and a few miles further back again there had been a village with a baker and a butcher and a hardware store. She didn't know that she'd ever want to live somewhere like this. It would be too quiet. And besides, she wouldn't be able to see the sea.

'So, what do you think, Emma?' Mr Smythe said.

A woman who Mr Smythe introduced as Phyllis Hannaford had served a luncheon of cold meats and potatoes with a trifle for pudding. After the meal, the boys – eager to be out on the moor amongst the wild ponies – had persuaded their father to go with them. And for Emma to go along. They had all enjoyed it far more than Emma had because her shoes had been inadequate for the rough terrain and she'd twisted her ankle – although not badly – a time or two. They had all returned to the house tired, and hungry again.

At 4 o'clock Mrs Hannaford who, it seemed, was the housekeeper of Bagstone House, had served a tea of scones with cream and jam. But now she'd been despatched to the garden with the children, who were wrapped up warm with scarves and hats. It *was* colder up here on the moor than it was by the sea.

'Think of what?' Emma said.

'This house.'

'It's very pretty. Well today it is, with the sun shining and I can see it would be warm enough in winter with the range in the kitchen and the big grate in this drawing-room. But I wouldn't want to live here. Whose is it anyway?'

'Mine. I've arranged for some alterations to be done, re-papering of rooms and so on. But I wanted you to see it. To see if you like it.'

'Oh,' Emma said. She hadn't expected that answer.

'I thought the boys might like to be here at weekends. The weekends are always busy at the hotel and they get under my feet rather.'

Ruby had been right – Mr Smythe didn't want to have much contact, if any, with his children.

'I do try to keep Sidney and Archie entertained,' Emma said. 'But short of gagging them I can't keep them silent.'

'No, no – of course not,' Mr Smythe said.

Emma thought he looked and sounded distracted. She couldn't think of a single thing to say, so she looked around the room. It was a shrine to brown – the table, the dresser, the couch, the cushions, the carpet; all various shades of the same, depressing colour. She hoped for the boys' sake there would be an injection of something bright into the room. Just being in it made her heart feel as though it was shrivelling, the way a conker shrivels with time.

'It had always been our plan,' Mr Smythe said slowly, clearly – as though he was explaining something to someone who had learning difficulties, 'Claudine's and mine, to have a country house for her to live in with the children and for me to join them at weekends once I had someone trained

256

up to run Nase Head House in my absence. The boys have never forgotten I promised them a pony.'

Was the surprise going to be that he wanted her to be that person – the one running the hotel while he was here with the children?

'Sometimes,' Emma said, knowing what thin ice she would be skating on by saying it, 'the plans we make have to change. Your new wife might not like the things Claudine ... I mean Mrs Smythe ... liked.'

Her plans had had to change after her parents died. Seth's had certainly changed after his pa and brothers had been put in prison. He'd had plans to go to Canada to work for his uncle but had had to stay in Devon to keep the fishing fleet going, and to keep Hilltop House from going to wrack and ruin if no one was living in it. So why shouldn't Mr Smythe's plans have to change, too?

'So I'm beginning to discover. But tell me, Emma what were *your* plans?'

'My mama wanted me to be a teacher. After she died I wasn't at all sure I wanted to be a teacher anyway if Mama wouldn't be there to see me get my certificate. But it's not only that. I don't understand why, once a woman marries, she has to leave teaching. What would be the point of all that training if I were to want to marry? And ...'

'Quite,' Mr Smythe said. 'But I have to tell you, you make a very good teacher, Emma, trained or not. The principal at Lupton House tells me the boys are well in advance for their age in terms of French grammar and punctuation and vocabulary. And even little Isabelle forgets which language she's using sometimes. Do you know she said to me only yesterday, "*J'ai soif, papa.*" Well, that's what it sounded like.'

'Did you get her a drink?' Emma asked.

'A drink?' Mr Smythe's eyebrows met in the middle in puzzlement.

'Yes. A drink. Isabelle was telling you she was thirsty.'

'Ah. There was never any need for me to learn French because my darling Claudine spoke English so deliciously perfectly.'

Whoever Mr Smythe was thinking of marrying, Emma was already feeling sorry for her – the man would never love her as he had so obviously very much loved his Claudine.

A sudden chill seemed to sweep through the room, despite the sun streaming in the windows, although Emma had a feeling it was only affecting her. A shiver ran up her spine and the hairs on the backs of her arms stood on end. The air was pregnant with something Emma couldn't define, but she had a feeling that whatever it was it would probably be life-changing for her.

So it was with some surprise that she heard Mr Smythe say, 'Sherry, Emma?'

He stood up and went to a cupboard in the corner, took out a bottle and two glasses and brought them back to the side-table.

'I've never drunk it on its own before,' Emma said. 'But it's very good in a *crème anglaise*.'

'It is indeed. It goes wonderfully with your wonderful tarte tatin. I wouldn't want to be without that.'

'So you're not going to tell me I have to look for another position now you'll be getting married again?'

'Goodness no, Emma. Haven't you worked it out for yourself yet? I had you down as a very bright young lady indeed.'

'You want me to run Nase Head House at the weekends once you're married? I could do it, I know I could if I was given some training. I'm sure I'd learn quickly. Oh, that would be just wonderful. I ...'

'Stop.' Mr Smythe reached for Emma's free hand and clutched it between his own. 'Your mind is running away on flights of fancy and you're wrong about all of them. What I'm proposing, Emma, is that you become my wife. When you turn eighteen in a few weeks' time, then we can announce the engagement officially. You will be of a good age to marry and I will have been seen to wait a respectable length of time before marrying again. The wait will give you time to get used to the idea. What do you say?'

Chapter Nineteen

'No!' Emma bit back 'over my dead body', her lips pressed tightly together. 'There must be someone more suitable than I would be ...'

'I'll be the judge of that,' Mr Smythe said. 'But for the life of me I can't see your objection. You have no family, and I'm offering you the chance to be part of mine.'

She was sitting on an over-stuffed, velvet-covered chair in Mr Smythe's private sitting-room, shaking with fury that he had expected she would say yes with alacrity to his proposal.

He had asked her daily for weeks now and every day she gave him the same answer. It would be a marriage of convenience if she accepted – but only convenient to Mr Smythe.

He let out a long sigh.

'What did you think the clothes allowance I gave you was for?'

'For clothes,' Emma said through gritted teeth. 'For when I'm out with the children, or with you on their behalf. I wouldn't have accepted it if I'd thought you only gave it to me so I could ... could be considered a replacement for your wife.'

'You could never replace her.' Mr Smythe glanced towards the photograph of his wife on the mantelpiece, but only for a moment.

'When I marry, Mr Smythe,' Emma said, 'I want it to be for love, not so I can be an unpaid nanny. And be dressed up and paraded in front of your business associates. And if telling you this means I have to find another position, then I will.'

'I wouldn't bother you if that's what you're meaning. You would have a separate room.'

'Separate room?'

The words were out of Emma's mouth before she could stop them. In saying them it made her sound as though she wouldn't want that if she married Mr Smythe – that she would want to share not only his room but his bed.

Emma had memories of her parents snuggled up together in the feather bed, and of movement in the night. Murmurings. A cry from her mama sometimes, but not of fright. The sounds of love-making. And in the morning her mama would have a smile on her face that even the range refusing to light, so that they had to have a cold breakfast, couldn't budge. And a softness – her mama would have a loving softness about her.

Emma knew she wanted that loving softness from marriage and not the cold business deal Mr Smythe was offering her.

'I wouldn't want to add to my family. Do you understand me?' Mr Smythe looked towards the fire in the grate as he spoke.

'I might want children myself one day, Mr Smythe. And when I do, I'd want them to be part of a loving union.'

She felt herself blush because Seth came into her mind as she said it – not that he was often out of her thoughts. She'd glimpsed him so rarely of late and when she had he'd been head down, scurrying somewhere, or talking on the quayside to one of his crewmen, and she hurried past lest he see her because she didn't know what sort of reception she'd get from him.

She still hoped, deep in her soul, they would get together again some day. Her heart still lurched with desire every time she saw him.

'Could you meet me half way?' Mr Smythe said. 'I think it would be a way for you to get used to the idea.'

Emma balled her hands together in her lap wondering

what might be coming next. Although he hadn't said 'Get out' had he?

'What do you propose?' she asked. 'Apart from marriage.'

Mr Smythe gave a wry smile. 'Number one, that you call me Rupert in private.'

'Rupert?' Emma thought she would explode saying the word, but realised she just had. It sounded alien and slightly ridiculous to be calling Mr Smythe by his Christian name.

'It's my name, Emma. Hardly anyone calls me by my Christian name. Claudine did, of course. And Matthew Caunter because he and I attended the same school for a while many years ago, but he's in America.'

So that's how Matthew was able to use Nase Head House to spy on the Jagos' smuggling activities. And possibly why Mr Smythe had agreed to Matthew's request to give her refuge.

'I know.'

Emma swallowed hard. She felt the loss of Matthew's friendship and the potential friendship she might have had with his wife had they not emigrated. Perhaps taking a giant leap of faith to go and live in another country wouldn't be so bad? Although maybe not just yet. Who would put flowers on her parents' and Johnnie's graves if she wasn't there to do it? And besides, she'd saved nowhere near enough money for that sort of adventure.

'And number two is that you take the children to Bagstone House at the weekends. When the alterations to the attic space to make it into a playroom for the children and the redecoration is finished, of course. I thought the children might like Christmas there this year, with the possibility of snow on the higher ground.'

Emma felt her heart plummet. She crossed her fingers behind her back the renovations wouldn't be finished by Christmas.

'At the price I'm paying Mr Maunder to do them I shall have something to say if the place hasn't been completed to my brief by then.'

And that's when Emma's heart plummeted further – Mr Maunder was Caroline Prentiss' father. Every day there was a reminder of Seth in her life – in this instance that he'd been very cosy with Caroline Prentiss at dinner. Emma wished now that she hadn't been so vehement in telling Seth not to ask to see her again.

'You could at least look a little more enthusiastic about this opportunity I'm offering you, Emma. I imagine you ate less well at Christmas in a fisherman's cottage?'

Emma didn't much like the rather sarcastic tone of his voice. 'My papa provided very well for us all, thank you.'

'Yes, yes. Of course. But Bagstone House – I'm sure you'll like it there once you've given it a try. I'm sure it will look lovely with a sprinkling of snow.'

And be marooned there for goodness knows how long? Emma thought. She tried to think of something to say but words eluded her. Mr Smythe seemed to take her silence for acquiescence – to Emma's horror.

'I'll see that Evans is taught to drive. He would take you to pick up Archie and Sidney from school in my motor and drive you on up.'

Evans? The gardener? He couldn't even drive a wheelbarrow in a straight line! *And* he was ancient. And what was more, Mr Smythe had taken on William Coote to help Mr Evans with the grass-cutting because he'd said it was too much for him.

'Mrs Hannaford will be there, of course,' Mr Smythe went on. 'To cook. I won't expect you to cook.'

'I might want to,' Emma said. 'I like cooking. I'd like to run a business some day with my cooking. I think I …'

What *did* she think? In saying she might want to cook at

263

Bagstone House had she just agreed to spend the weekends with the children in isolation on the moors? Was she mad?

'I think you're not averse to my request then, Emma – to spend weekends with the children at Bagstone House? And myself on occasion there, of course.'

'I didn't say that.'

Emma balled her hands together tighter in her lap.

'Well, it seems to me you have two alternatives – you can either agree to that suggestion and to call me Rupert in private, or you can cut your tutorial duties to my children. I'm sure a tutor could be found for them quite easily to continue their study of the French language. Ruby can take over the care of Isabelle. I *might* have a position as scullery maid you can take on but it *will* mean you vacating the tower room you seem to have made your own, and sharing with another girl.'

That was blackmail.

Emma gulped. But leave the tower room? She *had* made it – small as it was – her own. She'd hung pictures she'd picked up for pennies from the church jumble sale on the walls. And she'd covered cushions in fabric unpicked from a summer dress she'd grown out of. The room was her sanctuary now – the only place she really felt safe. She wasn't ready to up sticks and move anywhere just yet, despite what she had said to him in the heat of the moment earlier.

Emma hung her head. She felt like a puppet on a string being manipulated like this. And she hated herself for allowing that manipulation.

'I've become very fond of the children,' Emma said, raising her head to make eye contact with Mr Smythe. She stretched her lips into a smile, but she knew that smile came nowhere near her eyes because her heart felt heavier than all the lead on all the church roofs in the county, and there were hundreds of them. 'I don't think it would be in their interests for me to not be part of their lives and their understanding of their mother's language. At the moment.'

There, that wasn't agreeing to marry him exactly, was it?

'Clever girl. We need one another, you and I. And we both know it.'

'May I go now?' Emma said. 'Please.'

'When we've said goodnight in a civil manner. Goodnight, Emma.'

'Goodnight, Mr Smythe.'

'Oh, you can do better than that. "Goodnight, Rupert" is what I want to hear. A small price to pay for my kindnesses to you these past two years, I think. You'll find it springing from your lips quite naturally as the months go by, I'm sure of it.'

Drag by more like, Emma thought. She knew she had to put an end to this agony, and soon. He wasn't going to give up – not in getting her to call him by his Christian name, or in getting her to accept his proposal.

'Goodnight ... Rupert,' she said.

And then she ran from the room – gagging all the way until she had her bedroom door closed firmly behind her, and the key in the lock.

Seth woke as a flash of lightning lit up his room. He was used to sudden August storms after days of sultry heat, but this seemed louder and closer than usual. Then a clap of thunder boomed almost immediately afterwards. Rain that sounded as though it was nails hitting the roof rather than drops of water, was coming down in torrents now. The storm was right overhead.

He had a trawler out on its way back from fishing grounds around the Channel Islands. It was due in at first light. What time was it now? Switching on his bedside lamp Seth reached for his pocket watch. Twenty minutes past three.

Still too early for his crew to be back but he prayed the trawler would be near enough to come into harbour safely.

Seth got out of bed and went to the window. Lights glimmered in one of the rooms in Nase Head House on the other side of the harbour. Emma's room? He hoped not; hoped she wasn't disturbed by the storm.

More lightning fizzed and sparked, and ever closer thunder. This storm was sounding fiercer than any he'd experienced before. Seth thought he saw the flicker of lamps down in the harbour. Perhaps his trawler *was* back after all? If it was then his men would need help unloading in this weather. He pulled his nightshirt off over his head. Dressed quickly. He ran down the stairs, found his boots, grabbed his oilskin, and opened the back door. Another flash of lightning lit up the garden.

He ran out into the darkness. No time to find a lamp and light it.

'Jago?' someone said, startling him, as he reached the gate.

'Yes. Who is it?'

'Adam Narracott. And my brother, Peter. We wuz just coming to fetch you. God, but there's one unholy mess down there. Your boats ...'

'Then we're wasting time.' Seth raced towards the harbour, the older men following some distance behind now.

There seemed to be men running everywhere when he reached the quayside. Some had lamps, but most were without as he was. A loud crack of lightning lit up the scene – boats on their sides, boats upside down, masts broken, boxes floating before being smashed against hulls. Seth could see that what Adam Narracott had said was true and that one of those hulls was one of his crabbers.

'Better start praying, Mr Jago,' Adam Narracott said. He was breathing heavily – wheezing – from the exertion of running and from his battle with the elements. The wind seemed to be getting stronger by the minute.

'If He's listening,' Seth shouted back at him.

'My boy's out there on your trawler, Mr Jago, my Robbie.'

'I know,' Seth said. 'I'm praying for him. We must all pray.'

And then there came a shout: 'Man overboard! Look.'

The cry seemed to galvanise all the men to go towards the voice; a voice Seth didn't recognise.

'Where?' Seth yelled.

'The *Kittiwake*. Maunder's boat. Stupid bugger took the tender to go out to it for some damned stupid reason but five minutes past.'

'Charles Maunder?' Seth said.

'Of course. 'Tis *his* boat.'

Seth grabbed a lantern from someone and swung it out towards where the *Kittiwake* was moored. But it had broken its moorings and was now at a precarious angle. One strong blow and it would be right over.

'Help!' Charles Maunder's voice was surprisingly loud and strong in the circumstances. 'I can't …'

Another deafening crackle of lightning illuminated Charles Maunder centre stage as he cried for help. But his words were snatched from him as he disappeared beneath the water.

'No use me going,' Peter Narracott said. 'I can't swim.'

There were a few cries of 'Nor me.' It was common knowledge that not many fishermen could swim.

Seth made a vow that if his fleet ever recovered from this storm then he'd make sure all his crew were taught to swim before they went to sea.

Flinging aside his oilskin, Seth stripped himself of his jacket, kicked off his boots, pulled off his trousers. The tide was high, so he lowered himself over the wall and slipped into the water, the coldness of it taking his breath from his body for a few seconds. He gulped in air the way a fish does when it's thrown on the deck. Eventually the air reached his lungs.

Seth struggled to swim against the tide and the water being whipped into a frenzy by the storm. The harbour was flanked by steep hills on three sides but the wind was blowing from the east and they were about as much use as shelter as a bucket with a hole in it is for holding water. He battled on towards where he'd seen Charles Maunder go down, fully expecting him to bob up again, but he didn't. Dodging floating crates and loose buoys, Seth reached the spot he thought he'd last seen the drowning man.

He groped about for anything solid beneath him. Nothing. Frantically treading water with one leg now, he felt about with the other for Charles Maunder. Still nothing. Taking a deep breath, Seth dived down, reaching with arms and legs, hoping to come up against something solid.

But there was only seaweed and bits of rope which he pushed off as best he could so they didn't trap him underwater.

Seth came back up for air. More people seemed to have arrived at the harbour now. Someone shouted for the sergeant to be woken and dragged from his bed in the police station, the lazy bastard – his voice carrying across the water. How the sergeant hadn't heard the commotion going on, Seth couldn't understand – the police station was but a stone's throw away.

Then he felt something touch his leg, something soft. Then hands grabbed him pulling him further down. Charles Maunder. And obviously alive. Seth kicked for his life, grabbed for any part of Charles Maunder that he could and struggled to the surface. While the effort was making him hot inside, his skin seemed to be getting colder by the second. He could barely feel his face now – his lips felt numb as icy rain lashed them, and he bit them to bring them back to life.

But thank goodness the storm seemed to be moving away. The flashes of lightning were less intense, with longer breaks in between – the thunder a rumble that sounded further away.

Seth yelled for someone to throw a line.

'I've got you,' he told Charles Maunder, as Mr Maunder's head broke the surface of the water and the two men were face-to-face. Charles Maunder spluttered and coughed – thank God he was alive. 'Keep calm. Or we'll both drown.'

With his free hand, Seth caught the end of the rope, but it slipped from his grasp. It was tossed again and this time he managed to grab it and wrap it around a wrist – they'd be hauled ashore soon. But with the weight of two sodden men, and neither of them small men either, it seemed hours rather than minutes until they were.

Dr Shaw was waiting on the quayside. Seth assured him he was fine, if very wet and cold and would get himself home. Charles Maunder was in need of hospital care and Seth watched him being taken away in the doctor's car. Someone else said they'd call at the Maunder home and inform his wife what had happened. Seth was on the verge of saying 'And his daughter, Caroline,' but managed to stop himself – aware of what might people have read into his concern if he hadn't.

Men with lanterns were scanning the harbour, struggling with long and unwieldy hooked poles to haul in various items – buoys ripped from their moorings, wooden boxes, bits of broken mast.

'We'd best leave it 'til the morning,' someone said.

'The wind's got up again,' someone else joined the debate. 'Storm's not played out yet, I don't think.'

'Maunder's been saved anyhow,' another voice chimed in. ''Bout time one of the Jago bastards did something good.' The speaker disappeared into the darkness.

Seth sighed. How much more was expected of him, for goodness' sake? He'd just risked his own life for Charles Maunder – a man he barely knew – and he'd been working every hour God sent to keep the boats in the water and men employed, and yet there were some people who still couldn't realise he was nothing like his pa and brothers. Would they ever?

The landlord of The Blue Anchor thrust a bottle into Seth's hands. 'Get that down you, man.'

Seth put the neck of the bottle to his lips, tipped his head backwards and swallowed long and hard. Brandy. One of his own pa's smuggled bottles of brandy? He couldn't have cared less at that moment. It tasted like what it was – a life-saver – as he felt warmth return to his body.

Emma woke and rubbed sleep from her eyes. She'd had a bad night, woken by the storm. Wrapping her dressing-gown tightly around her she'd crept down to Isabelle's room to check on her four times. Usually, Isabelle slept through the night, but Emma knew Mr Smythe wouldn't be pleased if he had his sleep broken by a wailing baby. And she was glad she had, because as Emma had crept into the room for the fourth time Isabelle *had* woken, her eyes wide with alarm as a crack of lightning lit the sky. Emma brought the child to sleep beside her in her own bed.

Isabelle was sleeping peacefully now.

'You little vixen,' Emma said, dropping a kiss on the child's rosebud mouth. 'Here's me feeling like a washed-out dishrag and you look the picture of contentment.'

But it was time to return her to her own room now. Not that she was worried Mr Smythe would go in there and find his daughter missing. How dreadful that would be if he did, though. He might think the child kidnapped.

Not bothering to wash, Emma pulled off her night things, dressing hurriedly. Memories of the disturbed night were coming back to her and she sent up a silent prayer that no fisherman had drowned as her pa had – that no wife had been left a widow, no child an orphan.

She picked up Isabelle, stepped out into the corridor and made her way to the nursery.

She met Maisie Bellamy, the chambermaid Ruby had grumbled about, coming the other way with her arms laden with bed-linen. Emma hadn't done as Ruby had asked which was to tell Mr Smythe how useless Maisie was, because to Emma, Maisie was always friendly and kind.

'Blimey, Emma, what a night that was and all. I 'spect it woke the little miss there, didn't it?'

'It did,' Emma agreed. 'There was lots of commotion down on the harbour when I looked out of the window.'

'Commotion's not the half of it,' Maisie said. 'Rumour has it someone's drowned. Seth Jago …'

Emma didn't hear any more. It was as though everything happened in slow motion as her legs ceased to support her and she seemed to forget how to breathe. She saw Maisie drop the bed-linen and snatch Isabelle from her. And then blackness. Going down, down, down …

Now morning had arrived, there were more people on the quayside than there had been during the night. Many were salvaging what they could from boats that had been scuppered. Seth walked to the mooring for his trawler. Not back yet, although that didn't surprise him. No news had to be good news and he'd just have to strengthen his prayers that the skipper had dropped anchor in a more sheltered bay somewhere.

'There's going to be a lot of work for Olly Underwood,' someone said as Seth passed, not looking to see who the speaker was.

'That's right an' all,' someone else replied. 'It's a damned ill wind that does nobody any good.'

Seth had only had the one crabber tipped on its side. No doubt he would have lost tackle but as far as he could see from where he stood it hadn't been holed. At low tide he'd get his waders from the boat store and go and see.

He busied himself pulling in what flotsam and jetsam he could with a bar hook and waited for his boat to return.

'How are you feeling now, Emma?'

Emma opened her eyes. Ruby was sitting beside her bed with Isabelle on her lap. A very tired Isabelle, who yawned and rubbed her eyes.

'Oh, I didn't know you were there. I must have dozed off. I had a bad night.'

'Didn't we all. Anyway, I've been 'ere twenty minutes, I 'ave. Or thereabouts. You fainted clean away, Maisie Bellamy said. You were out for the count for a good five minutes, by all accounts. Then you came to before ...'

'Seth,' Emma said. She pushed herself down into the soft pillow and mattress, wanting to escape hearing from Ruby that Seth was dead.

'What about 'im?'

Emma reached for her friend's hand. 'Please, please, Ruby, tell me Seth hasn't drowned.'

'Seth hasn't drowned,' Ruby said, grinning.

'But Maisie said ...'

'You didn't let her finish 'er sentence before making a right spectacle of yourself. What 'er was going to say was that Seth swam out in the height of the storm to rescue

272

Mr Maunder. Rumours were flying that Mr Maunder had drowned, which was what Maisie was going to tell yer, but they weren't true.'

'Rumours almost never are,' Emma said.

'That's as maybe. You heard 'er say "Seth" and put two and two together and made a dozen of it, didn't yer?'

'Oh, oh my, I ...' Emma put her hands to her head.

'See that nose on your face?' Ruby said, tapping the end of Emma's nose with a finger.

'You know I can't.'

''Course you can't – not without looking in a mirror. Same as you can't see you're full of love for Seth Jago. What are you going to do about it, eh?'

'Do about it?' She'd told Seth not to speak to her again, hadn't she? But what must Seth have gone through if he'd battled raging waters to rescue Mr Maunder? And of *course* she knew she was in love with Seth – not that she was going to admit it to Ruby. 'Is Seth all right?'

'Very all right. More handsome than ever, if that's possible. Saw 'im meself, when I nipped down to the chemist's for some vapour rub, didn't I?'

Emma knew she ought to ask why – or for whom – Ruby had gone to the chemist's for vapour rub, but Seth and how he was, was more important.

'Seth's really all right?' Emma struggled to a sitting position. 'More handsome? Oh, I ...'

'*Very* all right. There. That bit of information's put colour back in your cheek, that's for sure,' Ruby laughed. 'So, one good turn deserves another. D'you think you could lie there looking wan and weak a bit longer, 'cos Mr Smythe's asked me to keep an eye on the children until you're up and about and I'd much rather do that than change beds and clear up after people.'

Emma lay back against the pillows, put the back of a

hand to her forehead and sighed theatrically. Inside she was bubbling with joy that Seth hadn't drowned.

'Oh dear, oh dear,' Emma giggled. 'I think I'm going to take at least a day to recover.'

'Good. And while you're at it give some serious thought to Seth Jago and 'ow you can win his heart before some other woman gets her claws in 'im. Give it some thought at least.'

'Oh, I will,' Emma said. 'I will.'

But Seth was alive and for the moment that was all that mattered.

Chapter Twenty

To Seth's great relief there was no loss of life from his own boat, or from any of the others that had been out in the storm – just very tired and wet crews. He set to unloading the catch with his men – something he'd never done for his father, and everyone knew it, which had gone a long way to absolving him of any part in the smuggling.

'Good catch, Mr Jago,' Robbie Narracott said. 'Kept fresh and all with the deluge.'

'There'll be an extra half-crown apiece in your pay packet,' Seth said. He put his hand in his trouser pocket, pulled out a handful of florins. 'But here's something to be going on with for a round of drinks for the crew in The Blue Anchor.'

'Thanks, Mr Jago,' Robbie said, grinning broadly. He pocketed the money. 'Best get this lot up to the sheds for sorting first, though. It'll be another day before it's done, else, if they get their ale first.'

There was lots of good-natured grumbling from the crew that they couldn't start drinking right away but they got on with unloading the boats fast enough as they always did, Seth thought, given they must have been frightened for their lives out there in Lyme Bay with the storm raging around them.

The job done, Seth made his way to the Maunder home, praying his rescue attempt hadn't been in vain and that Charles Maunder had made it through the night.

'Heaven only knows why my husband went down to the harbour, Mr Jago, it was a reckless thing to do in the height of the storm. I shall have something to say to him about that when I visit him at the hospital this afternoon.'

'He might have been making sure his yacht was secure …'

'It was still a reckless thing to do,' Mrs Maunder interrupted. 'But I'm so grateful *you* were there, Mr Jago. You saved his life.' She ushered him into the drawing-room.

'I'm only glad I was able to,' Seth said.

Mrs Maunder indicated for him to sit.

'No, no,' Seth said. 'I can't stop more than a few moments.'

'My daughter should be arriving shortly,' Mrs Maunder said. 'This has come as a huge shock to her.'

Seth wondered how soon shortly was – five minutes, one hour? He had no desire to see Caroline again. And he'd bet every penny he had that she wouldn't want to see him.

'From Plymouth,' Mrs Maunder said.

She looked, Seth thought, rather embarrassed, but whether it was because he seemed to have dried up and was having difficulty keeping a conversation flowing or because Caroline had been in Plymouth for whatever reason last night, he had no way of telling.

'Caroline moved to Plymouth six months ago,' Mrs Maunder said. 'Against her father's wishes, of course. They had a fierce argument, and she hasn't been back since. I'm sure she'll come now this has happened.'

So that was why he hadn't seen or heard anything of Caroline for some while.

'I'm sure she will,' Seth said, and he sincerely hoped she would – Mr Maunder was a good man, well liked in the town.

'Silly girl has gone to be a live-in companion to some titled lady for reasons best known to herself.' Mrs Maunder dabbed at her eyes with a lace-edged handkerchief. 'And here's me being so indiscreet. It's the shock of what happened to Charles, of course. I trust you won't repeat this conversation, Mr Jago.'

'Of course not,' Seth said, although he was fairly certain

Caroline hadn't told her parents the half of why she had gone to Plymouth.

But that was none of his business.

'If there's nothing I can do for you, Mrs Maunder, I'll be on my way.'

'No, nothing. Thank you. You must have had a long night. I'll let you get on your way. But rest assured, I'll tell Caroline what a hero you are. So unlike your brother, Miles ... oh.'

Mrs Maunder put her hands to her mouth. To stop another indiscretion escaping? Why, Seth wondered, had she brought Miles' name into the conversation? Not that he was going to ask. If he never heard his brother's name mentioned again, it would be too soon.

'Good day, Mrs Maunder,' Seth said. 'I can see myself out.'

'Ah, there you are, Emma,' Mr Smythe said, when Emma – now recovered from her faint – knocked on his open study door to tell him she was ready to resume her duties. She and Ruby had made the recovery stretch to four days, certain they'd be caught out in their subterfuge, but they hadn't been. 'I've been meaning to talk to you.'

'It was a faint,' Emma said. 'I was tired. I'd been up most of the night. When Dr Shaw came he said I was run-down.'

'Yes, yes, so he told me. I trust you're taking the tonic?'

'Yes,' Emma lied.

She was never going to take that stuff – it tasted like she imagined boot polish would taste if she was ever stupid enough to eat any. She flushed a tablespoon of it a day down the lavatory, just in case Mr Smythe should check on her.

'It's not your recovery I want to talk to you about. I think it's time you have a new frock to dance in. Something that sparkles as you will when you dance.'

'Dance?'

'You do know how?'

Not really, she thought. She'd only ever had that one, short, turn around the seat in the foyer with Matthew Caunter, and that had been almost two years ago.

'I didn't mean the knowing of it. I meant the dancing.'

The hotel had been hosting Friday night dinner dances for some months now but Emma had never been a part of it. Or wanted to be. Well, with no one to dance with, why would she?

'I don't need a new frock. To dance in or otherwise. My lilac one does me well enough for best, and besides, my amethyst necklace goes so prettily with it.'

'Possibly, possibly,' Mr Smythe said. 'But I think a frock to dance in and some suitable jewellery, and shoes, in the circumstances – since we're to be engaged shortly, once you are eighteen …'

'I apologise for interrupting, but I haven't said yes to your proposal,' Emma said.

'Not yet. I rather hope, once you become more a part of my life, that you will see my proposal as a good idea. I like to think I've been benevolent in affording you a safe haven, and that you are not unappreciative of that.'

'I do appreciate it, yes. Thank you. But I'm not sure other people – your business associates I mean – will think the same if you are seen dancing with … with your daughter's nursemaid unless I have your engagement ring on my finger …'

Oh God, what was she saying? That she wanted to wear his engagement ring? She wished she could swallow the words back but she couldn't – they were out now, hovering between them in the air. She saw Mr Smythe's lips quiver – the beginnings of a smile.

'French tutor, Emma,' he said. 'As well as nursemaid, of course. But I can assure you they will consider it totally appropriate for you to join me in that capacity.'

'I'd still rather not ...'

'You are an ungrateful little wretch,' Mr Smythe said. 'It's not a lot to ask, is it – that you dance with me?'

'Telling,' Emma said. 'You're telling me. Ordering me.'

'Would it hurt so very much?'

'Yes.'

He'd probably buy her a dress that was cut low and would show an awful lot of skin, wouldn't he?

'You'll come around to the idea, Emma, I'm sure you will. Where would you go if you went from here?'

And that, Mr Smythe, is emotional blackmail she thought, but even she wasn't brave enough to say so. But his question was valid – where indeed would she go? She had savings, but nowhere near enough to last beyond a few months if she couldn't secure another position straight away. Certainly she didn't have enough to start a business, which was all she dreamed about – well, that and Seth.

'I'll try the dancing, Mr Smythe,' Emma said. There was over a month to go before her eighteenth birthday – she'd save every penny, feather her nest as best she could before making her escape. But in truth, the thought of fending for herself completely was turning her blood to ice in her veins. She wasn't quite ready to strike out on her own and pursue her dream of having her own business just yet. 'Although I might not take to it ...'

Against her better judgement, Emma was dressed, ready for her first Friday night dance. But she'd acquiesced – however unwise she'd been in doing so – to Mr Smythe's request so she'd just have to get on with it.

Ruby came rushing into the room, holding Isabelle by the hand. 'Madamoiselle here wanted to see you in all your finery,' she said. 'And blimey, what finery, Em.'

Emma smoothed her hands down over the fabric of

her dress. A soft milky shade of satin embroidered with what looked like a million crystals. Mr Smythe had had Eve Grainger lay it on her bed as a surprise. No doubt the rest of the staff were downstairs now giggling about her and making up all sorts of stories about what she got up to with Mr Smythe if he'd spent that much on a dress for her.

She glanced at herself in the cheval glass, feeling naked and vulnerable without her mama's amethyst at her neck, and in its place a string of pearls with a huge pear-shaped pearl dropper. And earrings to match. On her feet were cream leather court shoes with a strap – the only part of the whole ensemble she liked and would have chosen for herself.

'Apart from the shoes,' Emma said. 'I look like a dowager.'

'A come again?' Ruby said.

'An aged, rich widow with too much money to spend on fripperies and too much time on her hands.'

Caroline Prentiss came to mind with the word 'widow' – not that Mrs Prentiss was that old. In her mid-thirties at the oldest.

'Well, you haven't got none of that, maid,' Ruby said. 'Have you? Me neither.' She scooped Isabelle into her arms, plonked her on one hip. 'She looks a right treat an' all, doesn't she, Belle?'

'Pretty dress. Belle want pretty dress. Dance with me, Emma.'

Emma pursed her lips. Ruby would persist in shortening Isabelle's name and now even the child was calling herself Belle. But she decided now was not the time for an argument with Ruby because in all fairness Ruby loved the child.

So, Emma took Isabelle from Ruby's arms and affected a polka with her around the room until the child's cheeks turned pink with laughing and delight. Another glance in the mirror and Emma saw that her own cheeks were flushed, too.

'Well, aren't you the beautiful one,' Ruby said, but there wasn't a hint of jealousy in her voice. 'My money is on Mr Smythe falling in love with you tonight, Em.'

Emma almost dropped Isabelle with the shock of Ruby's words. Carefully she set the child down on the rag rug.

Such a short time ago she'd dreamed of working and living in Nase Head House. And of dancing on the tiled floor. If she'd known she'd be in the position she was now she'd never have entertained the idea.

'Never,' Emma said, making for the door. 'His heart got buried with his wife.'

Chapter Twenty-One

'You look even more beautiful tonight, Emma,' Mr Smythe said, standing as she approached, before gesturing that she take the seat next to his. 'I see I've chosen well.'

Emma sat, grateful that she wouldn't have to be in his arms just yet. Whether he meant his choice of clothes and accessories for her, or in deciding he was going to make her his wife, she didn't know and certainly wasn't going to ask.

She should never have started this charade, should she? The days were ticking away to her eighteenth birthday and while her savings were adding up, they were still nowhere near the amount she would need to keep her from the workhouse.

Emma looked about her – anywhere but at Mr Smythe. The room was filling up with guests stopping at the hotel but also a few business people and richer residents from the town.

The cellist and the violinist were both leafing through sheet music and the pianist was playing a slow and rather dreamy piece of music. Chopin probably. Chopin was Mr Smythe's favourite composer. Emma had a feeling Chopin had been Claudine Smythe's favourite, too.

'I think it's time I asked the good Dr Shaw to come and take a look at you again, Emma,' Mr Smythe said. There was a joking lilt to his voice Emma hadn't heard there before. It made her uneasy.

'Dr Shaw? Why? There's nothing wrong with me.'

'No? Not going a little deaf?'

'Deaf? Of course not.'

'Then if you heard my compliment to you – and honestly given I have to say – it's only polite to respond. To say thank you at the very least.'

'I didn't ask you to buy me these things,' Emma said. 'And they wouldn't have been what I would have chosen. I think I look like a dowager.'

Rupert Smythe guffawed with laughter and heads turned to look towards him. Emma felt herself flush, felt the heat of it at the sides of her neck. If only she had her amethyst there to hold on to, to ground her, to remind herself she was Emma Le Goff and not someone Mr Smythe was doing his best to mould into a replica of his late wife.

'A dowager indeed. You look wonderful, Emma, and you know it.'

'It's how you want me to look,' Emma said.

'Now, stop this. I do believe you're an ungrateful wretch.'

Mr Smythe tapped Emma gently on the back of the hand in faux admonishment. She swiftly moved her hand into her lap, and again Mr Smythe guffawed with laughter. Emma wondered if he'd been at the eau de vie or something.

'I know I have things to be grateful for,' Emma said, choosing her words with care. To say she loved his choice of clothes for her would only mean he would buy her more. Own a little bit more of her. And she didn't want that. 'And I'm not a wretch.'

'No, of course you're not. You're by far the most beautiful woman in the room, and certainly the most expensively dressed. And I don't think I'm the ugliest escort either, am I?' Again that joking lilt in his voice.

Emma glanced at him, saw he was smiling, and yet there was still the sadness around the eyes he always had. He was – she was sure of it – thinking of his wife, as he always would.

'You know you're not,' Emma said. 'I saw that lady over there glancing at you admiringly a moment ago. The one in the silver frock with the diamanté around the neckline. Why don't you ask her to dance? I'm sure she wouldn't refuse.'

'Joanna Gillet?' Mr Smythe said, after a quick scan of the room to see which lady Emma was referring to. 'I don't have the slightest desire to dance with Joanna Gillet. I only want to dance with *you*, Emma.'

He reached for her hand. She wanted to whisk it away, hide it behind her back, but to do so might cause a fuss. She willed herself to relax under his touch. And then to her horror he lifted her hand to his lips and kissed the back of it. He'd definitely been at the eau de vie, hadn't he? There was always a bottle of it on a side table in his drawing-room.

So it was with some relief to Emma when the three-piece band began to play. She stood up, able to wriggle her hand free from his as she did so.

'Usually, Emma,' Mr Smythe said, standing beside her, 'the lady waits to be asked to dance.'

'Usually,' Emma said. 'But what you're forgetting is that I'm not a lady. I'm Emma Le Goff from a poor fishing family whose mother was considered a suicide and not fit to be buried in consecrated ground, even though she is. I doubt anyone in this room, bar a few of the locals, knows that, but if they did do you think they'd consider me a suitable companion for you? Most of them wouldn't consider me worthy of cleaning their shoes if they knew.'

What more could she do or say to put him off?

'And do you think any of that bothers me at all? Either the facts about your background, or about the people here knowing? I admire your drive to make the most of the cards dealt you in life. I admire the way you learn quickly and that you're an asset to the hotel in so many ways. And yes, I admire your beauty. You've flourished since you've been here, blossomed.'

'It's called growing up, Mr Smythe,' Emma said. 'I would have done that anyway, I expect. Now, shall we dance?'

Mr Smythe threw back his head and laughed loudly.

Goodness, what *had* got into him tonight? But the musicians had upped the tempo and the noise of dancers' feet on the polished floor and their chattering voices meant that no one noticed.

The rest of the evening passed slowly, so slowly. Emma was asked to dance by one of the hotel guests and from time to time, Mr Smythe excused himself to dance with guests or the wives of business associates, but always returning to Emma after each dance. Her heart had lifted a little when she'd seen Mr Smythe dance with Joanna Gillet. Although she'd wanted to laugh out loud when she saw the way he held Joanna – as though she was a muddy dog that needed to be kept at arms' length.

She declined a glass of sherry, even though Mr Smythe had pressed it into her hands. And when the champagne was brought round she declined that, too. She needed to keep a clear head.

'Last dance, Emma,' Mr Smythe said now.

'I'd like to sit this one out,' Emma said. With luck she could make her escape early. 'Ask Miss Gillet.'

Mr Smythe, fuelled now by more than a few glasses of sherry and at least two flutes of champagne, only laughed.

And then a man Emma hadn't seen before came rushing through the open double doors of the small ballroom. He stopped and looked about him. How strange to turn up at a dance the moment it was about to finish. Or perhaps he was a late-arrival hotel guest – but at this hour? But for whatever reason she was glad of his arrival. All eyes in the room seem to be on him, too.

'Oh, there's Howard Bettesworth. I wonder what he wants.'

Rupert Smythe – in a rather wobbly fashion – stood up and beckoned to the newcomer.

Emma recognised the name of the biggest law firm in the area.

Mr Bettesworth rushed on in. Couples cleared a pathway for him, stopped their chattering. Most of the locals present would know who he was and those that didn't would wonder at his reception.

A hush fell over the room as the three-piece band stopped playing.

'Smythe,' he said, holding out his hand. 'I know the hour is late but I thought you would want to know. Rum news. Carter Jago swung this afternoon. It's not a pretty sight witnessing a man hang. I don't suppose I could get a drink, could I?'

Emma's hand flew to her mouth. That Carter deserved to be hanged she was certain and the realisation that he had tried to kiss her, to assault her, made her feel faint. She sat back in her chair.

'A drink? Of course.' Mr Smythe signalled to a waiter.

'And that's not all,' Mr Bettesworth said. 'Seth Jago has instructed me in the sale of his fishing fleet.'

'And well he should,' Mr Smythe said. 'We don't want the brother of a murderer in the town.'

There were mutterings of 'Hear, hear' from the dancers.

'Seth's selling the boats?' Emma said. She hadn't meant to actually voice the words but they'd slipped out of their own volition.

'Hush, Emma,' Mr Smythe said. 'This is business.'

'I won't hush. Why's Seth selling up, Mr Bettesworth?'

The solicitor looked at Mr Smythe and raised an eyebrow as if to say, 'who's this and should I be answering her questions?' Mr Smythe gave a brief nod of his head.

'Because he has plans to go to Canada it seems. Vancouver. And that's all I'm telling you. But it will be round the town soon enough.'

Canada? Seth was going to Canada? Without telling her? Who was going to put flowers on his ma's grave? And who might he be going to Canada *with*?

Everyone seemed to be talking at once then. The name Jago echoed from people's lips all around the room.

'No better than he should be, that Seth Jago.'

'Tarred with the same brush as his father and brothers, no doubt.'

'Just lucky they couldn't pin anything on him.'

'Not his father's son at all, perhaps, if you get my meaning.'

The words washed over Emma like acid. Her skin prickled, her throat went dry. She felt cold, then hot, then cold again.

How would Seth be feeling now his brother had hanged? Poor Seth.

'Well at least that's solved one problem for me,' Mr Smythe said.

Mr Bettesworth laughed. 'What's that then?'

'Keeping him from my door. I've had him thrown out once tonight. He came ...'

'You threw him out? Why?'

Emma's voice rang loud and clear around the room as she jumped to her feet. All eyes were on her now – and her alone.

'I'll tell you again, Emma – keep out of this.' Mr Smythe turned towards Mr Bettesworth. 'I should never have let him in here the night of Mr Underwood's dinner, but he was a guest of a client. And besides, there were other influential people as Mr Underwood's guests that night.'

'It's all about what use people are to you isn't it, Mr Smythe?' Emma said.

The two men wheeled round to look at her, surprise on their faces – at her audacity in speaking her mind, probably.

'I told you to keep out of this.'

Mr Smythe tried to push her back down onto her chair but she side-stepped him.

'No. No, I won't keep out of it. Seth's done nothing wrong. He stood up for me against his brothers, and his father.

He got me food when I had none. And he bought a headstone for my parents' and my brother's graves. He's a good man. Haven't any of you stopped to think how he'll be feeling that his brother's been hanged for murder?' Emma knew her voice had reached screeching level but she couldn't stop. 'He …'

Mr Smythe lurched towards her and she could smell all the alcohol on his breath. He gripped her wrist.

'As it was you he came here asking for before I threw him out, you'd better go to him, hadn't you, young lady? Although maybe lady isn't the word I should be using?' The hardness was back in his eyes, his lips stretched over his teeth like taught wires. 'I can see I was wasting my time with you.'

He dropped Emma's wrist as though it was on fire.

'You have five minutes to collect a few belongings. Then go.'

Emma went. She should have gone months ago.

Beattie Drew stood with the door to Hilltop House open only a crack. She looked unsure as to whether to let Emma in or not.

Emma was certainly surprised to see her there so late at night.

'Well, look at you in all your finery, Emma Le Goff. Too proud and stuck-up to come and see your old friends, weren't you? What brings you here now? And at this hour?'

'I wasn't too proud and I'm not stuck-up. I had a lot to learn and I learned most of it in five minutes just now. I've just made myself homeless. My own doing this time, Mrs Drew.'

'Oh, lovie, you are a one.'

The old Mrs Drew Emma had known, and who had been so kind to her, was back.

'Can I see Seth? Please.'

'He's out.' Mrs Drew waved a hand down towards the inky blackness of the harbour, made an arc in the air to encompass the bay.

'I was told Seth called asking for me, but Mr Smythe threw him out.'

'Did he now? I can't imagine Seth took kindly to that.'

'I wouldn't know. I was prevented from seeing him. Where is Seth now? Do you know?'

'He said he was going to see Mr Underwood. He's had rum news today of his brother. I wouldn't be at all surprised if Mr Underwood hasn't taken him for a pint or two. To drown his sorrows.'

'Can I wait for him?' Emma said.

'He should have been back ages ago,' Mrs Drew said, as though Emma hadn't asked anything. 'It's why I'm not in my night things. He'll be wanting a hot drink when he gets back.'

'You're living here now?'

'Since my old man died, yes. Got my Edward here with me an' all. The others have got positions on farms. Accommodation, see.'

'I didn't know you'd been widowed, Mrs Drew. I'm sorry.'

''Twere a while ago, now. Had an accident at the quarry. Load of stone was unbalanced and that was that – it toppled and did for my ol' man. But there it is – I'm here now. And glad to be.'

Emma shivered in her thin dress. The five minutes Mr Smythe had given her to collect a few things had barely been enough to grab all her money from under the mattress, rip off the pearls and earrings Mr Smythe had bought her and put her mama's amethyst around her neck instead – only remembering to take her shawl from the back of the chair at the last moment. She hadn't worn it since arriving at Nase

Head House, but hadn't been able to part with it, either. She'd kept it on the back of the chair for old times' sake, and was glad of it now, as worn and threadbare as it was in places. She pulled it more tightly around her shoulders.

'You'd better come in and wait, lovie. You'll catch your death in that slip of a frock, so you will. You've heard about Carter, I reckon?'

Emma nodded.

'Now, in with you and let's get you warmed up.'

Emma stepped inside gratefully as Mrs Drew opened the door wider. She waited while Mrs Drew closed the door and locked it. It was a big house by anyone's standards but it seemed small when set against Nase Head House in her mind. Nothing seemed to have changed since the last time she'd stood in this hall – the same pictures were on the wall. The same smell of stew in the air.

'How did you find out about Carter?' Mrs Drew asked, walking towards the kitchen.

Emma followed closely behind.

'Mr Bettesworth called at the hotel this evening. The dance was just ending ...'

'The solicitor fellow? I expect you know him what with you mixing with the nobs and all?'

'I only knew his name. I've seen it in the papers a time or two.' She chose to ignore the 'mixing with the nobs' bit.

'Where could Seth be, Mrs Drew?' Perhaps she could go and find him if she knew?

'I've already told you, lovie. In an inn somewhere having a pint or two with Mr Underwood I expect. There's no one he trusts more. And no doubt the pair of 'em have gone to the back room of whatever inn it is they'm to after closing time.'

'And you've been expecting him back before now?'

'I have. Oh, but it's good to see you, Emma. I've often

looked over to Nase Head House and wondered how you were doing. Remember how we stood, you and me, in the bedroom looking at it and you said you were going to work there some day? Bet you never thought you would?'

And I wish now I never had, Emma thought, but didn't say.

'And it looks like you got to dance under them chandeliers with that fancy frock you've got on.' Emma let Mrs Drew prattle on. 'Not seen you in the town much.'

'Working in a hotel isn't so much a job, I've been fast finding out, as a way of life. I only had one half day a week and I used to spend that caring for Isabelle mostly.'

'I'm surprised a man like Mr Smythe didn't want to make an honest woman of you.' Mrs Drew laughed.

'It was nothing like that,' Emma said.

'But he had hopes?'

'Yes. But however many times I told him I wasn't interested in being the second Mrs Smythe, the more he kept on about it. Buying me things. Dancing with me ...' Emma let her voice trail away, swallowed back tears.

'There are men like that what do think it's their God-given right to have any women they choose. I'm glad you didn't fall for it though, lovie. He'd have sucked your soul dry, wouldn't he?'

Emma swallowed. That was exactly it. She'd stopped feeling like herself. She'd allowed herself to become someone she thought she wanted to be, but now knew she didn't want to.

She tried to stop the tears coming, but failed miserably. One by one they trickled down her cheeks until it felt there was a river running down the sides of her neck, slithering over her shoulder blades, and down the cleavage of her stupid, stupid dowager dress.

She swiped at the tears.

'Cocoa time, lovie,' Mrs Drew said. 'Not a lot a nice mug of hot cocoa can't cure, is there? Sugar?'

'Yes, please. Seth's going to be surprised to find me here, though. Do you think he'll mind?'

Emma was starting to have misgivings now. If he did mind, then she'd tell him how sorry she was about Carter and the effects it would have on him, and then she'd book herself into The Globe for the night. She had enough money, and thank heavens for that.

'Oh, I shouldn't think so for one minute,' Mrs Drew said. She put an arm around Emma's shoulders, gave them a squeeze, then set a saucepan of milk to boil. 'And you said yourself he'd called asking for you tonight. He must have wanted you for summat.' Mrs Drew giggled. 'And what's more, I'd like half a crown for every time Seth's asked if I've seen or heard anything of you.'

'Has he?'

'Didn't I just say? You always did have a habit of questioning things. But he'll be as pleased as punch that you're here.'

'Even though he's got the boats up for sale and is going to Canada?'

'Has he?' Mrs Drew said. There was genuine surprise in her voice. 'First I've heard of it. We'll ask him about it when he gets in. But between you and me I'm worried where he's got to, so I hope we don't have long to wait.'

So do I, Emma thought, so do I.

''Ere, Seth Jago. What's all this about the boats being up for sale?'

Seth looked up from his beer. Albie Holland – one of his crewmen. He took another sip of his beer and considered Albie's question. So, telling Bettesworth had done the trick – the rumour was spreading faster than fire through dried bracken. Would Emma have heard? Would it be enough for her to realise how much she'd miss him if he left? Or wouldn't she care?

'So is it true?' Albie demanded. ''Cos if it is I hope you'm making the provision the new owner keeps on us crew.'

'My boats might, and they might not, be for sale,' Seth said. His head was beginning to feel like it was floating independently of his body. Being denied access to Nase Head House to speak to Emma had come as a shock – a short, sharp shock. And the strong ale wasn't helping. 'But I won't see you out of work if I can help it.'

'Well, just as long as you keep your word,' Albie said.

'I will.'

'Good. Anyway, what're you doing in 'ere? The Blue Anchor's your usual drinking hole.'

'I fancied a change. And it looks like I'm drinking, Albie, doesn't it? Sh...ame as you. Sh...sh...sheeing as ...'

'Seeing as you'm obviously not used to downing quite so much.' Albie laughed and his mates joined in. 'Heard your brother was found guilty back along. He'll be swinging any day. I 'spect you're drowning your sorrows.'

Seth screwed his eyes shut tight, but the thought of Carter being led to the gallows wouldn't go away. He'd told Olly the news, but the rest of them would have to wait 'til the morning when, no doubt, the word would have got round. He swayed on his bar stool but Olly came to his rescue, put a steadying hand on Seth's shoulder.

'That's right, Albie. And if a man – for whatever reason – can't have a skinful of ale, and do it in peace, then it's a bad job. Now bugger off. And here's a half crown to do it with. Some place other than here, if you get my meaning.'

Olly Underwood took the coin from his pocket and pressed it into Albie's palm. The man went back to his drinking companions, said something and they all finished their pints and left the inn.

'Thanks, Olly,' Seth muttered. He must remember to pay him back the money, but would he? The way his head was he wasn't sure he'd be able to say his own name if asked.

'Drink up, Seth,' Olly said. 'It'll help you forget for a little while. But what's all this about Canada? I'm supposed to be your best friend and this is the first I've heard of it.'

'I set a sprat to catch a mackerel, Olly. Seeing as Smythe barred me from his premises.'

'Ah, one Miss Le Goff?' Olly said, his voice low, almost a mime.

Seth nodded.

'Well, much as I'd love to sit here and listen to you extolling the good Emma's charms, I must be off. My ma's been sick and I said I wouldn't be too late back. You'll be all right?'

'Yeah, 'course I will. With some good ale inside me.' Seth took a long swig of his pint.

'Good man,' Olly said. He patted Seth on the back and left.

'For a little while,' Seth mumbled into his tankard as he watched Olly go out through the door. 'For a little while. If I'm lucky.'

'Behave, you lot. I'm just going down the cellar for another barrel,' the landlord yelled.

The second he was out of sight all hell let loose. About half-a-dozen men surrounded Seth. Strangers to him, all of them. One rammed a hand into a pocket of Seth's trousers, removed the loose change he had in there.

'Heard you're a rich man,' one of the men said. 'You can share your riches out a bit.'

The speaker yanked back Seth's head and poured beer down his throat – it made him splutter and cough and he swallowed far more than he wanted to. He felt hands scrabbling in his other pocket, extracting coins.

'Now your mate's gone you're on your own.'

'Get off …'

The strength seemed to have seeped out of Seth. The ale was doing its job, making him whoozy. He knew he was no match for half-a-dozen men.

'Use that money you've just stolen from me to buy more drinks, lads.' Seth said. He took a £5 note from his inside pocket. 'And take this. Make that two pints. Keep the change.'

'Now you're talking sense,' someone said, and his tormentors left him in peace.

Seth set his unfinished tankard on the table, closed his eyes. A little doze and then he'd make his way home. It wasn't far. Although he had a sick feeling in his gut he hadn't seen the last of these men.

Chapter Twenty-Two

'Eyes bigger than your belly, were they, lovie?' Beattie Drew said. She patted the back of Emma's hand. 'Thought you wanted everything there was to be had at Nase Head House but now you've tasted it all it's not to your liking?'

Emma wished, just for a moment, for Mrs Drew to stop talking. Waiting for Seth was bad enough – the not knowing. She certainly didn't need her own bad judgement laid out before her for scrutiny, even if that's exactly what it had been – her ill thought-out yearning to be at Nase Head House.

'Some of it I liked well enough,' Emma said. 'I learned a lot about how to run a hotel. A business. Just by watching and listening. And I liked teaching the children. Oh ... oh ...'

'You're going to miss them?'

Emma nodded, too choked up to speak. She shouldn't have been so impetuous. Hadn't she told Mr Smythe herself that if he was going to change the arrangements for the children's tuition, their care, then he would have to do it slowly – let them get used to changes gradually. And now she'd upped sticks and left. How would the children feel to find her gone in the morning? And Ruby – she should have got word to her that she was leaving.

'I'll miss Ruby. She's been a good friend to me.'

'As no doubt you've been to her. Am I right?'

'I hope so. And she's good with Isabelle. The child will be all right with Ruby looking after her.' Emma knew that if she now had to spend more time with the children, it would be no hardship to Ruby.

'So, there's no need to fret about little Isabelle if she's got your friend, Ruby, there, is there? Until Mr Smythe finds himself a wife and then it'll all change, mark my words. He's waited a respectable two years before looking for a new wife and now you've refused the position, he'll find someone else soon enough.'

'Do you think so?'

'Know so.'

Emma yawned as a huge wave of tiredness enveloped her. She risked a glance at the clock and wished she hadn't – midnight had been and long gone. Beattie Drew saw the glance.

'Here we are talking about everything under the sun 'cept the person we should be talking about – Seth. I've got to admit I'm more worried than ever now. More cocoa, lovie?'

Emma, curled up in the chair by the range, shook her head. She didn't look up. The minute hand on the clock on the mantelpiece seemed to be going around so slowly. So very slowly. She didn't want to see that barely a minute might have passed since she'd last looked.

'No thanks.'

The chocolaty-ness of the cocoa she'd just finished had made the inside of her mouth feel dry. She didn't want any more, and didn't think she'd be able to swallow it anyway.

'I've just had a thought. With his balance all over the shop if he's had too much ale, he might have fallen in …'

'Stop it, Mrs Drew. You're frightening me.'

'I'm frightening meself, but summat's happened.'

Beattie Drew put a hand to her mouth, stifled a yawn. And now that Emma was looking at her properly she could see the woman was tired. There were large dark folds of skin resting on her ruddy cheeks.

'Don't let me keep you up,' Emma said.

'And leave you here to worry all by yourself?'

'I'll be fine.'

'Well, I'm not fine about leaving you. I'm sure Seth won't

mind you being here, but if he comes in and isn't too happy about seeing you in all your finery then I can help persuade him otherwise.'

Emma sighed – her shoulders heaving up towards her ears then down again. 'I always said I'd never come in this house again, and now here I am.'

'Well, them as who you didn't want to see aren't here any more. And good riddance to the lot of them. I know that Carter made a play for you in the drawing-room, didn't he? Touched you where he shouldn't?'

Emma nodded. Felt sick as the memory of it came back – it felt the way heartburn felt, only this was in her soul.

'Let it go, lovie, let it go. I hope Seth can, too.'

'And me. I'll stay until I know Seth's safe and then I'll move on.'

She told Beattie Drew how she had money and would find a room in a hotel in the morning and then work out what she was going to do next.

'But I couldn't just sit there and listen to Mr Smythe and the solicitor saying terrible things about Seth – how he'd been kept from going into Nase Head House because of the things his father and brothers did. I didn't want Seth to think I thought those things, too.'

''Course you didn't, lovie.'

Beattie Drew ran water into the milk pan, began to scour it out.

And then there was a banging on the front door. And shouting. Men's voices.

'That'll be the man of the house back and no doubt,' Beattie Drew said. She wiped her wet hands down the sides of her apron. 'Better go and let him in.'

Emma, stiff now from so long curled up in the chair, eased herself to a sitting position, then got up slowly and followed Beattie Drew out of the room. Their heels clicked on the tiled passage – an echoey sound in the stillness of the night, punctuated by random shouts from the men at the door.

Beattie Drew unlocked the door, but kept the chain on.

'Just as I thought,' she said, looking back over her shoulder at Emma. 'Drunk the lot of them. Can't see Seth yet, though.' She called through the crack to the men. 'Got Seth Jago there have you, lads?'

''Course we have, you old crone,' one of them said and laughed. The others joined in.

'Watch your language lads or I'll scour your mouths out with carbolic.'

Beattie Drew seemed unfazed by their rudeness. She took a candle in its holder from the side-table.

'Later,' another lad laughed. 'Best open up and let Mr Jago in 'cos he's in a bad way. We can't afford to lose a good boss, can we lads?'

His companions, very noisily, agreed that they couldn't.

'Bad way?' Emma said. She tried to get between Mrs Drew and the gap in the door but was pushed back.

'Drunk, lovie. Unable to stand. Made a mess of himself as well, no doubt.' Beattie Drew took the chain off the door and opened it wider.

Emma gasped. By the candlelight she could see Seth draped over a handcart with what looked like blood all over his face.

'Oh, lawks a mercy on us,' Beattie Drew said. 'What happened, lads?'

'Got in a bit of a fight, I'd say, wouldn't you?'

'Us was taking a short cut home and us found 'im lying in the alley. Broken glass all over the place there was. He …'

'Enough,' Beattie Drew shouted. 'Get him off that filthy handcart 'cos it idn' fit for rotting fish heads never mind a man, and take him through to the kitchen, then you can all clear off. And make sure you're quiet about it 'cos my

Edward's asleep upstairs an' if you waken 'im you'll know all about it.'

After much shushing of one another and theatrical walking on tiptoe by the men, Seth was at last propped up in the chair Emma had so recently vacated. Stupidly, she was glad it was still warm for him, even though she knew he probably wouldn't know whether it was a warm chair or a block of ice they used to chill the fish.

She tried to see where the blood was coming from that covered Seth's face. Some had either run into his hair, or had come from a head wound. His clothes were slowly soaking up the blood, some of it drying now to an orangey-brown on his shirt.

Emma rushed to the sink. Grabbed a dish from the plate rack on the wall and filled it with water. It felt cold – icy. Then she took a clean tea-towel that was airing on the overhead drying rack.

'Is there a drop of warm in the kettle?' she asked.

'Help yourself,' Beattie Drew said. 'I'll just go and see if I can find something to stop the bleeding. Compress or something. And a pillow for 'im to rest against. Oh, and iodine.' She bustled from the room, leaving Emma wincing at the word iodine. She knew iodine stung.

Carefully, Emma dabbed the dampened cloth on Seth's bloodied face. Blood seemed to have come from quite a few cuts – as though a glass had been pressed into Seth's face perhaps. Yes, glass. Carefully she picked two small shards from a sliver of a cut.

'Oh, Seth. Why ever did you let yourself get into this mess?'

Emma sent up a silent prayer that Seth wouldn't be permanently scarred. And that the cuts wouldn't be too deep and get infected.

'But I'd love you scars and all,' she whispered.

Seth groaned and squirmed under her touch, as light as it was. Even though he was in such a mess and stinking of drink, Emma's heart lurched at the sight of him, the feel of him under her fingers.

'Now then,' Beattie Drew said, bustling back into the room, her arms filled with the things they would need to tend to Seth. 'You hold 'is head forward and I'll slip this pillow in behind 'im.'

Emma did as she was told.

'Now then, what's the damage?'

'I think he's had a glass or a bottle pushed in his face,' Emma said. She pointed to the shards of glass she'd placed on the table. 'I've picked out two.'

'Well, keep picking them out, lovie. Look in his head as well.'

Emma did as she was told. Found three more shards on the cheekbone underneath Seth's left eye. She gulped. What if the glass had gone an inch or two higher? Seth could have been blinded, couldn't he?

But still she would have loved him. He'd come looking for her and been turned away, hadn't he? He did care for her – she knew it.

How strange it felt to Emma to be running her hands through Seth's hair, ministering to him when she hadn't spoken to him in a long while and seen him only across the harbour. She'd never touched him this intimately before and wondered what he would think if he knew she was. And yet it felt so right to be doing it. To be here when Seth needed her most.

Emma stood back and let Beattie Drew apply compresses to the deeper cuts until they stopped running with fresh blood.

'He'll live,' Beattie Drew said, at last. 'Now, let's get him undressed.'

'Undressed?'

'You heard, lovie. Shoes first.'

Emma pulled Seth's shoes off as gently as she could while Beattie Drew undid the buttons on the flies of his trousers. Emma could see white underwear and wondered if Beattie Drew intended to strip Seth of that, too.

'Good girl.' Beattie Drew bent down to feel Seth's stockinged feet. 'Well, they're dry so we'll leave them on. But you'll have to help me get these trousers off him.'

'I will?'

'You and your questioning, Emma Le Goff,' Beattie Drew said, but she said it with a smile on her face. 'Seen a man how God made him before, haven't you?'

'Only Johnnie when he was a baby. And Archie and Sidney Smythe but they're little boys. They're ...'

'Same thing, only bigger. Now I'll hold him up and you pull on the trouser legs. Gently now.'

Emma did as she was told, but to her horror Seth's underclothes came away with the trousers.

'Much bigger in Seth's case, I see,' Beattie Drew said. 'Now, you hold his feet up and I'll find a stool to put under 'em to support 'em.'

Emma did as she was told while Mrs Drew took a low stool from under the kitchen table.

'Well, what do you think, lovie?' Mrs Drew said when they'd got Seth settled as comfortably as they could. 'Won't *that* make a woman of a girl one day?'

'Mrs Drew.' Emma felt herself blush.

'Don't waste your blushes, lovie. Seth can't see how pretty they make you look, can he? Now undo those shirt buttons and we'll see if the blood on that shirt I ironed only yesterday has come from his face, or if someone's took a knife to him.'

'A knife?'

'Shirt buttons, Emma. I'm going to get some water on the

boil. We're going to have to clean these cuts a bit better and need sterilised water to do it, don't we?'

Emma nodded, began to unbutton Seth's shirt. Dark curls sprang out as she pulled the fabric away from his chest. She poked a baby finger in the curls and wound them round and round until her finger was caught fast. She closed her eyes then opened them again, let them run down over Seth's body. The hair around his man parts was curly too ... and long. Emma undid the last button of Seth's shirt and it was all she could do not to place a finger in those curls, feel how it felt ...

'Emma. Time for that later, my girl.'

'I don't know what you're talking about,' Emma said. She tore her gaze away from the amused face of Mrs Drew and began to examine Seth's chest for any cuts. To her relief there were none.

Between them, Emma and Mrs Drew tended Seth's wounds and then Mrs Drew unfolded a crisply ironed linen sheet from a pile on the dresser and covered Seth's nakedness.

'Now, I don't know where I'm going to put you for the night, lovie. My guess is you wouldn't want to sleep in a room that had been Carter's, or Miles', or that evil father of theirs. There's Seth's room, of course, seeing as he won't be wanting ...'

'I'll stay here,' Emma said. 'Watch over Seth. In case he's sick or anything ...'

'Oh yes? I saw the way you looked at him. You just want to peek under that sheet ...'

'No, I don't. I don't think it's right that I impose on Seth's hospitality any more than I already am. I'll sit in the chair the other side of the range if you can get me a blanket to sleep under, and then if he's sick or wakes in pain ...'

'You can tend to him?'

Mrs Drew grinned and to Emma's horror she found

303

herself grinning back. Now Seth was back in her life she didn't want to lose sight of him. Not for a minute. But what was he going to say when he found her there in the morning?

'Is this heaven?'

Seth lifted his head from the pillow, his words startling Emma from a half-doze. She shivered because her blanket had slid to the floor. She must have dozed for longer than she'd thought and fidgeted in her half-sleep because her dress had ridden up almost to her knees. One strap of her dress bodice had slipped down over her shoulder. What a sight she must look.

But oh, how good it was to hear his voice, even though he still sounded whoozy with drink. All through the night Emma had left her chair and gone to him at regular intervals to check on his breathing. She'd put her hand on top of the sheet and left it there until she could feel the rise and fall of his chest. And once, when it hadn't been discernible, she'd slid her hand underneath the sheet, let it rest at the bottom of his rib cage – his flesh warm and smooth beneath her palm.

'Heaven?' Emma said. 'What makes you think you're in heaven?'

'Because there's a beautiful woman looking at me who looks very much like I imagine angels to look.'

'With my colour hair? Angels are blonde.'

'Who says? Anyway, I don't go for blondes.'

'Who do you go for, as you put it, then?'

'Emma Le Goff. Let her slip through my fingers, I did.'

Seth peered at her through slitted eyelids, as though he was finding it hard to focus.

'You're still drunk, Seth Jago, and you should be ashamed of yourself.'

Seth's eyes widened then. 'It *is* you? I woke up just now

and thought it was you sitting in the chair. And then I thought, no it couldn't possibly be Emma Le Goff because she's over at Nase Head House and any day now she's going to marry Rupert Smythe, and ...'

'Oh no, I'm not,' Emma said. 'Whoever told you that?'

'Not going to say. But people talk.' Seth tapped the side of his nose. 'I went up to Nase Head House last night and asked to see you. I thought I'd point out you were making a mistake if you married Smythe. I was barred from entering. I ...'

'I'd *never* have married him, Seth. Never!'

'I'm relieved to hear it,' Seth said. 'And I know I'm probably more than a little hungover but ... why are you here?'

'Mr Smythe threw me out.'

'For?'

'Standing up for you.'

Seth looked at her for a long, long time. Emma almost stopped breathing waiting for him to say something.

'You might be better off marrying Smythe,' he said at last. 'There's no doubt more than a few would consider me untouchable goods with my brother hanged yesterday ...'

'I know about that,' Emma said, getting up from her chair, putting her clothes to rights as best she could. 'And I'm not one of your hypothetical "more than a few", Seth. I know the worth of you. And I'm definitely *not* going to marry Rupert Smythe.'

'But he's asked you?'

Time for the truth, Emma decided. 'Yes,' she said, ashamed now that she'd let herself be so malleable to Rupert Smythe's grooming and duping. And feeling stupid that she'd stayed at Nase Head House as long as she had. 'But I never would have.'

'Good,' Seth said. His mouth turned upwards in the beginnings of a smile. 'Ouch! It hurts to smile.'

'That'll teach you to temper your drinking, then,' Emma laughed.

Seth ran his fingers through his hair – they almost disappeared in the thickness of it, as though he hadn't been to a barber in a long time. Emma rather liked the length of his hair the way it was, wondered what it would be like to run her fingers through it and not be looking for blood and shards of glass.

Seth shifted, struggled to get himself into a better sitting position, then put his hands to his head and groaned, letting his head drop back onto the pillow.

'You've got a hangover,' Emma said.

'Yes, Miss,' Seth said. He flicked his tongue out between bruised lips at Emma.

'And put *that* back where it came from before I cut it off,' Emma said.

Seth raised his head from the pillow just a fraction but it was obvious the pain from his hangover and the bashing he'd been on the end of was too much for him.

'You just stay right there, Seth. I'll make you a cup of good, strong coffee and get you a bite of toast to eat.'

'Making yourself free in my kitchen, I see,' Seth said, but there was laughter in his voice. 'But I don't think I could eat or drink a thing, thank you.'

How good that laughter sounded to Emma – they were almost back to the way they'd been before circumstances and misunderstandings had parted them.

'You're pleased to see me, though?' Emma said.

'I am. And if I didn't think I'd die if I leapt from this chair ...' Seth took his hands from his head and slid them under the sheet. 'I haven't got anything on under here.'

'Except for your socks,' Emma said. 'And you look quite ridiculous if I may say so in just your socks.'

'And did you ... did you ...?'

'Yes.' Emma grinned. 'And I removed shards of glass from about your person.'

'Where?' Seth said. He felt about underneath the sheet.

'Higher up than that,' Emma said, laughing.

'But you saw me ...'

'I did. But I was too worried you were going to die on me to look properly.'

It was a lie. He hadn't looked in the least like he was going to die. And she had looked. And for longer than was seemly. Seth was beautiful, if a man's body could be called beautiful.

Emma felt herself blush and as the sun was way up now and the kitchen flooded with light she knew Seth would have noticed.

'You always did blush prettily, Emma,' Seth said.

'Do I?'

'There you go – forever questioning what a fellow says. But ...' Seth hauled himself upright in the chair. 'As delightful as this banter is and as wonderful as it is to see you sitting there looking like an angel, I have something to tell you. You might want to go when I have.'

'I think I know what it is. You've got the fishing fleet up for sale. You're going to Canada.'

'Ah, so that little snippet of information reached the spot I wanted it to reach.' Seth grinned at her.

'You mean me? You spread false stories?'

'Yes. For the best of reasons, Emma. I thought we had something very special, you and me, and my hope was that if you thought I was going to Canada then you'd come rushing back to me and beg to come with me.'

Emma laughed. 'I never had you down as so devious, Seth Jago.' But how thrilling it was to hear him laying his heart out before her.

'But that's not all I have to tell you. There's something else.

And, once I've told you, I'll understand if you don't want to have anything to do with me ...'

'Tell.'

'There's no easy way, Emma – Carter left a letter to be given to me after he was hanged. Howard Bettesworth had it delivered by hand just as I was going out last evening.

'The first thing I *want* to tell you is he confessed to pushing our ma down the cellar steps. There had been an argument about ...'

'Oh, Seth. I'm so sorry. You don't have to pain yourself telling me what it was about. But at least you know what happened to her.'

Emma placed a hand gently on Seth's shoulder.

'I do,' Seth said. 'But that's not all. The second thing he wrote to me about concerns you. But I don't want to tell you just yet. I'm feeling very undignified at the moment. I'll show you through to the dining-room – you can wait for me there while I get myself tidied up first.'

Reluctantly, Emma let him go – wrapped in the sheet. She would have to wait a little longer to hear the rest of what he had to say, wouldn't she?

Seth knew he was going to have to go back downstairs soon. He'd already taken far longer than need be. And Emma was waiting for him to give her the news he didn't really want to tell – or want her to hear. But it had to be done.

On high alert for the sound of the front door opening and closing – and Emma making her escape because, perhaps, she'd second-guessed what it was Seth had to tell her – Seth examined the cuts and bruises on his face. Cuts and bruises Emma had tended. But no sound of the door being opened and closed came.

Good, Emma was still waiting for him. A bittersweet thought because he'd promised to tell her everything that was in the letter Carter had written to him. What Emma wanted to do about it he'd leave up to her, and he'd abide by her decision. He'd thought about offering her money – he could afford it, after all – but had changed his mind; the Emma he knew so well would more than likely be too proud to accept it. And in any case, it was akin to blood money Seth realised now – and what price could you put on a mother and a brother, for goodness' sake?

Chapter Twenty-Three

Emma waited impatiently in the dining-room while Seth washed and dressed. Had she still been at Nase Head House she'd have breakfasted by now, and her stomach was beginning to grumble embarrassingly loudly.

When Seth at last appeared – with his hair clinging damply and deliciously to his neck, and looking handsome in a neatly pressed pair of trousers and a pale blue striped shirt, unbuttoned at the neck – Emma leapt to her feet. His wounds didn't look too bad now, either, in daylight.

'Has Mrs Drew been in yet?' Seth asked before Emma could say anything.

'No. She was up late last night. I expect she's sleeping on.'

'Ah yes – up late on my account. I won't disturb her. And Edward won't get up until his mother tells him to. He's a good lad but not the brightest of sparks.'

Just get on with it, Emma thought. She was becoming impatient now. But she could see Seth was anxious – he kept pushing his hair back off his forehead. She'd help him – get the conversational ball rolling.

'Seth, I think I know what you're going to tell me. Carter had something to do with Mama and Johnnie falling off the cliff, didn't he?'

If he'd pushed his ma down the cellar steps – his own ma – he probably wouldn't have thought twice about doing it again.

'There's the shortest of answers to that, Emma. And it grieves me to give it. But, yes. And I'm sorrier than you will ever know.'

So, she'd been right. She wished she could just leave it at that, but she couldn't.

'Why?' Emma asked, her whole being aching with sadness that her mama and Johnnie had lost their lives this way. 'Why?'

Seth held Carter's letter out towards her. 'You can read it for yourself. The answer's there. I'll go …'

'No. Stay.' She threw her arms behind her back, clenched her hands together. 'But I don't want to touch it. Can you put it down on the table? Please.'

'Of course. I'll find the page that concerns you.'

When he'd found the right page and finished smoothing out the creases, Emma took a deep breath and walked towards the table. Prison notepaper. Written in pencil.

She read. And afterwards was silent for a long while. Seth was silent, too, and she was grateful to him for staying and for not saying anything to try and make her feel better.

'He offered to waive the rent if Mama let him into her bed,' Emma said at last – having to say the words so she'd know they were true. 'I thought they were your father's properties?'

'They were. But Carter collected rents for Pa sometimes – if people were slow to pay …'

'Your brother threatened them,' Emma finished for him.

'That's the sum of it,' Seth said.

'And he says here that Mama said she was never going to do that, but it was mere chance they were both walking up on the cliff that day. They exchanged words – whatever he means by that – and she ran away from him, holding Johnnie's hand as she ran. But she tripped and they both fell … oh, Seth …'

'Don't read any more. Don't torture yourself.'

Emma ignored his advice.

'I already knew the Coroner's report said there were no marks to indicate that … she'd been interfered with,' Emma said. 'But something bad must have been said to make her run from him.'

'More than likely. Emma, I'm sorry.'

'It's not your fault. But I don't want to think about what Carter might have said he was going to do to her, how Mama would have felt …'

Emma pushed the pages of the letter across the table. From things Reuben Jago had said that night he was arrested at Nase Head House she'd always wondered if it had been him who had been responsible for her mama's and Johnnie's death. But it seemed not.

'I'm sorry you've had to read that,' Seth said.

'I'm glad I have. Not pleased to have read it, of course, but at least I know.'

'And from evidence given at his trial, it seems those who refused Carter were either raped or …'

'Murdered,' Emma finished for him. 'Like poor Sophie Ellison as bad as she was about drinking in inns and being free with her body with those she wanted to favour.'

'That was for Sophie to decide. But if you read on you'll see Carter has written about that, too.'

'No. I don't want to read it. You can tell me. If you want to, that is.'

'In brief, Emma – because as you can see there are pages and pages of it – Sophie was blackmailing Carter. She'd found out about the smuggling somehow. Carter stole your ma's amethyst necklace from Pa's desk and gave it to her to keep her quiet. He told her not to wear it ever in public or Pa would have recognised it. But she did. And she bragged about who had given it to her. One of Carter's cronies came to the house that night and told him what Sophie was up to in the inn. So he went after her. There was a struggle in the back alley. And he killed her.'

Seth hung his head, but indicated for Emma to sit back down. She didn't. She went to him. Put her hands on his upper arms.

'And he probably dropped my mama's necklace on the way home, which is why Matthew found it where he said he did?'

Seth nodded.

'Thank you for showing me, Seth. It's not your fault how your brother is. Was.'

Emma felt Seth stiffen at the word under her hands. How terrible it must be to have had a brother who'd been hanged. And only yesterday.

'And I'm sorry, too,' Emma went on, 'that you've got this terrible thing to deal with. It can't be easy.'

'Like you had to deal with a terrible thing when everyone thought your ma was a suicide and you were shunned and someone desecrated her grave. People thought her a murderess, I suppose, for taking your little brother with her.'

'But now we have the evidence that Carter was up on the cliff that day. He didn't push her as such – or so he says. Did that come out in the trial?'

'Not that I've been told, no. This letter, I should think, is the letter of a desperate man trying to save his soul before ...'

'Going to the gallows,' Emma whispered the end of his sentence for him.

Seth was looking so very pained. She ran her hands soothingly up and down his upper arms.

'You don't have to be nice to me, Emma. You can take your hands away if you want.'

'I don't want.' She gave Seth's arms a gentle squeeze. How muscled they were.

'It's going to take some getting used to – Carter gone. I'm glad he wrote to me, though.'

'Easing his conscience.'

'No doubt. But at least we both know the truth now.'

'We do,' Emma said. It was a comforting thought in a strange way. 'We can cope with what we know, but not with our imaginings.'

The sun escaped a cloud then and light flooded the room, bouncing off the mirrors, highlighting the sheen of the polished silver. The chandelier glittered overhead.

With Seth so close, her hands on him, feeling his breath ruffle her fringe as he breathed out, it seemed to Emma as though the past two years had never been. It was as though they'd each just gone out for a little while and come back in and the love between them was still there.

'It's never going to be easy for us, Emma,' Seth said. 'Too many people know too much about us …'

'We haven't done anything wrong,' Emma interrupted. 'Neither you nor me.'

'No. But there'll be others who will always think otherwise. When drink loosens men's tongues you hear the truth. They forget then that I've kept many men in work these past two years by running the fishing fleet – only honestly this time – even though it was the last thing I wanted to be doing. It was as though I could taste the badness of Pa and my brothers every time I loaded a crabber, or took fish off a trawler. Do you understand?'

'I think so,' Emma said. Seth looked so sad, so beaten, that it was easy to put his distress before her own. 'I could so easily have taken the sovereigns Matthew Caunter gave me and moved where no one knew me, where no one would have heard the rumours about my mama. But I didn't. I stayed and I learned new skills and …'

'You took a shine to Matthew Caunter, didn't you?'

'He was married, although he couldn't tell me he was at the time because of his job. But he was a gentleman.'

'You still took a shine to him, though, didn't you?'

'I don't deny that. Same as you took a shine to someone I saw you with that night – the night of Mr Underwood's dinner, I mean. Mrs Prentiss.'

Seth gently removed Emma's hands from his arms. He

walked over to the dining table, pulled out two chairs – side by side, Emma noticed.

'I ended my association with Caroline Prentiss the very next day,' Seth said. 'Come and sit down, Emma. Please.'

Emma went, thanked Seth when he held the chair out for her to sit.

'As long ago as that?' Emma said.

Why, then, didn't you call and tell me? Emma wanted to ask – but she knew why he hadn't. She'd told him, through stupidity and jealousy, not to speak to her again, hadn't she?

'Yes. And then almost immediately afterwards I saw you with Mr Smythe coming out of Rossiter's with armsful of parcels.'

'Oh, Seth. They were for the children. Did you think …'

'We're *both* guilty of doing too much thinking and not enough asking. But that's Mrs Drew crashing about in the kitchen,' Seth said. 'Knowing her, she'll have heard us talking and will be bringing breakfast in a minute.'

'She was worried about you last night, Seth.'

'And you weren't?' Seth said.

'I can't deny it.' Emma laughed. She felt almost light-headed with relief that she and Seth had cleared the air of misunderstandings.

But Seth was looking serious again. She hoped he wasn't going to tell her more than she would want to know about Caroline Prentiss.

'I'm a fairly wealthy man now, Emma,' he said. 'My pa turned his properties and the business over to me when I became twenty-one …'

'So the authorities couldn't take it from him if he was caught smuggling?'

'I suppose Pa knew his luck might run out sometime, although he was very cunning in how and where and with whom he landed his contraband.'

'And it did run out,' Emma said, remembering Matthew and his part in it. And how she had been a part of that in providing cover for Matthew, even if he hadn't intentionally used her. 'But, when he and Miles have finished their sentences, what then? Will they move back here? Will you let them?'

'They'll have something to say on the matter, without a doubt. But I'll cross that bridge when I come to it, although goodness only knows I've had enough trouble from them to last me a lifetime.'

'Mmm,' Emma said.

She knew Seth well enough to know he could be a soft touch. That he probably wouldn't want his pa and his brother to be homeless. And yet there was a new strength to Seth – as though his backbone had toughened and he was more of a man than before.

'What about Mrs Drew and Edward if your pa and Miles move back in? I can't see Mrs Drew living happily under the same roof as them. Where would they go?'

'My pa and Miles won't be moving back here. Not ever. Hilltop is my home now. But you don't have to worry about Mrs Drew – I'd always provide for her if my circumstances were to change. I couldn't possibly have managed without Mrs Drew lately. I own most of the row of cottages that your old home is in. She could have one of those. A gift.'

'Oh, Seth, that's a lovely thing to do.'

'What about you?'

'What about me, what?'

Was he going to offer her a cottage to live in? A gift? He'd just said he was a wealthy man, hadn't he?

'What will you do now?'

Kiss you, hug you, make love to you. Marry you. Have your babies. All those thoughts rushed into Emma's head. But she knew she wouldn't be able to say them. Now wasn't the time. What would Seth think of her if she did? But she wished with all her heart she could see inside Seth's head and know what *he* was thinking. She only hoped it was the same thing *she* was thinking. But she wasn't going to beg him for a home to live in. Or for him to marry her.

'Find somewhere to live. I've got money and can rent for a while. But I want to start my own business one day.' Emma clasped her hands together in front of her, rested them on the table. 'When ...' Emma was about to say 'when Matthew and his wife took me to Torquay' but couldn't. It would hurt Seth if she did, remind him of the time he'd sat waiting for her at Nase Head House and had seen her kiss Matthew, albeit that it was a goodbye kiss. 'When I went to Torquay once, I thought the puddings and cakes in the hotel where I ate were terrible. Stodgy pastry. Undercooked fillings. Too sweet. I know I can do better than that. With the boat ferry and the train I could get freshly made tarts – savoury and sweet – to the hotels there every day. Further afield even. Exeter. Plymouth. Why not?'

Emma knew her voice had risen. But she felt excited at the thought, now she'd put her ideas into words.

'A businesswoman?'

'Why not? Women can run businesses you know. Mrs Minifie runs the sweetshop and the Misses Rossiter the department store, so why shouldn't I run a business of my own?'

'Why not indeed?'

'You sound as though you don't approve.'

'It's not for me to approve or not, is it? But I've always thought of you as the sort of woman who would want to marry and have children. With whoever it is you choose to marry.'

With whoever she chose? Didn't he realise she was bursting with love for *him*? That she only really came alive

317

when she was in his company? That if he asked her to marry him right now she'd say yes? And that she'd be happy to have his children? However many he wanted. Emma had told him once that she didn't want to marry – not yet. Was Seth still taking her at her word? Please, God, if you're listening, don't let him do that.

'*Whoever* I choose to marry, I could do that *and* be a businesswoman, couldn't I?'

'Could you?'

'Yes. I want it enough so I'd make it work.'

'And who would look after your children?'

'Who? I could ask Mrs Drew …'

And at that precise moment Mrs Drew came into the room with a tray piled high with breakfast things – eggs and bacon and fried bread and hog's pudding. And toast. Three jars of preserves. A jug of coffee and cups and saucers. Emma's stomach rumbled and she put a hand against it to quieten it. How hungry she was. And how tired suddenly.

'Not taking my name in vain, I hope, Emma Le Goff,' Mrs Drew said.

Seth leapt from his chair and took the tray from her, placed it on the table.

'No, Mrs Drew. Emma was just putting your name forward as nanny to her children. Hypothetically, of course.'

'Hypo what?' Mrs Drew said.

'Hypothetically,' Seth said. 'It means Emma's thinking about the care of her future babies. When she has them. With whoever she has them with.'

'Only one way to have 'em, lovie,' Mrs Drew said. 'And I should know 'cos haven't I got enough of the varmints? Unless I haven't been looking and it's all changed since I had the last one.' She began to pour the coffee, guffawing at her joke. Then she became serious and turned to Emma. 'You never are, are you, Emma? In the family way?'

'Of course not,' Emma said.

'Best get married first, lovie,' Mrs Drew said. 'You've had enough slights and bad-mouthing around these parts to do it the other way.'

She handed Emma a cup of coffee. 'Now get that down you and all this breakfast here. I don't want a scrap left. Either of you. And seeing as she was up all night playing Florence Nightingale, I've turned the mattress in what was the housemaid's room and put fresh linens on it. Poor maid's worn out. She could sleep there, if that's all right with you, Seth?'

'Perfectly,' Seth said.

'Oh, I can't stay,' Emma said, flustered. She'd acted impulsively the night before and she was glad she had, pleased beyond anything that Seth hadn't come to any worse grief than a few cuts and bruises. But now she couldn't stay – she just couldn't. To be in the same house with Seth and not want to creep into his bed, feel his arms around her – well, it would all be too much. More than she wanted to cope with at the moment. 'It wouldn't be right. People will talk. Again.'

Seth looked as though she'd hit him with a barbed stick.

'Where'll you go then, lovie?' Mrs Drew said.

'A hotel. A boarding house somewhere. I need time to think. On my own.'

'Before you get down to having those hypo-whatever-you-called-them babies?' Mrs Drew said.

Emma pressed her lips together. Nodded. 'I've still got some things up at Nase Head House. Clothes. I'll need to see about getting them back. If Mr Smythe hasn't given an order for me not to be allowed on the premises.'

'Oh, I 'spect he has,' Mrs Drew said. 'Men like that don't like being slighted. Could you get in touch with Ruby? Ask her to squirrel them out of your old room?'

'I expect I could,' Emma said. 'But I wouldn't want her

to get into trouble on my account. Anyway, I don't know where to tell her to bring them.'

'Shingle Cottage is still empty,' Seth said. 'It's furnished. Aired. You can stop there. I'll get the key.'

He got up and strode over to a dresser, opened a drawer. Came back with the key to Shingle Cottage on the plaited threads that Emma had made for her papa.

'For as long as you like, Emma,' Seth said, holding the key out to her. 'I understand your need for time. Trust me, I understand that.' He turned to Mrs Drew. 'I'll take my breakfast in my room.'

And then he left.

Emma stared at the key in her hand for a long time. She'd turned full circle, hadn't she? If she went back to live in Shingle Cottage she'd be where she'd been two years ago and it would be as if all her struggle to survive, to better herself, to learn and to grow had been for nothing.

'I've upset him,' Emma said.

'Right an' all you have, lovie. That expression in his eyes when he looks at you is pure love. He drinks you in, lovie. And there's you refusing his offer to stay in this lovely big, warm house. You're so stubborn, Emma Le Goff, you can't see what's in front of your own nose sometimes.'

'I speak before I think. I …'

'Don't you just. You'll learn, though. But don't you worry. You'll be snug as a bug back in Shingle Cottage seeing as Seth got me to light the range once a week to keep the place aired in case you needed it. And a heated brick went in the bed once a week an' all. Oh, I know he was fearful you'd get snared by that Smythe fellow, but between you and me, I don't think he ever gave up hope that you wouldn't. Why else would he have told me to do all that? Now I'd best be getting Seth's share of this up to his room or you won't be the only one looking for a job.'

Mrs Drew placed half the breakfast she'd brought in on the table in front of Emma and left the room with the other half on the tray.

Emma ate every single scrap. She had lots to think about and she'd need good food inside her to give her the strength to do it.

Emma woke to daylight. She had no idea how long she'd slept. She remembered waking when it was dark; waking with her mouth dry and needing water, but she hadn't thought to bring any up with her. She'd gone back to sleep eventually. But now it was light outside again. So she must have slept through a whole day.

She eased herself from the bed. Stretched. Looked around her. She was in the room that had been her mama's and papa's and then later Matthew's.

The jug on the dressing table was empty and she badly wanted a wash. She'd have to go and draw water from the pump at the bottom of the back lane. And to think she'd had running water in taps at Nase Head House. And there'd been water from taps in Seth's house, too.

She felt grubby now, in need of a change of clothes. She only had the dance dress she'd run away from Nase Head House in. And she was going to look ridiculous walking about town in that at this hour of the day, wasn't she?

Barefoot, a blanket around her for modesty's sake in case anyone should look through the window, she went down the stairs.

To her surprise there was already water drawn in a bucket by the back door. And a loaf of bread on the dresser. A square of butter on a dish. A packet of tea. A jug of milk on the marble slab. And towels – three of them, neatly folded and piled one on top of the other. She picked up the top one and it smelled of lavender. Same as the towels in Seth's house did. Mrs Drew must have had a hand in this.

She smiled. Mrs Drew was such a good woman. How easy it would have been for her to be bitter seeing as she'd had such a drunk for a husband and life had been more than a struggle with six children to bring up with little money.

'Oh, and a skirt and blouse,' Emma said, as she spied both draped over the back of a chair. They looked new, and the fabric felt as though it had never been washed, when she fingered the stiff collar of the blouse.

She wondered whose they'd been, not that it mattered. Certainly they couldn't have been Mrs Drew's because she was a lot shorter and a lot rounder than Emma was. But Emma now had something to wear when she went out to look for somewhere she could start her fledgling business. She was determined to do that. She couldn't expect other people to come to her aid *all* the time, as grateful as she was for Mrs Drew's and Seth's help at that very moment.

Washed and dressed, two slices of bread and butter and a cup of tea inside her, Emma was ready to start her new life.

She'd told Seth she wanted to find premises to start a business, so she'd jolly well go out there and look for somewhere.

It wasn't easy for Seth not to go to Shingle Cottage. At least a dozen times a day he found himself walking that way. With superhuman effort he somehow managed to turn and go in another direction. He'd promised Emma time to think and he'd honour that promise – however long it took.

Now he was on his way to Nase Head House, determined to go in through the gate and up the drive to the front door, regardless of what reception he would get from Rupert Smythe when he got there. He'd had glimpses of Emma going about the town over the past two days and each time she'd been wearing the same skirt and blouse he'd asked Mrs Drew to take to Shingle Cottage. And her trusty shawl; Emma wore it for emotional protection rather than warmth, he was sure of it, because August was the hottest he could remember. Mrs Drew had told him that Emma hadn't got her things back from Nase Head House yet – well, he'd do his level best to get them back for her.

'Ah, Will,' Seth said, as he reached the entrance to the hotel. 'Fancy seeing you here. Just the chap I want to see.'

'Oh, Lordy, Seth. I've not been in this job long, helping Mr Evans out – he's getting on a bit. I'll get the sack quick as lightning if I let you in. Got orders to keep you out, haven't I?'

'Who says I'm coming in?'

'Eh? You've got me puzzled now.'

Seth grinned. Poor Will – he never had been the brightest star in the galaxy.

'Remember when we were at school, Will, and you fought the Ede gang with me when they pounced on me after school?'

'Right an' all I do. And you bought me sweets by way of thanks. Aniseed balls and gobstoppers. Kept buying 'em you did, long after the fight was over.'

'Glad you remember. But I need another favour now. I need to go to Emma Le Goff's room and clear all her possessions into this bag.' Seth unrolled the kitbag he'd had tucked under his arm.

'I can't let you do that, Seth. My job is to stay here and keep an eye out that Emma Le Goff doesn't come back for her things and that you don't come in, neither. And cut the grass and dead-head the flowers while I'm doing it.'

'D'you know which room was hers, Will?'

'Oh, I do. The tower room.' Will put two fingers to his lips. 'But I've just remembered – I wasn't supposed to tell you that.'

Seth smiled. 'I won't tell anyone you have.' Seth put a hand inside his jacket where he kept his wallet. He fingered out a £5 note and held it out towards Will. 'For your help.'

'Five pounds?'

'Ssh, keep your voice down.' Seth chuckled. 'I'll make it two five pound notes then.'

Seth took a second note from his wallet. He hoped and prayed Will wouldn't get the sack for aiding and abetting him.

'You always were a foundling in that house of yours,' Will said, reaching for the money. He jerked a thumb towards Hilltop House. Then he turned his back on Seth and began pruning a plant Seth knew didn't need pruning. 'In the back door'll be the quickest. Turn to the left. First flight of stairs you come to, keep going up 'til you can't go no further. On your way.'

Seth raced across the lawn and around the back of Nase Head House.

Chapter Twenty-Four

'You can't come in here, Emma,' William Coote said.

'I've got things in my old room,' Emma said.

She should have come for them before but she'd been plucking up the courage to do so. And if truth be told, that courage was rapidly leaking away.

'Might have,' William said. 'Might not. Lots of stuff been thrown out the back, ready for a bonfire.'

'Not my things, I hope,' Emma said. She made to push past – she just couldn't bear the thought that all her clothes and personal possessions would be burned again, as Reuben Jago had had her things burned after her parents' and Johnnie's deaths. But William Coote grabbed her arm and pushed her back towards the gates.

'I said you can't come in. I'm in enough trouble already for letting someone in I shouldn't have. Mr Evans found out and I had to give 'im one of the £5 notes I was given to look the other way.'

'Who gave you money, William?'

William Coote gave Emma a shove – not too hard, but not a gentle push either. 'I'm not saying.'

'Was it someone wanting to go to my room?'

'I'm not telling you that either. Now go.'

Emma didn't put up a fight. She didn't want to spend her savings on new clothes but if she had to, then so be it. 'They're only clothes and few bits,' she said. 'If Mr Smythe wants to sink so low as to burn them, then let him.'

And she marched off down the hill.

Seth was standing on the path by the front door when she returned to Shingle Cottage. And he was smiling. Eyes closed, face turned to the sun, but smiling. There was a canvas kitbag and a carpet bag propped up against the door jamb. Her carpet bag. The one she'd left behind at Nase Head House. How good it was to see it. To see *him*. Oh, how she'd missed him. She hoped that smile meant he'd missed her, too.

Seth had said he'd give her time and she'd always be grateful for that. She'd had enough time now – she was in love with Seth Jago and wanted him to know it. Even more so now that it looked as though he'd risked the wrath of Mr Smythe by going to collect her things.

Emma flung open the gate and it banged noisily against the wall, making Seth jump at the sound, eyes springing open in surprise. A huge grin spread across his face. He was as pleased to see her as she was to see him, Emma knew it. Especially when he opened his arms wide inviting her into them.

She thought she'd trip over her own feet she ran that fast towards him. 'Yes! Yes! Yes!' Emma said, 'I'll come to Canada with you. Anywhere.'

'Canada?' Seth said, looking mock-puzzled. 'What makes you think I'm going to Canada?'

'You have talked about it, you know you have …'

'And I also said I'd spread the rumour to make you realise how much you'd miss me if I went.' Seth grinned at her – how a smile transformed his face. 'The truth of it is, I couldn't go anywhere without you, Emma. *We*'ll go to Canada one day, perhaps. But not today.'

'Oh, Seth,' Emma said. 'That's a lovely thing to say. And you've got my things. From Nase Head House. It *was* you. I've just come from there. William Coote said he'd got into trouble for letting someone in he shouldn't have.'

She threw herself at Seth, not caring who saw her, and clasped her hands behind the back of his neck. Kissed his cheek. Then kissed it again.

'I took a kitbag but it wasn't big enough for everything. I saw your carpet bag and filled that. I thought you'd want that, too.'

'Oh, I do. Thank you, thank you, thank you,' Emma said. Then she kissed the other cheek.

'Well, *that* makes parting with £10 for Will to look the other way worthwhile.' Seth had put his arms around the back of Emma's waist now and was hugging her tightly.

'Good old William,' Emma said.

'I couldn't agree more. We went to school together, him and me. So, he pretended a rose, or somesuch, needed pruning urgently and I slipped past him. I saw Smythe with Gillet's daughter when I was coming down the stairs, but he was deep in conversation and didn't ...'

'Joanna Gillet?'

Mr Smythe hadn't wasted any time finding someone else to take her place, Emma thought. She'd been gone from the place less than a week.

'Gillet's only got one daughter. But are we going to stand here all day talking about people who don't really matter a jot to us, or ...'

'I don't want to let you go,' Emma said.

'Or me, you,' Seth said. 'But this isn't the best place to conduct a courtship, especially as I can see Mrs Phipps coming down the road.'

Emma giggled. 'Let's give her something to spread gossip about, shall we?' she said. She took her hands from behind Seth's neck, and placed them on his cheeks. Then she stood on tiptoe and kissed him on the mouth. Just a gentle kiss at first, but then it went deeper and it seemed to Emma as though their souls had melded together.

The kiss went on and on and on and Emma didn't want it ever to stop. That kiss was telling them everything they needed to know about what was in the other's heart.

And she knew that wherever it was they were going to go from here in life then it would be together.

'Filthy devils,' Mrs Phipps shouted as she reached the gate of Shingle Cottage. 'Out here so anyone can see.'

'And you've never done it yourself, Mrs Phipps?' Emma said, reluctantly releasing her lips from Seth's.

'Not in broad daylight. But then you're no better than you should be, Emma Le Goff. Like mother ...'

'I'd keep very quiet if I were you, Mrs Phipps,' Seth interrupted.

'And who's making me? Not a *criminal* Jago?'

'No,' Seth said. 'I'm not a criminal. But there is such a thing as slander and I'll have no qualms about accusing you of it if I hear you call me that ever again. D'you hear me?'

That made Mrs Phipps change her tune. Her scowl became a nervous smile. She twisted her hands together over and over. She flicked a greasy-looking, loose strand of hair back over the top of her head.

Seth turned his back on Mrs Phipps.

'Time I tasted one of your famous crab tarts, I think, Emma.' Seth bent to tap the top of his kitbag.

'You've never put a crab on top of my things?'

'Might have. Well wrapped in a bit of sacking if I have. But you'll have to take it indoors and look for yourself.' Seth kissed the top of Emma's head, reached for her hand. 'Come on, Emma.'

Emma took her key from the pocket of her skirt. 'You could have waited for me inside, Seth. Didn't you have a key to let yourself in?' she asked.

'I did. But I didn't want to use it. I wanted you to *want* me to come in.'

'Oh, I do, Seth, I do.'

Emma made Seth the crab tart he'd asked for, using herbs

she'd planted herself in the back garden which had run riot – a veritable forest – in the time she'd been away, to flavour the egg and milk filling.

For dessert Emma poached apples, picked from the tree in the back garden, in a toffee sauce and made Seth run to the dairy for clotted cream to serve with them.

Between eating they didn't talk much. They kissed instead. And just gazed at one another. And they repeated the cooking and the kissing and the gazing day after day for a whole week when Seth finished his day's work. Getting to know one another all over again, falling in love with one another a little more with each mouthful they fed one another; with each kiss.

They both knew they did have to talk. About their future. But talking in Shingle Cottage didn't seem to be the right place to be doing it, even though it held so many good memories for Emma.

When Seth suggested a walk before sunset, Emma knew where it was he would take her.

Crystal Cove. Emma was pleased to have her coat back and let Seth help her on with it. Seth suggested they take a blanket as, while it had been a warm day, once the sun set it would be considerably colder. What would they do on that blanket, Emma wondered as – arms linked – they made their way to Crystal Cove.

'This always was our special place, sweetheart, wasn't it?'

Sweetheart – his special name for her.

'It was. Is,' Emma said. 'I can't imagine not being able to come here.'

She spread her arms wide to take in the small cove, empty now of people. Not that many ventured down the rough steps and clambered over the sharp rocks to get to the sand, which became just a thin strip when the tide was high.

But the tide was far out now. Emma kicked off her shoes.

329

Then she unfastened her stockings and took them off, too – rolled them up and tucked them in her shoes. She wriggled her toes and let the sand, warmed by the sun in the day, push up between them.

'I'm beginning to think nowhere could be as lovely as this. Made lovelier because you're here, too.'

'Flatterer,' Emma said, tickling Seth in the ribs before running off.

Running off, knowing he would chase her.

He did. Caught her. Folded her into his arms.

'I was so jealous, Em,' Seth said, 'when I saw you in Matthew Caunter's arms that night. The night …'

'I was sixteen. I'm sorry you saw what you saw and especially after waiting so long for me, but it was an innocent kiss. A thank you, and a goodbye. You do believe me?'

'I do now.'

'And it was my birthday.'

'I hardly need reminding,' Seth said, kissing the tip of her nose. 'And you'll be having another one soon.'

'So I will,' Emma said. 'My eighteenth.'

'Almost a woman,' Seth said, grinning at her.

'And what's that supposed to mean?' Emma said, mock-outraged. Although she could guess. They had only just stopped short of making love more than once. It was only a matter of time before … Emma felt a frisson of excitement ripple through her.

'Oh, I think you know,' Seth said. 'What woman could resist a man who's kept all the letters she's written him?'

'You've kept all my letters?'

'Didn't I just say?' Seth said, stealing another quick kiss. 'Every single one. Got a bundle of them, I have, all tied with garden string because it was all I could find.'

'Well, there's a thing. I've kept the handful you wrote me, too.'

Thank goodness Seth had thought to look in the chest of drawers in her room and clear the contents into her carpet bag.

'And tied with garden string?'

'You know they're not. I used the ribbon from a petticoat I grew out of. I thought if I threw them away, burned them, then I would have lost the little bit I had of you – the paper you'd touched, the stamp you'd licked to put on the envelope.'

'D'you think we're destined to be together?'

'Because we've both been through rough times? Or because …'

Emma couldn't say the words that were in her head – *because we love one another.*

Seth hadn't said he loved her yet, even though he'd demonstrated that he did in so many other ways. And for her to say it first, well it would be too forward, wouldn't it? Not seemly.

'Because, Emma Le Goff, despite your quick tongue and your impulsiveness ….'

'The way I kissed you in front of Mrs Phipps?'

'Brazen hussy. Kiss me again because I've forgotten what it felt like.'

Emma duly obliged. And somehow in the kissing they had gone from a standing position, to sitting down – their arms wrapped around one another – on the sand. Seth's hand brushed her breast as they sat and it felt right to Emma; it was what she wanted – to start on her journey to become a woman.

If Seth wanted to lay her down on the sand, lift her skirt and make love to her right now then she probably wouldn't put up any resistance. Life was too short to live it by other people's standards – look how short her mama's had been. And her papa's. And Johnnie's. And Seth's ma's.

'I've been thinking, sweetheart,' Seth said as he kissed the top of her head. 'You won't have anyone to give you away when you get married.'

Emma snuggled deeper into Seth's arms – he'd say he loved her in a minute, she knew it.

'Dr Shaw might, if I asked him. He's always been kind to me. But getting married means a wedding. June's a lovely month for a wedding, I've always thought,' she said.

'But that's almost another year away now. Just before Christmas would be a lovely time.'

'Oh, no,' Emma said. She kissed the tip of Seth's nose to let him know she wasn't telling him off, only joking with him. 'I wouldn't want shop flowers, only wild ones. Wild sweet peas in a posy and dog roses in my hair …'

'You'd look beautiful carrying a cabbage,' Seth said.

'Oh you. Anyway, it's usually best if a girl's told that she's loved and that she's asked before she gets married. And I haven't heard you say either of those things yet.' Emma put a hand to her ear, pretended to listen hard.

'I didn't think I needed to, Em,' Seth said. 'But just so we set the record straight …'

'I love you, too,' Emma said.

There, she'd been the first to say it even if Seth had been the first to show it. Did it matter which way around the love came as long as they reached the same place together eventually?

'As much as I love you, Em?'

'Oh, I expect so,' Emma said. 'Every bit as much as that.'

Seth wrapped the blanket he'd brought around them.

'Show me,' he said.

So Emma did. As the sun began to slide down the sky and the sea turned crimson, she kissed Seth until her lips were sore and her face ached. Their bodies came together there on the sand, their souls and their hearts hungry for the union.

Then they drifted in and out of sleep, sated from their love-making. Emma opened her eyes to find the sun quite gone and the moon rising.

'Wake up, sleepyhead,' Seth said. 'Time to go. Time for me to make an honest woman of you.'

'Oh, not too honest,' Emma said. She dropped a gentle kiss on his lips. 'I quite enjoyed being dishonest just now ...'

About the Author

Linda Mitchelmore

Linda has lived in Devon all her life, where the wonderful
scenery and history give her endless ideas for novels and
short stories. Linda has over 200 short stories published
worldwide and has also won, or been short-listed,
in many short-story writing competitions.
In 2004 she was awarded The Katie Forde Bursary by
the Romantic Novelists' Association. In 2011 she won
the Short Story Radio Romance Prize.

Married to Roger for over 40 years, they have two
grown-up children and two grandchildren. As well as
her writing, Linda loves gardening, walking, cycling and
riding pillion on her husband's vintage motorbikes.

To Turn Full Circle is Linda's debut novel
and the first in her trilogy.

More Choc Lit

Why not try something else from the Choc Lit selection?
Here's a sample:

Please don't stop the music

Jane Lovering

 Winner of the 2012 Best Romantic Comedy Novel of the year

How much can you hide?

Jemima Hutton is determined to build a successful new life and keep her past a dark secret. Trouble is, her jewellery business looks set to fail – until enigmatic Ben Davies offers to stock her handmade belt buckles in his guitar shop and things start looking up, on all fronts.

But Ben has secrets too. When Jemima finds out he used to be the front man of hugely successful Indie rock band Willow Down, she wants to know more. Why did he desert the band on their US tour? Why is he now a semi-recluse?

And the curiosity is mutual – which means that her own secret is no longer safe ...

Visit www.choc-lit.com for more details including the first two chapters and reviews, or simply scan barcode using your mobile phone QR reader.

Highland Storms
Christina Courtenay

 Winner of the 2012 Best Historical Romantic Novel of the year

Who can you trust?

Betrayed by his brother and his childhood love, Brice Kinross needs a fresh start. So he welcomes the opportunity to leave Sweden for the Scottish Highlands to take over the family estate.

But there's trouble afoot at Rosyth in 1754 and Brice finds himself unwelcome. The estate's in ruin and money is disappearing. He discovers an ally in Marsaili Buchanan, the beautiful redheaded housekeeper, but can he trust her?

Marsaili is determined to build a good life. She works hard at being a housekeeper and harder still at avoiding men who want to take advantage of her. But she's irresistibly drawn to the new clan chief, even though he's made it plain he doesn't want to be shackled to anyone.

And the young laird has more than romance on his mind. His investigations are stirring up an enemy. Someone who will stop at nothing to get what he wants – including Marsaili – even if that means destroying Brice's life forever …

Sequel to Trade Winds

Visit www.choc-lit.com for more details including the first two chapters and reviews, or simply scan barcode using your mobile phone QR reader.

The Scarlet Kimono

Christina Courtenay

Winner of The Big Red Reads Historical Fiction Award 2011

Abducted by a Samurai warlord in 17th-century Japan – what happens when fear turns to love?

England, 1611, and young Hannah Marston envies her brother's adventurous life. But when she stows away on his merchant ship, her powers of endurance are stretched to their limit. Then they reach Japan and all her suffering seems worthwhile – until she is abducted by Taro Kumashiro's warriors.

In the far north of the country, warlord Kumashiro is waiting to see the girl who he has been warned about by a seer. When at last they meet, it's a clash of cultures and wills, but they're also fighting an instant attraction to each other.

With her brother desperate to find her and the jealous Lady Reiko equally desperate to kill her, Hannah faces the greatest adventure of her life. And Kumashiro has to choose between love and honour ...

Visit www.choc-lit.com for more details including the first two chapters and reviews, or simply scan barcode using your mobile phone QR reader.

Love & Freedom
Sue Moorcroft

*Winner of the Festival of Romance
Best Romantic Read Award 2011*

New start, new love.

That's what Honor Sontag needs after her life falls apart, leaving her reputation in tatters and her head all over the place. So she flees her native America and heads for Brighton, England.

Honor's hoping for a much-deserved break and the chance to find the mother who abandoned her as a baby. What she gets is an entanglement with a mysterious male whose family seems to have a finger in every pot in town.

Martyn Mayfair has sworn off women with strings attached, but is irresistibly drawn to Honor, the American who keeps popping up in his life. All he wants is an uncomplicated relationship built on honesty, but Honor's past threatens to undermine everything. Then secrets about her mother start to spill out ...

Honor has to make an agonising choice. Will she live up to her dutiful name and please others? Or will she choose freedom?

Visit www.choc-lit.com for more details including the first two chapters and reviews, or simply scan barcode using your mobile phone QR reader.

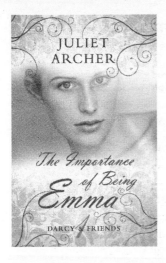

The Importance of Being Emma

Juliet Archer

Winner of The Big Red Reads Fiction Award 2011

A modern retelling of Jane Austen's *Emma*.

Mark Knightley – handsome, clever, rich – is used to women falling at his feet. Except Emma Woodhouse, who's like part of the family – and the furniture. When their relationship changes dramatically, is it an ending or a new beginning?

Emma's grown into a stunningly attractive young woman, full of ideas for modernising her family business. Then Mark gets involved and the sparks begin to fly. It's just like the old days, except that now he's seeing her through totally new eyes.

While Mark struggles to keep his feelings in check, Emma remains immune to the Knightley charm. She's never forgotten that embarrassing moment when he discovered her teenage crush on him. He's still pouring scorn on all her projects, especially her beautifully orchestrated campaign to find Mr Right for her ditzy PA. And finally, when the mysterious Flynn Churchill – the man of her dreams – turns up, how could she have eyes for anyone else? ...

Visit www.choc-lit.com for more details including the first two chapters and reviews, or simply scan barcode using your mobile phone QR reader.

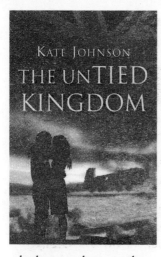

The UnTied Kingdom
Kate Johnson

Shortlisted for the 2012 RoNA Contemporary Romantic Novel Category Award

The portal to an alternate world was the start of all her troubles – or was it?

When Eve Carpenter lands with a splash in the Thames, it's not the London or England she's used to. No one has a telephone or knows what a computer is. England's a third-world country and Princess Di is still alive. But worst of all, everyone thinks Eve's a spy.

Including Major Harker who has his own problems. His sworn enemy is looking for a promotion. The General wants him to undertake some ridiculous mission to capture a computer, which Harker vaguely envisions running wild somewhere in Yorkshire. Turns out the best person to help him is Eve.

She claims to be a popstar. Harker doesn't know what a popstar is, although he suspects it's a fancy foreign word for 'spy'. Eve knows all about computers, and electricity. Eve is dangerous. There's every possibility she's mad.

And Harker is falling in love with her.

Visit www.choc-lit.com for more details including the first two chapters and reviews, or simply scan barcode using your mobile phone QR reader.

'A dramatic, moving and intensely romantic story'
TRISHA ASHLEY

The Silver Locket
Margaret James

2010 Single Titles Reviewers Choice Award Winner

Winner of CataNetwork Reviewers' Choice Award for Single Titles 2010

If life is cheap, how much is love worth?

It's 1914 and young Rose Courtenay has a decision to make. Please her wealthy parents by marrying the man of their choice – or play her part in the war effort?

The chance to escape proves irresistible and Rose becomes a nurse. Working in France, she meets Lieutenant Alex Denham, a dark figure from her past. He's the last man in the world she'd get involved with – especially now he's married.

But in wartime nothing is as it seems. Alex's marriage is a sham and Rose is the only woman he's ever wanted. As he recovers from his wounds, he sets out to win her trust. His gift of a silver locket is a far cry from the luxuries she's left behind.

What value will she put on his love?

First novel in the trilogy

Visit www.choc-lit.com for more details including the first two chapters and reviews, or simply scan barcode using your mobile phone QR reader.

Never Coming Home
Evonne Wareham

All she has left is hope.

When Kaz Elmore is told her five-year-old daughter Jamie has died in a car crash, she struggles to accept that she'll never see her little girl again. Then a stranger comes into her life offering the most dangerous substance in the world: hope.

Devlin, a security consultant and witness to the terrible accident scene, inadvertently reveals that Kaz's daughter might not have been the girl in the car after all.

What if Jamie is still alive? With no evidence, the police aren't interested, so Devlin and Kaz have little choice but to investigate themselves.

Devlin never gets involved with a client. Never. But the more time he spends with Kaz, the more he desires her – and the more his carefully constructed ice-man persona starts to unravel.

The desperate search for Jamie leads down dangerous paths – to a murderous acquaintance from Devlin's dark past, and all across Europe, to Italy, where deadly secrets await. But as long as Kaz has hope, she can't stop looking …

Visit www.choc-lit.com for more details including the first two chapters and reviews, or simply scan barcode using your mobile phone QR reader.

Turning the Tide
Christine Stovell

**All's fair in love and war?
Depends on who's making
the rules.**

Harry Watling has spent the
past five years keeping her
father's boat yard afloat,
despite its dying clientele.
Now all she wants to do is
enjoy the peace and quiet of
her sleepy backwater.

So when property developer Matthew Corrigan wants
to turn the boat yard into an upmarket housing complex for
his exotic new restaurant, it's like declaring war.

And the odds seem to be stacked in Matthew's favour.
He's got the colourful locals on board, his hard-to-please
girlfriend is warming to the idea and he has the means to
force Harry's hand. Meanwhile, Harry has to fight not just
his plans but also her feelings for the man himself.

Then a family secret from the past creates heartbreak for
Harry, and neither of them is prepared for what happens
next ...

Visit www.choc-lit.com for more details
including the first two chapters and
reviews, or simply scan barcode using
your mobile phone QR reader.

Introducing Choc Lit

We're an independent publisher creating
a delicious selection of fiction.
Where heroes are like chocolate – irresistible!
Quality stories with a romance at the heart.

Choc Lit novels are selected by genuine readers like yourself.
We only publish stories our Choc Lit Tasting Panel want to
see in print. Our reviews and awards speak for themselves.

Come and support our authors and join them in our
Author's Corner, read their interviews and see their latest
events, reviews and gossip.

Visit: www.choc-lit.com for more details.

Available in paperback and as ebooks from most stores.

We'd also love to hear how you enjoyed *To Turn Full Circle*.
Just visit www.choc-lit.com and give your feedback.
Describe Seth in terms of chocolate and you could win a
Choc Lit novel in our Flavour of the Month competition.

Follow us on twitter: www.twitter.com/
ChocLituk, or simply scan barcode using
your mobile phone QR reader.